REALITY CHECK

REALITY CHECK

IT'S WORTH FIGHTING FOR

DAVE McCREERY

WEIGHT OF THE WORLD BOOK 1

Cover design by Design for Writers
Book design by Design for Writers

ISBN 978-1-9168827-0-6 (paperback)
ISBN 978-1-9168827-1-3 (ebook)

Published by Dave McCreery
Davemccreery.co.uk

Acknowledgements

THERE ARE SO MANY people I need to thank for helping me get this book over the line – friends, family and even random strangers! Everyone who's offered a word of encouragement, a piece of advice or the criticism I needed to improve has been a big part of this project, and I appreciate all of you.

There are a few who went above and beyond this, however, and they deserve an extra mention.

Michael and Gail, my fellow travellers, you offered fantastic feedback as test readers and while many others read the book, your comments – reading this from different points of view – were incredibly valuable.

Kat, you've put up with me from the start and have seen this story evolve from its early days until now. You were a big part of its evolution and I couldn't have reached this point without you – and I appreciated you lifting my spirits on those low days.

Finally, Rachel Rowlands – my editor. I'm so glad I chose you to edit this story – and grateful you entered that line of work! Your comments and advice, on the story itself and the process as a whole, were just what I needed to make this the best book it can be.

For all of this, and so much more, thank you all.

Dave.

# PROLOGUE

"HOW MUCH LONGER?"

Teeth grinding. That was what the burst of static brought to mind. It rattled through the cockpit, drowning out the occasional beeps and clicks that had been Queen's main source of company for the last nine hours. The rook's volume was too high.

Comm chatter had been minimal throughout the journey. The mission was routine: escort a shuttle and repair crew to the malfunctioning deep space sensor and discover the reason for its failure. Simple, but something wasn't sitting right, and that unease had spread to the other pilots – especially the rook.

"Ask that one more time, Rook. I dare you." It wasn't the first time someone had said it during their flight, but it was becoming more frequent. Everyone was on edge.

"Just stay in formation, Rook. We're almost there," Fonn, her second in command, chimed in. Ever the peacekeeper.

"That's what you said an hour ago," he whined. Compared to the other rookies she'd trained, he hadn't complained as much as expected, but his first long space flight was getting to him. On any other day, on any other mission, she would have said something reassuring – not just for his sake but for the other pilots' as well. "Why are we the ones out here?"

"Not all of our missions are exciting," she reminded him, trying to keep her voice gentle. "Everyone needs field experience, and this is a good way to get it."

"Even Flare Squadron?"

"Even Flare Squadron." She nodded, despite no one being able to see it. That was proving a hard habit to break.

"Why do we even have sensors out here? Do they ever find anything?"

"Deep space sensors are used to look beyond our solar system. They pick up comets, debris, anomalies – and give us advance warning of any threats."

"What threats? There's nothing out there."

"Without the sensors, we wouldn't know for sure, would we?" She sighed. "Stay focused on your flying. Your movements are erratic; concentrate on staying in position, Rook."

The sensor sphere on her left showed nothing but friendlies. Her ship was in the middle with eleven behind, all V-shaped Valkyrie-class fighters, escorting a shuttle loaded with a repair crew and all the equipment needed to fix the sensor.

The waypoint on her display changed from blue to green as the group approached. Still, she couldn't shake the unease. Perhaps it had something to do with the return journey taking another nine hours on top of however long the repairs would take. With only a full day's worth of air on board, it left six hours before they'd have to turn back.

With a nervous rook, the return – and the waiting – wasn't likely to be peaceful.

"Flare One, this is *Veranda*," the shuttle's pilot said over the comm.

"Go ahead, *Veranda*," Queen responded.

"We are on course to the sensor, correct?"

"That's right. What's wrong?"

"It's not there."

"What?"

"It's gone. The sensor isn't damaged, it's vanished," the pilot said, confusion obvious.

"Listen up," she ordered, switching channels. "The sensor is missing. Break off in pairs and scout the area. Do not leave comm range and report in if you find anything."

Her sensor sphere showed five pairs of green dots peeling away and she could see the engines of two ships as they flew ahead. The shuttle remained behind while the other fighter, her lieutenant, tailed it. When they reached the target coordinates, the three pilots shut down their engines.

The minutes dragged, making the journey they'd made to the area feel like it had taken seconds. Her breathing became shallow. A pit opened in her stomach.

"Queen?"

His voice startled her. The harness dug into her skin through her flight suit. She switched to their private channel and answered. "Still not used to that call sign, Fonn. What is it?"

"Malfunctions are rare, and we usually know the cause of the damage before dispatch, but...the sensor is gone. Just gone. There's no debris either, so..."

"So you think it must have been taken?"

"Yeah. What I can't work out is by who." Fonn paused before continuing. "The area may not be as empty as we thought."

"We're on the same line. There's been no intel on any dissenter cells that have the resources to get this far into space, though."

"Yet. Unless Intelligence are holding out on us."

"I don't think so. Even if a dissenter cell had the tech and resources to reach this far into space, what would they get from it? Terraforming is nowhere near viable, and without a Warp Tunnel it'd take years. Something else has to be going on here."

"Like what?"

"I don't know. Keep your eyes open, Lieutenant. I don't want any surprises."

Instead of answering, Fonn clicked his comm as an acknowledgement. Queen went back to scanning the stars ahead as she looped around the shuttle but there was nothing unusual out there. The sensor sphere showed no other contacts.

"Captain! Captain! Hick's gone, I repeat, Hick is gone!" the rook said, his voice almost a scream.

"Calm down, Rook. What happened? Where is he?" Queen stared at her sensor again. Hick's dot had vanished, leaving the rook's alone. He was flying erratically around the zone they had been searching.

"He's gone! There was a flash of light and then…nothing. Just shrapnel. No ejection."

"Get back here, now. Flare Squadron, regroup. Two, stay with the shuttle. Have them record and relay everything that happens back to OSD. Be ready to evac the area."

Clicks answered. Queen powered up her engines and raced towards the rook. The pit in her stomach kept growing but even as she closed in on the panicked pilot, there was nothing out of the ordinary – other than Hick's disappearance.

To her left, a small cluster of stars winked out and she jerked her controls and sent the ship into a sharp dive and spin. Two lances of red light streaked above her and there was a cry over the comms, followed by more silence.

"What's out there? Why can't sensors see them?" Seven said.

"Whatever it is, it's black and I can't see any engine trails." That was Eight.

Queen pulled out of the dive and looked for the rook. She found him heading towards the shuttle and spun around, releasing a stream of blue needles into the black void behind him. None connected.

"Two? Get out of here. Take the shuttle and go," Queen ordered.

"I can help, One," Fonn said.

"No! We'll buy you time, but you need to warn OSD. Take whatever data you've got and get it to them."

"Understood. Good luck, Captain."

Her attention returned to the black ocean but there was nothing. The shadow flanking her moments ago... empty space.

With two pilots gone and a third escorting the shuttle, only nine remained to tackle the threat. Questions tore through her mind: what was it, who did it belong to and how many were there?

Too many questions and no answers.

Another flash from below and right was quickly followed by a cut-short scream. Eight left. Seven and a half if you counted the rook.

"Everyone spread out. Fire at will. Cover as much space as possible. If we can hit it, we have a chance," she ordered.

The area blazed to life as countless blue lances pierced through the blackness in all directions. After thirty seconds of constant firing, her nerves hit a whole new level. They should have hit something by now, even if there was only a single ship out there.

The sensor sphere flickered. A yellow dot appeared as a shot connected. Her pilots converged on that point without an order and another yellow dot appeared in the same place. Then another, and another.

As the eight pilots converged, she could see a shadow. It almost resembled a person but the arms were too fluid – and there were more than two. Queen transmitted the images to Fonn, hoping he was still in range, before turning her attention back to their attacker.

"Arm missiles," she ordered, flipping two switches above her. "Fire on my mark. Three, two, one, mark!"

All eight launched their warheads, two from each wing. They hit the shadow, engulfing it in blinding light and fire.

Her pilots cheered as the shadow vanished. The noise faded with the explosion before erupting again as debris spread from the cloud. Another shadow burst through the remains and the celebrations fell silent.

"Oh no, oh no, oh no!" the rook screamed.

"Open fire!"

Before they could, it whipped four long arms at the closest fighters while bright red beams absorbed another two.

Queen kicked her engines to full power as two arms wrapped around her ship, with the remaining pair grabbing the rook. They were going nowhere. She watched in horror as the rook's ship was crushed before it exploded. The screeching metal of her own ship cut through her shock right after.

In those final seconds, she found herself thinking of the rook, trying to recall his name. Her family followed, along with a hundred things she had never said. "Sorry..."

Fire engulfed her ship and her scream.

"Report," General Matthews ordered as he strode onto the outer ring of the Command Centre before the doors had fully opened.

It was the middle of the night but he looked sharp and pristine. His beard, lightly tinted with silver, was perfectly groomed but there were faint bags under his eyes.

"Sir," one of the operators on the innermost ring called. Matthews marched past the outer three circles of consoles and operators without hesitation to stand behind the young man. "Flare Squadron were sent to escort the shuttle *Veranda* and its maintenance crew to repair probe eight-nine-three-nine—"

"I know that," he snapped. "What was so urgent that you had to call me in the middle of the night?"

"They're gone, sir."

"Gone? Where?"

"No, sir. Flare Squadron, and the *Veranda*, have been destroyed."

"How? When did this happen?"

"Fifteen minutes ago. Flare Two contacted carrier one-sixteen with sensor readings, recordings and a verbal report. The sensor was missing, the squadron attacked and wiped out. Flare Two was escorting the

Veranda away when they came under fire too. That's when the report ended."

"What about carrier one-sixteen?" Matthews stroked his beard. His frown revealed his true feelings to everyone.

"It's returning now. I've assigned an operator to keep an open channel with them until they return, even beyond the Warp Tunnel."

"Good." Matthews fell silent, thinking of the pilots and crew lost on what should have been a routine repair mission. "You said they sent images. What kind of ship was it? Who does it belong to?"

"That's the thing, sir." The operator turned from his terminal to look at the general, his face pale. "It's not a ship. It's nothing we've ever seen before."

Matthews stared at the screen for over two minutes. The room was as quiet as a vacuum. No one had ever seen the general this shocked – and it scared them. The operator shifted uncomfortably in his chair.

Matthews turned and strode for the door again, calling back to the operator. "Send all data on this to my MOB-I. Level one encryption. No one else is to see this, understood?"

"Yes, sir!"

But the door had already closed.

CHAPTER ONE

It was race day.

Ryan normally skipped breakfast but that was never a good idea before a Cyber Cycle race. He grabbed the dark green blazer from the chair at his desk and ran out of his room, down the corridor towards the dining hall, excitement spurring him on.

It was always busy first thing in the morning and the noise hit him like a wall upon entering. All the tables were nearly full; he saw familiar faces on one at the far end. Grabbing a cooked breakfast tray on his way, he settled into a gap they made.

They allowed him one bite in peace before the bombardment.

"How you feeling?"

"Any nerves today?"

"Are you going to win?"

"What's the strategy?"

Each one spoke over the last, getting louder each time, but there was never a chance to answer. The noise started to catch the attention of students sitting close by or who were on their way past, and they added their own questions. Some gave up when no answer came, but not enough.

"Cut it out." Zack's voice was calm but sliced through the chaos instantly and silence fell as Ryan continued to eat. Zack took a seat opposite and nodded to his friend, who returned it. There was no need to say it again. Being a few years older, Zack had the respect of most students.

That meant Ryan had it too.

Ryan watched his friend work on a handheld device. Short, messy black hair dropped over his hazel eyes. Pale skin and thin lips accompanied permanent day-old stubble. He was meticulous about the style. Two silver studs pierced each eyebrow. He wore a white T-shirt and faded jeans, with his blazer draped over a shoulder. There was no food in front of him but Ryan could count on one hand the number of times he had seen his friend eat a morning meal over the last six years.

"You set for later?" Zack asked without looking up.

"Yeah," Ryan answered between mouthfuls. "I'm ready. Are you?"

"Yep. Don't crash this time. The gaps between the next races are much closer together than the last one and today's."

"I'll do my best. When are you heading over?"

"After breakfast."

"If I skip another lecture I'll be in big trouble. I'll be there this afternoon."

Zack nodded, finally looking up. "You'd better get a move on or Kinni will rip you."

Ryan followed his gaze to the digital clock on the far wall and cursed. Shovelling the last of his breakfast into his mouth, he waved to his friends and ran for the door, bouncing between a fresh wave of students.

The oval-shaped building of Institute 412 concealed a garden in the centre. Large social rooms were on the south side, away from the entrance, while lecture halls, workshops and other teaching facilities were on the lowest five floors. Both the north and south side had two main corridors, one towards the outer row of rooms and one along the inner. In between were large rooms that could be split into smaller spaces.

Floors six to eleven were student rooms and there was one dining hall per level, while the top two levels had all the facilities staff and students might need: shops, bars, gyms and more. The plan was to stop students from causing trouble outside of the school.

Ryan's left wrist vibrated. A quick shake activated a holo-display over the inside of his arm. It showed an alarm proving he was late. Again. A quick swipe silenced the alarm and the image vanished when his arm dropped.

Dashing through the outer curved corridor on the north side of the building after descending four levels, he saw his class filing into a lecture hall at the direction of Miss Kinni. When she caught sight of Ryan running, she shook her head dramatically and held the door as he swerved inside.

The tutor was one of the few people Ryan had seen wearing glasses, the narrow lenses just covering each eye. He suspected they included visual interfaces, but implants accomplished the same thing and were more common. He'd never been able to get an answer as to why she chose to wear what could be implanted. Despite being shorter than most of her students, she was no less fierce. Looking contrite during a scolding was difficult for him when he didn't see the value in the class.

A few laughs greeted him as he climbed the shallow stairs towards a seat at the back. Earth History wasn't his favourite lesson – it was one he normally skipped, but Kinni had noticed, despite his low profile. Many discussions and punishments later, he made a point to be in every lesson – even if he dozed off most of the time.

Today was preparation for end-of-year exams. Hearing things for the second, third or fourth time didn't make them any more enjoyable.

"Morning, everyone. Exams are coming and our next classes will be focused on what you might need to know," Miss Kinni started, and Ryan settled in for another numbingly boring three hours. "Who can tell me what important event will be celebrated in a couple of months?"

"Unity Day?" a voice said from the front rows.

"Correct! And what is Unity Day?"

"The celebration of the formation of the Globe," another student said. They didn't seem too excited with the lesson, either.

"That's right. Unity Day saw the end of hard borders between the nations of Earth just three years after World War Three, and this will be the hundredth and eighty-sixth celebration. Resources were pooled and shared, poverty ended and police, security and military forces merged into one organisation, the Enforcers."

"What about Asiazone?" someone closer to Ryan asked, and he heard more than a couple of groans. "They still have some borders."

"In more recent years, Asiazone has been more segregated than when the Globe first formed, yes, but each region has the power to focus on areas that need development, and that's what they're doing. Who can tell me why Unity Day is so important?"

"It's a reminder of the lives lost during the war," the first student answered.

"Exactly," Miss Kinni said, using the holographic display over her arm to activate a bigger image of the Earth behind her, green, blue and white. Two large areas of land were grey: the first covering the United States of America and the second over Russia. "Most of the damage was limited to these two areas, but lives from around the world were lost – many were under the age of twenty, before laws were changed. What did this mean?"

"A generational gap halted growth for two decades because of the young people lost." The girl was on a roll, answering before anyone else could.

"Which is a lesson we can't forget. It brought in new laws that kept our young adults in education and protected from conscription for longer, so we'd…"

Miss Kinni's voice bored him to sleep every week. She knew what she was talking about, that was clear, but she also knew how to lull her students into a false sense of security before showing them up in front of everyone. It kept most of them attentive no matter how dull the lecture.

After she hit her stride, Ryan lost interest, turning his head slightly so he could look outside. The weather was glorious. A bright day with clear skies and no wind – perfect for racing, or relaxing. Instead, he was stuck inside learning about the formation of the Globe, the world nation. It wasn't fair.

The final exam for this class was two months away and then it would be a part of his history forever. There were other classes and exams before he could graduate but that was a problem for later. Ryan was sure he knew enough to pass this class already. Sitting here now was a waste of time.

Unfortunately, he had to put up with months of recap lectures. It was only now he realised that if he had turned up enough previously, he might have been able to skip these instead.

Ryan's thoughts drifted to the race ahead. The track's location wouldn't be revealed until an hour before the start but the rumours spoke of a street circuit. That would reduce overall speed and introduce some tricky corners. Overtaking would be harder than on other tracks. After the last race, that would make things difficult.

"Ryan Fall!" The sharp call snapped him out of his thoughts. He straightened up in his chair, noting the giggling and whispers around him. Caught again. "Can you please repeat anything I've just said?"

"I could," he replied, desperately trying to think of a way out, "but I wouldn't want to bore everyone by recapping a recap."

Laughter echoed through the hall. Ryan cursed mentally, knowing he had just opened himself up to a world of pain after class. His tongue got him out of a lot of sticky situations, but it was also the reason he ended up in so much trouble.

"In that case," she answered in a sickly sweet voice he was very familiar with, "would you kindly wait outside?"

Yes, it was a question, and yes, he could have refused, but Ryan had lost this round. Everyone knew it. Better to live and fight another day.

Aware of the eyes on him, most waiting for another witty remark, Ryan deactivated the hologram on his desk, walked down the wooden steps and out the door on the left. In the corridor, he leaned against the wall and stared through another room's window into the garden.

Miss Kinni continued her lecture like nothing had happened. He was going to be here a while.

"Once in a blue moon," a soft voice said a few minutes later, "you find someone who has so much potential that they can do anything – if they put their mind to it, that is. How many times have you heard that?"

"Too many," he said, keeping his gaze ahead, "but I already know what I want to do. Why are you here, Sara? I thought grads were supposed to leave, not hang around."

"I still have friends here," she said, stepping in front of him to block his view. "Besides, this is a good place to get business advice...and keep an eye on the competition."

"Feeling threatened by me?"

"Please," she said with a laugh, stretching the word for effect. "I'll feel threatened when you complete a race without doing something stupid. There's more to the sport than taking coo risks. Come on, let's take a walk."

"Those risks have helped me win," Ryan retorted, but he followed Sara away from the lecture hall.

They walked through the corridors slowly, occasionally passing a caretaker. Sara's holographic visitor pass over her purple jacket meant the pair were left alone.

Through the windows, he caught glimpses of the courtyard and garden, hidden by the building's curved walls, and of the ponds and outdoor hot springs, which students used in their free time to unwind. It was one of the best features of the whole Institute, especially on such a gorgeous day.

They completed two circuits of the halls in silence, taking the stairs down until they reached the ground floor. Ryan cleared his throat and Sara smiled, turning sharply to lead him out to the garden.

The moment they left the building and emerged into the shade offered by leafy trees and rock walls, Ryan forgot about the lecture and what Miss Kinni would say to him. Birds fluttered from flower to branch and back again, and while some students had picked out the sunny spots, more were chilling in the shade as they passed grassy mounds and trees with nooks.

They walked to the edge of one of the smaller pools and stared at the calm water. Only one was a natural hot spring – the large one in the centre – and it was the best. The rest were activated at night mostly, although a couple were on during the day for anyone with a free block.

Ryan looked at his reflection. Short, dark blonde hair caught the sun and the light wind ruffled his fringe. It needed another trim already and he brushed it away from his eyes without thinking. He had grey eyes, like an ocean on a cloudy day. A crescent moon of pale skin on his left cheek caught the light and he looked away.

"So, you missed me that much you came back just to stand here in silence?" Ryan quipped.

"You're a real coo at times, you know that?" Sara snapped. With a sigh, she continued, "I miss this place. Everything changes after graduation."

"I can't wait to find out. I'm going crazy here."

"It's not as easy as you think—"

"That's what everyone says," Ryan cut her off, not ready for another lecture. "Life's been pretty easy so far, though."

"You haven't fulfilled your part of the bet," Sara said, changing strategy. She'd dyed her hair again. It was purple with red streaks now. Graduating had really changed her; she looked older, wiser. The smirk that both infuriated and relaxed him was still the same. "I beat you last time. When are those blue locks gonna make an appearance?"

"Probably when I won't get yelled at by a lecturer. You do remember what they're like here, right?"

"Not as well as I'd like. It was simpler here. Less decisions to make, and they didn't matter so much."

"I can't wait to get out of here. I want that freedom."

"Who says it's freedom? Where will you go?"

"I don't know yet. I haven't given it much thought. Just…somewhere."

"Better start. You'll be out of here before you know it and able to race freely. Until then, I'm still worried you'll be caught," Sara pressed. "There's an age restriction for a reason."

"I'm twenty-five next year, early next year," he said casually, staring at the water. "No one knows who I am or where I'm racing from. It'll be fine when I'm legal, but I just can't wait."

"Then be careful." She grabbed his hand and gave it a squeeze. "Good luck today. Just…cool off a bit first."

Before he could answer, Sara stepped back and placed a hand on his shoulder. A moment later she drove it forward. Ryan flailed in the air before crashing into the water.

# CHAPTER TWO

THE LUKEWARM WATER DID nothing to soften the sting from Ryan's belly flop. He reached the bottom of the pool quickly and pushed up to the surface. Even though it had only been a couple of seconds, his lungs were burning.

As he burst from the water, Ryan took a deep breath before coughing up liquid. The people closest to him sat up or turned in his direction but were content to point and laugh.

The four-foot-deep pool was surrounded by a row of clean-cut stones that made clambering out easy but didn't stop water cascading over the ledge and surrounding grass. He lay there, panting softly.

There was no sign of Sara.

When he finally got to his feet, the prospect of returning to the lecture loomed, but after a fleeting glance towards the door, Ryan chose to skip it. If Miss Kinni saw him like this she'd know he had left – if she didn't already – and that was hassle he didn't want.

Navigating the halls presented another problem. Caretakers prowled the corridors during classes to clean up any mess. The Institute prided itself on its clean aesthetic. The floors were wooden, and each wall featured wooden panels in different tones. They became the easiest way to identify what part of the building you were in.

If the caretakers caught him trailing water through the halls, he'd be in deep trub. Grumpy didn't do their demeaner justice, and a couple of times Ryan had to double back or take a sharp turn to avoid the grey jumpsuits. With each step, the puddles of water grew smaller, and he went up and down more stairs than he liked to confuse them but, eventually, he made it to his room on the eighth floor.

He had just enough time to shower and change into a new uniform before his next lecture began. With a flick of his left wrist, the hologram above his inner arm activated. Drawing a pattern with his right finger unlocked the display. Opening his finger and thumb on one bubble changed the screen into a list of messages.

There was one from Zack at the top but the second caught his eye. Another reverse pinch and it expanded to fill the rectangular display. It was the details of the Cyber Cycle race: the location of the track, the schedule and a list of competitors – he ignored the list.

Swiping the message away, Ryan opened Zack's message. It had the same details but with a line at the top: *See you at John's.*

He sent a one-word reply and crushed the hologram. His arm felt warm around the implant. It had been heating up with even the briefest use over the last couple of weeks. It needed to be checked but a MOB-I was illegal until graduation. They made life a lot easier than carrying a device which could be lost or stolen. Mobile implants were also harder to hack without biometric data.

Portable Communication Terminals, or PCTs, were used by everyone who didn't have an implant, from young children to retirees. They could access comm channels and information from around the Globe, process payments and act as identification, but an implant could do all of that, too. There were some people who didn't feel comfortable having technology implanted, which Ryan couldn't understand. He had no regrets.

Standard PCTs usually needed both hands to be used properly at ten by eight inches. Smaller versions were one-handed, much smaller and more compact. Other sizes were used for walls and desks that didn't have full terminals. These were created on demand. All were touchscreens with micro-cameras and holoprojectors, with new versions released every other year. They could bend without being damaged.

Opening a compartment next to his wardrobe, Ryan grabbed a small, clear patch and tucked it inside his ear. Further in was a single PCT. He checked the battery level and pushed the black frame together, collapsing the rectangular device and leaving a black cylinder that fit neatly into his pocket. They did have some uses.

Three sharp knocks on the door stopped him cold.

Quietly stepping back, he turned to his desk and activated the terminal. Selecting the camera outside his room, he saw two people in dark clothing.

"Who's there?" Ryan called.

"Is this room eight-seven-four?"

"Yeah."

"Ryan Fall?" the second person answered. "We need to speak with you. Urgently."

"One sec," Ryan said, shutting down the screen. They wouldn't wait long before getting suspicious. He opened the balcony door, which slid silently, and looked over the rail, but it was a long way down. "Who are you?"

"Agents Cresta and Flinn. Enforcers," the second person responded.

That sent Ryan's mind into overdrive. Two Enforcer agents weren't here for skipped classes and wet corridors. They were concerned with more serious crimes, such as illegal racing licences and underage implants.

"Is everything okay in there?" the first voice asked.

"Yeah. Yeah," he said, trying to think of another way out. "Just getting dressed. Hang on."

After pacing the room a couple of times, there was no way to avoid them any longer and he opened the door to find two men in black outfits, one a bit older than the other, blocking the doorway. On the left side of their uniform's chest was an image of the Globe in white with a slanted 'E' in black over the top.

Both agents studied him. One raised an eyebrow at his appearance, not convinced he had just gotten dressed.

"What can I do for you, agents?"

"Can we come in? This is something best discussed privately," the older one said, glancing at the few students passing by. No one bothered to hide their curiosity.

"Sure. Once I see some identification."

They both held out thin metallic cards and activated holograms with their names, agent numbers and holographic models above. Ryan studied them. Agent Cresta was the older man and Flinn the younger, but the scarred skin on his face aged him. Ryan stepped back and they followed him inside, closing the door.

"So, what's this about?" he said.

"We're under orders to bring you in for testing," Cresta said, watching him carefully. "You've been identified as a potential candidate for a new programme. It's not optional."

"I'm exempt from conscription until I'm twenty-five, when I'm recognised as an adult and compulsory education ends," Ryan shot back. "Even then, only under Emergency Protocols can you have me conscripted – and those aren't active as far as I know."

"This isn't conscription, it's testing," Flinn said, his voice low, eyes dark and narrow. He wasn't happy to be here. "As Agent Cresta said, it's not optional. You are coming with us."

"I'm not interested."

"We have been authorised to use force if necessary, boy," Flinn growled.

"Flinn…" Cresta said, stepping between the two.

"Force? On an unarmed minor? I'm sure your bosses will love the publicity from that, because I assure you, I will make it very public. Get out."

"Ryan, we don't want to make a scene, but we have our orders." Cresta was the diplomat. "You are required by law to follow the orders of an Enforcer."

"Wrong again." Miss Kinni's class did have some use after all. "As a minor, you must order my guardians, who must then make me comply. Have you done that?"

"Well, no. This is a discreet matter and—"

"Then we're done. I have other plans today and your tests don't make the cut."

"Listen here, boy!" Flinn yelled, reaching behind his back. Before he could do anything, Ryan turned, dashed across the room and leapt over the balcony rail.

By the time the two agents ran outside, all they saw were the waves from Ryan diving into the moat on the outside of the building and the dissipating strands from the SafeNet. He was climbing out and running through the crowds before either could decide what to do.

"What now?" Flinn asked.

"Call it in."

"But you're the senior agent!"

"And you're the one who spooked him," Cresta roared. After a couple of deep breaths, he lowered his voice and turned away from the balcony. "Things would be a lot easier if you just kept your coo mouth shut. Now call it in. We're in deep enough trub as it is."

Ryan didn't make a habit of jumping from buildings – especially those on the eighth floor – but no one would say he was the kind to think first and act later. He knew it wouldn't be deep enough to dive in from that height, but the SafeNet was designed for such accidents.

SafeNets were everywhere, removing the risk of injury from falling at any height. Tiny emitters formed a web of holographic strands that were strong enough to catch people, vehicles and debris. The ultimate safety feature Ryan knew would catch him before hitting the water, slowing his fall enough to avoid injury before the strands vanished and he dropped the last few feet with a splash. It made his jump far less stupid than it looked.

The edge of the moat was higher than the hot springs and took more effort to climb. A quick glance up showed the agents were still on the balcony. Ryan ran into a crowd of people on the stone path leading to the Institute's main entrance, ignoring complaints and questions.

At the edge of campus was a transport terminal. Two sets of wide escalators gave access to a box on stilts with a number of rails extending in different directions.

A train arrived every few minutes, a series of carriages running along the beams like an inverted monorail. Miss Kinni had told them there was a lot of scepticism when they were first introduced because of the weight the beams had to hold, but the compound was strong enough to support the skytowers each zone held – although Ryan had never figured out how that actually worked. The doubts were forgotten when no accidents occurred, and the carriages proved reliable. Upgrades were few and shaved a few seconds off the journey while smoothening the ride.

Ryan found himself pacing the platform, waiting for a train that would take him to Zone-718. If the Enforcers had chased him, they might have caught up.

He took a seat in the front carriage when it arrived and slouched down in his sodden clothes. People threw funny looks in his direction because of the squelching shoes but he ignored them. The agents' story made no sense. If they knew enough to decide he was a suitable candidate for anything, they must know the rest. That gave them reason to arrest him and use it as leverage to get him to do their tests.

So, why not arrest him first?

The journey took twenty minutes and in that time Ryan came up with nothing. Emerging from an identical terminal to the one at his campus, he took a moment to adjust. Zone-718 was full of skytowers and criss-crossing pedestrian lanes connecting them. The ground was a jungle of people and mobile retailers, while hovercars and transports flew through invisible lanes above, a web moving in delicate synchronisation.

With all the people around, it would be impossible to track him, and Ryan wasted no time in diving into the biggest crowd he could find. According to the morning's message, he had about two hours before he had to meet Zack at John's, and if he was being tracked by those – or other – Enforcers, he didn't want to lead them straight there.

There were cameras everywhere, making blind spots non-existent. If the Enforcers wanted to find someone, they could. It was only a matter of time until the suspect slipped up, missed a camera or did something unusual. Ryan's best bet was to keep moving and stick to big crowds where he could keep his head down and blend in.

That meant killing time. His wet clothes caused people to push away from him, not wanting to get damp themselves. Bright colours were the fashion of the moment—yellows, blues and pinks—and his uniform would only draw more attention.

He crossed the plaza and picked a shop under one of the angular skytowers, its glass panels as bright as the sun above, to change his clothes in.

Every store entrance required an ID scan. Avoiding it set off alarms, and giving away his location would attract agents to the shop. He wouldn't have long to get out. He passed his arm over the scanner when a few others entered, keeping his head lowered, away from the cameras above.

Finding a hooded jacket without a logo or any other distinctive markings wasn't easy. The shop floor was littered with terminals and a holographic display of products that would scan for dimensions when activated. It meant the perfect fit for every piece of clothing, although you could manually override the selection for something else.

Once he had chosen a new outfit and used his MOB-I to pay, he walked to a white tube where his clothes waited, neatly folded, on the bench. He changed into dark denim jeans, a blue T-shirt and a reversible hooded jacket. Keeping the grey fabric on the inside, he wore the yellow side out to help him blend into the crowds but to make him forgettable next to anyone else with more standout styles – which was most people.

He threw the old clothes into the disposal chute and left the store. No agents were obvious to him as he did so. Ryan grabbed the folded PCT from his pocket, opened it and commed Zack.

"What's wrong?" Zack asked, his voice clear in his ear thanks to the patch.

"Enforcers came to my room," Ryan answered, holding the device by his side. He wanted to find a spot to stand and talk properly but knew it was better to keep moving. The steady churn of people offered a sea of faces to hide in and he slipped into the middle when a gap appeared.

"Hence the PCT."

"Yeah," Ryan said, finding it hard to avoid the people passing him – in both directions – without actually going anywhere. He couldn't stand still without drawing attention to himself, either.

"Ditch it. I'm heading to John's now. What did they want?"

"I'll tell you when I see you. Just watch out for tails as they might hope you'll lead them to me." Ryan grunted as a shoulder knocked him back a step and into the person behind. "There were two, but I didn't see them chase me so they might still be at the Institute."

"And more could turn up. I'll keep an eye out. You okay?"

"Yeah, just had a second swim of the day. Hopefully John will let me use his shower," Ryan said, spotting a group break away from the crowd and towards a plaza on the other side of one of the smaller towers. The walk would give him a direction and by keeping his head down he'd be hard to identify.

"What? Wait – forget it. John won't be happy if he finds out Enforcers are after you."

"Believe me, I'm not happy Enforcers are after me!" Ryan said, looking around after the outburst to make sure no one was staring at him.

"Good point. Lay low for a while. Anywhere you can go?"

"Yeah, see you soon."

"Be careful."

Ryan pulled the device's frame apart and threw each piece into a different bin along the way before changing direction. If the Enforcers were tracking him, he didn't want to be too easy to find.

John's place was on the other side of the area, crossing into Zone-719. That left enough time to grab something to eat and still be early. With no sign of him being followed, Ryan relaxed.

CHAPTER THREE

Enough happened in Zone-718 and the surrounding areas to stave off boredom for days, but when a race came around Ryan found it hard to focus on anything else. A big breakfast was normally enough to keep him going, sometimes with a light snack before the race, but the day's excitement had left a hole to fill.

Sticking to the crowds couldn't hide him forever and navigating the endless swarm of people would wear him out. Beyond the skytowers were smaller buildings that, from a distance, created a rising mountain of glass. His destination was towards the outer edge of this formation, down a side street with few people.

Unlike the plaza, with its holographic advertisements and dynamic shopping terminals, the doorways in this street were dull and lifeless.

Ryan stopped at an open door with no sign or indication of where the stairs led, but this place had become his favourite diner since he'd discovered it. You couldn't find it on any maps or in a directory. All their custom came from recommendations and word of mouth. The quirkiness added to the appeal, a break from the personalised ads on every public screen or display. It was one of his favourite secrets, shared only with Zack and Sara in the five years since he'd found it.

The steep, slightly uneven stairs led to the basement. The lighting dimmed as his descent continued. At the bottom, the gloom was enhanced by murky red lights in the shape of candles and lanterns before a dark-wood door. A faded brass sign revealed the name of the diner: Great Grub. Not original, but it lived up to its name, which was all Ryan cared about.

The door was surprisingly easy to open given how old and heavy it looked. Inside, the room was brighter but nowhere near normal levels. He was told on his first visit it was mood lighting. It added a secluded feeling regardless of how close the tables were.

Ryan stopped three steps inside. His usual table was occupied by a group of four men dressed in greys and browns, all crowded around one side of the table with their backs to the rest of the room – the booth seats were empty. Frowning, he stalked to the other end of the room and chose a booth where he could see the door. With no other exit, it wouldn't do anything more than give him time if Enforcers turned up.

There weren't many people eating – he had missed the lunch rush – but the evenings brought bigger crowds. Ryan scanned the room to see a couple sitting near the door—probably their first time here given how often they were looking around—and a few people sitting at tables alone. Then there was the group at his table. They were ignoring everything and everyone. That made Ryan nervous. Enforcers?

"We normally don't see you again so soon," one of the waiters said as he sat down. "Shame about your table."

Ryan searched for the name of the tall man who had been working during almost every visit he'd made for the last two years. In place of his eyebrows were metal studs, silver this time, six on each side, above bright sapphire eyes. Today he wore pink eyeshadow, exaggerating the corners of his eyes. Too long a silence would give away that Ryan had forgotten his name – again – so he turned to look at the group of men sat in his normal spot to buy himself an extra few seconds.

"Do you ever take a day off, Marcus?" Ryan asked, just as the waiter was about to speak – probably to chastise him for forgetting again. "Or are you stalking me to make sure you're here when I am?"

"Don't flatter yourself, Ryan. I enjoy you but you're so full of it, y'know that?"

"I've been told."

"More than once, I bet. The usual?"

"Just half."

"Half? What's wrong? Are you ill? I'll send someone else if you are."

"I'm not ill. It's just been a…strange day." That seemed to do nothing to reassure Marcus and he sighed before adding, "It's a long story. Go and get my food, you coo."

"Careful, or I'll wash that mouth out with soap," Marcus called on his way to the kitchen, hips swaying as he left.

A chime in his ear synced with a vibration in his arm startled Ryan. Activating the MOB-I, he saw another message from Zack: *Reported increased solar activity for the coming week. APS is being activated soon.*

That was bad news. The possible interference caused by the Atmospheric Protection Shield threw up a number of unpredictable scenarios for the race later. No matter how hard Ryan and Zack tried, a new problem they hadn't thought of always caught them out, and at the worst time.

The clang of metal on wood brought Ryan back to the diner. Marcus stood next to his table, grinning. The tray was piled high with pulled pork, vegetables and an artistic drizzle of sauce.

Compared to photos from his history classes, it looked just like the real thing, but all food had been synthesised since before World War Three using proteins and nutrients to make sure no matter what anyone ate, it provided benefits. Even dessert. Animal slaughter was outlawed, and the space used for crop and vegetable harvests reclaimed for wildlife. It meant mutations from growth hormones were no longer a factor. No one knew the difference between the natural and synthesised foods anymore.

"I said half!" Ryan said.

"Well, this is what the chef gave me. Maybe he knows something I don't?" Marcus said.

"It's race day," Ryan sighed.

"Ohhh. Maybe he's a fan? Don't worry, I won't say anything."

"About what?"

"Exactly. Swipe." Marcus pulled a scanner from the pocket of his blue apron and Ryan passed his left arm over it. The MOB-I chip registered the transaction and a double chime in his ear told him the payment had cleared. "Enjoy!"

For those without an implant, any PCT could process the transaction. Ryan had ditched his, so he had no choice but to use his implant. No physical currency existed outside of museums and private collections.

Even though he only wanted a light meal, Ryan devoured the whole plate in minutes and was sitting contemplating his next move when a horrifying thought struck – the Enforcers may have tracked the transaction.

Before Marcus could return, he headed for the door and passed his arm over the scanner to leave a tip. He glanced at his usual table through the dulled mirror.

With that brief look, he decided they weren't Enforcers. Agents were uniformed, obvious to everyone. Off duty, they had limited powers until backup arrived. It made no sense for four Enforcers to be out of uniform and following him.

One man held sheets of paper, with more on the table before him, and none had PCTs or were using implants. That was unusual too, and he noticed they all looked tired and ragged. He only stared for a couple of seconds to avoid suspicion. One of the men stared at him. The rest had their backs to the room, as they had done for his entire visit, but this man, older than both agents from the Institute, watched him carefully.

Pretending not to notice, Ryan opened the door and climbed the long flight of stairs to the street.

The APS had already activated. The sky was peach instead of blue and the buildings tinged with orange. He wandered through Zone-718, noticing the more subdued atmosphere, as if people were uneasy with the shield protecting them despite how often it happened. Ryan liked the change. It made everything feel new and different, like a prolonged twilight.

With only an hour before race registration, he cut through buildings, shopping arcades and plazas on his way to John's.

When the APS was active, Ryan felt like the air was heavier, more humid. He had the same thought each time.

John's was as far from a transport terminal as possible – although the man denied that was on purpose – in an area full of warehouses and storage space. As an industrial area, Zone-719 never stopped; haulers dragged containers through the air, people in high-visibility gear directed processes from control points, and there was a lot of to and fro, even on the fringes.

His destination was one of the first buildings across the border between zones. Above the entrance were well-kept, but very old, letters spelling *John's* and radiating white light. The colour could be changed on a whim. At first glance, it looked seedy and potentially dangerous, but nothing was further from the truth.

Four pairs of tinted glass doors stood underneath the bright letters; the white light turned orange because of the APS. Pushing one open, Ryan braced himself for the wave of noise to wash over him and let his eyes adjust to the dim glow.

The floor was an open space and packed with more people than Ryan would have thought possible. The building held every kind of gaming device that had ever existed, from ancient arcade machines and consoles right through to augmented and virtual reality modern simulators of all sizes. There were small children with their parents, and groups of teens and adults all competing on some of the newest and oldest video games available.

Ryan walked through the crowds at a snail's pace, soaking up the excitement. Players cheered when they won while their opponents were consoled by friends or let loose angry rants aimed at no one in particular. It brought a smile to his face as a few memories surfaced – although some of the curses annoyed him when young children were close.

At the back of the large room, he found his man. Boasting a large stomach and thinning hair on top of his head, brown fading to grey, John stood behind two teenagers, barking instructions as they fired plastic shotguns at a screen.

"That one. No! On the left – not his left, your left! Careful, now…"

"Maybe you're working them too hard," Ryan said, standing just behind the older man and watching with delight as he jumped.

"Ryan! Don't do that!"

"You should be used to it by now. You haven't forgotten what day it is, right?"

"No, no, no. Of course not. Come on," John said as he regained his composure and turned to the back corner of the room. Leaving the two minors, he called to them, "Keep at it, boys. I expect some real progress when I get back."

In the far corner stood a black metal staircase to the upper level. With little lighting nearby, it was almost invisible to anyone who didn't know it existed. They climbed in silence and John opened a red door with a metal key – the kind that belonged in a museum – to reveal a stretching corridor.

"Zack got here a while ago." John lit a cigarette that had appeared from nowhere after the door closed. "He's not happy the APS has been activated."

"The conspiracy theory again?"

"I stopped listening. He just wanted to get to work. Is this round twelve or thirteen?"

"Fifteen. Where've you been the last two months?"

"Wish I knew. When you get to my age, days and weeks seem to merge together and you're left wondering how you got so old."

"You make it sound so much fun," Ryan quipped.

"Oi. Happens to us all." John sighed heavily after taking a drag on the white stick. The corridor was long, running from one end of the building to the other, with black doors on either side. Without warning John stopped, and Ryan ploughed straight into him. "Are you being straight with me, Ryan?"

"What do you mean?"

"There's been some talk that the Enforcers have been recruiting sim users. You're not the only underage racer out there but our agreement is based on no Enforcer activity. I do not want them poking around here," John said, turning around. The seriousness in his eyes seemed to make him taller, as if he loomed over Ryan, despite Ryan being taller. "You both promised to be careful and warn me of anything suspicious. Has anything happened recently?"

"No," Ryan blurted, trying to keep his face neutral. "Of course not. We don't want to bring the Enforcers here, either."

"You're sure?"

"You don't trust me?"

"I don't trust many people. That's how leaks happen. If you see anything suspicious, you tell me straight away, you hear?"

Ryan nodded and John turned back down the corridor, his demeanour reverting back to what Ryan knew.

Whatever talk he'd heard had spooked the owner more than he was letting on.

There were no numbers or markings on the doors, but John stopped outside one and used another key to open it. "Your sim, sir," he said with a mocking bow and tone of voice.

"Not going to wish me luck?" Ryan said, trying to keep the levity.

"Only if you agree not to crash this time."

"Can't promise that. Where's the fun without a little risk?"

John shook his head and walked back down the corridor, letting the black door slam shut. The sim room was square and beige with a black sphere in the middle, twice as big as Ryan was tall. In one corner, a terminal with a holographic display had been divided into a series of square windows. Zack was tapping away, swiping, closing them down and opening new ones with such speed that he couldn't keep up.

"You made it," Zack said before Ryan could speak, not looking away.

"Plenty of time. Went to Great Grub for a bite but got enough to feed my entire class."

"So, you're feeling sluggish. Register, then take a nap. This looks a tough grid."

"You've found out who's racing?"

"Just the numbers they use. You're about halfway down the order if they choose that line-up."

"Could make things interesting."

"Yeah, and the APS is going to help with that."

"It's been, what, over a hundred years, and they still haven't been able to fix the power surges it causes from being online more than an hour or two?" Ryan asked with a sigh.

"They're annoying, but it's the interference caused to comm signals over long distances. You might find controls sluggish every so often, but I'll try and keep on top of it."

"Maybe they need more satellites up there? Would that cut out the interference?"

"Some, maybe, but the field itself is the problem. There must be increased solar flare or plasma expulsion soon."

"We're using it for longer each month. Invent a time machine and I'll go back and tell them how much they're screwing things up for us."

"I'll add it to the list." Zack chuckled. "At least we have enough power to use it without harming the planet even more."

"Nah, it's just my race that's getting messed up." Ryan shrugged, dropping his arm after finishing the registration with his implant.

"I've logged in to some backup relays. Let's hope that's enough. Did you tell John about your visitors?"

"Nope, and I'm not going to. Hopefully, this all blows over."

"Sure." Zack shook his head. "So, what happened this morning? Why are Enforcers after you?"

"You make it sound so ominous," Ryan complained, but Zack had always spoken in a direct manner. He could be tactful but mostly didn't see the point. "They want to test me. Something to do with my skills and experience relating to whatever it is. That can only mean they know I'm racing. They threatened to arrest me."

"That does sound ominous. How'd you get away?"

"One was pulling an Enforcex, I think. I ran for the balcony and jumped," Ryan said, then paused. "You already knew."

"Just wanted to see if you were going to spice it up."

"I had no idea how deep the water was, if that helps." Ryan said with a grin.

"It does. If not for the SafeNet, you could have died."

"What's life without a little risk? Besides, the SafeNet doesn't fail."

"It could," Zack countered. "Sometimes I worry you're going to take it too far."

"You worry too much." He walked to the dark leather sofa in the corner. Flopping onto it face down, he muttered, "Wake me in an hour."

It felt like only a few minutes had passed by the time Zack was shaking him, telling him to wake up. Muttering incoherently stopped the shaking but the cold water woke him instantly.

"Three times! Three damned times! What's with people getting me wet today?"

"Then wake up when I tell you. Get in the sim and prep," Zack said, putting the empty glass down and thrusting a white bag at him. "Grid order's sorted. They chose racer number rather than the previous result. Lucky for you."

The sim's hatch faced the door but required Zack to open it from his station. Lines of white light appeared in the shell as it opened, and Ryan stepped inside. Before it closed, he started changing into the blue jumpsuit. The cycle floated in the middle of the sphere with his blue-and-purple helmet on the seat and he ran his hand along it. It did nothing but help him relax; his own routine.

He put his own clothes in the bag and stowed it under a floor panel. Then he donned the helmet, leaving the visor up, and opened the channel to Zack; not that there was anything to say yet. As he stood next to the cycle, the sim burst into life with lines of colour stretching and distorting until they created a whole new scene.

The curved walls showed the starting grid of the track, but in seconds the scene masked the walls completely with perfect depth perception. In the following seconds, the rest of the space changed, filling and creating the area entirely until it looked, sounded and felt like Ryan was standing right next to a real bike on a stretch of road with forty-nine other racers. Each one stood in the same position next to their vehicles as all the sims synchronised.

Zack gave him the all-clear and he waved to the cameras and crowds above. Each racer's image was superimposed over an artificial avatar for a lifelike impression. No one liked races without riders. A few cameras dropped down to get close-ups of some racers. One swooped towards him and he swiped it away impatiently. With the helmet on, no one could see who he was, but that was one risk he wouldn't take.

There was an announcer saying something, but Ryan ignored it. When the horn bellowed, he climbed onto his motorcycle, like everyone else. The one in the sim was an exact replica of the one on the track – minus wheels. This helped with elevation changes. Looking down, he saw wheels attached by the sim unit, but they were holo images of the real machine. He knew there was nothing there. Any conditions would be relayed to him, with all the difficulty or ease that offered, while his movements and controls were matched instantly. Lag was measured in fractions of seconds.

"You ready?" Zack's voice rang through his helmet.

"Too loud!"

"Better?"

"Yeah."

"Don't forget the APS is up. There may be some glitches."

"Got it. Ready."

# CHAPTER FOUR

RYAN COULD FEEL THE cycle shuddering gently.

Zack had calibrated the sim to a high level of sensitivity, based on time spent on real motorcycles. It felt just like the real thing. The controls, the weather, the heat from the engine – all as lifelike as possible.

As close to a real race as possible.

Yet, it could still be better. He'd bring it up later. His friend had delved into the sim's hardware and programming to reach this level, but that didn't stop them trying to improve it. The bigger challenge was convincing John to keep this sim just for them.

Spectators only knew a rider's name – their screens could show on-track action, positions, footage from a single racer, rider information and more. Ryan was listed as Wesley Ellis; a random name to hide his real age.

To keep interest, riders were assigned different races at random in their tours. It made for a complicated scoring system, but everyone had the same chances to race unless they opted to miss one. With no travel involved, all equipment equal and transport not being an issue, it made each race a pure test of skill.

Raindrops splattered his visor as they waited to start – another element the simulator replicated. Zack would have an update but comm messages were restricted before the race and throughout the opening laps. He would get one message before the start, like everyone else.

The first few were always chaotic.

At the front of the grid, three red lights hovered above the racers. One by one they turned to green and the pack set off for the recon lap. This would be the first chance they had to see the circuit.

It felt familiar, with a series of tight corners right after the straight reminding him of a past race. Skytowers loomed over the racers as they cruised around the circuit while the APS cast a dull orange light over them.

It took over two and a half minutes to complete. Ninety-degree corners, three long straights and two short, two s-type chicanes and no run-off areas. The final section was a series of sweeping corners; he counted at least eight before losing count after almost running up the exhaust of another racer.

The last part would be the most difficult – and the most fun – but the rain increased the challenge. He shook the thoughts from his head. The start needed all of his attention.

"Forty-seven laps," Zack told him as he stopped at the white line. "Target time of two minutes seven seconds. Rain will increase before easing off. Watch for dozers."

It felt like it took an eternity for the rest of the racers to line up, but it was only thirty seconds. Maybe forty. There was no looking back; those in front were more important. He spent a few seconds looking at the way those closest to him had stopped, what angle they had taken and where they hoped to go. Everyone would be doing the same.

Finally, the three LED lights returned, which signalled everyone was in position and the race was about to begin. The first blinked out and a chime in his ear confirmed it – at the back you couldn't always see them.

Up and down the grid, the racers revved their engines as they waited for the lights to go out. Ryan had seen recordings where the noise was almost musical. Supposedly it was chance, but he wasn't convinced. It must have been staged or altered.

The second light blinked out with another chime.

It led to the longest moment of Ryan's life to date. It was the same every race. The short space of time between the second and third lights going out dragged. It gave him enough time to live through every possible scenario. Zack didn't understand, but Sara agreed, although her version was nowhere near as long as Ryan's.

The last light went out.

Tyres screeched and engines roared as he lurched forward. Everything else fell behind as the adrenaline kicked in.

A few riders ahead stuttered in the first second, making Ryan weave between them to avoid collisions. Everyone picked up speed as they charged towards the first corner and the tricky sequence that followed. The braking points became even more crucial.

The spray from the rider ahead made it hard to see what was coming. He needed to be in the lead to escape the grey mist before missing the entry to a corner.

Ryan swept through the fourth corner and heard metal scream, followed by the thud of an impact. Seconds later he arrived at a scene with two bikes in the barrier and three more strewn along the track. He took the clear line to the right, but had to brake hard to make the corner, skimming the barrier with his knee.

With his heart lodged in his throat, Ryan pushed forward.

Corner after corner, the rest of the lap unfolded without incident. On the second, he came across more accidents with debris across the tarmac. He was too fast to count the ruined bikes.

At the end of the third lap, the racers gained more confidence with the track, the weather and each other. Each rider swung to the side to avoid the worst of the spray and look for an overtake.

"Okay, talk to me," Ryan ordered as he crossed the line for the fifth time.

"Eleven out in first lap crashes," Zack answered. "Three retired with mechanical issues. There have been some pit stops too. You're sitting twelfth."

"I can barely see – this mist is coo!"

"The rain should clear in the next ten minutes. The track won't dry completely but a line should emerge. Switching tyres at the right time is crucial. Forty-one laps to go. Push."

"Cha."

With the chaos of the start behind them, the race settled down a little. Ryan found a groove – braking later and later on each corner and getting on the throttle earlier – as he tried to reach the racers ahead. Sim technology was so advanced that every time he leaned into a corner, he could feel the friction if his suit brushed the floor or skimmed a barrier. Even the rain hitting his helmet came with real patters.

With each corner, Ryan grew bolder. He knew nothing could hurt him in the sim.

He caught two racers jostling for position on the next lap. On the long sweeping curves in the middle section his chance arrived, and Ryan swooped around the outside. A third racer emerged from the mist and Ryan swerved, braking late and hard to cut inside on the next corner.

He met a sterner challenge soon after. His opponent defended the corners well but couldn't stop Ryan pulling alongside on the straights. Neither had the speed, or the nerves, to brake later than they should, so Ryan fell in behind for the last part of the lap. It began a cat-and-mouse game, with neither giving an inch, and Ryan's frustration showed as he made sharper moves to try to scare the other into making a mistake.

"Calm down. There's plenty of time. As the track dries, you can brake later with more confidence," Zack said in a lull between corners.

Ryan stayed quiet, focused. He knew that but didn't want to wait. The longer he fought here, the further ahead the leaders pulled.

Leaning into the next corner, he felt a strain as the cycle resisted. It lasted only a second, but his heart shot from his chest. Only one thing could cause that...

"Did you see that?" Ryan yelled.

"I did. I've activated the booster. That APS is coo."

The smoothness returned before Zack finished speaking. It increased the risk of their signal being tracked, and John wouldn't be happy, but Ryan had no time to think about it.

His chance to pass his rival arrived seconds later.

At the last corner, the rider, in yellow and black, hit the brakes a fraction too late, and too hard. Their turn was slower, and Ryan took the chance to draw up alongside.

The rain had eased up, and with everyone sticking to the same areas of the track, a dry line was beginning to form. Ryan moved to the wet areas to keep the tyres working better and pulled ahead before returning to the dry line to slide into the first corner of the next lap.

"This dry line is eating up my tyres. Has anyone started to switch yet?"

"No," Zack said.

Ryan cursed. Wet tyres relied on water through the grooves. Without it, the tyres would wear out. The weather was random, and it was a gamble to change tyres. Pit stops cost a lot of time.

"Let's switch," Ryan decided.

"Okay. Dry tyres."

No one wanted to pit first. It would tell the other racers what tyres to be on. His call would raise eyebrows. Ryan knew it was a gamble, and he would drop down the field, but if it was the right call, he'd make more time on the leaders.

The pit lane ran parallel to the main straight. As he pulled into his assigned slot, the cycle jerked into the air as two metal arms grabbed it. The wheels were replaced by two more. He dropped with a jolt and tore away again.

The dry tyres meant he couldn't go wide, or he'd risk losing control on the wet surfaces. That would be the end of his race. Overtakes would be more difficult.

He could feel the difference straight away with better braking and speed.

It didn't take long to catch up, and Ryan eased past two riders on the next two straights.

"More are switching to slicks," Zack's voice rang through his helmet. In the confusion, Ryan found himself alone for two laps until an update arrived. "We're halfway there. You're in seventh. Get on with it."

Ryan caught sight of black-and-white overalls and grinned beneath his helmet. He could soon make out the red thirteen on their back. Like Ryan's 111, their number was all over their race suits and cycles so spectators could identify them easily.

"Easy now," Zack warned as Ryan closed the gap. "Don't do anything reckless."

Seeing Thirteen reminded him of previous races, where Ryan had lost out more often than not. Sara never let him live it down.

He closed the gap quickly. Both racers started braking later and later with each corner. Ryan drew up alongside his rival on the straights but backed down when he couldn't reclaim the best line. The back and forth continued until the board at the side of the finish line showed only fourteen laps left.

In that moment, Ryan made a choice.

He kept up the pressure, jinking left and right, braking at the usual spots and drawing level on the straights. The tight and twisty section at the end was his target. One bend in particular.

Three corners from the end and they reached the hairpin. Ryan hit the brakes hard and late to dive up the inside. It worked until Thirteen's better exit drew them level, putting them both neck and neck and trying to take the same dry piece of track.

Ryan sneaked ahead at the next corner but reached the last one of the lap, a ninety-degree turn, off the dry line. His rear tyre spun. He wobbled...and lost traction.

Leaning to the side to try to make the corner, Ryan's leg scraped along the road. It was no use. His wheels left the surface and he tipped, his leg between the surface and the cycle.

Ryan's leg dragged along the track, the friction burning. A sudden jolt from behind told him it was over.

He briefly caught a glimpse of rider Thirteen and their bike flipping over him and hitting the SafeNet in front of the barrier just before he did. Ryan's bike bounced away from him and he slammed back to the ground with a thud, gasping for air.

It took a few moments for him to move. Breathing proved painful as he got up, but other than a throbbing hand and leg there was nothing serious. The race suits were so advanced that everything he felt was only a fraction of what it would have been in the past, when sims weren't even around. A quick glance made him wince as he saw the two bikes mangled in the barriers.

Thirteen stared at him until the holographic avatar disappeared and the lifeless avatar turned to the barrier. It didn't take a genius to work out he wasn't going to win any popularity contests.

Ryan dusted himself off and gave a quick wave to a descending hovercam before Zack cut the signal. His hologram disappeared from the track and the simulator fell dark for a few seconds until the lights activated, revealing the grey panels of the sphere. The cycle hovered in the middle, back in its normal position. Grabbing the bag from under the panel, Ryan opened the hatch and walked out.

Zack stood at the terminal, working as hard as he had been before the race. He said nothing, but his thin lips and furrowed brow told the story.

"The silent treatment?" Ryan asked, trying to lighten the mood. "You're getting too predictable."

"So are you. That's the fourth race in a row you've crashed out. If you're not careful, you'll never get a contract for next year."

"I was one of the most exciting racers out there."

"Great for the audience but sponsors want wins. That's how they make money. You can't win if you crash."

"I know, I know."

"You say that, but you're not learning. You've got a twenty-place penalty for the next race because of this. That's going to make it even harder to get a good result."

"Unless we get a good starting position—"

"At best, twenty-one. Not likely."

Silence stretched between them. Ryan took a long drink from the water bottle Zack offered while Zack shook his head. They had the same conversation every time Ryan crashed. Even a penalty was no deterrent. While he felt like he had a chance, he was going to take it. The pro Cyber Cycle racers knew when to pull out of a move, but with no risk of severe injury, Ryan wasn't worried about the consequences.

"I've got more bad news for you," Zack said, returning his attention to the terminal. "Enforcers are here. Every exit is covered and there are three out in the corridor with John."

"Coo. He's not gonna like that. How long have they been there?"

"They got here soon after the race started. The ones at the door? About ten minutes."

"No windows to jump out of this time," Ryan muttered as he made his way over to the sofa and flopped onto it. "Give me a few minutes and let them in, I guess."

CHAPTER FIVE

"ARE YOU SURE THEY'RE in here?" General Matthews asked. They'd been standing at the door for twenty minutes. The race had ended a while ago and there'd been no sign of movement.

"Yes, General. They always use this room, there's no other way out," John wheezed, rubbing his hands over and over.

"And they know we're here?"

"They always know when I'm coming after a race." He waved to the black domes overlooking the corridor from the ceiling. "I think they monitor the cameras."

"Clever boys," Matthews muttered.

Ryan Fall was a gamble. The criteria for this project were a lot more flexible than he normally worked with, but they needed more recruits. Given the objective, and his resources, he had decided it was worth the risk and what he'd seen of the race confirmed it. He handed a PCT to one of his companions with a frown.

How Ryan's race ended was a problem. It needed to be discussed.

He took a step towards the door and grabbed the brass handle. Very antiquated. The lock clicked before he could try to open it, and Matthews supressed a smile. They had been waiting for him to make the first move.

"You two wait here," the general said to his agents. He turned to John. "Thank you for your assistance. No further action will be taken on supporting an underage Cyber Cycle racer."

The agents took positions on either side of the door as John sagged in relief. He turned and staggered down the corridor, muttering.

The general pushed the door open, expecting both occupants to be alert and ready for a confrontation.

They weren't.

Zack stood in the corner to his left, working furiously at a workstation. He wore a frown that Matthews guessed was because of the race. The simulator stood in the middle of the room but there was no sign of his target.

The door slammed behind him but didn't lock. Before he could speak, Zack pointed to a corner where the end of a sofa poked out from behind the sim. The general slowly walked around it and saw Ryan sprawled out on the side hidden from the door.

He didn't react when Matthews stopped in front of him, nor when he cleared his throat. Ryan's eyes remained closed behind sweat-stained hair.

"Can I sit?" Matthews finally asked.

The racer opened his eyes. He sat up slowly and swung his legs to the floor before gesturing to the other half of the sofa.

"Thank you."

They locked eyes in silence. Ryan, still breathing heavier than normal as he recovered from the race, hadn't changed out of his overalls. The red 111 could be seen on both legs but because the top half of the suit had been rolled down, he couldn't see where else the number was placed.

Matthews, on the other hand, wore a sharp-edged uniform that came from a lifetime of service and discipline. The jacket trims were silver and, as befitting his rank, six silver triangles were pinned on the left side of his collar. Over his heart was the Enforcers logo, an image of the planet with the slanted letter "E" cut through it. Unlike the white worn by most agents, this was also silver.

"My name is General Steven Matthews," he said. "You are Ryan Fall."

Ryan said nothing.

"You caused those agents some trouble today," Matthews continued, leaning forward and interlocking his fingers. "Most people, unless they have something to hide, do not jump from balconies. You, however, chose to be difficult. You chose to jump from the eighth floor.

"We tracked you through Zone-718 easily – did you think your tactics helped? This room has only one exit, so it was clear that if we waited for you to arrive, you'd have no choice but to hear me out. You didn't stall for long, so why stop running now? Do you have something to hide, or had you not planned past the race?"

Still, Ryan said nothing.

"Not very talkative? That's fine; you can listen for the moment." Matthews shrugged, leaning back. "Let's look at the situation here. I'm sitting with you, a twenty-four-year-old minor who's just finished a Cyber Cycle race. I'm sure you're aware the minimum age to participate in professional races is twenty-five. This is when you finish compulsory education and become an adult in the eyes of society and the law. Is there a reason you think you're special enough to get away with breaking this law?"

Ryan shrugged. Matthews wasn't sure what the silence was for at this stage, but it didn't matter.

"The truth is, we've known from your first race you were underage. Can you think of a reason we chose not to do anything about it?" Matthews waited, in case Ryan chose to speak. "No? Would it surprise you to learn you're not the first underage racer on record? Nor will you be the last. In fact, in the race you were just in, there were three others – two younger than you, and one of them younger than you were in your first race."

Ryan's eyes widened a fraction. It was enough to tell Matthews he was making progress.

"In the grand scheme of things, it's not high on our list of priorities. You people have made your choice. The only times we'll intervene are when an institution informs us your education is suffering, when your guardians complain or if it leads you to crime – none of which have happened to you, but that doesn't mean we can't take action. Remember that."

"Is the silver on your uniform because you're a general, or did you just want to stand out?" The question came so abruptly it took Matthews by surprise.

"It serves a purpose—"

"Which is?"

"It shows I'm not a regular Enforcer. I'm part of a special division," Matthews answered slowly. The boy was curious. That had been in his profile, but he had obviously noticed the difference and thought on it since Matthews sat down. He was sharp. "My agents explained what we wanted you for, correct?"

"Some sort of test." Ryan shrugged again, looking around the base of the sofa. He looked up at Zack, but before he could say anything, his friend tossed a water bottle to him and he took a swig. "They didn't say what for."

"They were under orders not to say anything. At least they managed that," Matthews muttered, ignoring the smirk on Ryan's face. "We wanted to test your ability to use a sim."

"Why?" Ryan asked, confusion clear in his voice. "You already said you've known I've been racing for the last two years, so you know I can."

"We know you can race but the test is more than that," Matthews explained. "It's about how you can use the sim in a number of scenarios and what you'd do in demanding situations. By looking at past footage, and the race you've just finished, I'm satisfied you'd pass, although..."

"Let me guess, you think I'm reckless," sighed Ryan.

"What makes you say that?"

"You wouldn't be the first."

"They're not wrong, are they?"

The only response Ryan offered was a chilly stare.

"Don't misunderstand, you put on a fantastic show and made great progress throughout the race, but... you don't think of the consequences much. Am I correct?"

"Once I make a decision, I follow it through. To the end."

"Admirable, but how are you to learn? If you'd been on that track—"

"I might be dead right now, I know. I've been told," Ryan snapped. Matthews realised he had hit a nerve. "Here's the kicker: we're not on the track, we're in sims. The worst that'll happen to us is a knock when we're thrown to the ground. It's the same everywhere.

The SafeNet means I'll never die from jumping off a balcony. Synchro units prevent cars and bikes crashing. Enforcers can track our every movement, crime is almost non-existent, implants are making us faster and more connected to everyone. We live wrapped in blanket after blanket. Why do I need to worry about the risks or consequences when they don't matter?"

"Perhaps for the good of the race, and the sport?"

"And now you sound like a sentimental old man."

It was exactly the response Matthews expected. Ryan may be close to being an adult by law, but he was far from the finished product.

Matthews interlocked his fingers again as he analysed Ryan and their conversation. The boy was brimming with talent and skill, and there was intelligence to go with it, but he lacked discipline. He would go far if he could learn to take responsibility for his actions and how they affected others.

The dilemma was clear. One day, Ryan would be a fantastic candidate, but not now, and there was no way of knowing how long it would take to make him into what they needed. Unfortunately, time was short and, purely on data, he was one of the best still available.

That cemented Matthews' decision. Even Ryan's risks sometimes paid off.

"Given you've already missed the tests, I'm prepared to use your racing experience as a suitable alternative," Matthews said, taking the plunge. Ryan met his gaze – all they needed were cards to go with the poker faces. "I want you to join the programme."

"It would help if you told me what it was."

"I can't do that. It's need-to-know and, until you agree, you don't need to know."

"How am I supposed to make a choice with that much information?" Ryan asked incredulously.

"You're a racer, let your instincts decide for you," Matthews said simply. "What I can tell you is this is a challenge unlike any other, that less than one percent of the population will ever experience in your lifetime. All the excitement and adrenaline you get from Cyber Cycle won't compare to what I'm offering."

"And if I refuse?"

"We'll take action for underage racing. There will be a custodial service and fine. I expect you'll miss the final exams and graduation, so you'll have to repeat this year. Your parents will be informed, and that could prove embarrassing for everyone. I can contact them now, if you'd like?"

"I'd rather you didn't."

"I thought so," Matthews said with a smile. "I hope we won't have to go through all of that, though. There's enough going on."

"If I agree…" Ryan said slowly. He shot a look at his friend, and Matthews had no doubt Zack had been listening carefully while working at the terminal. "I want Zack to come. He knows how I work, and vice versa."

"Agreed."

Too easy, Matthews realised instantly. He had always planned for Zack to come along – his skills hadn't gone unnoticed either – but the general didn't want Ryan to think he had all the power.

"I've made all the necessary arrangements," Matthews continued, and pulled a PCT from inside his jacket. "This has the instructions and ticket information you need. The shuttle will leave in one week, so you have until then to decide."

"You act like I have a choice," Ryan said glumly.

"We always have a choice, son," Matthews responded. He stood and started walking around the sim, leaving the device on the sofa. "This time, I've been kind enough to explain the consequences of both options. Not everyone's so lucky."

A moment later, Matthews was on the other side of the door and let it close quietly before exhaling slowly. The agents looked at him for orders and he motioned down the corridor.

There was only one logical choice for someone like Ryan. He was always looking for a way out, even if it meant taking the easy option until another came along.

Matthews was certain that once he saw what the programme offered, Ryan wouldn't want to leave. There was something much bigger than adrenaline the young man hadn't realised he wanted yet. Whether it was the right choice or not, only time would tell. That was where the real problem lay. There wasn't much time left before everyone knew the extent of the threat they faced.

# CHAPTER SIX

"THOUGHTS?"

Ryan didn't answer, his gaze glued to the PCT General Matthews had placed on the sofa. Zack left the terminal and stood in front of him, waiting for his friend to come back to reality.

After a few moments of silence, Zack sighed, picked it up and activated it. Ryan's gaze didn't shift.

"What does it say?" Ryan asked eventually, raising his head.

"A lot. Read it yourself," Zack said, tossing the device onto Ryan's lap before returning to his work. "I don't like it."

"What you read or what you heard?"

"Pick one."

Ryan flipped the PCT over with a sigh. The information, displayed on multiple windows, was overwhelming. The thought of going through it all now gave him a headache. Shaking his head, he flung it back onto the sofa and stood, stretching his back and arms before combing his hair with his fingers.

Zack raised an eyebrow and Ryan frowned. They both knew there was too much to read so quickly.

"Is there anything I need to know about before tomorrow?" said Ryan.

Zack replied with a silent shake of the head.

"Good. I'll read it then. My brain is frazzled."

By the time Ryan had rolled up the screen and tucked it in his bag, Zack had shut down his station and was waiting by the door. The race had taken a lot out of them; fatigue was setting in. They ambled along the corridor, through the door and down the jet-black staircase. They passed John on the way and waved to the older man to show there were no hard feelings. He smiled feebly in return. Zack strode off to get their ride as Ryan took another look around. A part of him wanted to ignore everything else and play the games John had collected but he knew Zack wouldn't let him.

The sun had dipped below the buildings when Ryan walked outside, but with the APS active the sky would have been shades of orange and amber regardless. He stared up at it while waiting for Zack to return and clambered into the passenger seat of the white hovercar when it arrived.

The take-off was smooth and silent. Within a minute they joined a lane of traffic passing through Zone-718 and its steadily rising and descending buildings on the way back to the Institute.

Skylanes kept traffic regulated. Before their introduction, hovercars flew wherever their drivers wanted, and at any height. It led to so many accidents that all traffic was banned for months until the lanes were implemented, and autopilots improved enough to predict routes and potential accidents.

"Shall I call traffic control for permission to switch to manual?" Ryan asked, still looking up at the sky, where the first stars had peeked through the orange shield.

"Not tonight, I'm beat. No issues with the satellite's link to the autopilot."

The lanes were visible through the windscreen's display as a series of lights on either side, and they could see the markings for other lanes as they passed by. It could be confusing to navigate at first, and there were no physical markers outside of the digital display. The theory behind it was that there would be less maintenance to do on beacons or signs and everything could be managed from centralised locations. The displays also offered helpful information and guidance without blocking the view a pilot or driver needed. Zack leaned back and joined Ryan in watching the sky darken.

By the time they reached the Institute, both were dead on their feet. Grunting goodnight to his friend, Ryan shuffled back to his room. There wasn't any obvious disruption from the agents, so maybe the general could be trusted.

There was no more thinking, however, as Ryan flopped onto his bed and fell asleep.

A cold breeze stirred him from what felt like his best night's sleep in years. Without opening his eyes, Ryan groped for the duvet but gave up after a few attempts and opened an eye. The balcony door was wide open; the Enforcer coos hadn't bothered to close it when they left.

He was about to sigh but realised he wasn't on his bed – at least, not properly.

Ryan's legs sprawled down to the floor, which explained why his back felt so stiff. He must have been incredibly tired to have slept like that. Most races didn't exhaust him like...

The race!

Memories of the event flooded back: the start, the chaos, the sweeping corners, the pit stop and his crash. Thirteen was standing next to the wreckage, looking in his direction, and even though he couldn't see behind the visor, Ryan knew he was being blamed.

A surge of anger made him clench his fist and slam it on the mattress. Then it was gone.

Of course it was his fault, and he knew it. It was his move. The track was too wet. He should have known. Ryan also knew everyone watching would have held their breath to see if he would make it. No one got hurt, so no problem. Right?

Next time, he'd make the move stick.

Forcing himself to his feet, Ryan staggered to the shower. The stress evaporated from his muscles quickly but instead of him feeling fresh, exhaustion crept back. It took an arm against the wall for him to stay on his feet.

The PCT General Matthews had left was sticking out of the bag near his desk. He reached for it, stopped, and pulled back. Not yet – breakfast first.

When his arm vibrated, he activated the MOB-I automatically to read the message. It was Zack: *You're suspended again. For skipping yesterday. Also, there's an investigation into your crash and conduct. Read the info.*

"How do you always know?" Ryan muttered.

A knock on his door alerted him to breakfast. Suspension meant he was confined to his room, but no one would be guarding the door – unless Enforcers were back.

No agents were outside, just a member of security in their maroon uniform, holding a tray of food. It wasn't very appealing: porridge, fruit and milk. The tray would be collected an hour later.

Ryan tried to read reports of the race, but they annoyed him so much he switched them off before he started ranting. The reporters knew nothing. Obviously they weren't good enough to be racers themselves, so they criticised everyone's performance. Even the winner's.

The PCT caught his eye again. Pushing aside the lumpy porridge, he took a bite of apple and pulled the PCT from the bag, reading through the first window.

A brief introduction covered what Matthews had told them yesterday, including the tests he was supposed to take. The next part covered the two outcomes of the test. If failed, the results would be stored, and the participant returned to a destination of their choice, but if successful, the participant would be invited to join a new Enforcer programme.

Ryan had been offered that chance, with a little blackmail.

The following tab was a list of instructions: directions to Zone-311's Space Port, where the recruits were to meet. From there, they would be transported to an undisclosed location for a period of six months to a year, at least. Further details would be revealed then.

The third window was a contract Ryan had to sign and present when he arrived at the destination.

The final tab had the terms of travel and a cost code. This would authorise Ryan's transportation, within reason, as long as the journey took him to the Space Port.

Ryan put the PCT down and walked out onto the balcony, relishing the wind now that he wasn't so cold. It had already warmed up a little, even with his hair being damp. From his eighth-floor vantage, the students and staff walking in and out of the Institute looked like children. It was tempting to jump over the rail and run, but where to? There was no going home – he'd burned that bridge years ago – and Matthews would still find him.

He could try to hide for a while, but what would he do? There'd be no more Cyber Cycle. Could he live with that?

The answer was a resounding no. With six days until he had to be in Zone-311, he was in no rush to make a decision – not that there was one to make, really. Ryan knew he had to go. Whether he could convince Zack to join him was another question.

His friend was three years older and only failed to graduate because he didn't apply himself enough. Each year he got closer to the pass score without trying any harder. Would he really want to repeat the year again just to see Ryan join a programme that, so far, offered him nothing?

He wouldn't know for sure until Zack contacted him. Suspension also meant no visitors or comm access, but they'd been finding ways to get around the rules ever since they met. Having a MOB-I helped, as did disposable PCTs.

Ryan knew his way around comm systems, but Zack was the expert. He needed to figure out the what, how and why things worked to solve any problems that popped up. Firewalls, flawed code, missing parts and broken technology – the man had a gift for understanding, fixing and improving everything.

It made no sense for Ryan to try to match him. His skills were best used in other ways.

Ryan grabbed a holdall from a wall compartment and began to stuff it with clothes for the journey. Halfway through packing, the door opened and he braced himself for the strict voice of Principal Grove. Another lecture about how important education was and what kind of future he was likely to have by messing it up was surely coming.

It didn't come.

With the bag almost full, Ryan turned to face his visitor and was surprised to see Miss Kinni. She stood in the doorway, leaning against the frame and watching him with a serious expression. He had only seen that a handful of times. It didn't bode well.

"What are you doing?" she asked after an uncomfortable, drawn-out silence.

"Packing."

"For the love of…" she whispered, closing her eyes and taking a breath to stay calm. It didn't work. Her eyes opened a moment later as narrow slits. This was the first time he had seen her without glasses. "A long, long time ago, we were allowed to whack students with a cane if they answered back or gave teachers attitude. Sometimes I wonder if that would have worked on you."

"We'll never know. Come in or get out – there's a breeze."

Miss Kinni stepped inside. Her gaze flew to the open balcony doors and back to Ryan. He wasn't cold anymore, just deflecting her attempts to find out what was going on, although it was getting him nowhere.

"How much trouble are you in?" Miss Kinni asked, crossing the room and reaching for the device on the bed, but Ryan scooped it up before she could grab it. "It's not often Enforcers come for one of our students."

"I'm not in any trouble," Ryan said, waving his tutor to the chair at his desk while he sat on the bed. "They wanted me for testing, but it turns out I already passed."

"Then why did they order an extended absence for you?"

"I've been *invited* to join a new programme based on sim technology. I won't know what it is until I get there."

"Why did you say it like that, with emphasis on 'invited'?"

"If I don't go, they'll charge me with underage Cyber Cycle racing. That'll be worse than having to resit this year."

"That's blackmail!"

"Yes, it is." Ryan nodded. "Unfortunately, that's the situation. I was told the consequences of the options available to me. Apparently, that's a rare event and I should feel lucky."

"There must be something we can do." Miss Kinni stood and started pacing. "Maybe with the media's help we can fight this."

"And here I thought you were coming to lecture me for skipping class."

"There'll be time for that once this is sorted out. The whole Institute is talking about this – and your leap from the balcony. I've not forgotten about it either, you damned coo."

"Yes, ma'am."

"Don't act contrite. It doesn't suit you."

"Fine. Then you should know I'm not going to fight this." Her reaction was priceless, and any other time Ryan would have savoured it. "I'm bored here. That's no secret, and racing is the only thing that's kept me from leaving. Now that's at risk and I don't know what I'd do without it. I can't afford to get into a fight with the Enforcers that could threaten my future as a racer."

"But—"

"Besides, the Enforcer general promised this programme would make Cyber Cycle look like a child's game. I've tried not to let it get to me, but it has. I have to find out what this is."

"Ryan—"

"You can't stop me; I've made up my mind. Granted, it's not often I think about my future, but I don't have a choice here."

"Okay, okay. I won't try and stop you. Truth be told, Principal Grove has had enough. He's trying to find a way to get you out of the Institute already. Not even your parents' influence will be able to stop him." Before Ryan could answer, Miss Kinni held up her hands and continued, "I know, I know. You've never wanted your parents' help, but you might need it now. When are you planning to leave?"

"I have to be in Zone-311 in six days."

"You might not have that much time."

"Then I'll get there early. I need to speak to Zack."

"You're not thinking of dragging him into this too? Come on, Ryan. There's no reason he has to be involved!"

"I'm not here to ruin people's lives but I think he has to. This programme is based on sim technology and I don't know anyone who's as good with it as Zack. When I was talking to the general, I said I'd want Zack with me, and he agreed straight away. There was no objection. I think he wants him there as well."

"Why can't I get through to either of you? You're two of the most annoying students I've ever taught."

Ryan looked at her like she had lost her mind but let her continue.

"You could do anything, but you don't care. You only want to race. It's the adrenaline. I've seen it before. You need to find something else, something that grounds you, or you'll end up dying for a thrill you can never achieve."

"And Zack?"

"That stays between me and him, just like this stays between us." She pulled a PCT from her pocket, like the one he'd destroyed yesterday in Zone-718. "He gave me this to give to you. You'll have to leave today, before Grove sends you back to your parents." Miss Kinni turned to leave, her fingers tracing lines across the desk as she turned. "Don't do anything to get yourself arrested or killed. I expect to see you here next year." At the door, she turned and smiled. The same smile Ryan had learned to fear because it never meant good things for him. "Maybe then you'll be ready to actually apply yourself."

The door slid shut behind her and Ryan was alone again. Miss Kinni had always been pushing him, but he assumed that was because he was so disinterested in what she was teaching. It never occurred to him that she saw something in him. Maybe other tutors did too.

Ryan rolled up the PCT from Matthews and put it in one of the bag's side pockets. He grabbed the bag and placed it on the bed...and sat down next to it.

Zack had managed to get him a new device. It was a big risk to go to Miss Kinni – and an even bigger one for her to bring it to him. Getting out of the room wouldn't be easy. He was sure people would be watching his balcony to make sure he didn't jump again. The door wasn't locked but security would find him in an instant if he wandered into the hall. He had to wait for his friend to share his plan.

And Ryan wasn't patient at the best of times.

It took another three hours for Zack to call. Lunch had come and gone, a cold salad that felt like he was eating air, and his impatience was tempting him to jump again. The bag was waterproof, after all.

"You took your sweet time!" Ryan said when Zack finally called.

"Been sorting things out. You ready to go?"

"Sure, there's just one problem," Ryan said, looking around his room.

"Check your desk."

"What?"

"Do it," Zack said with the smallest sigh.

Ryan reached his desk but saw nothing. He was about to turn away when something caught his eye in the light. A closer look revealed a small square of clear plastic camouflaged perfectly on the desk's surface, half the size of his little fingernail.

"How did you get Miss Kinni to drop this off?"

"Another time. Scan that piece of plastic to get through any door in the Institute. Start with your door – it'll fool security. Get out quickly and meet me in the transport terminal."

"Okay, when—"

"Don't make me wait," Zack cut him off.

The piece of plastic was small and thin enough to hide in his palm easily without it bending or breaking.

The corridors were empty since everyone had class. He kept his head down and walked with a purpose he normally lacked. That might be why the few people he passed didn't react. They'd remember later, when everyone realised he had vanished.

At every corner, he expected campus security to be there and escort him back to his room, but they never appeared.

Ryan almost dropped the square at the worst time. His heart leapt into his throat and his legs turned to lead as he approached the main entrance where scanners checked each entry and exit. The plastic slipped and when he passed his hand over the scanner it didn't read properly. Ryan held his breath as he tried again before being cleared through. No one stopped him. Whoever he was pretending to be, they'd have some explaining to do later.

The walk to the transport terminal was uneventful and Zack was waiting by the entrance. He didn't say a word when Ryan raised a hand, just turned and walked inside. He followed in silence.

Trains arrived and left but Zack didn't take any of them. Ten minutes passed. Then twenty. Thirty. Finally, after forty-five minutes of waiting in silence, a train arrived. This one had three levels of seating and orange markings across every compartment.

Zack led the way to a pair of seats on the top level at the end of the carriage. Only then did he let out a deep breath, smile, and begin to talk.

# CHAPTER SEVEN

Sprint trains were much quicker than their interzone counterparts, having to cross larger distances where they could reach higher speeds. Ryan and Zack's journey took them from Zone-713 to Zone-676 in little over an hour. For the first half, Zack talked the journey away. Ryan couldn't remember the last time he had heard his friend speak so much. It was mostly nonsense to deter anyone who might be listening. They were both being cautious.

Ryan had become the quiet one. So much had happened since the previous morning and he still hadn't processed it all. Zack seemed to realise this and did his best to be a distraction.

He was partly successful.

It took another twenty minutes to travel across the zones of the island's former capital and reach the Europort – the only way of getting to mainland Eurozone without flying. The underground train system still existed for anyone who wanted to experience what public transport used to be like at the turn of the millennium – most of the custom being tourists.

The former Channel Tunnel had taken two decades to upgrade but it started the transformation of transport infrastructure across the island and mainland Eurozone. It became the most popular method of transport across the water, taking between fifteen minutes and two hours to reach a number of destinations.

There had been many attempts to take hovercars across the water but they'd all failed, first due to tech limitations and then new laws. Crossing the shore instantly activated the autopilot and returned the vehicle to land. While borders had disappeared into zones, everything was monitored and only agreed routes were permitted for long-distance travel.

Wounds from the past healed but weren't forgotten. There were scars that reminded the world daily of the past, according to Miss Kinni.

The Europort was always busy, with long queues of people waiting for the next available train. The tracks were designed for different sprint trains, and while they traversed mainland Eurozone, each region had their own intercity routes. These services never stopped running, which helped keep people – mostly – content.

Ryan and Zack stood in a large hall covered by an opaque white bubble. People piled out of stairways at the far end leading to underground platforms, while others were shepherded into ragged lines by pacing staff. Even more queued at counters for tickets, information or food, and swarms of people were milling about in the remaining space.

"Hold up," Zack said as he walked towards a line of people queuing to speak to an attendant.

"Where are you going?"

"To get us some seats without waiting three hours."

"Here," Ryan said, opening his bag and pulling the PCT out. He activated it, swiped through the tabs until he found the right one and handed it over. "Matthews left this."

Zack smiled as he read it. "Missed that. That'll make things easier. Come on."

Ryan followed his friend towards the ticket office but instead of waiting at the back of the queue, Zack walked around the side and straight to a counter someone had just left. Before the man could object, he pushed the device into his hands. By the time Ryan caught up, the attendant's face had paled past the colour of milk and a stammer replaced his confidence, brown eyes filled with panic at the sight of them.

"P-p-p-please w-wait just a moment," the man said, standing and turning. "I'll b-be right b-back."

He might have said more but it was lost as he vanished into a back room. A few seconds later, a stocky woman with a stony expression marched out with the man tripping over his feet behind her. She took a long look at the pair, as if deciding whether this was a scam, before telling them to follow.

A smug grin spread across Zack's face that Ryan couldn't help but mirror. They followed the woman to the far end of the hall where six stairways descended to the underground platforms.

"Where is it you boys are heading?" she asked without looking back, the impatience clear for all to hear.

"Zone-311," Ryan said.

Her only reply was a grunt. Whatever she thought they were doing, it wasn't enough to impress her. She led them to the stairs at the far left, walking so confidently that people moved out of her way. Ryan and Zack weren't so fortunate. The gaps closed before they could get through, making them weave in and out of the crowds to keep up.

She didn't wait at the top of the stairs and they ran down them two at a time to catch up.

At the bottom, she led them to the end of Platform Four and spoke to another man quietly. He looked them over suspiciously before waving them through a gate with a few other people. Ryan could feel the stares from people on the platform they had skipped.

"This is the premium area," Zack murmured. "Quite an upgrade."

It only took a few minutes for the sprint train to arrive. It was a similar shape and style to the carriages used above ground but smaller and split into just two levels. Rather than the white foam seats they had occupied since leaving the Institute, now they were treated to red recliners with a table for every four seats and dedicated staff to make their journey comfortable.

The man who let them through the gate spoke to a steward, who asked them to follow her and showed them to two seats away from everyone else.

"I've never travelled in luxury like this," Zack said as they sat. It was one of the few times Ryan could remember him being in awe of something. "Only people with influence and power get to sit in these seats. And a lot of money."

"I've done it once or twice."

"With your parents?"

"Good guess," Ryan said as he leaned back and closed his eyes. "What's our next step?"

"Get to Zone-311's Space Port."

"You make it sound so simple."

"It is."

"Fine. I'm going to get some sleep. Wake me when we get to the mainland."

Ryan didn't sleep well. The journey through the underwater tunnel was smoother than overland but the air felt heavier. The carriage was silent other than when the occasional attendant asked if anyone needed anything. Synthol was generally the answer.

It felt far too soon when Zack shook his arm. They had emerged from the tunnel onto the mainland. "Are we close?" Ryan said.

"About half an hour from the edge of three eleven."

"What happened to waking me when we got to the mainland?"

"We're on the mainland. You're awake."

Ryan cursed quietly. "Why do I put up with you?"

His friend only smiled. When he didn't say anything, Ryan turned to the window and watched the world pass by. More of mainland Eurozone was devoid of residential and industrial zones, unlike the island they'd left, and he could see populated zones in the distance.

On one side, close to the horizon, he could make out the sea, but with the raised track they were travelling along, Ryan wasn't sure if it could be seen from the ground. Their journey did curve them towards the coast every so often, but not enough for a good view.

Inland, a quarry was in the distance, with machines tilling the earth for materials of some kind and automated carts taking whatever they found to another zone for processing. These stations were managed from afar. People were sent in to conduct maintenance and repairs when required but this was rare.

"We're going to have to change trains," Zack said as they approached Zone-306. Ryan grabbed his bag and they headed to the door. The steward for their section pointed them to another platform and they got there just as an interzone train arrived.

"How long will this one take?" Ryan asked when they settled into their new seats.

"It's the last stop on this route. About forty minutes."

Soon after leaving the station, rain started to fall and worsened as they continued. It created a dull and lifeless view.

"Why are we doing this?" Zack asked.

"What?" Ryan said. The question caught him off guard.

"Why are we leaving the Institute for an unknown Enforcer programme?"

"I wasn't exactly given a choice."

"You could have given up racing."

"You know I couldn't do that. I'd have nothing."

"Except me. And Sara. And your future."

"A future without racing? What would that even look like?"

"Whatever you wanted it to. You have options."

"I don't see it," Ryan sighed, avoiding Zack's gaze. "It's all I know I want."

"What about it do you want? The fame? The excitement?"

"The feeling I belong," Ryan said quietly. "I belong on that track. It feels right. The excitement helps, but I feel like I have a purpose there that I don't have away from the track."

"That feeling comes from people, not a place or activity. The people you do the racing with, or those around you when you're there. Until you realise that, you'll never get that sense of belonging you want – no matter where you are or what you do."

"How do you know?" Ryan shot back, harsher than he meant it to be.

"Experience. Have you told your parents where you're going?"

"What do you think?"

"Maybe you should. We have no idea what we're getting into."

"They wouldn't care. We haven't spoken since they left Eurozone. It's been nearly eleven years." Ryan tried to keep the bitterness from his voice but knew he failed. Zack didn't say anything about it, though. "Have you told yours?"

"Left them a message. They might see it in a month or two. Depends when they next take a break from work."

"Can we drop it?" Ryan asked, feeling the emotions bubble. "Let's just get through the programme and get back to racing. Everything will be back to normal then."

Zack obliged and they spent the rest of the ride in silence. Ryan could feel his friend's gaze on him a few times, but he kept his eyes glued to the window and the darkening landscape.

It wasn't late but the stormy clouds continued and the APS above blocked some of the light. By the time they arrived at the end of the route, despite it being mid-afternoon, anyone would be forgiven for thinking it was much later in the day.

They left the transport terminal in Zone-311 without speaking. Unlike Zone-714 or 718, very little filled the area. Across from the terminal's entrance was a metal archway, creating an opening onto a large, fenced area. The closest building, inside the fence, was also the only one they could see in the gloom. They would get soaked trying to reach it.

"Now what?" Ryan said.

"You tell me." Zack shrugged.

"I don't know!"

"Surely the PCT Matthews gave you should tell you what you need to know."

Ryan grumbled as he pulled it from his bag again. The pair stood in the entrance to the transport terminal as they hid from the rain.

Shaking his head, he passed it to Zack, but neither could find anything that told them where to go next. With a shrug, Zack followed Ryan out into the rain, pulling the collar of his jacket tight. They were only in the open for a few minutes as they ran but it was long enough to soak them completely by the time they reached the building.

It was a lot quieter than Ryan expected. A few people were waiting on scattered chairs and two men were working on the reception desk. The pair working ignored the newcomers when they approached. Even after Ryan cleared his throat, they still didn't look up from the terminals in front of them.

Ryan looked around. Almost everyone here was older than them, other than a group of three in the far corner. They looked far too young. These weren't workers; they were passengers with bags similar to Ryan's and Zack's. Everyone was waiting for something.

A few minutes later, Ryan tried to get the attention of the two behind the desk again. After more failures, he tried to grab the closest man, but his hand went right through, disrupting the holographic image.

"A shuttle is arriving imminently," a muffled voice announced over the intercom. "All programme partici-pants should make their way outside and board without delay. Thank you for your cooperation."

"I guess that answers that," Zack said as he turned back towards the door.

The shuttle was landing as they – and everyone else in the room – piled through the far door and crowded outside in the small shelter the building offered from the rain.

As soon as it settled and the door opened, everyone rushed forward. The first two seats available were on the second row from the front and they took them silently. No one spoke. The lights dimmed and the windows darkened as the shuttle rose gently.

They wouldn't be able to see where they were going but it was too late to turn back now. Ryan couldn't see a way to the pilot even if it had been an option.

The journey took just over ten minutes and the silence was unnerving. Someone behind them coughed and everyone turned to look. There seemed to be an unwritten rule not to make any noise until they arrived and found out more about what was going on.

A tall, slender man stood waiting for them outside the shuttle. His beard was neatly trimmed, braided and as black as the hair remaining on his head. At first glance, the man's eyes looked black too, but as his own adjusted to the low light, Ryan could see they were very dark brown. Those eyes were hard. He wasn't a happy man. His uniform was similar to the general's – black with a silver trim but only two metal triangles on the collar.

They were in an underground launch bay with dull metal on all sides and white light rods that could be used to direct or launch traffic from. This bay was just large enough for the shuttle but the hatch above was already closed.

"Welcome to Delta Space Port. I am Officer Jenkins, and I'll be your liaison during your stay here. I didn't expect so many of you this early. As the week progresses, you'll find things get a little cramped." Jenkins barely took a breath. "Let's get one thing straight; I don't care about your complaints or comments. You'll deal with it until the general arrives and takes you to Orbital Station Delta."

"When will that be?" Ryan asked, drawing a stern gaze from Jenkins.

"In six days. Until then, you wait here. You will not leave without authorisation. You will not access restricted areas. You will not get in the way of routine operations. If this is clear, then follow me to your rooms. If you wish to opt out, and this is your last chance to so, the shuttle will return you to the Europort."

Jenkins didn't wait for an answer. He turned on his heel and marched to the wall. A door opened as he approached, camouflaged until lines of light shone through the seams.

Everyone followed.

They were shown to cramped rooms deeper in the compound – each room slept two people, so Ryan and Zack took one of the first ones they passed – and directed to the food hall one level up.

The next six days dragged. There was nothing to do except sleep, eat, exercise and talk. No one knew anything more than they did about what they were doing there, and it was clear there was a mix of Enforcers and civilians, if skewed in balance.

Throughout the week more participants arrived and asked the usual questions only to be given the same answers. It wasn't until the fifth day, when a group of eight arrived, that things changed.

Rather than Jenkins, it was Matthews who greeted them. He didn't give them any more information but now Ryan and Zack knew he was here. A message was delivered to each room that night with a time and location for the following morning. It was time to leave.

The next morning, General Matthews stood outside watching the sunrise. The sky, dark behind him and light in front, was orange, but not just because of the APS. Waves and swirls went from jet black to deep purple and royal to baby blue. The shield played a part but wisps of cloud added to the effect. Behind the orange, it created an artist's landscape that was one of his favourite sights.

As the sun crept up, the streaks of light took a golden hue. It was a sight he rarely had a chance to see. He was used to a different view of the sun from Orbital Station Delta and his time on the surface was often scheduled down to the minute.

Moments like this were precious.

It took an age for the first recruits to join him. Thirty-three out of forty-eight had arrived and there was no time to search for more. Some were freshly trained agents from the academies while others had years of experience behind them.

The rest were civilians of varying ages and backgrounds. The last two to join them were Ryan Fall and Zack Wendall, the former yawning loudly. He didn't like mornings, judging from the bedhead and half-open eyes. Zack, on the other hand, was wide awake and much better groomed.

Without a word, the general led them to a large rectangular hole in the ground with a metal walkway descending to the hatch of their shuttle. The ship was long, with a flat underside and a curved top. Two wings would extend in flight, creating a triangular shape. The blue chrome patterns identified it as personnel transport rather than a warship but that didn't always stop dissenters from attacking.

The group proceeded straight to the passenger lounge, where they stored their bags under their seats and buckled in. With the ship standing vertically, they had to walk on extended panels from the floor and use rungs to get around.

The plush blue seats threatened to swallow them whole, but Matthews knew from experience the extra padding would be needed during launch. After the first few minutes, the compensators would kick in and ease the g-forces.

Matthews looked at a number of faces and could pick out the ones who had been in space before. They were calm, staring out the windows – although all they could see were the dirty walls of the launch chamber – while others were rechecking harnesses, bags or looking at the screen counting down to launch. With only a few minutes left, the general debated saying something, but the pilot saved him the trouble.

"Preparing for launch. Ensure all loose items are secure and everyone is strapped in. For those who haven't flown before, things are going to get bumpy." She signed off with a laugh and Matthews smiled despite trying not to. Bumpy.

A murmur ran through the lounge and Matthews noticed Ryan and Zack talking to each other quietly. No one paid them any attention. Their records didn't mention excursions into space but neither seemed nervous. That was interesting.

The noise dropped as the countdown continued. For the last five seconds, no one spoke, and the pilot's voice stopped coming through with three to go.

The rumbling started, quiet at first, and almost everyone missed it. It grew steadily louder and stronger. Even Matthews found himself gripping the arms of his seat. Old habits.

Then came the launch, and while the noise was dampened inside the ship, the general watched as the first-timers jumped, their harnesses digging into their shoulders as they kept them in their seats. A couple of squeals escaped. The lurch shoved everyone back into their seats as the ship raced towards the sky.

He was taking them home.

# CHAPTER EIGHT

THE LAUNCH WAS AWFUL.

Other than General Matthews and the pilots, it was clear most of the passengers had never flown into space. The reactions ranged from quiet gasps to wails. It didn't help that the general had barely spoken a word since they'd all gathered that morning. Ryan didn't think he was alone in feeling uncomfortable.

He managed to keep the noise to a minimum. His stomach was still back on the surface, and keeping his mouth closed was the best way to ensure what he brought with him didn't escape. Ryan didn't want to be that guy.

Zack was more vocal, swearing loudly for the initial phase of the launch. It would have been hilarious had Ryan not wanted to do the same – his past launches had been a lot smoother.

By the time everyone calmed down the shuttle had levelled off. Thankfully, no one's breakfast made an appearance, but judging from some of the faces, they weren't out of the woods yet.

Matthews was the first to unbuckle his harness, but without a word he entered a code into the door at the front and disappeared. The screens on either side blinked to life, showing the shuttle's position relative to the surface and their flight plan to a space station named Orbital Station Delta.

It was a long, curved arc, which wouldn't take them into space until the last hour or so. They had about two hours of atmospheric flight before that. It seemed odd they wouldn't head straight up instead of taking this longer route, but Ryan wasn't going to object with the pilot's decision.

Quiet conversations were spreading throughout the lounge as everyone relaxed and recovered from the launch. Without the general looming, theories were shared about why they were going to Orbital Station Delta in the first place – some Ryan had heard on the surface, others new.

"I reckon it's to solve some really important problem or equation," one man was saying to the two next to him, who nodded vigorously. "Those tests were based on complex scenarios and given how many people are here, it must take a high level of intelligence to solve them correctly."

"I can't say I really got all the situations," a woman was telling those on her row, with the row in front looking back between the seats. "I felt way out of my depth, so I'm not sure my answers were right."

"You're here, though," said one man in front with a smile. Ryan nudged Zack and nodded to them with a grin. His friend grunted and turned back to the window.

"We don't know why, though," she continued, ignoring the charm. "Maybe it's something other than right answers, like how you think or what you're trying to do."

There were a number of theories, but they all seemed to miss one thing; everything was to do with sim technology. Matthews had confirmed that with Ryan during their meeting but since he hadn't done the tests like everyone else, he had no way of knowing how obvious it was just from those. Was this another test? Ryan couldn't decide whether he should share.

No one had paid any attention to them beyond initial glances. It was the same with the other younger candidates but that didn't bring them together. If anything, it kept them apart. They had something to prove.

"Take a look out of your windows," Matthews announced. Ryan did his best to hide his surprise – he hadn't noticed the general return. "It's better on the starboard side but you'll see it from either."

"What is it we're looking for, sir?" an older man asked. His posture and tone suggested he had received Enforcer training.

"If you can't figure it out, you shouldn't be here," Matthews answered softly.

Everyone crowded around the windows, most heading for the starboard side. A few tried to get close to Ryan and Zack but were met with stern glances and sharp kicks. They wanted a clear view.

Above them were stars. Hundreds, thousands, millions of tiny points of light against a darkness so vast it threatened to swallow you whole, but they were beyond the orange boundary of the APS. Below, the sky brightened to blue with a wash of white, silver and dark grey clouds blocking the ground beneath them. Some were thin and wispy, others thick and menacing.

It took a moment of searching until Ryan saw it. A glance at Zack told him he had found it as well.

There were gasps from the lounge as the rest caught on, pointing down for the ones who hadn't realised.

It was strange to see, especially from such a height. Most of the pictures Ryan had seen at the Institute were close-ups of ruined cities and barren wastelands, decaying bodies and mutated animals. There were only two areas like this on the planet: the Western Scar and its counterpart in the east.

"We're flying over the Eastern Scar," Matthews said as everyone fell quiet. "Millions died in Russia, just like they did in the United States of America. This is the result when nuclear warheads are used. People, cities, economies, environments and ecosystems – all laid to waste."

It was hard to see the true size of the Eastern Scar. Clouds covered a good chunk of the land, but Ryan could make out large piles of grey on the brown waste and some smaller piles too. Rubble. The only clues of once great cities.

"As a planet, we learned a lot from World War Three," the general continued. "It taught us that using these weapons against each other was only going to cause more pain. It helped unify nations and put in safeguards for the future."

"You mean the Enforcers?" someone asked. Ryan couldn't see who.

"That was one, yes. Another was to increase the age at which children become adults. A lot of eighteen to thirty-year-olds died in that war. Conscription played a big part but so did propaganda. It played on emotions and their lack of worldly experience to fill out the frontlines. They were cannon fodder. Subsequent generations suffered a lot and skills shortages were rife in the years after. We had to stop that from happening again."

"I never knew he was such a history buff," Ryan muttered.

"Everyone needs a major," Zack responded.

"History stops us from making the same mistakes again, Ryan Fall," Matthews called out, and Ryan could feel everyone's eyes on him as he tried not to blush. And failed. "Maybe that's something you should keep in mind, judging by your recent races. I chose this route specifically so you could see this. Every action has a consequence, some of them severe and devastating. You may all find yourselves faced with difficult choices in the future and I want you to keep in mind what even the smallest action can do."

"Sir?" a woman asked, waiting for the general to nod before continuing. "What if we're just following orders?"

"The people who caused this flipped a switch. They might not have built the weapon, or have given the order to fire it, but they pushed the button that caused this. Following orders is not an excuse for genocide."

"How do you ensure your agents do what they're supposed to without following orders?" Zack asked quietly.

"I could order you to walk out of the airlock right now, Zack Wendall. Would you do it?" Matthews smiled as Zack shook his head. "Exactly. Some orders shouldn't be followed. When the situation changes, the orders must too. If an agent is not able to get updated orders, they must use their experience and judgement to best fulfil the mission directives."

"So, that's why I had to jump from the eighth-floor balcony to escape your agents!" Ryan exclaimed, drawing some quiet laughs from around the room.

"Those agents weren't prepared to deal with you, it seems. That was a learning experience for us all – and one new recruits will be studying for years to come."

"Fantastic." His sarcasm was obvious.

Ryan turned back to the window as Matthews sat in his seat at the front. A few of the other candidates moved closer to him so they could talk. He couldn't hear whether it was questions about where they were going, about the Eastern Scar or more history lessons.

"Strange, isn't it?" Zack said after a silence. "This was a tragedy on every possible level, both for this and the other Scar, yet it brought about an end to nuclear technology. Sustainable energy, new laws and research into other areas helped create the world we live in. Maybe there's good to be found in even the darkest of moments."

"Depends who you ask. Maybe it happened too long ago for us to be directly affected anymore. Besides, there are still groups rebelling against the Globe. It can't be perfect if not everyone likes it."

"I'm not saying it's perfect, but I prefer grey clouds to dark ones."

Ryan had no answer. He watched as they travelled over the wasteland, edging towards space.

More commotion erupted when the gravity faded and everyone started floating, save for two who remained seated with their harnesses on. It was utter chaos as only a few knew what to do other than Matthews, who floated quietly, watching the flailing and shouting and collisions with a bemused expression.

Zack strapped himself in quickly but his face lost what little colour it had regained since launch. Ryan let himself drift, occasionally pushing off a wall or chair and rolling in the middle of the lounge. Whenever someone came close, he pushed them away before realising that was pushing him away as well. He had never experienced zero-g before.

Every time he passed a window, he looked for the surface and was amazed to see how far away it was. It was strange, as the distances were on the screen, but seeing it first-hand always took his breath away.

A bright orange light filled the room as the shuttle passed through the APS. The line didn't pierce the ship's hull but passed each window in turn, creating a lighthouse effect.

"You seem to be handling this well," Matthews commented as they floated past one another.

"It's strange. It's the complete opposite to when I'm racing. I feel so sluggish."

"That's a common reaction, although you may be noticing it more. It depends on how sensitive your sim is, I've been told. Aren't the sensory settings standardised?"

"Yeah, but every racer finds what works best for them in time. I like to feel as much as possible, as I would actually being there."

The conversation ended there as they drifted away from each other. Ryan didn't feel like yelling out for everyone to hear, despite Matthews making it clear he was a racer.

It felt like they had only been floating for minutes when Matthews told them to find a seat. They were approaching Orbital Station Delta and the artificial gravity would activate shortly.

Everyone tried to make it back to their original seats but when the display started counting down from ten, it turned into a fight for the nearest ones. Ryan pulled himself into one on the port side not far from the front and buckled himself in as a woman a few years older landed gently beside him.

She had long brown hair in a ponytail, sharp green eyes and a slender build beneath a red-and-green jump-suit. That last detail tugged at his memory. She was scrutinising him the same way.

"Kendra Jackson," she said, offering her hand. Her accent was European, but Ryan couldn't place where.

"Ryan Fall," he said, accepting the handshake. It was brief but strong.

"Everyone calls me Jackson."

"Everyone calls me reckless."

"Got it," she said with a laugh. "General Matthews said you're a racer. A little young, aren't you?"

"When you're good enough, you find a way," Ryan said, nodding at her race suit. "You're either a racer yourself or a fan."

"What if they're just comfortable?"

"That's a lie."

That made her laugh and her expression softened up enough for Ryan to realise she was trying to figure him out just as he was doing with her. He couldn't blame her. He and Zack hadn't exactly been forthcoming either.

He shot a glance back and saw his friend engaged with a group of three: two men and a woman. All were older but he didn't seem to be talking much, just listen-ing. There must be something of interest.

"Fine, they're not comfortable but I was racing last night, and it was a bit of a rush to get here on time," she conceded.

"How'd it go?"

"Not well. Heavy wind and rain so we stopped around half distance. I'm waiting for it to be resched-uled but if I'm up here I might not make it."

"Or the rest of the season?"

"Yeah…"

The pilot's voice came over the intercom and announced they'd be landing in a few minutes, which made everyone lean towards the windows again.

Jackson leaned a little too close for Ryan's liking but as he looked at her in hopes of making her move away, he noticed Matthews watching them. That made him more uncomfortable than her closeness.

Giving up, he turned to the window and watched the space station fill the view.

Five large rings surrounded a cylinder with eight spokes connecting each ring to the central shaft and four to each other. On their approach vector, it made each ring look like a wheel. Two sails were deployed at each end of the central shaft to absorb light from the sun. It wasn't the sole source of power but research in that area helped improve solar collectors used on the surface.

A number of ships patrolled the area. Some stayed close while others were in orbit around the planet. Furthest from the station were the Carriers, large crescent-shaped ships designed to transport and launch smaller ships like fighters and shuttles without depleting their fuel on long journeys. Carriers had only defensive weapons but in most situations they'd arrive, launch and depart quickly – and wouldn't return until the area was secure.

Each one was accompanied by between three and five Battle Cruisers. These ships, long and narrow, were bristling with firepower and occasionally entered the atmosphere for training and demonstrations. There were two Battle Cruisers at either end of Orbital Station Delta, and Ryan got a good look as they approached.

They were sleek and curved, until the weapons were deployed, and designed to move into position quickly and take out any weapons before Carriers launched shuttles to deploy agents. What they made up for in firepower, they lacked in armour.

Some frigates patrolled the space in between the ships and space station, usually in pairs. Each one looked different, formed of a central block and various additions related to its purpose: cargo, firepower, exploration, equipment and any number of others. Even the lightest-armed boasted heavy armaments and armour but limited soldier and fighter space. They were slow to travel long distances but could manoeuvre quickly to get the best attack position.

In the distance was another ship under construction – bigger than the rest, most likely a deep space explorer or something similar.

On the side of the station they were approaching, Ryan could see a number of external hatches, with some open, allowing shuttles and smaller ships to fly in and out. He could also see a number of bigger closed hatches.

The Enforcers had never been portrayed as an overly offensive or military force. They policed the Globe and the other three space stations, and while Ryan and Zack had been taught about the three ship classifications he'd noticed, it was something else to see them. This raised even more questions about what they were doing here, at the newest station of the four, not available for civilian residents.

Matthews hadn't been forthcoming with answers. A few passengers exclaimed about the shuttle spinning to match the rotation of the station before slowly turning in to one of the open hatches and the hangar beyond.

As their ship passed through the hatch, a faint blue light appeared at the point where the ship met the containment field keeping the atmosphere inside. The light travelled along the ship and was blindingly bright as it passed Ryan and Jackson's seats, then it was gone.

It took only a couple of minutes for the shuttle to turn, descend and land on the hangar deck before everyone burst into motion.

CHAPTER NINE

THE GROUP FOLLOWED GENERAL Matthews down a set of metal steps pushed against the side of the shuttle. Jackson led Ryan and Zack was at the front of his group, about halfway back in line.

The deck was a flurry of activity. Pilots in grey flight gear were talking to men and women in orange jumpsuits or working on a ship. Half a dozen silver V-shaped fighters were being prepared for launch or being checked over after returning from a mission. The cockpit sat at the back of the ship, where the two wings met, with weapons and engines protruding from each. Ladders provided access to the components and controls since the landing struts were taller than average height.

More fighters were stacked vertically against the wall, facing the floor. It made them look more like arrows pointing to the ceiling than an upside-down letter "V".

When they gathered at the bottom of the steps, Matthews turned to face them. "I know you all have a lot of questions and you probably want to rest and freshen up but I'm afraid there's no time. Leave your bags with the crew and they'll be taken to your quarters. Follow me."

Ryan dropped his bag, as did Jackson, Zack and everyone else. From nowhere, men and women in black uniforms carried them away.

The general was already walking away and everyone rushed after him. The hangar was larger than it looked from the shuttle and more than once their group was speared by agents in black, techs, carts of equipment and cables connecting to various ships.

After the obstacle course, they entered a corridor wide enough for five or six people to walk side by side without feeling cramped. The walls were white with black panels in the middle – terminals providing instant access to maps, communications and information. They could track everyone's position and guide you to your destination with a series of lights. The floor was a matte black material designed to prevent slips and trips.

Matthews didn't need help to reach their destination. They followed him through a series of identical corridors, turning left, right, right, left, going up two levels and then along more corridors. Ryan soon lost track of where they were in relation to the hangar deck.

"General?" he called, waiting until the older man looked over his shoulder before continuing. "Orbital Station Delta is a cylinder with rings around it – and we're on one of them. I haven't noticed slanted walls or changes in elevation in any of these corridors. I can't even tell the station is rotating."

"Is there a question in there?" Matthews asked, but when Ryan didn't respond, he sighed and explained. "New arrivals are limited to one third of the station, the one they land in, to help them adapt. The central shaft is area A, with the rings B to F. There are levels for each area and sections to help narrow it down. Right now, we're on C-fourteen-six. The sections are mirrored on each ring but different in area A.

"There are curves and elevation changes on each ring, so subtle you'll probably never notice them. It's a fantastic piece of engineering that goes beyond me – and probably most of you as well. The gravity plating in the floor keeps you grounded and compensates for the rotation. If you were to look outside, you'd notice it – and that takes some getting used to. Just accept it, Fall."

"So, why a cylinder?" Jackson asked.

"I didn't design the station; I just make the best use of it I can."

That was as clear an end to a conversation as Ryan had ever heard. He shared a quick glance with Jackson and both rolled their eyes, prompting a double grin.

Whether this was the most direct way to their destination, no one other than the general knew, but it certainly helped impress upon them just how large the station was.

They rounded another corner and were faced with two surly Enforcer agents in their black uniforms, one on each side of a large door. They held Enforcexes in one hand, resting them on the floor. The standard Enforcer weapon was a handheld rod that extended into a staff for close combat but could fire energy blasts to stun targets in its shorter form. It could also kill when needed. Ryan wasn't the only one who took a step back.

Matthews didn't break his stride and returned their salute without making eye contact. The door opened as he approached and the group quickly followed him inside. When it closed, Ryan let out a breath – as did Jackson and a few others.

The room was large and white. Blindingly white. It was so crisp and clean that it had to be the medical centre; a lingering chemical smell reinforced that impression.

The general spoke to one woman and she scurried off. Her blue overalls, partially hidden by a white coat, indicated a doctor or medic, and there was a rolled-up PCT in her pocket. She returned a few seconds later with an older woman emerging from an office to the left. She wore the same uniform but her loose black hair was streaked with white. Hazel eyes surrounded by faint wrinkles regarded the candidates coolly.

"I'm Doctor Kayo," she stated. "I don't want you in here as much as you don't want to be here but it's procedure. I want no fuss from anyone. One of my team will take you through a full workout and examination. The more you help us, the quicker you'll be done. When I call your name, go with the attendant on my left."

Activating a MOB-I on her right arm, Kayo started calling names. Ryan watched the first man walk over to the attendant and the pair left the room through a door to the right. A new attendant appeared for the next name, and the following.

The names were called in alphabetical order, so Ryan was paired with a man in his late thirties early on and followed the other pairs through the door. They arrived at a room and headed for a bed where the curtains were drawn closed. This closed-off space had a screen on the wall next to it and curtains separating it from the beds on either side and the rest of the room. There were clothes folded on the bed and he was told to change into them: a light grey vest and matching sweats baggy enough for him to wear over all the other clothes he had packed.

The attendant went about his work while Ryan changed and then had him sit on the bed. He inserted a needle into his arm to draw eight samples of blood.

"Your boss seems quite strict," Ryan noted.

"Only to the rooks. She likes to intimidate you but she's actually very nice. This is the most popular of the seven medical centres – all because of her."

"Who's in charge of them all?"

"They're run by committee, but Kayo's probably got the most influence. She sits on the general's council too."

"You got a name, doc?" Ryan asked, wincing slightly as the needle was removed.

"Alan."

"Doctor Alan?"

"Alan Himmes," he said with a smile. There were tattoos on his wrist, faded with time. He explained when Ryan saw them: "Mementos from my youth. I was only a year or two older than you. Those were the days; loud music, long hair, beards and tattoos – pretty much the opposite of my life now."

"Why not have them removed?"

"Good memories."

"I'd never have guessed," Ryan quipped.

Doctor Himmes went to work examining every appendage, joint, muscle and organ he could. It was quiet work and Ryan gave up trying to make conversation. The answers he received were vague or misleading.

"What's this scar?" the doctor asked, then answered his own question. "A MOB-I? You shouldn't have one of these yet. Where'd you get it?"

"I don't think you'd know it."

"Ryan, this is serious. The scar is proof it hasn't been implanted properly. Is it acting strangely?"

"It's getting warm every time I activate it," Ryan said glumly. "Has been for a few weeks."

"Okay, we'll get it replaced in a couple of weeks. Try to avoid using it until then, or it could begin to damage the nerves. That'll reduce its effectiveness and reduce your arm's effectiveness."

"Replaced? You'd give me a new one?"

"Top of the line. You've experience of using one and you'll be legal next year. They're valuable tools for agents. I suppose you could keep the scar. Some people like it."

"No, get rid of it," Ryan said before another idea occurred. He pointed to the crescent-shaped area of pale skin on his left cheek. "I don't suppose you can do anything about this too?"

"Not without knowing what caused it, and there's no mention of it in your file. Sorry."

"Typical."

It took over an hour, by which time he was ready to fall asleep. Occasionally he needed to lift an arm or leg, turn his body or answer yes or no to a question. Once, he was asked to stand. That was as exciting as the examination got. Given how far they had travelled to get here, it was underwhelming.

When Himmes finally stopped entering notes on his PCT and stood up, Ryan jumped to his feet. The action startled the doctor so much it drew an apology from Ryan.

Ryan followed his attendant back to the main part of the medical centre where a group of other candidates were waiting, about a third of the total number. Kayo walked out of her office and nodded to the attendants, who swiftly disappeared.

"You're the first group to finish with the examination. We now need to establish your fitness levels. You are going to be pushed to your limits in all areas so I can promise you one thing with certainty – you'll sleep well tonight."

She led the group out of the medical centre and navigated the corridors like an expert. How anyone knew their way through this maze was beyond Ryan – and the others in his group, judging by their expressions.

They arrived at another door with two more armed guards, which seemed like overkill. Inside was a fitness facility with machines of every kind to test and train your body, surrounded by a running track and climbing walls which carried on to parts of the ceiling. Swing rings, weights, running, rowing, cycling machines and much more. New attendants were in this room but no one else. The candidates were ushered inside.

It was doubtful it was used solely for testing and there would be no reason for armed guards just for a fitness facility. Something else was going on.

"Your bloodwork will be done by the morning and you will receive a copy of the results. General Matthews will also be informed," Kayo said, before pairing them up with another attendant and leaving the facility.

The next four hours were the most exhausting of Ryan's life. He was taken from machine to machine by his new attendant, who identified herself as Rae and spoke only to instruct him on what to do and when to start and stop. Occasionally she'd point him to a bench, or a tap to get some water, but the breaks were never longer than a couple of minutes.

The rest of the candidates came in two groups, about twenty minutes apart. Jackson arrived with the last. She caught his eye, but her attendant kept them at opposite ends of the room.

After completing a circuit on the machines, Ryan ran laps. Six laps of three hundred metres and he faltered. He managed one and half more before stopping. A brief look of annoyance flashed across his attendant's face before she led him to the next station.

Starting at one end of the room, Ryan was to climb the wall, traverse the ceiling and descend on the other side. He made it to the top easily but when he reached the roof and tried to make his way across, he fell after a couple of metres. Even the station had SafeNet emitters to stop him getting hurt.

He wasn't the only one to fail at this task, but another attempt saw him get a bit further. It wasn't enough to appease his instructor.

After the second hour, every muscle in his body felt like it was burning. Ryan wasn't unfit but physical activities like these weren't his idea of fun. He had to keep going, though. Doctor Kayo had said this was going to be hard, as his attendant kept reminding him.

Sweat dripped off him and the light grey clothes grew darker every minute. Ryan's hair was plastered to his head and face, but his breaks felt like they were getting shorter rather than longer. Others in his group were showing similar signs of exhaustion, although it became crystal clear who had been trained as an Enforcer and who hadn't. Whenever one of the candidates did well the attendants would point it out to the rest, showing it could be done.

Ryan's favourite activity, if he had to pick, was the rings. Starting on a platform at one side, he'd swing his way to the opposite platform. Finding a rhythm was easy but his strength faded fast after so much exertion. He made it across the first time easily, but on the return some of the rings withdrew into the ceiling at the last second, forcing him to change direction. The surprise nearly made him fall but he cursed his way through.

He failed on the fourth. He was so close to the platform he tried to skip the last ring as it vanished. Ryan's fingers skimmed the edge of the platform and he landed with a thud on the floor, yelling as pain seared through his leg. The station had no SafeNet, it seemed, and he landed awkwardly.

For once his instructor didn't have a look of disapproval on her face. It wasn't satisfaction but it was better than every other result. It made him feel a little better.

"No more, no more," he wheezed as his legs gave way during another set of laps. "I'm done. Totally done."

When she didn't say anything, he looked up from the ground and saw her coming back with a cup of water. It was ridiculously small for how thirsty he was but better than nothing.

She helped him to a bench. He looked around the fitness facility while taking small sips. Everyone had been in here for more than three hours now – close to four for Ryan's group – and only a couple of them were still going.

"Where's Zack?" he asked the instructor as she made notes on her PCT. "He never came in. Is he alright?"

Ryan thought she wouldn't answer but eventually she looked him straight in the eye and said, "He's with Doctor Kayo. He's undergoing different testing."

"Why?"

"You're a candidate for a specific programme. Your friend is here for a different reason, so he needs to have different checks to ensure he's fit for it. That's all I know."

Despite him insisting he was done, the instructor told him to finish the laps he had started. He got about two hundred metres around the first one before dropping to his knees, breathing hard.

With a final tut, she told Ryan to take a shower.

There were three others in the changing room when he entered. The water was cold and cooled him quickly before he turned the heat up. A lot. The steam cleared his head, although his legs buckled after a minute. He was forced to sit on the floor and let the water cascade over him.

He lost track of time as his mind tried to process everything he had seen and heard so far, and by the time he got out and dried off, his skin was wrinkled and the changing room full with the rest of the candidates.

Everyone was too tired to talk. He left the changing rooms and found a group of grey-uniformed staff waiting near the door. All the instructors had left. One waved him over and confirmed his name before taking him on another tour of the station.

They ventured deeper into the station before arriving at an unmarked door. The man opened it and showed him how to activate all of the systems he may need. Ryan nodded absently, his mind already drifting to sleep.

"Hey, is there any news on my friend? Zack Wendall?" Ryan asked before the man could leave.

"He's still with Doctor Kayo, I'm afraid. You'll find out more tomorrow."

The door closed and Ryan took a few seconds to explore, although when he found the bed it was over. He pushed his bag to the floor and flopped down face first.

CHAPTER TEN

RYAN WOKE UP BURNING.

Panic took over until he realised the room was fine. Dark, with cool air blowing from the vents. His muscles, on the other hand, were on fire. They ached. Every movement stoked the flame as he rolled onto his side, gingerly swung his legs to the floor and waddled into the main room.

"Lights."

There wasn't much to see. One square room with a glass desk, a chair and an L-shaped sofa in one corner and two adjoining rooms, one with a bed and the other with a toilet, sink and shower. The basics. Ryan suspected the other three stations had much more spacious living arrangements.

There were cupboards and drawers at the end of his bed. It took a minute to unpack his bag and store his belongings. They looked sparse, pathetic.

The holographic clock over his desk told him it was just after eight in the morning. Yesterday's journey and tests must have taken a lot out of him if he needed eleven hours' sleep.

Zack hadn't left any messages. That was worrying. He hadn't seen or heard from his friend since they entered the medical centre.

Activating the console at the desk pushed the time display to the side and a number of windows opened. A schedule for the day showed nothing. There were maintenance updates from the sections and levels near his room, a mailbox with no messages and weather updates from across the surface.

Even in space the weather was important. Miss Kinni had said that had been the same for hundreds of years. No matter where you were, it made good small talk.

There was no indication of what to do next. Ryan left his room, emerging into one of the many identical corridors of Orbital Station Delta.

The screens on the wall were blank until touched. Ryan was greeted with his name and a query asking what he needed. Selecting destinations, he scrolled through the list by swiping down. When he couldn't find what he wanted, he typed in a word and a room code flashed: C-4-8-12.

Another tap and the displays to his left lit up with a blue light at the bottom. Ryan followed as the light led him through the corridors, staying one panel ahead. It guided him through the labyrinth of white-walled halls, up a few levels on the station and then through another series of twists. Some of the corridors were long and seemingly never-ending but with enough intersections to make it easy to get lost without the flashing lights as a guide.

There were plenty of people in the corridors as he tailed the blue guide. Most were in Enforcer uniforms of various colours, but a few wore casual clothes, presumably off duty.

Most paid Ryan no more attention than a cursory glance, while others let their gaze linger. He stood out like a sore thumb. While there were people of various ages, skin and hair colours, accents and other features, Ryan's uncertainty was obvious. It marked him as an outsider.

Room 12 in C-4-8 was on a busy corridor, but no one paid any attention to it. Ryan waved his hand over the sensor, the door slid open without a sound and he stepped inside.

It was a dark room with only half a dozen small floor lights Ryan could see. Once his eyes adjusted, he could make out ten padded benches on a stepped floor. The observation room was one of the more comfortable areas he had seen on the station so far but it was still designed to be as efficient as possible.

The focus of the room was a large viewport but all he could see were stars. Ryan took a seat on the front row of benches before swinging around and lying on his back, turning his head to watch the darkness beyond.

It was oddly relaxing as he realised the stars were moving because of the station's rotation. They disappeared at the top of the viewport and new ones crept into view at the bottom. It made him feel nauseous, but he refused to close his eyes. Stargazing had never been one of his hobbies but without the APS and light pollution of the surface, the beauty of what he was seeing wasn't lost on him.

He only meant to stay for a little while before finding something to eat but the view proved mesmerising.

Every so often a ship would obscure his view; sometimes in the distance, while others were close enough to touch.

"Aha!" a voice yelled from the back of the room, causing Ryan to leap to his feet and spin around to see a silhouette in the doorway. "There you are."

The speaker stepped inside and the door closed, restoring the dimness. That made it easier to see once his eyes adjusted again. Dark skin, dark hair and wide, dark eyes – probably not helped by the poor lighting. The man was only a couple of years older than Ryan, with very short, shaved hair.

"You're Ryan, right?" he asked when Ryan didn't say anything, stopping two steps up from him, leaving him an inch or two taller. Ryan nodded and the new-comer grinned, revealing slightly yellow teeth. "I'm Mac, your tech. Been looking for you for an hour. I see you've found a viewing deck. What do you think?"

"My tech? For what?"

"That'll be explained this afternoon," Mac said cheerfully. "Until then, I'm to show you around a bit, help you get used to OSD – um, Orbital Station Delta – and make sure you know how to use the terminals. I guess you've figured those out already, eh?"

"Where's Zack? My deal with Matthews was that he'd be working with me," Ryan said, his eyes narrowing.

"I don't know anything about that, I'm just follow-ing orders," Mac said with a shrug before stepping down to Ryan's level and sitting on the bench. "I bet you're hungry but there's something you're going to want to see before we leave. Trust me," he said before Ryan could object.

Curiosity got the better of him and he sat on the bench, leaving a healthy gap between them. After a brief silence, Ryan had to ask. "Where's the accent from?"

"Aha! You hear it? I can barely tell it's there anymore; I've been away from home for years. It's Scottish." The last remnant of the older borders. Identifying accents by zone proved troublesome and confusing. The old names were a nod to a more divided time.

"And your name is…Mac?"

"Yup. Well, Maxwell MacConn."

"Not the most imaginative nickname."

"I'm a tech. As long as my pilot knows me, that's all that matters. Any second now."

They waited in silence for the event. Mac leaned forward with even wider eyes. He had seen this before, but his eagerness was infectious.

Ryan grew impatient. It was fine being here by himself, on his own terms. Mac's presence changed things.

Just as he was about to say something, Mac beat him to it. "Here it comes." Something blurry appeared at the bottom of the viewport and time slowed to a crawl as Ryan figured it out.

Blue oceans, green land and white clouds slowly filled the viewport and Ryan's breath caught. Seeing the planet like this wasn't something he'd expected.

Without the commotion of ground and low-air traffic, the Globe was peaceful and serene. One of the Scars peeked out from some dense cloud cover but Ryan couldn't tell which one. Even that wasteland, combined with the rest of the view, was stunning.

"Whenever we need to remind ourselves why we're here, we watch this," Mac said quietly. "It puts everything into perspective. We're all they've got, you know? You should see a sunrise up here. That makes this seem ordinary. Okay. Let's go!"

Mac stood and walked up the steps to the door. Ryan lingered, burning the view into his mind. He'd tell Zack about it later.

By the time he caught up, Mac was waiting for him in the corridor. He didn't use the terminals to take them to their destination. Time on the station had obviously helped him get used to the smallest details of each corridor to find out where he was and wanted to go.

Ryan followed the tech deeper into OSD. He was getting tired of these endless corridors. Surely there had to be an easier way to traverse the station – so far hardly anyone else had used the stairwells when he had. It was no different now.

Mac finally turned to an open doorway and the noise washed over them like a wave. The mess hall was made up of six long metal tables with people sitting at them all. Some were in groups while others were alone. On one wall was a row of food dispensers – different to the Institute, where people served the food.

They walked to one of them. Mac placed his palm on the sensor and waited for the light behind it to fade after a couple of seconds. A tray popped out from the back with six compartments, food on five and a glass on the other. When it stopped moving, water poured into the glass. He took the tray, stepped back and waited for Ryan to do the same.

"The dispenser scans you and provides the food you need for this meal. We have medicals every month to make sure it's always accurate," Mac informed him as the display lit up and scanned. A tray appeared with food and a glass.

They found two empty seats at a table to eat. It wasn't the most exciting meal; oats and nuts with a paste, some dried fruit, bread, chopped banana and dry cereal flakes – all with a glass of water.

"No accounting for taste, I guess," Ryan commented. It didn't stop him from eating it all, with Mac providing a breakdown of the station and its core systems.

Ryan half listened. He didn't like not knowing anything about Zack and felt isolated without him. They weren't telling him what they knew. There wasn't much he could do but keep asking and wait for an answer.

Even with all his chattering, Mac wasn't giving him anything useful about why he was here. Whatever the reason was, it needed a tech and he was it. There was a physical element, too, or they wouldn't have been pushed so hard in the fitness facility yesterday.

Despite the bland breakfast, he finished it quickly. They returned their trays to the dispenser, scanned their hands again and left the hall. People had come and gone in that time, but it still seemed as busy and loud as before. Mac saw him looking and told him shifts changed at different hours to make sure there were always people on duty, with different teams starting midway through another's shift. It meant fatigue and exhaustion could be managed and helped with productivity. Ryan couldn't argue.

They returned to the maze of corridors. This journey was a lot shorter than the others and their destination was even on the same level as the mess hall, just in a different section.

The pair arrived at a door and Mac turned to face him. "This is it, for now. General Matthews will speak to you all in there."

"Thanks, Mac. It's been...interesting."

"Aha! You'll get used to me. I'm your tech. See you later. There's a lot of work to do to get you ready."

Mac turned and walked down the corridor. It was only now Ryan noticed the slight spring in his step. A chipper Scot. Very rare.

Smiling despite himself, and shaking his head, Ryan opened the door and walked in to find another room with a stepped floor and row upon row of seats. Only the first few rows were occupied but not all of the other candidates had arrived yet. Ryan sat on the fourth row from the back and stared at the men and women in silver-trimmed Enforcer uniforms standing against the wall. The podium was unoccupied.

Over the next ten minutes, the last of the candidates entered. Everyone except Zack. A few moments later, Matthews walked in and the few whispers creeping through the room died. The general walked to the podium and touched a button. The lights dimmed and the screen behind him activated.

CHAPTER ELEVEN

"GOOD MORNING," GENERAL MATTHEWS started. "We have a lot to go through. First, I want to thank you for your participation during yesterday's tests. Most of you haven't had the training our agents have, so that would have been a rigorous session. Your commitment made the process easier.

"With that in mind, know it was easy compared to what's in store. This briefing will answer the questions you've been asking since agreeing to come to Orbital Station Delta. You have all agreed to join this programme; however, if you wish to withdraw after hearing what I have to say you may do so, but you will have to remain onboard. Regardless of your choice, all comm traffic will be monitored and censored if needed. This information cannot reach the public under any circumstances."

Matthews let that hang in the air.

Ryan looked at the men and women standing behind the general. Four on either side, all wearing black Enforcer uniforms. Their collars and shoulders had the same silver lining as Matthews' but four pins on the left side of the collar instead of six.

The one on the far right met his gaze. Whether by chance or on purpose, Ryan didn't know. Her eyes were blue. Cold and hostile. Like ice.

He couldn't look away. There was something in those eyes that disturbed him. Beyond the frostiness, the distance, it was clear she was angry – but why? Despite willing himself not to, Ryan broke the stalemate and looked away but her expression didn't change.

Those moments felt like hours but no one else noticed, and Matthews started talking again.

"This isn't a regular Enforcer division. Most agents are trained surface-side, with only a small number sent to space. Exploring the solar system has allowed us to expand our space forces, selecting the best for the most difficult missions and environment. However, most of our work is on the ground.

"Eight months ago, a mission to the far edge of the system revealed just how vulnerable we are. In the months since, all efforts have been taken to upgrade our resources – ships, weapons and agents – to wipe out this deficit.

"Today, you will be joining the Mechanical Enforcer Combat Hardware unit," Matthews went on before one of the men interrupted.

"Or, as we've taken to calling it, the Mech Force."

"This unit is not just made up of rank-and-file agents," the general continued, ignoring the statement. "Everyone has their own unique skills and personality. It causes problems but also creates solutions. When the best are made to fit a mould, they lose the qualities that made them stand out in the first place. It's why you're here; it's why you're not going through standard training.

"Before we continue, I want you to be absolutely clear on what we're up against," Matthews said. He pushed a button on the podium. The lights dimmed and the Enforcer logo faded from the screen. "Or, as clear as the rest of us are."

A slight murmur crept among the candidates as the last of the light vanished and the display changed to a view of space. The bottom of the image was a white haze, presumably from the thrusters of the ship.

There was nothing except moving stars for a few minutes. Ryan found himself edging forward, waiting for whatever it was Matthews wanted them to see appear. He refused to blink.

A number of fighters, shrinking by the second, closed in on a point of pure darkness in the centre. Multiple needles of blue converged on a shadow. There were no stars in this spot, but the laser barrage didn't stop until all the fighters launched missiles, creating a burning orb. The scene turned quiet.

Six fighters exploded.

They flashed red, yellow and orange as the explosions expanded before dissipating. Ryan could make out a silhouette, but it faded to black. It looked like a person – a giant that could survive in space. It made no sense.

The final two fighters exploded in crescendo. When the last disintegrated, the woman who had been staring at him earlier winced. There was no sound to accompany the footage, making the whispers as loud as Matthews had been minutes before. Most of them hadn't noticed the footage was still playing, so focused they were on the explosions.

Ryan had. He was glued to it. Whatever was happening, it wasn't done.

"The comm chatter was quite lively throughout until this point," Matthews said. "We removed it to make the footage easier to watch. Right now, this pilot is making a report to us."

The general's voice sounded distant, so intent was Ryan on the footage. The pilot was flying straight. There was no evasive action or frantic changes in direction. Something else was happening besides the attack. The audio might have shed more light on the situation.

It was like racing without Zack in his ear. It felt strange.

Nothing happened in the footage over the next two minutes. The recruits were growing restless, Ryan included. All nine at the front watched the recruits closely. He felt those icy eyes on him again, but something was going to happen in the vid and it needed his full attention.

Ryan saw it before most of the others, judging from the conversations they were having. The dark area the fighters had been firing on was growing. More stars vanished each second. The shadow was gaining on the pilot, whether they knew or not.

By the time it got close enough to cover most of the tiny points of light, the white haze from the engines revealed a partial outline. The image jarred and the fighter stopped moving. A few shudders later and blinding light covered everything, drawing gasps from around the room.

None of the people underneath the screen moved a muscle. They were still watching the recruits. Ryan continued to ignore the piercing stare trying to carve through his soul.

"That incident gave this unit a purpose," Matthews said, drawing their attention back to the podium. "It made us realise how inferior we really are. Weapon research has been low on the priority list since World

War Three but some of the technology being developed, and now in use, is staggering. We've even found new uses for other resources. It's not completely finished and it's not all pretty, but it's what we have."

The lights came up too quickly as the screen switched off and Ryan wasn't the only one blinking rapidly until he adjusted. His mind was in overdrive; questions, theories, and problems were coming and going before he could properly comprehend them.

He still felt eyes on him. It was unnerving.

"We have people. Agents, pilots, engineers, officers and more are here. They've been trained to the highest standards but it's not enough," Matthews said, not fazed by the change in lighting. "We've drilled into them what we expect and in the three encounters we've had since the footage you've just seen we've learned a lot, but we've lost every single battle. We're improving, but our resources are limited and we don't know the full scale of what we're up against yet.

"We're also predictable. We all come from the same background, and while I spoke about individuality, it's slow to emerge. That's where you come in – and other groups like you. We need new ideas, new views. You'll be joining this unit not as Enforcer agents, although we will train you in the time we have, but as specialists in your fields.

"We don't know who they are, or what they want, but they are heading to the planet. Our messages have gone unanswered. Our losses during those three encounters were considerable, which is another reason we need you. Our weapons can defeat them, but their numbers dwarf ours. We don't know the extent of their technology, or the limits, but they haven't slowed down.

"Before we lost the deep space sensors, more were still coming into range. We don't have a full picture of the size of their force, but we are treating this as a full-scale invasion. Our current tactics aren't working, and we need fresh eyes to give us a chance to defend ourselves from what, until now, were only theories and conspiracies. We are not alone, and they are dangerous."

The silence following the general's last sentence hung ominously in the room, which suddenly felt a lot smaller than before. Apprehension was ripe, filling the air with tension. No one knew what to make of it and there wasn't anyone who wanted to speak up first.

"You want us to put our lives on the line, basically," Jackson spoke up at last, "for a war we might not even be able to win?"

"Yes and no," Matthews answered. "All our lives are on the line. Every one of us, on this and other stations, the ships and the Globe, is in danger. If we lose, there might be nothing left of the human race. We just don't know. However, while the units you control will be on the frontline, you won't be. There's a reason you were chosen: mainly your familiarity with sim technology."

"They're remotely operated," Ryan said, without meaning to speak aloud as it dawned on him. "Like in Cyber Cycle?"

"In racing, construction and demolition, transport and many other areas you might not even realise." The general nodded. "Most new candidates come from these backgrounds."

"And these units?" someone in front of Ryan asked. "How did they even come into existence if weapon research was so low on the list of priorities?"

A good question, and Matthews' reaction made it clear this was what he wanted. Enforcer agents probably wouldn't think that was important; they'd be focused on the capabilities of their units and enemies.

"They were designed for space labour; heavy-duty lifting and transport, ship and station construction and similar tasks. They're powerful but bulky, making this environment perfect for them. Only recently have we been arming them, improving their defences and speed – making them more versatile and useful to our mission. The remote link has taken some time to stabilise but improves with each mission. We're still working on it."

This information did nothing to help Ryan's mind relax. Each new piece of information mixed with his existing thoughts. It was dizzying.

More questions were asked, and the answers came just as quickly, but none of it reached him. Information overload drowned the conversation in white noise.

One thing Ryan was sure of was that the general hadn't lied to him after his race. This was an opportunity unlike any other and it made racing look childish. It was a challenge with real danger and adrenaline. If he had any doubts about accepting General Matthews' offer, they vanished here. Even without the leverage Matthews used to bring him to the station, this wasn't something he wanted to miss out on.

"I'm in," Ryan said, cutting another question short and drawing the eyes of everyone in the room. Matthews let slip a small smile, but the eight behind him remained neutral. The rest of the recruits had expressions ranging from annoyance to disbelief.

All except one.

"I'm not about to be outdone by a kid," Jackson said with a grin. "I'm in too."

That opened the floodgates. All questions fell, forgotten, and the group declared themselves in or out. Mostly in. Of the thirty-three in the room, twenty-seven joined. The six who opted out had faces as pale as the moon. Matthews pressed another button on the podium and an officer walked in and guided them out. They looked in shock and ignored the few goodbyes as they left.

When everyone settled down, Matthews spoke again. "You certainly made your minds up quicker than the other groups. Time will tell if that's a good sign. One of the men and women behind me will be your commanding officer from this point on. They each have a squad you'll be joining and will be responsible for your training and conduct while on board. They are all seasoned Enforcers with the best records."

General Matthews wasted no time in calling out names, going through the candidates in alphabetical order, before naming one of the captains behind him. Ryan was sixth.

"Fall, Ryan. Captain Ryder."

Jackson was called not long after and assigned to the same squad. They shared a quick glance and nod. No one else in the list was matched with them, with most captains being assigned three candidates. One was given four but another was given six. That caught Ryan's attention, but the general hadn't revealed anything about the captains. There was a growing feeling in his gut that Icy Eyes would be his.

She definitely wasn't happy about something.

"The captains will take over from here. You're in their hands," Matthews said after the last name was called. "I'll be receiving regular reports on your progress and look forward to seeing your contributions. Welcome to the Mechanical Enforcer Combat Hardware unit."

"Or Mech Force," the captain who had spoken up earlier repeated as the general marched out of the same door he'd entered from. "Okay, you lot. I'm Captain Dixon. Call me Dixy at your peril. Rooks, with me."

Three candidates stood and followed Dixon out of the same door Matthews used. The next captain took four with him and the following four took three each. The seventh captain took six but there was nothing in her stance or look to suggest anything unusual – that Ryan could see.

That left one captain and the pit in Ryan's gut dived as Icy Eyes, Captain Ryder, motioned for Jackson and himself to step forward.

Without a word, she turned and marched for the door everyone else had used, leaving them to follow as she navigated the maze of corridors and levels through the station. Ryan thought about commenting on how he was always playing catch-up but Ryder's demeanour was serious. All work.

"Captain," Jackson said, after they caught up and settled into a regular pace, "what's a rook?"

"Rookie. It tells others in the squad you need to be coddled for a while. When you prove yourself, you get a call sign," she said curtly, without looking at them.

Ryan shrugged at his squadmate before asking the next question. "What if there's more than one rook, or there's rooks from different squads together?"

"There shouldn't be more than one rook in a squad, but these are…unusual times. You'll either be called Rook or something else – probably your forename. That's up to the squad. With multiple rooks from different squads, the squad name will separate you. Anything else?"

She wasn't the most talkative person. Whatever was eating at her, it wouldn't do well to make it worse and they both knew it, so they walked in silence.

A few minutes later and they arrived at a door. Ryder waved a hand in front of the panel, waited for the doors to slide open quietly and they stepped into a small box. She tapped a room combination into the controls on the wall and the doors closed.

The floor vibrated then fell still as the transporter carried them to another part of the station. The awkward silence held throughout the journey and back into more of the identical corridors Ryan had been getting lost in since his arrival.

Navigating a series of corners and short stretches, Ryder stopped in the middle of a corridor in between two doors and turned to face them. "These are your new rooms. Fall, in here," she pointed to her left before motioning to the right, "and Jackson here. Your belongings have been brought here already. You'll find information on your terminals to familiarise yourselves with for the rest of the day. Be ready for oh-six-hundred tomorrow."

"Why do we have new rooms?" Ryan asked.

"All of our squad's pilots are in this section. You're closer to our briefing and sim rooms, too. It's more convenient."

"Has there been any news on Zack Wendall? My friend? He's supposed to be working with me."

"I haven't heard anything, but I'll check with the general the next time we speak."

Without waiting for a reply, Ryder spun on her right

foot and marched off. Ryan and Jackson looked at each other, shrugged and entered their rooms.

The first thing he noticed was that it was almost identical to his last, if a little smaller. His bag was in the same spot in this room he had left it in in the last, and each storage compartment had the same belongings inside – with new additions: grey training gear and black and navy uniforms. The desk was smaller too and he instantly regretted activating the workstation.

Window after window after window popped up. Information on the squadron, the station, the units, the enemy and more. There were at least twenty. Ryan sighed and turned for the shower. He needed to process and unwind.

Twenty minutes later he sat at the desk and began to absorb the huge amount of information waiting for him. It was going to be a very long day.

# CHAPTER TWELVE

THERE WAS A LOT of reading. For every window Ryan closed, another took its place. He didn't understand a lot of it and marked the files to be read again later, mostly technical documents and Enforcer jargon. Codes and abbreviations appeared often, and the context didn't clear everything up. After two hours, his concentration waned and his eyes glazed over.

Taking a short break seemed to be the best plan and he checked again for a message from Zack.

Nothing.

It was worrying that no one would tell him anything. Ryan had a good impression of Matthews; he seemed a decent man – beyond the blackmail – which made the lack of information even more confusing. Nothing made him suspect foul play but there was definitely something wrong and it was distracting.

Ryan spent ten minutes pacing back and forth, trying to order the chaos. Imagining the whole situation as a jigsaw helped and he started by creating the outline of the picture using all the information he had been given so far.

The footage from the briefing, what Matthews had told them and all the information on his screen started to fill the void, but after all that, there was no way to make complete sense of it all. Too many unanswered questions.

His break over, he returned to the desk and started working through more windows. Field reports now. There had been three other encounters and none of them had gone well. The last two, with the introduction of new hardware units, brought a change. The first skirmish was lost but the enemy suffered heavy casualties and it took a lot longer for them to engage again. In that time, the units were upgraded with stronger armour and better weapons. It still ended in a loss but the invaders pulled back to the outer edges of the solar system.

The most interesting line stated the sim technology allowed for bolder strategies. The enemy units always outnumbered the Enforcers, but their weapons and armour were weaker. Quantity over quality.

That was strange. For a race of aliens to have travelled so far and remain undetected, Ryan would have expected their weapons and tech to be much more advanced, but it wasn't his place to dispute the facts. If that was the situation, he had to accept it.

After the reports from commanding and senior officers came personal accounts from those involved. Given the numbers lost, it made sense there weren't a huge amount of these. It didn't make for exciting reading and there was a definite pattern emerging, where Ryan could tell who had been trained as an Enforcer and who hadn't.

Despite the tediousness, the information here was much more valuable than technical documents and official reports. It gave a real feel for the battles, the enemy and the equipment he'd be using. There were no rules about what could go into these logs and they had audio. When his eyes glazed over again, he resumed his pacing and activated the next report's audio, mentally moving jigsaw pieces around.

Some accents were stronger than others and he had to repeat sections to make sure he understood. Sometimes he repeated the entire log. These people came from around the Globe and while everyone spoke a single language, regional dialects differed. Every so often, an old foreign word slipped in too.

Ryan fell into a groove, like when he prepared for a race, and the lapses in concentration stopped. He reacted to the words and atmosphere of the reports on instinct, pacing himself slowly for the dull voices and boring moments and picking up speed when the tension grew. Some pilots had the gift of storytelling and he was soon breathing faster than normal. Through it all, his mind didn't stop looking for pivotal pieces of information that might have been overlooked.

It was easy to lose track of time and Ryan did. It wasn't until his stomach rumbled and his legs moved from aching to throbbing that he paused the recording of a female pilot with a thick, drawling accent, taking deep breaths and letting his brain catch up.

A quick scout turned up nothing. There was no food in either of the rooms he had been assigned. That meant a venture to a mess hall – not something he had planned.

There was another shock when he checked the time; past one-thirty in the morning! Ryder had made it clear she was expecting an early start and didn't seem like a captain to accept excuses. How he was supposed to get through all those reports and logs in one day baffled him, but there was now no time for food.

Ryan didn't bother to shut down his display – it would go into standby on its own. He dragged his heavy body to bed, killed the lights and fell asleep.

While sleep came easy, it wasn't peaceful. Ryan woke to a constant beeping throughout his quarters with his limbs tangled in the bed sheets. By the time he'd shrugged off his drowsiness, he was cursing himself for moving so much through the night.

Eventually breaking free, Ryan staggered to the wall and slapped the panel to stop the beeps and check the time. He had managed four hours but it felt like a lot less. That didn't bode well for the day.

Unlike his last room, this one had half a dozen grey sweats hanging up. They included the Enforcer logo, and the number of them told Ryan he'd be wearing them a lot. Next to them were a couple of navy outfits, thicker, with armoured sections. At the far end of the rail were two black Enforcer uniforms with the silver trim he'd seen a lot of on OSD. No silver pins on either but perfect fits. Medical had been thorough in collecting every possible piece of information on his physical state – and his mental and emotional attitudes.

He chose the grey sweats and finished getting dressed just as the door chimed. Right on time.

The door opened to reveal a bewildered Jackson standing opposite, wearing an identical outfit. Both wore their own jackets over the vest. His fellow rook's was half zipped from the bottom while Ryan's was completely open. If she was tired it didn't show, but she clearly noticed his fatigue. Thankfully, she didn't say anything.

"Over here, rooks," a deep but quiet voice to Ryan's left called. Poking his head out into the corridor, he saw the speaker – a giant of a man with braided black-and-blue hair, a neat beard and eyes as dark as his skin. Unlike Ryder, there was a playful glint in those eyes.

He was leaning against the wall a bit further down the corridor to avoid being seen by either of them straight away. His arms were folded but the uniform had a single silver pin on his collar, marking him as a trained agent.

"I'm Wisp. I get the honour of babysitting until you get used to how things work around here. Come on, let's go – and keep up!"

Without waiting, he ran down the corridor. Ryan and Jackson shared a glance. She shrugged before running after him. Ryan sighed and followed.

They caught up with Wisp a few seconds later when he slowed to a jog. Before they could say anything, he sprinted again. This happened a few times, across different levels and sections, but Ryan wasn't paying attention to where they were going as keeping track of the man – he wasn't using the station navigation system – required his full attention. Most people he saw didn't use it, but he still wasn't able to tell each corridor apart.

"What kind of name is Wisp?" Jackson asked, as they caught up to him for the fourth time.

"I tend not to talk loudly...or a lot. It started as 'Whisper' and eventually shortened to this. As a rule, call signs aren't as funny or clever when explained. I wouldn't ask everyone you meet to explain theirs."

There was no time for more questions as Wisp ran off again. By this point, Ryan had no idea where on OSD they were or where they were heading...or why they were running. Ryder had told them their quarters were closer to the squad's facilities, but if they had to make this journey every day, he didn't believe it.

The grin he glimpsed on Wisp's face made it feel like their "babysitter" was making fun of them, but the joke was lost on the pair. It felt like they'd travelled half the station over the last two days; not that he would say anything or people might think he was complaining.

Which he was. Kind of.

After a few more short runs, Wisp stopped at a double door and turned to face them. "Piece of advice: whatever you're expecting, don't."

The door opened as he finished talking and a wave of noise escaped, but it died as Wisp walked inside with the rooks hot on his heels.

Seven people rushed over with eager and excited faces, while an eighth hung back. Some were old and others young – still older than Ryan and Jackson – but six wore the same grey clothes as Ryan and Jackson. Wisp and two others had black Enforcer outfits with silver trims and collar pins.

The room was split across three levels. At the far end, the bottom, was a podium in front of a screen and three rows of benches, much like yesterday's briefing room. In the middle, slightly raised, was an open space with lockers and benches around the sides and a white mat in the centre. The closest area to the door was full of sofas, chairs and tables, with a small food dispenser in the corner. Everyone had gathered here, staring at the newcomers.

Ryan felt like a spotlight had focused on him, intense and hot. When the staring ended, questions and comments flew at the rooks like a tsunami, leaving them no time to answer before the next.

"How old are they?"

"Wow! Have they resorted to recruiting children?"

"What was it they picked you for?"

"They look so green – how are they going to handle combat?"

"Combat? I doubt they'll even be able to get a shot off before they pass out."

"Come on, give them a break. Even we were green once."

"Not that green!"

"Are they trying to make us look stupid or something?"

"We don't need any help with you here, Oaf."

"Hey!"

"Enough," the man at the back ordered, and everyone fell silent. "Rooks, get over here!"

Wisp grabbed Ryan and Jackson by the shoulders and shoved them forward. By then the man had made his way to the front of the crowd, sizing them up. The three pins on his uniform's collar showed he was a lieutenant. Ryan could feel the man's breath on his skin, hot and muggy. It took everything he had to stand still and look ahead.

"Hmmm. Bet the captain was thrilled with the pair of you. Still, you might not be lost causes if you work hard. Then again, neither of you look to know what that means. Am I right?"

Jackson spluttered while Ryan shrugged. Sharp, green eyes narrowed, but rather than bursting into an angry tirade, the man cursed under his breath and turned away.

"Oooh!" followed the encounter, with most of the squad members joining in. Ryan berated himself for making his usual first impression. That wouldn't help him – especially not with an officer. Matthews might have put up with him so far, but this man was cut from similar cloth to Ryder, he could tell.

"Oaf, is it?" Ryan asked eventually, facing the rest of the squad and looking at the big blonde man. "How did you get a call sign when you're still training?"

"Who says I'm still training?"

"We all are, you great coo!" another squad member answered, kicking his shin at the same time and drawing a yelp. She was just over half Oaf's size, but it was clear she wasn't to be messed with. Short black hair, sharp eyes that noticed everything, and of Asiazone. She was the first person from that part of the Globe he'd seen on OSD. "Of course he knows you're still training!"

"It's not about finishing training, Rook," another said, an older man. An officer. "It's a squad decision."

There was no time for further discussion as the door opened again and Ryder marched inside without sparing a glance at the crowd. She crossed the room quickly and took position at the podium while the rest of the squad took their seats in the lowest section of the room.

Wisp motioned for Ryan and Jackson to follow and led them to the side of the room before taking a seat himself. Ryder was joined at the podium by the lieutenant who had inspected them when they arrived.

Taking a step towards an empty space on the bench, Ryan saw Wisp shake his head. Instead, he leaned against the wall and folded his arms; Jackson followed suit. Their casual attitude drew the captain's stare. She wasn't happy but Ryan had already made his first impressions. There was no point pretending otherwise.

"Morning," Ryder said. "We have a busy day ahead so let's not waste any time."

CHAPTER THIRTEEN

"Rooks, welcome to Flare Squadron," Captain Ryder continued, looking at Ryan and Jackson. "With you, we have a full complement. Respect your team and you'll get the same in return. From all of us. I'm sure you'll do your best. Get down here and introduce yourselves."

As an underage racer, Ryan had avoided stepping into the spotlight. The few occasions he was required to show himself, Zack created a holo-display to hide his true appearance. They hadn't decided whether to keep it once he reached the legal age to race. The biggest advantage was keeping his privacy, unlike what Ryder was doing to him now. The seconds stretched as he searched for a way out but all he could think of was a flat refusal.

That wasn't an option. According to the general, an order shouldn't be disobeyed without good reason.

With legs of lead, Ryan followed Jackson to the front, where they faced the captain and stood at attention. A curt nod signalled them to turn around and face the eight members of the squad on the benches.

"I'm Kendra Jackson but everyone, other than my mother, calls me Jackson. Twenty-seven and a better racer than any of you could ever hope to be. I've won races in the Eurozone Cyber Cycle Circuit and like to party in between. I've always wanted to travel more – but I never expected to end up in space!"

The last remark drew a couple of laughs, which seemed enough for her. Ryan took a few more moments before deciding what to say.

"Ryan Fall, twenty-four, racer on the Eurozone Cyber Cycle Circuit. A better racer than her."

Silence answered him. Ryan would have loved to say that didn't bother him, but it did. Even a small reaction would make him feel better but they gave him nothing. Before they could see his disappointment, he turned back to the captain. Jackson did the same.

"I'm Eleanor Ryder, captain of Flare Squadron. This is Lieutenant Leon Toomes, my second in command. You will follow his orders like they are my own. We've worked together for a long time, so you won't find any conflict between us. When we're done, there'll be time for the squad to introduce themselves. Take a seat."

The lead in his legs gone, Ryan took a seat at the back. Jackson dropped down beside him. It was all he could do not to ask all the questions burning at the front of his mind; something about the captain stopped him. She seemed rigid, the opposite of what General Matthews said the Mech Force was looking for. Was this a balancing act or the start of a greater swing?

The lights dimmed and Ryder started. The screen behind her activated, first showing the squadron's logo, an orange circle with lines of various sizes stretching from the perimeter and the slanted "E" in the middle, followed by a technical diagram of the mech unit. It looked like one that had been sent to him the previous day.

"I won't go into detail, as everyone other than the rooks knows this information already, but these are the units you'll be piloting. The ME-1 was originally a space utility unit, used for construction, demolition and anything else you can think of. They were slow and bulky, but since we requisitioned them, speed and manoeuvrability have been improved as well as armaments and defences.

"Our Valkyrie-class fighters, the ones you saw in the footage yesterday, are faster but can't match the firepower of this hardware. None of our single-pilot ships can, but we have seen better results with the new Vanga model, which sacrifices speed for better armour and weapons. You will be trained to pilot both the ME-1 and the Vanga during your time here, but the former will be your primary unit.

"ME-1 loadouts can be changed depending on a pilot's particular skills and preferences, as well as the mission objectives. Once you've accustomed yourself to the units, we'll determine the best options for you, your flight and the squad."

None of what the captain said surprised Ryan. This was included in the files he had been reading for most of the previous day. Jackson was paying more attention but that didn't mean she hadn't done any reading.

If all Ryder was going to tell them was what he had already learned, it was going to be a boring lecture. He preferred to do things rather than listen. That had been the case for as long as he could remember.

"Using sim technology, we pilot the mechs remotely. This means our pilots are safe from harm. This is new tech for the Enforcers, and the distance has caused some problems. Unlike on the surface, there are fewer satellites for signals to transmit between. However, it has allowed our pilots to learn from previous experiences.

It's easier to build new units than train new pilots. That being said, we have a finite number of both available so reckless actions are not advised."

Ryan felt that was a jibe at him but couldn't be sure. He knew other racers weren't happy with some of his tactics on the track, but it kept things interesting for the audience whether they admitted it or not. Without knowing everyone's background, there was no way to know who the comment was aimed at, if anyone, but Ryder already seemed to have taken a disliking to him.

"Your tech will go through the workings of the units this afternoon, Rooks. Once you've been briefed, we will, as a squad, help you learn how to pilot the mechs in space and atmosphere. The focus will be on the former as that's where we envision most encounters to take place, but we can't say that with certainty. Preparation is the key."

"Captain?" Jackson's voice took Ryan by surprise – and the rest of the squad by the look of it. Interrupting the captain obviously wasn't a common occurrence. "What about setup and system preferences?"

"That will come in time." Ryder looked more surprised than annoyed at the question. "You're both racers, and you're used to having a particular 'feel' in the sims that's as close to real as possible, I understand. The mechs will be different. The compensators are necessary to give you the optimum level of control. You won't have time to change each setting during a mission so pre-set levels can be stored and adjusted where possible."

"What's the lag time?" Ryan asked as soon as she finished. The annoyance was clear. Definitely personal.

"Small enough that you won't notice." Her reply was curt. "Now, when the techs have finished introducing you to the units, we have a full—"

"With respect," Ryan cut in, ignoring everyone staring at him, most in disbelief. "It may not be noticeable to you, but we're racers. We deal in fractions of a second for a living. If there's a delay between actions in the sim and the mech, I'd like to know."

"There is a small amount of lag," Ryder said after a few moments. "Your tech will tell you the exact amount but it's constantly reducing as more work on the link is completed. At last check, it was about half a second. Does that help you, Rook?"

There was a threat to that question. She was daring him to push further. Ryan was tempted – there wasn't much he could say or do to make her feelings toward him any worse. On the other hand, the consequences she could bring down on him were likely to be harsher than any he had faced at the Institute, and he wasn't a fan of those.

"Yes," Ryan said, forcing a smile. "Thank you, Captain."

"We have a training schedule beyond the basic piloting simulations. With a full roster, we will work on formations and group assaults. I intend to break us down into four flights of three, as is the case with most squads. Each flight will have a specific purpose in the squad, to complement your skills and abilities, allowing us to present a range of offensive and defensive options. Doing this will make Flare Squadron one of the first choices for any mission. Experience will help us become a real team. Questions?"

Silence answered and when Ryder was sure none were coming, she ended the briefing. "Very well. Reconvene in the sim room in six hours. Rooks, you'll head to the hangar with Lieutenant Toomes and Wisp in one hour. You're free until then."

The lights came up after she finished speaking and, without waiting, Ryder marched out of the closest door with Toomes hot on her heels. The moment it closed the room erupted, with Ryan and Jackson surrounded by their new squadmates. It was impossible to make out anything they said, with everyone talking over one another.

"Give it a rest," Wisp ordered, and the crowd fell quiet. "Let them breathe. Go and get some food or something. They've introduced themselves to you. I'll introduce you to them. You can speak to them later, when you remember how to act like people. Go on, get moving."

There was an authority to his voice that left no room for discussion and, reluctantly, the squad dispersed to the middle level of the room. Ryan noticed Wisp didn't raise his voice; it was as quiet as ever – just stricter.

Their protector let out a sigh once they were alone and motioned towards the top of the room. Ryan and Jackson followed and sat around a table in a corner opposite the door. Wisp brought three glasses with a thick amber liquid inside to the table and sat with them. He raised his glass and clinked it once against each of theirs.

"Welcome to the squad," he said, and took a sip.

Jackson did the same. Ryan drank a fraction later, coughing and spluttering after only the smallest mouthful. "Synthol?" he asked after catching his breath.

"Synthol; takes a lot to get drunk but no hangovers or physical debilitation. Alcohol is rare and you won't find any on the station. That's one of the biggest rules we have. Can't risk being at anything but our best."

"I'm surprised you have Ambrosii up here. I haven't seen it much outside of southern Eurozone," Jackson said, swirling the syrupy liquid.

"It's quite popular on the station, more so within the squad. There are about five bottles in this room alone. I have another hidden away and others probably do too."

"What is this stuff?" Ryan asked. Like most students, he'd drunk synthol before, but racing required him to have a clear head, so it wasn't something he pursued as vigorously as his peers.

"You don't like it?" Wisp asked with raised eyebrows.

"He's underage," Jackson said. "And I don't think Ambrosii is common that far north."

"Synthol, blood orange, melon and a healthy dose of cinnamon. Sweet at first, with a hefty kick to follow through." Wisp smiled after another sip.

"From the cinnamon?" Ryan asked.

"Partly, but it's also a lot stronger than most on the market. The extra synthol adds to the burn."

"I'm beginning to see why it's so popular," Ryan remarked dryly.

"If you don't want it…" Wisp reached towards Ryan's glass.

Pride kicked in. Ryan raised his glass and downed the contents in one. His companions stared at him and for a moment, he thought he'd won. Then the burning took over. His mouth, throat and stomach erupted as the scorched sensation spread, and while he tried to keep his composure, it didn't work.

Jackson and Wisp laughed uncontrollably, drawing confused looks from the remaining squad members in the room. Ryan's objections were lost to gasps for air, which they found funnier.

"Looks like the kid can't hold his drink." Jackson giggled as she started to regain some control.

"He's still young. Give him a year and he'll be drinking like a pro," Wisp agreed. "Just remember, Rooks, what happens in here stays in here. I'm not sure if underage drinking is a rule we can bend but the captain won't get you in trub unless you piss her off – or get wasted."

"You can drink five glasses of this and not notice a thing," Jackson said, patting Ryan's shoulder. "Drink a bottle or two and you'll feel it. More than that, yeah, you'll probably get drunk. Stupidly so if you don't have a good tolerance."

"What the…" Ryan spluttered. "Okay, don't drink a full bottle. Or down it in one. Anything else?"

"Plenty, but we'll save those for another time."

Ryan turned to watch the squad one section below as Wisp and Jackson kept talking. The one in black sat alone, watching the others separate into pairs and edge closer to the white mat.

"He's going to kick your ass again, Oaf." The shorter woman shook her head. "I'm calling it now."

"Have a little faith, Teach," Oaf grunted, raising his hand above her head.

"Pat me one more time and I'll break every bone in your giant bear paw."

Ryan winced at the words, but Oaf laughed, a bellow that filled the room. No one else seemed to take any notice. Oaf walked to the edge of the mat and folded his arms.

"Fine, but I'll be here to laugh when you're face down on the floor," Teach scolded. Something about her tone reminded him of Miss Kinni.

"Settle down, Teach. Let him work it out," the uniformed man said.

Across the mat, two men started playing rock-paper-scissors to decide who'd step in to face Oaf. Seeing this, one of the women from the final pair decided to beat them to it and tried to hop over the bench. Her foot caught and she fell over it, faceplanting on the floor.

"Oh, Ricochet..." her partner sighed, stepping around the bench to help her up.

"I'm good, I'm good. Ready to go!"

"You missed it."

"What? No!" Ricochet yelled as one of the men stepped onto the mat and squared up to Oaf.

Neither moved for a moment and the bigger man charged in, extending his arms to grapple his opponent. At the last moment, as Oaf's arms closed in, his opponent ducked and spun to the right, delivering a blow straight to his side.

It didn't hurt Oaf, as far as Ryan could tell, but it drew his attention and his arms. With a grin, his opponent dropped to the ground and swung a leg at Oaf's leg and brought the big man down to a knee. The speed at which he moved seemed to give him the edge, but Oaf blocked the next blow and spun as the man jumped at him.

He caught his sparring partner in mid-air and slammed him onto the mat.

"Enough," the uniformed man shouted. "Oaf beats Rig. Well done."

"You call that a strategy?" Teach shouted. "Let him hit you until you can catch him? What's that about?"

Ryan didn't hear the rest of the conversation as a clang drew his attention back to Ricochet, who had leapt from the bench and clattered against the lockers on her way to the mat. She squared off against the other man in Rig's pair and the two grappled.

"Okay, it's time to go," Wisp said, leading them out of the room.

On the way to the outer levels of Orbital Station Delta, Wisp listed the squad members by call sign. Sometimes they were a play on someone's name, or to do with their personality. Others would focus on a specific event since they'd joined the Mech Force.

Wisp was fourth in command but was never expected to take the role – sims cut the danger of engagements to close to zero. It was impossible to read the man—his dark eyes betrayed nothing—so Ryan couldn't guess whether he was angry about that or glad.

Jackson and Ryan would be under his command in Flight Four, which explained why he was spending so much time with them. The squad was made up of their group and three others.

They could check personnel files on each squad member at another time, but Wisp wanted them to be able to put names to the voices they'd hear later so he provided brief introductions.

"Flight Three is led by Bishop, our chief strategist, and includes Oaf and Teach – the comedy act you saw before. Flight Two is made up of Tombstone, or Lieutenant Toomes, Rig and Wrecker. I'll give you one guess as to what they did before joining. Then we have Flight One, led by our captain, with Ricochet and Sketcher. You'll get to know them all soon enough."

"What's the captain's call sign?" Ryan asked.

Wisp smiled and said, "It used to be Princess. Her older sister was a captain too, called Queen, and they were both expected to rise to the top. Now, our captain's the queen – I wouldn't say it to her face, though."

Before Ryan could ask anything else, they arrived at a hangar. Wisp swiped his hand across the panel to open the doors. The scene drew curses from the rooks and a wry smile from their flight leader.

CHAPTER FOURTEEN

THE HANGAR WAS AT least four times bigger than the one the shuttle had landed in – and it needed to be.

Their reactions must have been expected as their flight leader had the biggest smile Ryan had seen on him since they met.

At the opposite end, the hangar doors were closed. Nothing was launching or landing any time soon but the floor remained a hive of activity. Mechanics and techs moved swiftly with tools, cables and supplies, but no pilots were around other than Wisp, the two rooks and Toomes, who emerged from the crowd shortly after the doors to the corridor closed.

Of more interest were the mech units. Two rows of six, one against each wall to Ryan's left and right. They were huge. His late-night reading meant he knew the details of their size, speed, weapon capacity and more, but it was different to actually see them.

Each one stood eighty metres from head to foot, a faceless metal statue. Sharp lines and edges had been smoothed for a more fluid skeleton. Most of the joints were covered with armour plates but the specification made it clear this wouldn't restrict movement and, in theory, these giants had more flexibility than any human. Each joint had its own propulsion system that would make learning to do anything a lot more difficult, but until he saw the control system, Ryan had no idea how he was expected to manage so many variables at once.

Each mech looked identical – chrome-coloured, electric-blue eyes – but the lack of nose and mouth was off-putting. The squad logo could be seen on both shoulder plates and in between the thrusters on the back.

Only one weapon was permanently attached: the rail gun, a powerful laser weapon that could be set for long or short bursts with varying recharge times. It drew energy from the power core, so it wasn't suitable as a main weapon, but tests against salvaged alien units proved it to be effective. The heat generated made it perfect for space, but any atmospheric combat would render it useless after one or two blasts – the shoulder mount would simply break apart. When not in use, it rested on the left of the mech's back, pointing up.

Other weapons were available to choose from before each mission, both laser and projectile-based. These, both long and short-range weapons, as well as melee options, were stored in an adjacent chamber. Some mechs had weapons attached and more were being worked on across the hangar floor. It was down to the pilot and squadron to meet each mission objective with the right loadouts.

"Rooks," Toomes called, when he was within a few paces. "Time to introduce you to your mechs. Come."

The lieutenant led them to the three units furthest from the large external door on the left wall. The sea of bodies swerved around them with incredible speed and Toomes never broke his stride. The other three dogged his heels in order to enjoy the same priority.

"This is mine," Wisp announced, stopping in front of the middle of three mechs. "The other two are blank, so take your pick."

"Any preference?" Ryan asked.

"I'll take this one," Jackson said, gazing up at the one on the right. That left Ryan with the unit in the corner.

"Ready to take a look inside?" Ryan turned to see Mac. "They look bland, I know, but when we get the squad colours on and give you a full loadout, there'll be plenty of life in it. Some pilots even give their mechs a name."

"Why? Never mind. Let's go take a look," he said, before speaking to Toomes. "What's our job here?"

"Sir," Toomes shot back. "You'll get a tour of the controls, which are replicated in the sims. Get a rudimentary setup ready, which your tech will load onto your sim. Once that's done, we'll teach you how to pilot your mech and then integrate you into training programmes with the rest of the squadron."

"Fine," Ryan said, deliberately forgetting to say "sir". To Mac, he said, "After you."

Just above the mech's shoulders hovered a metal walkway in front and behind the six units, with connecting walkways in between. It was the same on the other wall, with three bridges stretching across the hangar. Mac led Ryan around the back of his mech to a ladder on the wall and started climbing. On the way up, his tech informed him the railing would rise to the ceiling when the mechs were being deployed. Each mech had its own ladder in the hangar but in the field a cable could raise or lower the pilot in or out.

By the time they reached the walkway, Ryan's arms were aching, and he was out of breath, although Mac didn't seem fazed. How many times he must climb up and down these rungs every day he couldn't guess. The tech himself might not even know.

A quick glance told him Jackson had made it up first with her tech. They were deep in discussion about something. That was when Ryan realised Mac was talking to him.

"Sorry. Say again?"

"I said this is the access hatch – at the base of the neck. It needs a code to be accessed. Only the pilot and their tech have that code, to prevent anyone messing with your system. Once open, there's a ladder to take you down to the controls."

"Down? Not up?"

"Why up? Having controls in the head would be coo – one lucky hit and the mech's finished. The body is better protected. Besides, the head is your escape pod."

"So, the controls are right above the power source. That sounds safe."

"If anything goes wrong, being in the head wouldn't help. You won't use the escape pod since you're in the sims but that's how they were designed."

"Fair enough," Ryan said. "What's the code?"

"Watch." Mac punched a twelve-digit code into the controls. Ryan activated his MOB-I and stored the code. He made a note to find a way to unlock the hatch with his implant in the future.

The hatch opened and revealed a dark tunnel that slowly lit up with a ring of lights every five rungs. Mac climbed down and Ryan followed, careful not to step on his hands.

He needn't have worried. There was a thud as the tech landed while he was only halfway down. To save time, he slid the rest of the way and felt the shudder through his legs as his feet hit metal grates covering the wires and power core.

Mac was standing beside a chair and motioned for him to sit.

It was padded, which was a mercy, but of more interest were the four control points. Mac showed him how to lock in, first by putting his feet in the grips and closing the metal frames around his ankles and lower legs.

A series of commands on the consoles in front of him were next, although most did nothing while the unit was disconnected from the power core. There were more switches above for weapons and communications but most of the systems were handled from the main consoles. The entire front wall was a large screen presenting a panoramic view ahead and to the sides, from the head's perspective to make it easier to adjust.

With that part of the sequence completed, the seat moved. Ryan was pushed to a standing position and the chair became a wall. From behind, two metal gauntlets swung round.

It took a moment to get his fingers in the right slots. Unlike his legs, these frames weren't locked in. He could move almost normally but to reach the consoles, one of his arms had to leave its frame. Not perfect but it made sense.

"The arms and legs of the mech will mimic the movements you make in these frames," Mac explained. "Notice the slate behind you has moved back. It will support you during acceleration if you need it, or just drop into the floor. Certain movements can be calibrated to different functions. One is the thrusters. Press down with your toes and they'll activate. Reverse thrusters with the heel. Get it?"

It sounded far-fetched, even for Ryan, who was used to sims and technology that adapted to the user's needs, but he nodded.

"What's the lag time?" he asked as he swung his arms across his body in a mock punch, testing the limits of his movement.

"Miniscule. You won't notice it."

"I prefer details to vague answers," he answered dryly. Zack would have given him the answer.

"If you were piloting the mech from here, point zero three of a second. Even a racer like you wouldn't notice it." Ryan knew that was true. "From the sim, we've made improvements already but there's more to come. Right now, you can expect point four-nine of a second."

"Not disastrous, but it could be better."

"The researchers are doing their best to eliminate it, but this kind of application is more complicated than a racing avatar."

Ryan couldn't argue with that. Mac ran through the power-down procedure next, disconnecting his arms first, then his legs once the chair had returned to its original mode and he was seated again. That much was predictable.

From there, they took another ladder down to the power core and one up to the escape pod. There wasn't much else to see inside and they used the consoles to find Ryan's preferred setup. They started with compensator levels, providing enough of a feel for what was happening without putting too much strain on his body or too much resistance in making movements or commands.

Communication and alarm volume followed, as did screen focus, targeting controls and sensor visual levels. It took three hours to get a balance Ryan felt comfortable working from. He thought about Zack and how quickly this might have gone with his friend, using his experience of how Ryan liked to race – which was all Mac had to go off.

"Happy?" Wisp asked as they climbed out of the mech and back onto the walkway. Jackson was waiting nearby with Toomes behind her.

Ryan shrugged. "You fill me with confidence. You certainly took long enough."

"I won't know how good it is until we power up and test it."

"You're in luck," Toomes said. "That's what we're doing next, after we eat."

Flare Squadron's sim room was one level below the hangar but deeper in the station. It was a long, rectangular room with twelve large sim pods, two screens on the short walls at either end and two doors onto adjoining corridors.

The rest of the squad were already in the room by the time the four turned up.

"All set, rooks?" Captain Ryder asked, breaking off from the main group but not waiting for an answer before barking orders. "Get to your sims – it's time to put the rooks through their paces. Wisp, show them to their pods."

"Yes, Captain."

He led them to the far end of the room, passing others who nodded at them, smiled encouragingly or patted shoulders. There still hadn't been any real introductions yet but Ryder was more concerned with staying on schedule than building team spirit.

Wisp ushered them to the last three pods in the room. He stopped at the first of the three and climbed to the top, as the rest of the squad were doing. Jackson and Ryan followed suit with their own sims, opened the hatches and climbed into a replica of the mech's control system.

The hatch closed behind him, plunging Ryan in darkness until the lights activated. They were dim, floor level, but just enough to show where he needed to be.

The start-up procedure proved more tedious than difficult. Ryan locked in his legs, pushed buttons on the console in front and this time wasn't surprised when the chair pushed him to a standing position. His right arm slipped into the wire gauntlet while his left flipped the final switches and finished powering up his controls.

It took a few seconds for anything to happen but the message on his screen showed a timer ticking down while the sims synchronised with each other and brought up their training scenario. Mac came over the comm system briefly to inform him of the progress and point out a few other system controls they hadn't covered before.

"Rooks, you're going to be starting in an atmospheric environment while you learn the basic movement methods. If you progress as quickly as the general expects, you'll be given some weapons and flight training. Then we'll move on to a zero-g environment," Captain Ryder explained. "Don't think this is going to be easy. Your techs will walk you through the initial exercises while Wisp and I observe. The rest of the squad have their own schedule to follow."

"Yes, Captain," Jackson said.

Ryan reached up and flicked a switch to activate his comm system, set to default on the squad channel. "Understood."

Silence greeted him. It was slightly unnerving but not surprising given her strictness. Whether or not any of the liveliness he saw from the squad earlier ever made it through to their comm channel was unknown and Ryan didn't want to push it.

The sim went black again. Ryan stood in the darkness. He was aware of the uncomfortable metal frames clamped to his feet and legs, and the metal gauntlets that weren't a perfect fit. His nerves were mounting, just like before a race. Only this time it was a giant robot rather than a motorcycle.

The sim finally synced, his controls lit up and the screen burst into life as the environment loaded. It looked as real as any location Ryan had seen but it was quiet, until Mac's voice filled the sim with the first set of instructions.

CHAPTER FIFTEEN

"Ryan." Mac's voice could shatter glass at that volume, prompting Ryan to forget about the field he could see. They'd sorted volume levels not long ago. How had he got them wrong? "Ryan? Are you listening to me? Oi!"

"I'm here," he said, adjusting the volume. "A little deaf, but here."

"What? Never mind. We're going to run through basic controls now. We'll see how the initial settings feel and make any changes before the next exercise. Okay?"

"Yeah."

"Don't do anything unless I say so. This is the most efficient method we have for training. In a couple of hours, you'll be walking like a pro."

Ryan had never considered walking to be an activity anyone would need to be a professional at, but Mac was in his element. Better not to point that out even though he wanted to. He really wanted to.

"Start by moving your arms," Mac ordered. "One at a time, up and down, slowly. Then a horizontal swing. Let's check the resistance levels."

"What about the start-up procedure?"

"Don't worry about that, you'll get faster in time. After a few weeks it'll be second nature. Arms. Go."

That seemed smart enough. Everything Ryan had learned so far implied time was not on their side so priorities had to be made.

Clenching and unclenching his fist, he raised his arm from his side until it reached out horizontally. It took longer than expected; the initial movement was hard, like the gauntlet was stuck. Before he could tell Mac about it, he came on the line to note it.

Then he told Ryan to do it again.

He let his arm fall to his side, bouncing from his leg. An alarm screamed through the sim and the impact area flashed on the three-dimensional model of the mech he was piloting – or would be, if this wasn't a training simulation.

"What are you doing?" Mac yelled. "It may be a machine but that came down with some real force. Be more careful!"

"If it can't handle it, how is it going to help us on missions?" Ryan muttered, before replying to the tech. "There's a lot of difference in the resistance between my arm going up and coming down. Set it somewhere in the middle and we'll go from there."

With that in place, the training progressed much smoother. It took half an hour of raising his arm up and down and swinging it across his body to find the right level of resistance. Mac informed him most pilots liked almost no resistance so it was easy to move their limbs. Ryan was different. He wanted a small amount of resistance since the gauntlets were going to slow him down, even by fractions of a second, and to get the best reactions he needed his mech to respond the same way.

"Okay, I'll apply the same levels to the left arm, and we'll move on to the—"

"No, I want different settings for the left arm," Ryan interrupted.

"What? Why? That's coo."

"I'm right-handed, so it's my dominant arm. The mech should respond as I do or it'll throw me off with this control system."

"That's not normal procedure. Most pilots use the same settings," Mac explained, but Ryan wasn't having it.

"I'm not a normal pilot. Trust me on this." Working out the finer details of his setup was Zack's speciality. It would be much easier if his friend was working with him.

"Do it, Mac," Ryder ordered, "but Fall, if this hinders your progress, we'll revert to using the same settings on both arms."

"Understood."

Ryder's voice sounded a bit warmer than normal. Whether she preferred to be in this environment or was happy to see how much effort he was putting in, Ryan wasn't sure. He'd take any positivity at this stage.

Mac gave him no time to dwell on those thoughts as the next task came through. With the arms ready, leg movements were next on the list. If this wasn't done right, Ryan could find himself in a very awkward position due to the nature of the control system. While the running commentary had some benefits, Ryan preferred to work things out on his own.

"How about letting me try to figure this one out?" Ryan suggested.

"Nope." That was the end of that.

After how long it had taken to properly calibrate the arms, Ryan didn't expect the legs to be any quicker. The gauntlets made moving his arms awkward and it would be the same with his legs even though the controls were designed to give full movement. That didn't make them easy to learn.

Mac applied the same resistance levels to his legs as a starting point. The first task was to lift one leg and bend the knee, then repeat with the other. Hardly exciting stuff but his tech wouldn't budge from routine. Ryan's centre of balance was off, and he wobbled on the first few attempts but kept his footing. Mac gave his approval and asked him to speed up. All the while, they exchanged feedback on the settings, finding the right levels of responsiveness until it was as close to natural as possible.

Then Ryan added more resistance, creating the same feelings he had found with his arms. Mac didn't like it but obliged. It felt strange thinking of resistance and movement times for his own body – never something he had considered before.

"Right, time for baby's first step." Mac's joke was bad but fitting. Moving the limbs alone had taken a lot of concentration and effort so this wouldn't be easy.

It started fine. The right leg lifted just as he'd planned. It moved forward as well, although not as much as his leg would have normally. It didn't rest on the ground where and when Ryan expected it to and suddenly the world was falling. The display showed the grass rushing to meet him, with the right side of the mech closest to impact. A few seconds later the screen shuddered, and the unit landed on its side.

Ryan, however, was not.

The displays showed the mech lying on the ground at an odd angle, face down and leaning heavily on its right side, but Ryan was upright in the sim.

"This is coo," he told his tech.

"What do you mean?"

"I'm supposed to be on my side yet I'm standing the right way up. My orientation is screwed just looking at this. I need to feel like I'm in that position."

"You'll adapt."

"Not in time. I race by feeling, Mac. To lean in close to the ground and feel the scrape of kneepads on tarmac. For the sharp turns, the acceleration and braking. This is too stale. Turn down the compensators and any adjustment settings. I need to be in as close a position to the mech as possible."

"That isn't a good idea. You'll be really disadvantaged by the changes in battle. You don't stay in one position and you'll want to get your bearings quickly. Trust me."

"You let me worry about that."

"Ryan, listen—"

"Enough," Captain Ryder cut in. "Do as he says. His unit, his call. Rook, if you want this to happen, get up on your own. No assistance."

"Cha, Captain." Ryan was suddenly less confident of his decision. Her voice was back to being cold. Was this her way of teaching him a lesson? If so, he was determined not to lose.

"Okay, hold on to your breakfast," Mac warned.

Nothing happened for a few moments, then the screens blacked out. In the darkness, Ryan felt trapped, but a moment later he was in motion as the simulator flipped to the side. By the time the screens activated again, the view was the same but he was now positioned at the same angle as the mech. The gauntlets around his arms had also moved them into new positions to match the mech's current position. It wasn't comfortable, and if anyone could see him, they'd probably have plenty of jokes.

"Okay, Rook," Ryder commed. "Get on with it. Up."

Muttering under his breath, Ryan pushed against the ground – or what his sim knew to be the ground. Even though he was pushing at thin air with the gauntlets, the system registered where the ground should be and stopped his movements at a realistic point. In combat, that would mean he couldn't expect to swing his arm and have it carry on even if the mech's arm stopped – his arm would stop too. How jarring that would be was something else to discover.

The first attempt was laughable. He pushed up onto his elbow, but twisting the mech's body was harder than he thought. There would be a knack to it, but Ryan couldn't figure it out straight away. He landed with a thud and his body bounced in the air, suspended from his limbs in their control sockets against an invisible barrier.

The second attempt was better. He managed to get on one knee after pushing up from his elbow. He knew the next step was to stand but his other leg couldn't find level footing and he fell again.

Laughter sounded over the comm, although it wasn't clear who from. "Do you mind? I'm working here," Ryan grumbled, and it clicked off instantly. He obviously wasn't supposed to hear that.

Gritting his teeth, Ryan pushed up with both arms. He was face-first on the ground this time and once his arms were fully extended, he realised what this could look like. Deciding to give his spectators something to really laugh about, Ryan lowered himself down again, stopping just before the display went black from flattening the virtual grass. Then he straightened his arms, pushing back up.

He did this again and again. Ten virtual push-ups – the effort was real, but much harder than outside of a mech. He'd have to see if Mac could get a visual for him.

From this position he was able to stand. The first leg bent and found stable footing, then the other. He pushed up and used the momentum to plant his mechanical foot firmly on the ground.

Ryan smiled. He was standing again. However, his other leg kept going and he saw his continued movement. He hadn't stopped. It was such a natural thing with his body but the sims were different. Without thinking, he pushed back with one foot. It wasn't a real step, more like a shuffle. The screen jerked and stopped.

He took a deep breath. Instead of trying to take a step forward to stand normally again, he tried to bring his foot back with the same shuffle. It took two attempts, but he dragged it back into place.

"Well done, Rook. Looks like you'll be of some use after all."

The captain's praise took him by surprise, making him stumble as he tried to take another step.

"Okay, Ryan," Mac said sheepishly. "Maybe you do have some idea of what you're doing."

"Is that an apology?"

"As close as you're getting. Ready to try again?"

"What does it look like I'm doing?"

It took half an hour for Ryan to take a successful first step. He mastered shuffling quickly but it wouldn't help in combat, nor was it practical enough for most situations. There were more falls, but each time it was easier to get back on his feet. The last time, he even managed to push himself onto his back and try to get up that way. No one objected or asked what he was doing since it must have been obvious; he was learning.

His attempts didn't work. The mech's body, built with thousands and thousands of moving parts, was more flexible than his own but limited by the control system. Jumping from his back to his feet was out of the question for now. At best, he looked like a fish out of water.

"Good job, rooks. We're going to give you a break and bring you over to our environment. I want you to watch how we work together, the tactics we use and just what the mechs can do. Stand by."

Everything went dark for a few seconds and lit up with an aerial view of another grassy plain. There were ten mechs below in two rows of five. They stood motionless until the comm channel came alive with Ryder and Toomes giving orders to their teams. A lot of it sounded like jargon but Ryan was able to pick out a few names and their orders.

After adjusting to the chaos, he picked out individual mechs and their pilots by linking their actions to the comm messages.

Oaf was a spearhead for Ryder's team while Toomes opted for a three-pronged attack. The weapons being used were similar until they closed in and the rifles were ditched for short-range options. Explosions and flashing metal made it hard to see what was going on.

Slipping out of the gauntlets, Ryan flipped switches and tapped the console. It took some doing but the sensor sphere soon showed blue and red dots while the screen highlighted each mech with a name using the same colours on the sphere.

That made it easier to track what was happening but any thoughts he had of a quick finish to the session vanished when the skirmish ended and the mechs reset, lining up again in teams of five. He enjoyed peace and quiet for a couple of minutes before they started again. How long they would go at it, Ryan wasn't sure.

He settled in to watch, listen and make notes. Every so often Mac would speak over the comm and explain more about the mech's systems or what was happening in the exercise, but for the most part, Ryan stood in silence. He wondered what Jackson made of all this and what progress she had made.

All he had to do now was find out how to get the sim's chair back for the times he was left to watch – Ryan didn't want to hang there for however long the rest of the session took. That was something he didn't want to ask Mac in case Ryder overheard and lowered her opinion of him even further.

General Matthews leaned back in his chair. The wall in front of his desk was a large screen, split into a main window in the centre and surrounded by smaller squares. Each small window was split again into a simulator view and what the mech – pilot – could see.

It was the first time any of them had piloted anything like this, but all the rooks had some experience with sim technology. That was one of the criteria for their selection. What the general had seen today was nothing unusual; some had performed well and others had not.

The real test was how long it took them to become proficient. They were working against the clock but no one knew how much time they had. It could be days, weeks or, with a little luck, months. It was unlikely there would be time to train more pilots after this group.

With the newest recruits, they had seven hundred and eight pilots in fifty-nine squadrons of twelve. That was alongside over eleven hundred Valkyrie pilots on OSD and the surrounding ships, which had considerable firepower too. How it would match up against the enemy when they arrived in full force, he couldn't say. Nor did he want to think about it until then.

"Cadet," Matthews said, pressing a button on his desk. "Remind the squad captains I want daily updates on the rooks' progress. Book each captain in for a meeting every two weeks, starting in two days."

"Yes, sir."

This one was greener than the last, but it was becoming harder and harder to keep cadets around for more than a couple of months when they realised the extent of the looming threat. Matthews had tried to keep it from them in the past but they always found out. His assistants were sought out for gossip and most were too inexperienced to know when to keep their mouths shut. The experienced ones were sometimes worse.

Returning his attention to the screen, he selected another pilot and watched as they struggled to get to grips with moving properly.

It was a common problem with new pilots. No one in this group avoided falling over during their first steps, although one managed to have some fun with it. Ryan Fall was an interesting candidate. He had a lot of potential but no discipline. The squad's other rookie, Kendra

Jackson, was much better in that regard. She recovered from her falls quickly but took less care of the details Ryan spent so much time on. Her technique was better, so she made progress through the tasks faster, but Ryan was more comfortable with the controls already and what he managed looked more...natural.

The push-ups were proof of that.

Theirs would be an interesting rivalry if it had time to develop. Unfortunately, that would have to take a back seat. The sooner they were up to speed the better.

"One more thing, Cadet. I want you to find out the status of Zack Wendall. Give me an update first thing in the morning."

"Yes, sir."

It wouldn't be this cadet who gave him the update. By morning, she would have rotated with the other, a young man looking to be an officer on the station. He had been here for three weeks already. If he followed the pattern of the last few, he'd be gone in the next two, but there hadn't been any signs of him wanting to move on so far.

The one on duty now was more of a researcher but every Enforcer needed field experience. She had that look in her eye, though. One very few agents had early on. She knew loss.

Matthews picked up the glass on his desk, swirled the brown liquid gently and took a sip, savouring the taste. A few more taps on his desk and the next rook filled the gap in the centre of the wall. You could learn a lot from first attempts, and he watched them all.

There were still eight to go before he finished.

CHAPTER SIXTEEN

FLARE SQUADRON TRAINED FOR seven hours. By the time he finished his own exercises, Ryan was bored and hungry and then he had to watch the rest of the squad. He had given up watching the manoeuvres and formations, relying on quick glances to respond whenever Mac spoke to him.

The sim was a remote cockpit for the mech, making the controls the same, and he used this time to further explore the unit's functions. Each joint was constructed of gears and motors that responded to the pilot's movements. Actions not directly tied to the four limbs had activation commands requiring specific actions or console input and Ryan set himself the task of studying them.

Of more interest were the propulsion systems. Each joint included a small thruster for faster and quicker actions or, as the database told him, increased damage with physical attacks.

These worked alongside two main thrusters in the lower legs for primary movement, such as running and jumping on a surface. There were three more on the back of the mech's body, allowing the unit to hover or fly for short amounts of time when gravity was present before they needed to recharge.

Zero gravity environments used these propulsion systems in tandem, which, when combined with moving and combat, could be overwhelming. It made sense to start learning like this even if Ryan didn't expect to pilot a mech on the planet any time soon.

When the order came to disconnect, Ryan was skimming over information on the power systems. He had been able to work out that the mechs were powered by a plasma-based power core, although the details were lost on him. He was no scientist, but it was unlike anything he had encountered on the surface. The self-charging system, while hard to produce, could last for decades if what he'd learned was right.

That presented a unique challenge. They could push the mech to the limits but once depleted, the plasma would take hours to recharge, and replacing a core took days. They couldn't drop to below ten percent before shutting down to recharge. Even at full power, that was several hours of use.

Power management would be a critical factor.

Disconnecting was awkward on his own but he managed. By then, Mac had severed the link and left him in near darkness. The hatch opened, providing a halo of light which he used to guide himself up the ladder and into the rectangular sim room.

There was a congregation at the far end with the captain evaluating performances. The rooks were left alone.

"How'd it go?" he asked, covering the distance to Jackson quickly.

"It's not like riding a bike. I can't even walk properly."

Ryan laughed. "Not just me then."

She smiled but her exhaustion was clear. Ryan couldn't blame her; he felt the same. Beyond the physical exertion of piloting the mech, it was mentally draining. The concentration required to make your limbs move the right way was enormous. People took such actions for granted when they did anything; walking, running, sitting, standing, jumping. Once learned, they didn't require as much conscious coordination or concentration.

Athletes would disagree. They made their living doing things most couldn't, but Ryan doubted even they would be able to reach their high standards with this control system.

"Well done, rooks," Captain Ryder said, breaking off from the rest of the squad and joining them, Wisp just behind her. "That's not a bad first day but there's plenty to work on."

"Yes, ma'am," Jackson said, leaning against her sim. Ryan stayed quiet. The captain's eyes were ice cold again and her voice had an edge.

"When you get back to your quarters, you'll see a schedule has been sent to your terminals. You'll train with the squad, eat with them and get to know them as well as you know yourselves."

"Sounds fun," Ryan commented before he could stop himself. The mistake was all too apparent when Ryder's glare settled on him.

"You're not here to have fun, Fall. You're here to learn and fight. Squad tactics work better when you know the people you fight with, and vice versa. This isn't a social gathering. Keep that in mind."

"So, we're not friends but you want them to know me as a friend would. That's a bit of a contradiction. Sir."

"Figure it out," Ryder said curtly before turning to the rest of the squad. "Same time tomorrow. No briefing. Dismissed."

The captain and the lieutenant marched from the room and the rest of the squad pressed in around the rooks. They didn't look as tired as Ryan and Jackson and soon decided it was time for food. There was no chance to escape as the group kept them in the middle. Wisp followed, watching closely.

Their flight leader rescued them in the transporter. The squad filed out but before the rooks could follow, Wisp closed the door and sent them on their way. Ryan glanced at him and received a shrug. When the doors opened again, he strode into the corridor, leaving the two rooks to follow.

Ryan was too tired to notice where they were going but it wasn't long before Wisp stopped outside two doors and turned to face them.

"I know the captain's said this already but..." He paused. This clearly made him uncomfortable. "Good job today. It might not feel it, but you made a lot of progress, more than expected. It's going to be a long journey but we'll get you ready. If you want food brought to you tell them I authorised it. From tomorrow you'll eat with the squad. Until then."

"Hey," Jackson called to him as he walked away. "What's your name?"

"Andre Tanner," he said without stopping.

He vanished around a corner and his footsteps faded.

The pair looked at each other and entered their rooms. It took all of Ryan's will not to flop onto his bed. Instead, he sat at the desk and activated the console. There were the messages from Ryder, but nothing else, and his MOB-I had nothing from Zack either.

After his experience in the sim, going over more mech specifications and schematics didn't appeal. Instead, he loaded Flare Squadron's personnel files. Ryan didn't want to go in blind.

Other than the four flight leaders, none of Flare Squadron had received Enforcer training. They were drafted in from civilian life to join the programme. Without access to more records Ryan couldn't be sure how common that was.

There were pictures in the files, but some were so old they could have belonged to someone else. Thankfully, Wisp had pointed out each member after the morning briefing.

Another yawn told him it was time to sleep, but not before checking his schedule. Ryder was right; the days were routine, with physical conditioning in the morning before sim sessions in the afternoon and short breaks for eating in between. The evenings were free but a note at the bottom made it clear this was for extra physical training or studying the mech's advanced controls and features.

Free time was something the captain didn't seem to value very much. Ryan had doubts about that approach. It would work for fully trained Enforcers but most of the squad were civilians.

Sleep came easily again. It was one of the few things that did on OSD.

There was no word of Zack the next morning and the gym session was gruelling thanks to his new instructor.

After a brief introduction they set to work. The circuit was similar to the first one he had done as part of the medical exam, only this time he had to improve. Ryan had to go further, last longer and beat every old time or count he had achieved. Pain was a necessary part of the process, he was told.

Throughout the morning, Ryan saw other members of his squad come and go for their own sessions. They'd smile and wave and he'd do the same when he could. He spotted some other recruits from his group but mostly the gym was full of people he hadn't seen before: pilots, officers, mechanics and other agents on the station.

Lunch followed training, where the rest of the squad would assemble. There wasn't much time to talk and they were soon on their way to the sims.

Ryan and Jackson worked on getting the basics down for most of the session before tuning in to watch and listen to the rest of the squad at work.

It took a full week for Ryan to walk without falling or stumbling.

Sidestepping took longer and running was even harder. Jumping was easy once he learned how the controls responded to simple things like tensing a leg. Studying the advanced controls every night helped him master the basics.

Jackson was faster. She was walking within a few days, but it was an awkward gait. From their discussions, it was clear she could learn skills quickly, but refining them slowed her down. Her setup wasn't perfect. It was something else to overcome but given how much they had to learn it was hard to say whose approach was better.

Every session started the same way. Cover the basics they'd learned previously then move on to something new. Repetition was important according to Mac – something about muscle memory. Compared to relying on instinct, like Ryan did during a race, this wasn't as fun. A different kind of challenge.

In their third week of training, Ryan and Jackson moved on to joint exercises and how to use their mechs together to achieve objectives. Results were good but their actions in hand-to-hand combat needed improvement.

"Good job," Wisp said as they ended another session. "Your speed is good."

"Your movements are sloppy, and you both lack coordination," Captain Ryder countered. "Given your sim experience, I expected you to be in full squad drills by now."

"They're doing better than any of us did at this stage," Bishop said from behind her.

"It's not enough. You'll begin training with the squad tomorrow, but your evenings will be here. Ricochet, Teach and Oaf will be with you. They'll help you get up to speed so you don't slow the rest of us down."

"Why not just help us?" Ryan asked, unable to stop himself. "Tell us what we're doing wrong."

"Would you listen? You're both racers. You learn by doing and feeling. More sim time will help. The general agrees. Dismissed."

"You're not staying, either?" Jackson asked Wisp as he followed the rest of the squad out of the sim room.

"You guys have got this. Relax, and stop treating the mechs like machines. Cycles are an extension of you, right? These should be, too."

"Okay," Teach said, her energetic voice another reminder of Miss Kinni's attempts to rally a class out of a slump. "Let's get started."

"Why did the captain choose you three?" Jackson asked. Teach's energy hadn't rubbed off on her.

"We all had trouble with different aspects of the mech's control systems, too," Oaf answered. "By working with us, I'm guessing she's hoping you'll learn from us."

"Do you know why I'm called Ricochet?" Ricochet asked, brushing hair from her eyes. "My coordination isn't great, both in and out of the mechs. I spent the first month unable to walk in a straight line, and I still bounce off walls and objects—"

"And us," Oaf added.

"—if I don't focus. As soon as I'm distracted by something, it happens."

"Whereas I can track everything that's going on, and I can relay that," Teach followed up, "but deciding what to do in the sim is overwhelming. With my classes, I didn't have that."

"And what about you?" Ryan asked Oaf.

"I found the dimensions off-putting. I'm bigger than the rest of the squad and a lot of pilots. I had to overcome that in my mind before the controls clicked."

"You're not alone. You're one of us now," Ricochet added. "We'll help you find a way that works for you before you know it."

"We started as outsiders – me most of all," Teach said, before pointing to Ricochet. "Helen relied on simulators for social contact so people couldn't see how clumsy or uncoordinated she was. Sketcher used her coordination to make art, expressing and educating people across the Globe through simulators."

"Paula Reed Art. Look it up – she's really good," Ricochet winked.

"Oscar here spent most of his time away from people in case he hurt them. I'm from Asiazone. Our leaders have tried to keep us separate from the Globe for years, sharing technology and research but not people. How many of us have you seen beyond the border?"

"It doesn't matter where you came from, or what your life was before. You're here now, and accepting that means a clean slate," Ricochet finished.

"Thanks, guys," Ryan said.

Jackson nodded, and he wondered if she was thinking about what had caused their problems in the mechs, like he was.

They managed a few moments of quiet before Oaf turned them around towards the sims. "We're all still growing. Don't get worked up over what you can't do but focus on what you can. Come on, let's get started."

CHAPTER SEVENTEEN

His view from the desk was impressive but not real. The stars didn't move as the station revolved, nor were they blocked by passing ships. A command from the desk would change it to another of the library, making it easy to spend hours searching the archives – something General Matthews stopped himself from doing daily.

A single command could split it into any number of windows. A full view was relaxing but not always practical. The screen could show anything happening on the station as well as communications with the Globe, the ships and any part of OSD.

Most of the general's time was spent in this office, especially since the latest rooks had arrived. He didn't like being cooped up in one place for so long but agreeing to build the division brought compromises.

Over the years, Orbital Station Delta had become more of a home to him than the surface, even if it all looked the same.

That didn't make being confined to the office for most of his days easier. It allowed others to find him and that was crucial at times. His mornings were routine: breakfast with department heads for news and updates, gym sessions and reports from Colonels Seethe and Granya on their watches.

Afternoons were dedicated to squadron captains, both mech and fighter. They had all seen their numbers increase recently, and not with trained agents but civilians. It was hard for some to take but even harder to handle the lack of discipline. Matthews found himself smoothing over problems more than he liked, even speaking to some of the rooks in person.

The next appointment would prove to be difficult.

With the last week's reports in front of him, Matthews bore into them while he waited for the captain. When it was time for their meeting, a double beep sounded. A quick tap on the desk and the door opened to reveal Captain Ryder at attention.

"Captain," he said, waving her in. "Sit, please."

"Thank you, sir."

"Are you well? Still enjoying your command?"

"Yes, sir, thank you," she said stiffly. Rebecca had been better at small talk. "I'm dealing with the changes, but I don't think command is something to be enjoyed."

"Oh? Why not?"

"Well…it's, uh, complicated. Sir."

Matthews waited for her to continue. He had noticed this discomfort soon after Ryder's promotion and each meeting brought it closer to the surface. The rooks' arrival had pushed it even further. Now she might finally open up.

"I don't believe a leader should get too close to their subordinates," she said.

"Why's that?"

"Complacency. It's an easy trap to fall into. I've seen it happen. Leaders get too close and the rules become less important. Discipline drops and when the time comes, it ends badly."

"Interesting. Leadership isn't easy by any means. Some of the most capable agents have crumbled under its pressure. There isn't one right or wrong way to be a good leader, no matter what anyone says. It's finding what works for you but also what works for those under your command." The puzzled look on Ryder's face said it all and Matthews smiled before continuing. "We're not drones, Eleanor. Despite our training, we're still people. We have feelings, beliefs, preferences and such. They need to be embraced. It's most obvious with the rooks as they haven't had the training we have. We can control this to an extent but to pretend they don't exist goes against our very nature.

"Perhaps the training takes it too far already. Discipline is important, yes, but we serve civilians. We keep them safe. They have to trust and relate to us, even up here. It's why I put a lot of thought into the squads the rooks joined."

"I'm not sure my rooks are the right fit for me."

"Perhaps. Or, maybe, they're the perfect fit for you."

Silence descended as Matthews studied the captain. Rebecca had handled it so easily, so naturally. Eleanor had more talent as a pilot and agent, with growing leadership skills, but she was distant.

The air around Eleanor was cold, even on the rare occasions she smiled. Behind hard eyes lay a burning desire for revenge and Matthews couldn't blame her. If tempered, such emotions were powerful weapons, but she was a raging storm, unpredictable. It could be dangerous for her and those around her, but the general hoped any destructive force would be aimed at their enemies.

"Do you know my secrets to command?" he asked Ryder, who shook her head slowly. The barriers were back up. "Loyalty and competence, with a little brilliance added in."

He stood, walked around the desk and stared at the stars on the wall. "I'm not the best pilot, nor the best strategist, researcher, mechanic or anything else. I understand people, though. I know what makes them tick and I know how to utilise them in the best way. Every single person on this station is better than me in their field and I make sure they know it. By rewarding their talents, I gain their respect and loyalty. They thank me by doing everything I need them to do and, occasionally, I find someone brilliant. Someone who can do things no one else can or will. Just like Rebecca."

The captain's sharp intake of breath betrayed the touched nerve. It was quiet but Matthews wanted to confirm his suspicion. Underneath it all, Rebecca was the problem. Perhaps she always had been.

"Come look at this," he said softly, waiting for the captain to stand next to him. "Rebecca was brilliant in almost every way. I believe she understood more than anyone told her, more than they saw. Her biggest asset, like mine, was understanding people. Yes, she got close to her squad but that made it easy for them to follow her orders in the face of uncertainty and death."

"They failed her."

"Or did she fail them? By your logic, both arguments could be made. I believe neither. It could have been any squad out there and the result would have been the same. If not for her quick thinking, we wouldn't have had any warning at all. She gave us a chance and I intend to use it. Do you recognise this scene? It's from her lieutenant. It's beautiful. Calm. Dangerous." He pointed to a black spot. "That's the enemy. I've stared at this for hours. I made the decision to send her squadron on this mission and every day I wish I hadn't. Rebecca was a good friend; one I could use now.

"I see a lot of her in you, Eleanor. You have even more potential than your sister. You haven't yet come into your own. I hoped command would help. Maybe I was wrong again. Regardless, I need your skills just like your squad needs your support and discipline. If we make it through this, none of us will be the same. We'll all lose something. Or someone."

Matthews turned away from the display and returned to his chair. Ryder joined him. He brought up the reports from the last week so they could go through them but a look in her eyes told him something had changed, or was changing.

Some of the ice in her eyes had melted but the storm behind them hadn't withered. That conflict would take longer to resolve and he could only hope it would turn out in her favour. And his.

"Give me an overview, Captain," he said.

"The squad is performing well in simulations, sir. Each week they improve and work together better. Given only four of us have had the training this division requires, it's quite a feat."

"One you repeat every fortnight."

"They have exceeded my expectations and more. It's growing hard to keep them challenged and I fear they may lose interest without that, especially the rooks."

"I see. How are they progressing?"

"They've become better pilots than half the Mech Force in just two months. Their ability to learn, adapt and improve is astounding. They'll easily establish themselves among the best pilots we have – both mech and fighter – in half a year, if they have that long."

"I sense a but…" Matthews said, interlocking his fingers and resting his elbows on the desk.

"Their lack of discipline causes problems. They see things differently than the rest of us. That's not always a bad thing; some of their solutions are incredible, but they clash quite a lot."

"With each other or the squad? You mean their personalities?"

"They understand each other well and their flight leader has a rapport with them. They will be formidable. The clashes are with the squad and are more… physical in nature."

"You mean like this?" General Matthews worked his terminal and opened one of the files. The view they had just been staring at changed to a virtual moon with six silver mechs moving in formation, firing at targets in the distance. "It seemed to start off well."

"It did," Ryder agreed, half turning to see the screen without presenting her back to the general. "The formation held well, and the rooks adapted to the change in gravity quickly. There were a few stumbles—"

"And jumps."

"Yes. Fall explores the limits. Better here than on a real mission. What surprised me is that while they're acquiring targets and firing, the rooks have a fantastic sense of timing and targeting that makes them suited for long-range weaponry. With targeting computers, their accuracy is well above eighty-seven percent on most missions – the rooks are looking for ways to complete the mission quickly and effectively."

"That's why they're here."

"It results in this," Ryder sighed.

The mechs jumped as one, unleashing a barrage of laser fire into the distance. The returning fire followed them up, striking the frontline units repeatedly. Two of the mechs at the back moved forward, reached a unit in front and pushed upwards, while the front units plummeted towards the surface.

The two jumpers soared high, using their thrusters to carry them even further. When their momentum slowed, one of the pair jumped off the other.

As the mech continued to rise, the image pulled back so the whole squadron was visible, with lances of light criss-crossing as the two sides continued to exchange fire. At the height of its jump, the mech unleashed a barrage of missiles into the distance, lighting the horizon with orange that soon blurred grey as dust and debris took over. The returning fire died instantly.

"Fall and Jackson?" Matthews asked. "Did you impose limits on the thrusters for this sim?"

"Yes, sir. I believe it was Fall's plan. From that height, he was able to get a direct shot at the enemy while their attention was focused on the rest of the squad."

"Although it took out three mechs: the two they first jumped from and then the partner. Quick thinking to realise how high he had to get in that gravity and what the thrusters could manage. Who else suffered?"

"Lieutenant Toomes and Rig."

"They must have been thrilled."

"There were some strong words after. Fall was not put off. His plan worked and Jackson backed him. Surprisingly, so did Bishop."

Matthews smiled; it was the kind of thing his old friend would have thought of. In their youth.

"While the mechs were damaged and the pilots shaken, the objectives were met with no casualties and minimal damage. Very few pilots have completed this scenario so quickly. That Jackson bought into this, and was content to be the second boost, shows how good they are already."

"And they're fitting in well?" Matthews asked.

"Well enough. The squad likes them. They train together, eat together, pilot together – even socialise – but the rooks like their own space. Ryan's found a viewing deck near his quarters and spends time there every day. Jackson sits in her mech – not the sim, the actual unit – every day. Usually, it's after the sim sessions when they do this. Everyone's accepted it now, but it caused a stir at first."

"But not for you?"

"I think I get it," Ryder said, nodding slowly. Matthews assumed she'd been thinking about this for a while. "They're learning and processing a lot. It's their ways of coping."

"You're nearly right. Don't forget they're racers. They're both used to making decisions in fractions of a second and that's no easy task," Matthews said, leaning back and unlocking his fingers. He replayed the vid of the mechs jumping from each other. "The time after a race, when the adrenaline fades, allows them to process their choices and consequences; what worked, what didn't, what can be improved. They're still doing that here. You make decisions in seconds, but they've made five or six in that time."

"That's insane."

"It's what we need. Don't underestimate their abilities or the toll it takes on them. In those moments they need more support than anyone else."

"I'll keep that in mind, sir," Ryder said with a nod.

"Good. I'll speak to both rooks soon enough. While their intentions are good, they need to learn the chain of command. It's your role to make decisions on strategies and formations. They need to understand that."

"Rebecca told me there are always exceptions."

"Who do you think told her?" Matthews smiled. "Yes, there are always exceptions and it will take time for them to learn when those arise, but it's the same for everyone. Even you. My advice, Captain, is to be flexible with them. Agents know what to expect from someone in your position. They don't."

"Yes, sir. One more thing; Fall keeps asking about Wendall. He tries to hide it but he's growing more worried by the day and it's beginning to affect him. I think we need to tell him something."

"I see. Yes, I've had messages from numerous agents about this. I'll bring it up when I speak to him. I'm meeting Kayo today. I'll get an update then. What's next?"

It was rare to find Doctor Kayo so quickly. More often than not she was with a patient and left most of the admin work to junior staff. There weren't many serious cases that required her attention, mostly injuries from training or accidents.

The door to her office was open and he stopped outside to analyse the woman behind her desk. She didn't spend a lot of time here but there were clothes and PCTs all over the place, a sharp contrast to the usual tidy and ordered layout.

"When did you last get a full night's sleep?" he asked.

Kayo's head jerked up and her eyes snapped open. Her black hair, normally in a bun, was hastily tied back, with loose strands everywhere, and the bags under those hazel eyes were almost as dark as her hair. Once she was aware of who had spoken, her eyelids dropped. She was running on empty.

"I'll sleep when I'm dead," she grunted.

"Carry on like this and it won't be long. You can't care for patients as an empty shell."

"Since when did you become a physician?"

"Oh, two years ago?" Matthews stroked his beard in feigned contemplation. "After twenty years of listening to you, it's not hard to pick up the basics."

Kayo smiled for an instant. She stood, wobbled and regained her balance. "I assume you want to see him?"

"That's right. I'm sure you've had your fair share of messages too."

"Probably. I haven't checked. The staff have passed some on to me. He's persistent."

Kayo led them through the centre, past rows of beds that occasionally had an occupant and a doctor, or just one. They headed into the depths, far beyond the prying eyes of any casual visitor or patient.

They stepped into a small room with a large window looking into a larger, white room. There were screens on every wall, full of data from the occupant. The young man looked nothing like he had when he'd arrived on the station. With grey skin, saggy and hanging from his bones in places, he looked like a corpse. Only the rise and fall of his chest proved he was alive.

"Coo..." Matthews breathed. Kayo turned to him. It was rare he used that language. "How is he?"

"He's on the mend. It was close more than once but I'm confident the danger has passed. It'll take some time for him to get back on his feet. I'm also worried about his immune system."

"What happened?"

"We installed the implants like we did for every other tech on the station. His body rejected them. That does happen occasionally but another procedure can help us trick the body into accepting them – or we use different implants. Neither option worked with Wendall. If that wasn't enough, he caught an infection."

"That's some luck. How did you solve it?"

"The infection was easy once identified, but to reduce recovery time we've administered a strong dose of supplements intravenously. That should help his body recover within a couple of weeks. As for the implants, we've had to use the new ones from research. Wendall had a MOB-I; not unusual for someone his age, in his profession and with his abilities, but an older model – the same one Fall had before we replaced it. It makes his proficiency even more impressive, but I suspect there's a reason for it.

"Perhaps it's a reaction to the alloys used, or the impulses sent from the implants to the body. I haven't run those tests. The new implants are introduced to the body directly to the nervous system as nanites and form from there. We don't know why traditional implants were rejected but these provide the same functions with better potential for upgrades."

"Did the boy consent to this?" Matthews asked, frowning.

"He did. The nanites did their part to help him recover."

"Good. I'll tell Fall not to worry."

"Don't say too much. I don't want him barging in here to see him. My patient needs rest."

"Understood," Matthews said. They turned back down the corridor. "Is anyone having adverse reactions to the supplements?"

"No. They're much less potent when ingested. By now, even the rooks will be benefitting from them, although I doubt they or anyone else will have noticed anything. If they do, we put it down to a healthier and more structured lifestyle. Any answer is better than nothing."

Matthews paused. "I'm not convinced this is right."

"It had to be done, especially for the pilots. Trying to distinguish between groups would take more time. They'll need the extra support when the enemy arrives. You know this."

"I know. I still don't like it."

"The effects will stay with them forever but there are no negative consequences here," Kayo stated as they returned to the centre's entrance. "The longer they're taken, the better the effects."

"Thank you, Doctor. Get some rest tonight. That's an order."

"Yes, sir."

# CHAPTER EIGHTEEN

THE SIM FELL DARK after the exercise. In those brief seconds Ryan took deep breaths. Physically, the simulations weren't too demanding compared to the first sessions, but over the weeks Captain Ryder had increased the intensity of combat. It was still too easy, and Jackson agreed.

During the sessions, both pointed this out to their techs and captain, but the process was to ease them in and their complaints were ignored. Over the weeks, this changed. The increased intensity was taking a lot more out of all of the squad, not just the rooks.

Mentally, piloting a mech was much harder than a bike, with more to monitor and control. Racing was an individual sport but working in a squad and flight team required more awareness. The general was right to call it a challenge, not that Ryan had any regrets about joining.

This session, like most before it, hadn't been incident-free. From using friendly mechs as shields to jumping from them for a clear target lock, or creating diversions to sacrificing a unit for the benefit of the mission, there were usually strong words aimed at him and sometimes Jackson. They had a similar attitude to the missions, although Ryan's ideas were wilder.

Lieutenant Toomes had fallen victim to his latest idea. Again. This was the fourteenth time he had been the pawn. Not because Ryan had a problem with him; it was just the way the flights were organised. The lieutenant's flight was always in front with heavier armour and short-range weapons. That meant Toomes, Rig and Wrecker were the pilots and mechs Ryan made use of. It just so happened that by the time he was ready to put the plan into action Toomes was often the closest.

Not that the lieutenant believed him.

Light flooded the sim from above, signalling it was time to leave. Ryan dragged himself to the hatch, cursing the ladder, his exhaustion and the sim's likeness to the mech's actual control system. When his boots hit the floor, it took all his strength to stop his legs folding.

"Fall!" Toomes' voice carried across the long room sharply. "What kind of coo move was that?" His lips were pressed into a thin white line and the lieutenant had both fists clenched tighter than Ryan had ever seen them. It proved he was really angry this time.

Ryan couldn't blame him. That had been one of his riskier plans. In a real mission he wouldn't have tried it, but it was perfect for a training exercise. The lieutenant would calm down after a couple of hours, perhaps on the other side of some drinks, but the initial fury was hard to take.

Not all his plans caused outrage in their aftermath, even from those in the squad sacrificed in the process. Some were so crazy Ryan was met with shock instead of rage. The failures became jokes. The ones in between were met with anger most of the time, with varying degrees of heat.

"I needed a shield," Ryan said wearily. "You moved around too much. I couldn't get more than two shots off before having to retarget."

"It kept me in the fight."

"It made the fight longer and increased the risk of casualties. You were only going to be in the fight if the enemy got close enough, which would have meant we failed. You were better as a shield with your extra armour."

"That I can understand, but there was no need to disable my mech from behind and hold me in place!"

"It let me rest my rifle."

Toomes looked like a volcano, his face red and set to erupt. Ryan wouldn't have been surprised if smoke escaped his ears.

"That's enough," Captain Ryder interrupted. She liked the squad to remain as neutral as possible when it came to their exercises but it didn't mean she agreed with Ryan all the time either. "You both have valid points here, but we need better communication. The two of you can sit down later and work out how we can turn this into a viable strategy. Then we'll see how well it holds up in other scenarios."

"Sir!" Toomes and Ryan answered together.

"Captain, has there been any news—"

"If you ask me about Wendall again…" Ryder started, but the words trailed off and she moved on. "That's enough for today. You're all free until tomorrow. Enjoy it but don't do anything stupid. Dismissed."

On occasion, Ryder would mingle. She was trying to open up and create bonds with the squad. Remarkably, the icy glares aimed at Ryan sometimes melted. She never neglected the rooks, nor did she make any special effort with them. The captain would talk with them, instruct, advise and teach them but any attempt to talk beyond their duties was shut down swiftly.

"So, food?" Rig asked. It was a post-sim tradition now regardless of the time. There were always at least a few takers. Today everyone agreed – bar the captain and lieutenant, who had already left.

The pilots left the sim room together. It didn't take long for them to relax and begin talking loudly as they made their way to the mess hall. Ryan took his usual position at the back of the group, watching them interact.

Each flight's pilots had formed close bonds and it was these groups the squad broke into, even off duty. They were happy being all together but given how much time the flights spent together, it felt normal to spend more time with others in their flight. Jackson integrated into the large group better than him but that was partly his fault. The distance stopped feelings from clouding his judgement when his ideas called for hard choices.

Not that all the choices were hard. With no real consequences outside of the sims other than anger and jokes, there were no limits.

"Maybe you should try talking to them," Jackson said when she noticed he was walking alone. Wisp looked back and nodded in agreement before returning to his conversation.

"I'm learning from a distance."

"That distance could be a problem when we go on a real mission. You'll learn more talking to them directly."

"I'll pass on the criticism," he said dryly.

"Not everyone is against your ideas, Ryan. I've seen how tired you are after a session – it's the same for all of us. We all say things in the heat of the moment, it's a vent. Don't let it turn you against us."

"When did it become me against the squad?"

"We're all one squad, but you, me and Wisp are a team too. We've got your back. Besides, your plans make us look good," Jackson added with a wink.

"You've had some good ideas yourself; you just don't act on them as much."

"That's the chain of command for you."

Before he could answer, the group reached the mess hall. Ryan stopped at the door, deciding whether to slip away or stay. He wasn't hungry, and the food they received was meant to sustain them for a certain amount of time, taking into account their schedules and exertion. Eating early would disrupt that.

The food didn't appeal, either. It contained all the nutrients and vitamins needed but it was no replacement for a bloody steak, a greasy burger, fresh vegetables or the countless other things Ryan was craving. It didn't matter that everything he ate was artificial. Nothing was grown or slaughtered anymore – taste, texture, shape, colour; it was all created. An illusion. No one cared.

Despite that, he wolfed down the beige, bland food every meal like he would his favourite dishes.

He wasn't going to do that now.

He squeezed Jackson's shoulder and turned from the door. He could feel her disappointed gaze as he left to navigate the corridors. While they were still confusing, it was becoming easier to find his way between the main areas he frequented: the fitness facility, his quarters, the mess hall, the sim room, Flare Squadron's hall and his favourite observation deck.

It didn't stop him from being turned around at an intersection every so often and relying on OSD's nav interface to find his way. No one he passed said anything despite it proving he was a rook.

The observation room was empty, the silence welcoming. It wasn't often Ryan found people in here and no one he encountered stayed as long as him. Sometimes he was called away, but it was rare training exercises were unscheduled.

It was easy to lose track of time watching the stars. When the door slid open with a whisper there was no reason to look and see who had joined him. No one came here to interrupt him.

"What is it about this room that keeps bringing you back?" Matthews asked. The voice startled him; he hadn't expected the general.

"The view doesn't get old."

"The stars or Earth?"

"Both. Every time the planet comes into view, it reminds me what I'm doing here. Why we're all working so hard."

"I thought it was the challenge driving you forward."

"Sure, there's that. And it's important." Ryan paused, searching for the words. "But it's not the only reason I have to be here. The Globe is huge and there's a lot I haven't seen. Up here, it looks smaller. I feel like my actions can make a difference to something that size, even just a little. I want to protect it so I can see it in the future. I want to protect the people I care about. Then I can belong somewhere."

"It's good to have a reason like that," Matthews agreed, taking a seat behind him. "It's important to understand, though, that everyone has different reasons and motives. Sometimes it's protecting people, a place or an ideal, but others use revenge. The anger fuels them, drives them forward."

"I don't have that desire."

"Some of your squadmates do. It might help you understand them better to know their motivations."

"I'm a racer. I work better alone."

"But now you're a pilot working in a squad. A flight. You need to adapt to this just like they do to you. If you really want to belong here, with them, you need to accept this. It isn't a one-way street."

Silence descended again as Ryan thought over the words. Matthews let them sink in.

"Who complained this time?" Ryan asked after the minutes had dragged.

"Shrewd," Matthews allowed, "but wrong. No complaints other than the ones you know of and expect. I've been following the progress of all squads since the start, and I keep a close eye on the rooks to make sure they're progressing well and adapting to the new dynamic."

"So...I'm not?"

"I didn't say that. Your abilities aren't in question. Your attitude is."

"I get the job done."

"That's not enough. This isn't a race. You sacrifice your squad without a second thought. You need to think ahead and plan for what will happen should your ideas fail. You might need their support later."

"You brought me here to come up with solutions other pilots couldn't."

"You need to learn moderation. There are times when your ideas are just what we need but others call for tried-and-tested measures. That's a leader's decision. They know when to listen and when to act. Captain Ryder is still finding her feet in this role and you need to help her."

"And how am I supposed to do that?" Ryan asked, turning to look the general in the eye.

"Support her decisions but challenge them when you feel strongly. She has to make the call, but with all cards on the table the chances of making the right, or best, choice improve. We only learn from experience."

"Which is what I'm doing with the sims. They're the perfect place to experiment and try new ideas."

"And they're also good for training rooks on what they need to know: piloting skills, technical controls, team formations and more. You're here to learn as much as you're here to inspire," Matthews said, standing and walking to the door. "Don't run before you can walk, Fall."

Ryan turned back to the stars, where Earth was just edging into view. Talks with Matthews always left him with a lot to process. It made him miss Miss Kinni.

"One last thing," Matthews said. "Using sims is a great way to reduce the danger for mech pilots but it's more likely to make you do things you otherwise wouldn't. They're a tool and might not always be available. Visualise yourself in the real thing, with you and your squad in real danger. You might be less inclined to take so many risks."

CHAPTER NINETEEN

AFTER NUMEROUS SIM SESSIONS, Captain Ryder sprung a surprise on them by changing the schedule. Ryan and Jackson were confident piloting the mechs in space although surface combat manoeuvres sometimes proved tricky. They hadn't spent any time learning about the other ships used by the Mech Force and that was about to change.

"Listen up," Ryder commed, her voice as steely as ever. "It's time to add training for shuttles and fighters. All pilots have to be able to fly these ships, it's procedure. Flight leaders will lead shuttle training, but you'll be assigned a mentor to teach you to pilot one of our Vanga-class fighters. Then it's missions – anything from dogfights to races."

"The top pilot gets a prize," the lieutenant added gruffly.

"Oh! What kind of prize?" Ricochet asked. She was easy to distract.

"Win and find out," Ryder said. "While I won't be able to monitor you all in real time, I'll review the records later. Don't slack off."

Ryan powered down his sim and clambered out. By the time his feet hit the deck, Wisp was already there. Jackson joined a few seconds later. The rest of the squad were filing

out of the room and they followed. A few metres down
the corridor was another room full of simulators, but
much larger and with a lot more pods than their room.

Other squads were using some of the sims and the
agents nodded to each other in passing but the pilots
kept to themselves. The captain picked a row of sims
and the twelve pilots climbed in.

Ryan took the seat in the middle of the pod. A holographic screen and console materialised in front of him
but before he could do anything, a scenario was chosen.
The simulator transformed around him to resemble the
cockpit of a single-pilot shuttle. The viewports, consoles and controls burst into existence from light and
solidified. A message on the screen informed him the
simulator was calibrated and ready to use.

It was a stark difference from the mech simulators,
which were obviously designed for a single purpose.

He spent the next hour following Wisp's instructions,
going through the pre-flight checklist in a painstakingly
slow process. There was less to do compared to a mech
but that didn't stop him making a mistake, lighting the
sim red for a few seconds and setting off wailing sirens.
Everything went dark as the shuttle exploded.

Wisp's chuckle told him all he needed to know. They
started again.

Flying the shuttle proved much easier. It was slow
and sluggish compared to a bike – even to a mech –
and they spent some time in obstacle courses to learn
the new dimensions. Using a console for all controls
slowed him down; he couldn't be as intuitive with it as
everything had precise settings and calculations.

"Come on, land the shuttle already," a voice he didn't
recognise said over the comm.

That piled on the pressure as he lined up the landing. Ryan tried to push it from his mind as he reached the zone, spun around and descended slowly. "Man, if this were a battle, you'd be smoke right now," the voice said. Ryan cut power to the thrusters too soon and the shuttle dropped the last few metres to the ground. Not a perfect landing but it didn't result in an explosion. As he started the post-flight checks, the sim went dark and a face appeared to his right, with an infectious grin from ear to ear.

"My name's Ash," he said, "from Blink Squadron. I'll be training you to fly one of our new Vanga fighters."

"Why is it called the Vanga? It's not a name that fills me with fear."

"They're faster and lighter than the Valkyrie and Vulture classes, which is true of the bird."

The pre-flight was similar to the shuttle and Ryan didn't blow himself up, but leaving the hangar was trickier. Pedals at his feet controlled each engine and there was a single joystick for both hands, but one hand – or both – would also be needed for the switches and consoles.

"Don't worry, leaving the hangar is tricky for everyone," Ash said. "Getting the hang of those pedals takes a while. You won't be flying in a straight line for a while."

"You fill me with confidence, Ash."

"Just wait until we can kick it. That's where the fun begins."

The fighters were much faster and more manoeuvrable than shuttles and mechs, but they didn't feel like a match for the bikes he raced. Their size and shape were different and it was hard to remember what space he needed in each situation for each ship. The fact that the ship's wings could spin added another factor. The mechs were simpler.

Out in open space, Ryan found he enjoyed flying. Most of his experience with the mechs didn't help but whether through racing or natural talent, he was good at it. It was a different feeling to racing, without elements like wind or rain, but every time he increased speed, the forces brought a new kind of thrill.

"Nice little wing spin," Ash approved as Ryan blasted another target. "You're going faster than I said."

"This speed is unreal."

"I see." His mentor laughed. "You're just like me. That rush from the acceleration is insane. You want to try something cool?"

"Definitely."

"Transfer power from the weapons to the engines and then kick it as hard as you can."

It took Ryan a few moments to transfer the power as he explored the consoles. Before activating the thrusters, he took a breath and pushed back into the chair to brace himself.

Pushing hard on both pedals, he noticed the stars streak as the sim caught up to the sudden acceleration. Even bracing himself didn't help as he felt like the chair was going to absorb him and only a slight shuddering showed the speed was unsustainable for long.

When the safety protocols activated and the ship slowed, Ryan found himself out of breath and unable to pry his hands from the control stick. He expected laughter from Ash, but none came.

"That. Was. Awesome," Ryan breathed when he found the words.

"Now you know why I'm a pilot." Ash nodded, his face returning on the right.

"I didn't ask."

"But you wanted to." That was true. After that rush, Ash told him to return to the hangar and land, which proved harder than with the shuttle and ended with another explosion. "Don't worry," Ash wheezed. "Everyone crashes the first time, although not quite so spectacularly. We're done for the day, but I'll be here next time to help you stop that."

"Any way we can go faster?"

"Maybe. If you do well, I'll show you a few more tricks. Later!"

When Ryan and the others emerged from the sims, Ryder was speaking to another captain. The man was tall with an easy smile, glancing in their direction regularly. It took a minute, but he got what he wanted, judging by the grin covering his face when he left. Ryder looked furious.

"We've been challenged," she grunted, "by Shadow Squadron."

That drew a gasp and some whispers. Ryan didn't know much about the squad other than they were tipped for the frontlines. Most were experienced and Enforcer-trained pilots, with one or two highly skilled civilians. The rumours told of their high sim scores and active recon missions. Most pilots he spoke to, while happy in their own squadron, would happily transfer to Shadow.

"You didn't accept?" Toomes asked, and for the first time, Ryder shot her second in command a famous icy glare.

"I did. Report to our room in one hour. I'll brief you then. Dismissed."

The hour flew. As the seconds ticked, Ryan's nerves grew but he couldn't explain why. He believed in his abilities, and those of his flight and squad, but this would be the first time they were tested by an unknown force.

He couldn't focus on much of the briefing beyond the basics; a squad-versus-squad simulation with the last mech standing taking glory for their team. It sounded simple enough and they didn't have time to devise a full strategy. A reactive response was their best bet. A glance at Jackson showed she'd figured it out too – seconds before Ryder said so.

With the briefing over, all twelve climbed into their pods and went through their power-up procedures. The sims synced and their battlefield was revealed – a ruined town with a barren wasteland beyond. It was how he imagined the Scars would look.

A blue clock appeared with a two-minute countdown. That was all the time they had to get ready. Shadow Squadron had the same amount of time.

"Four flight formation," Ryder said over the squad channel. "Flights One and Two in front, Flight Three behind. Flight Four will provide long-range support. We'll take position in the ruins until they show themselves. Keep comm chatter down."

Ryan and Jackson followed Wisp to a ruined building due south of their starting point and took positions on the third floor. Wisp kneeled behind a broken wall while Ryan and Jackson stood to either side of their flight leader, with the building's sides offering shelter.

Ahead of them, Bishop, Teach and Oaf spread themselves along the street of the deserted town, looking behind and to the sides to spot a surprise attack. The first two flights were waiting for a head-on attack. No one spoke and Ryan didn't want to break the silence, so he sent a text message to his flight: *Even waiting for an ambush can still result in an ambush. If they find one of us, they get us all.*

Agreed was Jackson's response.

Orders are orders, from Wisp.

To keep himself occupied, he used his rifle's targeting scope to scout the ruins. The dull grey rubble would make it harder to spot a metal mech, but he tried, looking for movement or bright eyes.

It took a few minutes, but Shadow Squad revealed themselves before they could be discovered. A barrage of laser fire rained down on them, with the first two flights taking the brunt of the damage. Their heavier armour helped them weather the storm and they returned fire, blindly at first, until they were able to pinpoint the locations. These were shared with the rest of the squad and Ryan, Jackson and Wisp opened fire.

The frontline mechs had all taken damage – every single shot had hit their target, which was remarkable. Ryan's thoughts were disturbed by an explosion. He scanned the sensor and noticed a green dot had vanished. Oaf.

Teach wouldn't like that, but already she and Bishop were repositioning. More mechs were firing on them now and it wasn't long before Ricochet's mech was also up in flames.

"Focus fire on one target," Bishop said, surprisingly calm. "We need to overwhelm their armour."

"Then pick one and call it," Ryan yelled. "Keeping track of them is getting difficult."

A red target appeared on his display and he wasted no time in opening fire. The debris got in the way, providing much better cover than expected. It was useless trying to fire at that mech and he switched to another, sharing it with the squad as a secondary target.

It worked for a few seconds as the ten mechs focused fire on either target, but they weren't as accurate as Shadow, nor causing enough damage.

Ryan was trying to find another option but the incoming barrage proved they were being approached in a wide arc and the Shadow mechs could target most of them with ease. Their positions meant they had no way of helping each other and could be picked off.

The reactive approach wasn't working. A third Flare mech exploded; another from the frontline. Ryan didn't check to see which flight it had come from or who they had lost. He tapped the console furiously with his left hand, absently firing with the right despite the recoil. When he finished coming up with his plan, he sent it to the others. It only took a couple of seconds for Ryder to reject it and another mech was lost. They were now eight strong facing twelve. There wasn't much time left.

He armed missiles and set them all to launch together. He identified two targets and focused each side's armament on one each.

Ryan fired his thrusters and launched into the air. When he reached the right elevation, his projectiles launched. They streaked to the two targets and detonated together, creating two huge balls of fire. They burned like twin suns from an old sci-fi vid, flames licking the air. It didn't last long before the spheres started to shrink.

Once the flames subsided, there was nothing but twisted metal. Each missile had struck a specific area. It was enough to destroy the enemy mechs completely.

Launching alone made him a target and before he could move, the remaining ten mechs focused their fire on him. His mech was completely destroyed. The pod lit with red but the alarm didn't last long before it ended.

That left Ryan to watch the rest of the engagement. Ten Shadow Squadron mechs versus seven, then six, Flare mechs. The rest dropped quickly. They tried to regroup into a new formation, but it was too late. It didn't take long for the whole sim to end. A ruthless display of skill from their opponents.

It wasn't going to be a fun debrief. When the result displayed and the scene faded, Ryan powered down the sim and disconnected from the controls. He composed himself. He was sweating after the battle – it was the most real experience yet.

"That was embarrassing," Ricochet was saying as Ryan left his pod. "We didn't stand a chance out there."

"It does seem like they had every avenue covered," Bishop agreed, opening his mouth to say more but deciding against it.

"They were so disciplined and precise. I didn't spot a single mistake in their formation or any wasted shots," Teach added. She was holding a PCT and staring intently at whatever it showed.

"They missed a couple at the end," Ryan said casually. He knew what was coming. The captain was standing at the back of the group, watching quietly.

"Oh, really? I didn't notice, since the cover fire you were supposed to provide never materialised!"

"It was there at the start."

"And then? You just decided to stop? We had a strategy."

"That wasn't working. It would only have ended with us losing."

"In case you didn't notice, Rook, we lost!" Teach yelled, her shoulders shaking with rage. The rest held their tongues, but avoided looking at him – except Toomes, who stood with his arms folded and with a grim expression. Wisp and Jackson kept a neutral expression. Surprisingly, Captain Ryder didn't look angry or upset.

"Following a losing strategy doesn't make sense," Ryan said. "It was last mech standing. We weren't buying time and we weren't holding a position. It was destroy or be destroyed. We were instantly on the defensive and lost two mechs in thirty seconds. When it became clear our strategy wouldn't work, I came up with an alternative. I sent it and you all ignored it."

"But you—"

"I took out two mechs. If every flight followed my plan, it could have been eight. At worst, it would have left us on equal footing and in a better position to win."

"That's beside the point," Teach argued back. "It wasn't the plan. You cost us mechs by not following the plan, don't you see? You're a coo!"

"Enough," Ryder cut in. "You're both right. The strategy was flawed from the beginning and it wasn't going to work, not against Shadow. The alternative was risky, but Fall was the only one to score a kill – two, in fact – which means it has to be given merit. We were too slow to react. We'll work on that from tomorrow. Under the circumstances, you did well. We'll call it a day and pick up at the usual time tomorrow."

Ryan left the room straight away, before even Ryder had a chance to leave. He wanted to be alone. It made no sense that Teach would fight so hard to defend a losing strategy. His plan provided a result.

He wanted a rematch.

Matthews strode into the hangar with such purpose no one dared get in his way, even before they realised who he was. The whispers that followed were silenced by senior agents and they continued their work, perhaps with more care than before.

He marched to the left wall, where six Flare Squadron mechs stood in a line, surrounded by technicians and mechanics making changes based on recent training sessions, pilot feedback and system enhancements. There weren't many pilots present but the ones nearby did offer a quick salute before returning to their duties.

The pilot he wanted was on the metal walkway above. It had been a while since his last visit up there – not since the mechs first arrived and he was given a tour of their systems.

Not that there was time for luxuries like that anymore.

Gloves stopped the cold metal from biting his skin as he climbed the rungs. Either the walkway was higher than he remembered or he was out of shape from sitting behind a desk all day. The general couldn't hide his heavy breathing when he finally reached the top but everyone pretended not to notice.

Wisp was inside his mech with a tech. After waiting a minute for them to finish, Matthews grabbed a passer-by and whispered in his ear. The young man looked terrified as he jumped into the unit. Seconds later, the three of them were on the walkway in front of him. They stood at attention, saluting in sync. Once he returned the salute, the two agents departed, leaving him alone with Wisp.

"Burning the midnight oil?" Matthews asked, adding, "At ease."

"Thank you, sir. Just a few details. I don't like to leave things when they can be done now."

"Good attitude. With an ethic like that, it makes me wonder why you've turned down every promotion offered. You could be a lieutenant by now, possibly a captain. Why?"

"Following orders is simple. Even if I have objections, they're recorded. I take my share of the blame for anything that goes south but, ultimately, it's the captain's call. I'm a better mentor than a leader."

Matthews walked along the walkway and Wisp followed a step behind. "That's true, but you'll never reach your full potential without pushing yourself."

"I challenge myself in other ways. Who would have thought someone as quiet as me would enjoy supervising rooks, making sure they settle in okay? Not everyone follows the same path."

"So, you don't want to be a pilot forever?"

"Did you, sir?"

"No, I suppose not." Matthews laughed, stroking his beard. "But I can imagine the rooks assigned to you probably do."

"They have a unique take on life. If they're not talking about racing, it's the mechs. They're so...focused."

"That troubles you?"

"It did at first. I worried they'd shut out everything else, but their perception is astounding. They absorb everything and store it until needed. They're probably more aware than most others and have learned to focus on the task at hand. Maybe we should all be racers."

"Perhaps, but then we'd lack the discipline needed from Enforcers. Everything must have balance," Matthews said, stopping at the end of the walkway and grabbing a cable running down to the floor. "It's obvious the civilians have had an effect on us." He wrapped his legs around the cable and stepped away from the walkway, sliding to the floor and landing with a thud. Hiding the shock and pain took more effort than he expected but Wisp was already following him and a quick sidestep moved him out of the way.

They continued their walk through the hangar as Matthews continued, "I've been made aware you're spending a lot of time with Kendra Jackson."

"She's a member of my flight team."

"Do you spend the same amount of time with Ryan Fall?"

"Ryan prefers to be by himself."

"Judging from how often he enquires about his friend, I don't believe that to be the case."

"Is there a problem, sir?" Wisp asked after a silence. The small talk was over.

"That's what I want to establish. We've come a long way from the days of banning relationships between Enforcer agents, but this isn't a normal case. Jackson is a civilian."

"Which should remove any concerns. There aren't any barriers in rank, either, since we're both pilots."

"You're her superior; you lead the flight. That in itself is a concern. Would you value her life over another, over multiple lives? These are the questions we face. Relationships aren't banned but there are rules to be followed – for both of you."

They stopped at the hangar door. "Are you ordering me to stop this...whatever this is, sir?" Wisp said.

"No. I'm asking you to think about the situation carefully and discuss it with Jackson. Both of you should be clear on your priorities and keep our objectives in mind. What you do in your own time is of no concern to me as long as it doesn't impact your performance. However, Captain Ryder and Lieutenant Toomes will keep an eye on you both and report back to me on how this develops. This is a new situation for us, and I trust my people to do what's right, but I'll step in if I have to."

The general moved towards the door. "I'm not unreasonable, Tanner. Keep me updated yourself and I'll help you both to pursue this in the right way, if it's what you want. Believe it or not, I was young once too."

Matthews left, leaving Wisp looking lost in thought among the bustle of the hangar.

CHAPTER TWENTY

THE ATMOSPHERE IN THE squad cooled in the days following Shadow Squadron's domination. Despite Captain Ryder's involvement after the session, and her analysis the following day, which concluded Ryan's plan had the most impact, the rest of the squad still blamed him.

Losing to each other was one thing but losing to another squad – who made it public knowledge straight away – was something else. Ryan had learned Shadow hadn't lost a single battle in any of the squad-versus-squad simulations they'd fought.

That didn't matter to his comrades.

Jackson and Wisp stood by him, sometimes in silence, against the comments and remarks. Ryan suspected they agreed with the rest of the squad but they supported him in public, which made it easier. He had noticed them getting closer although they were careful to keep it professional with others around. Sometimes too professional.

After the third day, the three of them were back to normal. It was water under the bridge according to Wisp and the situation had an effect on their sim sessions – everyone was working together better and there was a new level of determination and enthusiasm to all exercises.

Surprisingly, one of Ryan's plans was approved during an exercise, and their team emerged victorious. That brought one half of the squad closer but the other side was still unhappy.

Even in their squad hall, he took to sitting in his flight or being alone most of the time. He'd acquired a taste for Ambrosii and found Wisp's stash – not that his friend realised. When alone, he'd decline offers to join others and focus on the PCT in front of him, which had enough data to occupy him for a month without distraction.

On the fifth day, when someone took a seat opposite him, Ryan assumed it was Jackson. Wisp would usually sit to the side. The newcomer said nothing. Ryan looked up and couldn't hide his surprise to see Bishop staring at him over interlocked fingers.

Ryan tried not to be distracted by his gleaming head. He had a light layer of white stubble and orange eyes – ocular implants. Anyone with those implants had to choose either orange or purple to make it clear what they were, even though not all implants altered vision. They connected to a MOB-I, offered sensors and filters, and had many other uses.

They hadn't spent much time together. Ryan's plans were wilder than Bishop's and Ryder valued the older man's ideas more. They exchanged words sometimes but the officer never seemed flustered. If anything, Ryan amused him more often than not.

"How are you, Ryan?" Bishop asked.

"Fine. You?"

"Very well, thank you. I've noticed you're keeping to yourself a lot. Is that due to last week's match?"

"I'm not the most popular person right now."

"Do you know why?"

"I don't really care. I'm here to do a job, and it doesn't include a lecture from you."

"Oh, this isn't a lecture. I knew from day one those wouldn't work on you. The other rook...possibly, given the right circumstances. You, however, you need something else."

"And what's that?"

"An intervention." Bishop held a hand up to stop his protest before it began. "An intervention in the form of a challenge."

"A challenge?"

"That's right. You still have no idea why everyone is against you right now. I could explain, but..."

"What kind of challenge do you have in mind?"

"One suited to both of us – a one-on-one battle."

"You can't be serious," Ryan cried out, standing so suddenly his chair toppled over, drawing stares from everyone in the hall. "There's no way you could beat me!"

"Then accept. What do you have to lose?"

"Why are you doing this, Bishop?" Ryan asked, his eyes narrow. "What's the real reason?"

"Perhaps I just want a friendly match to test my skills?" Bishop mused, a small smile behind his fingers. "Or maybe I'm trying to do you a favour. Does it matter?"

It didn't. He could have refused if he'd managed to stay quiet but now that everyone knew something was going on there was only one decision. Ryan picked his chair up and sat down. "Fine. When?"

"I've cleared it with the captain. When our first session starts, you'll sync with me directly. Better get ready."

Bishop stood and walked away. There were puzzled looks around the room, but the captain arrived for their morning briefing and they marched to the sim room in silence. Ryan wondered if Ryder enjoyed the silence; it seemed more disciplined.

His nerves grew as he climbed into his sim. The power-up procedure was interrupted by his numb hands but he couldn't explain why. When the screen flickered to life, he saw the option to link with Bishop.

Once he'd accepted, Ryan took in the battlefield. An ocean of stars surrounded him but there was no sign of his opponent. An asteroid field materialised ahead and his sensor sphere registered Bishop on the far side.

"Asteroids? That's a new one," Ryan remarked over a comm channel directed at his opponent.

"You never know what might happen in space," Bishop replied, straight to the point. "Are you ready?"

"Yeah. Let's go."

It was an anti-climactic start, something a race organiser would be fired for. Ryan kicked his thrusters to life and started to fly above the asteroid field but Bishop responded by moving underneath him, keeping the floating rocks between them. When Ryan tried going to the left, Bishop moved right. He wanted to fight amongst the floating rubble.

There was one other option Ryan considered: the rail gun. It was the only weapon that would cut through the asteroids, but a sustained burst could only last for seven seconds and the distance was too great. If he fired now, Bishop would be able to evade it easily and he wouldn't be able to fire again until it recharged.

With a sigh, Ryan flew into the asteroid field.

Bishop followed suit and both flew towards each other in the most erratic of lines, making full use of their thrusters to pull sharp turns and flips to avoid the drifting rock. His sensors wailed constantly with a new impending collision every other second.

That was probably what Bishop was hoping for. Ryan aimed his rifle and let loose a barrage of needles. Most of them hit passing rock or streaked off into the darkness. Bishop didn't take any notice.

An asteroid cut across Ryan. When it passed, Bishop was gone. The sensor sphere was no help with all the dots moving around. He could be anywhere.

His damage alarm told him he was too slow. Bishop struck with his beam blade, cutting into the rear armour. By the time Ryan spun, his opponent had vanished again. He flew deeper into the maze of rock but it took only a few seconds for Bishop to strike again, and in the same place.

Bishop was winning and Ryan panicked. He took a breath and armed missiles for continuous launch. Squeezing both trigger fingers, he turned slowly, creating a space clear of large rocks. His sensors showed Bishop approaching and he had just enough time to activate his own beam blade for an awkward parry.

The attack didn't end there. Bishop kicked him, using joint thrusters to add more power. It sent Ryan spinning, bouncing off rock and away from his safe zone.

Bishop kept coming and it was all Ryan could do to defend. He had no missiles left so when his opponent drew close to attack again, he powered his engines and drove straight into the other mech. It bought him a second, which he used to draw his scatter gun and fire three quick shots. Some of the smaller projectiles made contact but asteroids kept getting in the way.

A missile hit him and he lost track of his position again. A quick glance at the sphere to his right showed his armour weakening. A few more hits and Bishop would win.

Ryan armed the rail gun and steadied himself just in time for another attack. Instead of parrying, he grabbed the other mech and waited for the weapon to lock on.

Bishop was a step ahead and fired his own rail gun. Ryan's screen went white, then black.

It was over.

"Damn..." he whispered, leaning back against the support.

"Indeed," Bishop answered, his breathing slightly ragged. The comm channel was still open. "That took longer than I thought. You're a great pilot. Quite unconventional. That does make you predictable at times – only because I've faced off against people like you before. I knew you'd resort to the rail gun."

"What's your point?"

"Sometimes the obvious plan is the best one. Trying to be different all the time will let you down. We've all learned that – you should too."

Bishop closed the channel and left the link, leaving Ryan alone to calm down and sync with the rest of the squad. Bishop was there already, and no one asked about his delay in joining.

Captain Ryder reorganised the squad and they continued with their session, but Ryan couldn't settle. When he re-joined the squad, he was jumpy and eager. That brought more mistakes, which frustrated him even more. He tried everything to focus and get back to his usual form, to prove his defeat against Bishop wasn't an indication of a bigger problem.

He failed.

Any hopes no one was watching or hadn't found out about his battle were dashed upon leaving the sim. Bishop was in the middle of a huddle, not looking too comfortable, and the glances sent his way proved this was a squad-wide intervention.

Wisp and Jackson didn't join in, although he could tell they knew about the plan. Whether they agreed with it was another question.

Before anyone could speak to him, Ryan left the sim room and made for his viewport. He couldn't even relax there and ended up pacing his room. He wanted to talk to someone. Zack was his first choice but there was no news on him. Ryder had been trying to keep him busy enough to distract him from asking and when he did, she told him nothing.

Wisp and Jackson would listen, and the latter would probably understand more because of their shared background, but they were a flight. Ryan didn't want to create any friction with them or his performances would get worse.

Sketcher, Oaf, even Bishop – they would listen, too. He was getting closer to the squad but it was clear they were on the other side of the fence this time.

Suddenly, it dawned on him.

At his desk, he opened a comm channel to the surface. It took a few minutes before a familiar face appeared on the screen. She looked pale, tired.

"What the hell are you doing, calling at this hour?" Sara grunted.

"Is it that late? It's only just gone seven!"

"Time zones, Ryan. It's four thirty in the morning here."

"Oh." It hadn't even occurred to him that the time difference would be so large, although it did make sense. "Sorry, do you want to go back to bed?"

"Yes," Sara said with a sigh. "But seeing how I'm awake, what's up?" Now he had someone to talk to, Ryan didn't know what to say, where to start. "If you just want to look at my face, I'll send a holo."

"I'm just having a rough day. Thought a familiar face would help."

"It must be serious if you called me. Where am I on the list, just above your parents?"

"Around there, yeah." Ryan laughed. "Maybe a bit higher."

"I'm honoured. So, what's ripping you?"

"I just got schooled by an old guy. He's good, a brilliant strategist, but I know I'm better. I can't figure out how I lost."

"At what?"

"Can't say."

"What? Never mind, it's too early." Sara rubbed her eyes. "Do you go around picking fights with old men often?"

"Actually, he picked one with me." Ryan got up and resumed his pacing. Sara's image moved to the wall and she watched him walk back and forth. "My... colleagues...and I have been butting heads recently. It feels like I'm totally isolated from them sometimes, yet we're supposed to work together. It's why I was brought here – I can't tell you where I am, don't ask – but they don't seem very accepting of it."

"Why should they be?"

"What?"

"You're the new guy, right? Why should they just accept your way of doing things if you won't do the same? Teamwork is all about compromise, and as the newbie, you've got to make the first move."

"That makes no…" Ryan's words faded as he pieced it together. "I'm causing the problem."

"You've been causing me problems for years, coo. At least you're smart enough to realise it. Eventually."

"Cha."

"You're used to doing things your own way after years of refusing help. Even with Zack, he adapts to you more than the other way around. Why do you think that is?"

"I don't want to feel like I'm useless, or that I'll be replaced," Ryan said, staring at the floor.

"Exactly. Deep down, you want the bonds that come with a team but you're afraid of opening up and getting hurt. That's not something you can avoid forever," Sara continued, struggling to keep her eyes open. "Look, I'm happy to go twelve rounds over this and knock it into that thick skull of yours, but at a more reasonable time. The bottom line is this: make the effort with them and they'll make the effort with you. You're going to have to do more than usual if you've already pushed yourself away. You're good at digging holes but even better at getting out of them."

"That sounded like a compliment."

"Don't let it go to your head – probably just the lack of sleep."

"Even so, cha."

"Don't mention it. Now, where's Zack?"

"I don't know. I haven't heard from him in months. No one is telling me anything."

"So? Go and find out. That's what you'd do any other time. Why would this be different?" Sara yawned. "Oh, and next time, check the time difference before calling."

"Sure, or just get those implants that stop you sleeping so much."

"Shut up. G'night."

When the transmission ended, Ryan sat at his desk and rested his head in his hands. He lasted five seconds before opening another comm line. "Mac? Meet me in the hangar in ten minutes."

"What? Why?"

"I'll explain when I see you. We've got work to do."

He closed the channel before his tech could ask any more questions and left the room. The station was manned twenty-four hours a day, so Ryan had never seen any change in the number of personnel he encountered in the corridors. He expected that would change during an operation.

By the time he reached the hangar Mac was already there, waiting by the door. The tech yawned when he got close.

"I've not slept for twenty hours," he drawled as they entered the hangar, which was as busy as ever. "This had better be good."

"If things were good, you'd be in bed. I need your help but...it's not a normal job."

"Hey hey hey," Mac said nervously. "I don't know what you're into, but I can promise you, I'm not!"

"Shut it, coo! Nothing like that."

They reached Ryan's mech and climbed the ladder to the metal walkaway around the shoulders. There were only a few people up here and they were working on their own or their pilot's mechs. When they reached the hatch, Ryan motioned for them to go inside. Mac hesitated, unsure as to what was going on, but followed.

"Right, this is creeping me out," Mac said when they were inside the control unit. "What are we doing here?"

"Something's been bothering me since I started the mech training," Ryan answered, running his hands over the pilot's chair. There was a thin layer of dust. "I can't hear anything."

"Is something wrong with the comm?"

"No, the comm's fine – how else would I speak to you?"

"Oh, yeah…"

"It's everything else," Ryan said, motioning to his surroundings. "There's nothing."

"Everything…else?"

"Sounds. Noises."

"Wouldn't they be distracting?"

"When was the last time you met a deaf person? Science has pretty much eradicated it. Sure, they adapted, but I can only imagine how hard it must have been to go from hearing nothing to everything – and it's the opposite of what I feel like in the sim."

"So, you want to hear things when you're in there? Like what?"

"When I'm racing, I can hear everything. The engines, the brakes, tyres, wind, rain, crashes – all of it. It helps me keep track. I can tell if someone's coming up behind me, or if I have to adapt to a strong gust, even in a sim. I want that same sense of sound, of place, here."

"That's crazy! Trub! Coo! There are so many things wrong with this idea…I don't know where to begin!" Mac yelled, pacing around the mech's control unit. "I mean, sure, the sound of a missile can be recorded, but a rifle blast? I don't think anyone's bothered to try, and you do know there's no sound in space, right?"

"I know."

"So, you want the impossible?" Mac threw his arms up in exasperation. "You pilots are all the same. You want everything you don't have, can't have, and don't care about what you do have. You've done fine so far so why now? Is it because you got your ass handed to you today?"

"How do you – never mind. Yeah, that was when I realised what was missing."

"Is there any way I can convince you not to make me do this?" Mac asked, and Ryan shook his head. The tech sighed, letting his own head drop. "Do you at least have an idea of where we start?"

"Sure. We take what we can from the archives. I'm even up for running some live tests if we can get authorisation. If not, there used to be a lot of vids."

"Vids. You want to rip sound files from vids."

"They might not be realistic but…"

"I'm going to have to get those files, build a programme to adjust for distance and source and try to make sure it doesn't overwhelm you all at once."

"And block it from the comm system – I don't want anyone else to hear it."

"Coo. You know what? I wish you were into some other stuff. That would have been easier to deal with."

"Cha, Mac. Let's get started."

"I never agreed," the tech protested, but Ryan was already on his way out of the mech. "Damnit. Fine, but this is not a good idea!"

It became clear this wasn't going to be a quick fix. After three hours of scouring OSD's archives, they called it a night. Both agreed to keep working on it whenever they had time, although Mac needed a few nudges. Ryan was sure this would help his reaction times.

When it was finished, he would challenge Bishop again and the result would be different. That promise gave Ryan the drive to keep working.

CHAPTER TWENTY-ONE

AFTER TWO MINUTES OF pacing, Ryan stopped and faced the door to the medical centre. His arms, held rigid at his sides, felt too unnatural, so he clasped his left hand around his right wrist behind him, but that reminded him too much of General Matthews. He settled on folding his arms across his chest, his right hand resting under his open jacket.

On the other side of the door, Zack was waiting for him. It had taken days of investigating, speaking to people from different teams and departments across Orbital Station Delta. Everything had led here, and remembering all the vague answers and deflections cemented the feeling that something was wrong. None of his messages had been answered, and that wasn't like him.

Sara was right. He needed to take matters into his own hands. That's what he'd have done before joining the Enforcers and the Mech Force.

He managed just one step towards the door. Crossing the threshold would put his position in Flare Squadron at risk. Even if they were at odds, for the first time since meeting Zack and discovering Cyber Cycle, he belonged somewhere.

The moment passed and Ryan shook those thoughts

away. He wouldn't give up his best friend. Staying without Zack wasn't an option.

With a deep breath, he walked straight into the middle of the medical centre, his arms still folded. No one paid him any attention until he stopped and looked at the three doors leading out of the main room.

The one on the right led to examination cubicles, and he knew another would take him to the bigger testing equipment they used. That meant the third door would be for patients they were watching, unless he'd missed something.

"Fall?" one of the medical staff asked. "Your implant replacement isn't until tomorrow. What's wrong?"

"I'm here to see one of your patients," Ryan said, his gaze switching between the two doors. "Zack Wendall. Where is he?"

"I'm sorry, but he's in quarantine. I'd suggest speaking to Doctor Kayo for mor—"

"I'm done being passed around," Ryan cut him off. "Take me to see him. Now."

"That's not poss—"

"Now," Ryan said, dropping his arms and unclenching his fists. With his cuff unblocked, a metal cylinder slipped from his sleeve and he caught it in his right hand. In one swinging movement, he pointed it at the doctor, who took a small step back and raised his hands up.

"Where did you—"

"I'm going to ask one more time," Ryan stated, keeping his voice low even though staff were starting to look at them. "Where is Zack Wendall?"

The doctor's conflict was clear: follow orders and refuse to cooperate with the man holding a weapon or answer and go against his superior.

He couldn't show it, but Ryan sympathised with him. The Enforcex he held had a variety of uses, with stun blasts being used the most, but it could fire lethal shots, discharge electricity and extend into a staff. The doctor had no idea what setting Ryan's weapon was on, and to have an ally wield it had to call into question their state of mind.

"The door behind me," the doctor relented.

"Open it for me," Ryan ordered. He followed as the man turned and used his implant to open it.

Before anyone could react, Ryan entered the corridor and slammed the controls to close it behind him. He walked down the pristine corridor. There was no one else around, and the eerie silence engulfed him. None of the doors opened when he tried them, and, knowing he didn't have long before security arrived, he kept moving forward.

A T-junction ended the corridor, leaving him with a choice and no clue as to which way to go.

"There he is," a voice behind him called out. "You, stop!"

Ryan ran to the right. He made it two steps before the thuds echoed through the corridor as the Enforcer agents chased him. None of the doors opened as he passed and there was no indication of where the patients would be. It made him wonder if the doctor had lied to him.

Another turn took him left but there was nowhere he could hide if the doors didn't open. It wouldn't take long for them to catch up and he'd only taken the Enforcex for show – not once had Ryan considered using it.

The biggest problem lay ahead as the corridor ended. Before reaching the wall, Ryan stopped, turned and extended the Enforcex into a staff almost as long as him. Hand-to-hand combat formed just a small part of his training, but he adopted a pose with his knees bent and feet planted. They hadn't fired at him, and maybe he could use that to buy time.

Four Enforcers from OSD's security force slid to a stop, their boots screeching on the polished floor, ten feet away. All four aimed their weapons at him.

"Drop it," the lead agent ordered, her voice full of steel. Her face betrayed no emotion, but the expressions on the others ranged from shocked to bewildered. "Let's end this peacefully."

Ryan didn't answer. He studied the four opposite him and looked for another option. More footsteps approached the group. As soon as they reached the last junction, there'd be no way for him to find Zack.

The muscles in his legs tensed and he mapped out his path. If he could cross the distance to the first group quickly enough, they wouldn't have time to react.

"Don't," the woman ordered. She was watching his every move. Ryan knew then that no matter what he tried she'd be ready for it. He had no chance against a fully trained Enforcer in this situation.

"Stand down, Lieutenant," Matthews said, rounding the corner. The four agents stood to the side as the general stopped paces away from Ryan, with Kayo a few steps behind him. "Hand it over, Fall."

With a sigh, Ryan relaxed his stance and held the Enforcex out to Matthews.

He took it and dropped it into a holster at his waist. "I didn't expect this behaviour from you."

"I want to see Zack."

"You're in no position to make demands, Agent."

"We had a deal, and you're not keeping your end. Where is he?"

"He's recovering," Kayo said, taking a step forward.

"From what? Why won't anyone tell me what's going on?"

"What business is it of yours? He deserves privacy."

"Did he tell you that?" Ryan countered.

"No, but—"

"Then don't speak for him," he cut in. "He's like a brother to me, and not knowing has taken a toll. He should be helping me with the mechs but all I get is the runaround. How am I supposed to focus without knowing anything?"

"Try trusting us," Kayo said.

"What reason do I have to trust you?"

"How can we trust you after this?" Matthews gestured to the group of people gathered around. "Using an Enforcex to gain access to a restricted area, threatening an ally and ignoring orders to stop. It's not what I'd expect of any of my pilots."

"You wanted unpredictable." Ryan shrugged.

"I want creativity! A new perspective, fresh ideas – not chaos!" Matthews yelled, before closing his eyes to think. The moments dragged, but when he opened his eyes, he dismissed the security personnel before returning his attention to Ryan. "Perhaps I expected too much from you. Come, we'll visit Zack."

"General!" Kayo said, her tone showing her disapproval.

"If it puts this to rest and keeps us united, it's worth it," the general reasoned. "He's not a trained agent, and we can't expect the behaviour and discipline we're used to from them. Trust has to start somewhere. Agreed?"

Kayo offered a curt nod, and they both looked at Ryan before she said, "Agreed."

Without waiting, the doctor turned on her heel and marched back down the corridor. Matthews waited until Ryan reached him before they followed the doctor in silence.

The corridors looked identical to the rest of OSD, but there were no panels to guide people to their destinations here. That didn't stop Kayo, who led them through a series of corridors without hesitation until they arrived at an unmarked door and she waved her hand over the sensor to make it slide open.

When neither of his companions moved, Ryan walked into a dim room with another door to his right; a large window took up the remainder of the wall. On the other side was a white room with a single bed and screens on three walls, showing information about the patient.

Ryan's heart lurched up into his throat as he realised the frail body on the bed was Zack. He remembered his friend as toned and healthy, but he seemed to have shrunk, with sagging faint grey skin. Tubes from the floor and walls were inserted at various points of his body, and if it weren't for the steady but shallow rise and fall of his chest, Ryan could have sworn there was no life left in him.

"What happened to him?" Ryan choked out when the door closed behind Matthews and Kayo.

"Techs working on the mechs use more advanced implants than the MOB-I you and the other pilots have," Kayo said. "This is the DAPI, or Direct Access Point Interface. Rather than a single device in the arm or hand, multiple devices work together throughout the body, and ports on the back of the neck allow for wired connections for improved sensitivity and better control. It's an invasive process and the body takes time to recover from it, but the interfacing directly with the tech in question provides better results for the pilots."

"That's how Mac interfaced with my mech and dialled it in so quickly?"

"That's right." Matthews nodded.

"And this is a normal part of recovery? Why not just tell me this from the start?"

"No." Kayo shook her head and took a moment to pick her next words. "There were complications. At first, the DAPI performed correctly, but within a few hours his body rejected the implants. We think it's because of the MOB-I he had previously, as it wasn't a registered device, and the implantation damaged it, which had an adverse effect on his neural system. By the time we found the damage and removed the MOB-I, his body had started to shut down. We placed him in stasis while we repaired the damage and we're now stimulating the repaired areas until we're confident they'll function independently. Then we can begin waking him."

"It'll be a long road of rehabilitation but we're confident the danger has passed," Matthews added. "We didn't tell you because we didn't want to distract you from your training. I see now that was the wrong way to handle this, and I'm sorry."

"You're damn right it was wrong," Ryan snapped, his hand pressed against the glass, "but – thank you for telling me. I'm glad he's in safe hands. Will you keep me updated on his condition? I'd like to be here when he comes around."

"I can do that," Kayo said, "as long as you don't point a weapon at my staff again."

"With that out of the way," Matthews said, after Ryan nodded at the doctor, "we need to talk about the consequences of your actions. Regardless of the situation, I can't condone an untrained agent carrying a weapon and using it to gain access to restricted areas. Everyone on this station needs to be able to trust each other, and your actions have put that at risk."

"I understand."

"You'll be confined to quarters for the next three weeks whenever you're not in training. Use this time to reflect on what it means to be a part of a team, not just a squad. If this happens again, I won't hesitate to send you back to the surface. Dismissed."

"That one's going to be trouble in the future," Doctor Kayo stated once the door to her office closed behind them. Matthews didn't bother to answer, instead taking a seat at her desk, interlocking his fingers and resting his head against them. "If he can't control his impulses, he'll never make it as an agent."

"This isn't a simple case, Doctor. We're expecting him to act like an agent who's undergone three years of training in just a few months. He's come a long way – all the rooks have – but we can't forget there's a lot we've had to skip to make sure he's ready."

"You may be right, but I get the feeling he's not going to accept whatever we say no matter how much training he has."

"Is that such a bad thing?" Matthews asked, looking over his hands. "This threat has made us question and change a lot, and maybe for the better. We've grown stale as an organisation, especially over the last few decades. New thinking could be the way to revitalise us and keep us relevant in the future."

"You sound like you're questioning your decisions."

"It's no secret we don't have the numbers we used to. The public line is we don't need them, threats are decreasing, but we both know that's not true. People regularly question our relevance in a world of peace."

"They don't know what we do."

"And maybe that's the wrong approach. Take Fall; he tried to get answers through the proper systems and protocols and got nowhere, yet by taking action none of us expected, he got what he wanted."

"He could have killed someone."

"Look," Matthews said, as he pulled the Enforcex from the holster and laid it on the desk between them. "It's on stun. I don't think he ever intended to use it beyond letting people think he would. He's never been in a situation where's he had to even stun someone – yet."

"You...you admire him," Kayo gasped.

"A little." The general shrugged. "He reminds me of what it's like to be in training, pushing the limits and challenging the wrongs we see. I don't want him to lose that quality, but temper it into something better, stronger. Agents like him will change the Enforcers and perhaps do something the rest of us cannot."

"If we survive the coming storm."

"Yes. If."

CHAPTER TWENTY-TWO

"ARE YOU SURE I should be here?" Ryan asked as he sat down with Wisp and Jackson in the mess hall a few days later.

"Don't worry." Wisp shrugged. "Call it a reward for good behaviour."

"Hey," Jackson piped up with a mouthful of food. "What's my reward for good behaviour?"

"Not being confined to your room outside of training. Besides, all the officers are busy today."

"But not you?"

"I'm busy with you two," Wisp answered. "My job is to train you and keep you out of trouble. Something I'm not doing too well with one of you."

Ryan accepted the scolding without remark. Holding his tongue wasn't easy but it was something he had been working on since his punishment started, as he practised a new level of discipline. He wanted to be a better pilot and teammate, and that meant knowing when to act and when to hold back.

"Does this taste a bit...strange to you?" Jackson asked, breaking the silence and staring at her tray.

"No more than usual," Wisp said after another bite.

"I always think it tastes strange," Ryan said.

"Ugh. Don't tell me I'm starting to agree with you," Jackson mocked. Despite the question, she continued to eat at a hurried pace.

A vibration in Ryan's arm stopped him from taking another bite. Wisp and Jackson stopped, too, and a quick look around showed the others in the room opening their MOB-Is.

"This must be the list," Wisp muttered, activating his own implant's holographic display.

"What list?" Jackson asked. "What are these names?"

"Agents who didn't make it back from the last mission."

The boulder that landed in Ryan's stomach stole any reply, and the look on Jackson's face showed she felt the same weight.

Wisp, and other trained agents nearby, had a different look. Resignation.

"How often have you seen a list like this?" Ryan asked as he read each name. They included their rank, assignment and photo.

"More often than I'd like," Wisp said, his eyes not leaving the display over his arm.

"How can you be so calm?" Jackson asked. "This is horrible."

"These aren't the first people we've lost, and they won't be the last. All we can do is focus on the tasks at hand."

"I...I never realised you were so...so cold," Jackson struggled, shaking her head. "I've got to go."

With glazed eyes, Jackson stood to leave the room, avoiding getting too close to anyone else as she returned her tray to the dispenser. Wisp watched her go and sighed before turning back to Ryan, who stopped scrolling through the list and fixated on one name.

"What is it? Ryan?"

Wisp's words sounded hollow and distant as Ryan stood and left the mess hall. The maze of pristine corridors absorbed him as he walked, without a guide, back to his quarters. He swiped the list from his implant's display to the terminal at his desk and stared. The weight in his stomach plummeted into a hole that grew larger every second. He didn't know how much time he lost.

"So, that's it," Wisp stated from the doorway. Ryan hadn't realised his flight leader had followed him. "You know someone on the list."

Ryan didn't answer or take his gaze away from the image of his Vanga fighter trainer. The smile on Ash's face looked like the one he had flashed the first time they met, when they bonded over the thrill of hitting those top speeds. That they would never talk about that feeling again hit him like a gut punch.

"You've never lost anyone before, have you?" Wisp asked in a soft voice, not moving from the door. "That feeling you have, the emptiness, is natural. It's proof you're connected to someone, and in an organisation like this, that's important."

"Who'd ever want to feel like this?"

"No one does, but it shows we're a part of something. That we belong here. We— hold on." Wisp crossed the hall and summoned Jackson from her quarters, ushering her inside Ryan's. He took position between Ryan and the hologram. "Sit. Both of you."

A dejected Jackson picked the closest chair and dropped onto it, her vacant expression from the mess hall still on her face. It took Ryan a while to get his legs to move and take the seat next to her. Wisp studied them both carefully before speaking.

"Listen to me. You've been lulled into a lie that death is rare. Old age is the most common cause of death across the Globe, but for an Enforcer, death is part of our lives. Every mission we go on has a level of risk, but this is relative to our skills and experience.

"It's different in the Mech Force. We're in unchartered territory here, and every mission we go on results in death for some of us. I've lost more friends since coming to OSD than I could have imagined. It's not being cold to prepare. If we let this take over, we'll hesitate in the field and that's going to get us killed. Worse, it will get others killed. We have to be strong."

"We're not machines," Jackson whispered. "We don't know how to deal with this."

"There's training for this you haven't had, and that's because the mechs are operated through sims. You won't be on the frontline, but others will. The fighter pilots and ship crews don't have that safety net, and you'll be on one of those ships when we're deployed. Protect them and they'll protect you, but know that you – or someone you know – might not make it back."

"So, what do we do?" Ryan asked.

"Confront the fact that no one's infallible," Wisp said. "No one's immortal. There are consequences to everything, and some of those are our own mortality. It won't make it hurt less when someone is lost, but it won't cripple you. If you need to talk, I'm here – and so is the squad. There are doctors you can speak to, too."

"And what about out there?" Jackson asked, refusing to make eye contact with either of them.

"I can't tell you what the best solution is, but if I don't have time to talk or vent in a healthy way, I put those feelings in a box until I can. Keep my focus and stay alive until the chance arrives. That's all any of us can do out there."

No one spoke for a minute. Ryan took another look at Ash's face and used his MOB-I to close the list before nodding. Jackson took longer, and her nod was slower, but Wisp seemed satisfied with it.

"This isn't a game, and I think you both understand that now. If you want to take some time to process tonight, I'll understand, but if you'd like to do something, meet me in the sim room in an hour. We'll do some training and let you channel those emotions into something. Your call."

When neither replied, he left. Jackson took a few seconds to compose herself before standing and giving Ryan a small nod. The vacant look had gone, replaced by something harder and more determined. He hadn't seen that look before. She closed the door after her, leaving him alone until he reached the sim room an hour later. Jackson had already arrived. Wisp nodded and the three climbed into their sims to work through the whirlwind of feelings each faced.

In a dim observation room, General Matthews waited with crossed arms. A holographic display filled the wall in front of him with a map of OSD. A cluster of blue dots surrounded a single red one, moving through empty corridors towards the adjoining room.

More than one hundred agents being coordinated from the Command Centre ensured this group could move through the station without being seen. It would raise suspicions among some, but the risk was worth it.

Something good had to come from this.

The dots moved slower than he'd have liked, but this wasn't a journey that could be rushed. It was a miracle they had something to analyse at all.

Every mission saw his forcers perform better but they still lost, and the lives lost added to the burden the general carried. At least this time, some of their pilots survived – and they hadn't returned empty-handed.

The map disappeared as the group reached the door and light flooded the room on the other side of the screen.

Through the comm, Matthews heard the door slide open and footsteps, in unison, marched through the door. Six agents escorted three medical staff inside, followed immediately by a hoverpod they guided to the table in the middle of the room.

Without a word, the six escorts left, while the doctors readied their equipment. At least two would remain outside but as they didn't know what was inside the pod, and to minimise the risk of rumours spreading through the station, only a few people were privy to the true purpose of the operation.

"Have they started?" Doctor Kayo asked, stepping inside the observation booth.

"They're just about to."

"I hope this is worth it."

"Between this and the salvage in the hangar, we have a chance to learn more about the invaders in a single day than we have since they first appeared. It's worth the risk."

"We're ready," one of the doctors said. All three were around the pod and facing the observation room.

"Proceed, Doctor." Matthews nodded.

The woman turned back to the pod, shared a look with her companions and tapped a code into the side. There was a hiss as the air was released and the top of the pod popped up, letting the trio gingerly lift it up and stack it against a wall. It left the base of the pod on the table, giving the doctors full access to the alien body.

Kayo gasped, her fists clenched inside her white coat, while Matthews felt the hair across his body stand on end.

"We have a humanoid figure," Doctor Himmes said to the room, walking around the table slowly with a handheld scanner. "Armour covers the entire body, and there are...green markings across the chest plate. There is no order or repetition I can see. They are stacked on top of each other, maybe due to a lack of space. The symbols are sharp, angular and jagged. I can't see any circular lines—"

"The armour is blocking our scans," the lead doctor said, talking over her companion. "Whatever this material is, we can't identify it, nor can we see what's underneath."

"There are no arms, but four tentacles from the shoulder area," Himmes continued as he kept walking around the alien. "The skin looks to be folded over, creating rings every few millimetres. That could indicate an ability to extend. Further scans should reveal more about the internal structure of these appendages..."

"The armour is attached seamlessly to a mask. This could be breathing apparatus. Analysing it should reveal what they need to survive, and that might give us an idea of what they're doing here," the lead doctor said. The implants of both doctors would record their notes clearly, but for the general listening, it was getting confusing. He didn't know which one to focus on.

"Three eyes; one in the centre and one on each side. They're large, black and without eyelids, but there is a glass-like screen protecting them. I can't see any pupils. The skin is a dark red, but it's unknown if this is normal colouration. There's no hair of any kind. Skin feels rubbery to touch…" Himmes continued his monologue.

"The armour is like a bodysuit; there are no joints or connections I can find," the third doctor said, grabbing a small cylinder and activating it to reveal a laser blade in the shape of a scalpel. She turned back to the body and leaned closer as she continued, "I'm going to try and separate the mask."

While the other two kept making observations, Matthews focused on the woman as she moved the scalpel closer. Sparks flew, accompanied by a sizzling noise, as the laser struggled to pierce the armour. The general held his breath until the knife moved along the edge of the mask.

The words of the other doctors faded away as Matthews and Kayo watched the laser scalpel work. Every second dragged slower than the tool through the armour, becoming more unbearable as each passed.

A small pop revealed the scalpel had done its job. Matthews noted the doctor's hands were shaking as she reached for the mask and pulled it away from the alien's face. The initial lift looked easy before she slowed and a tube emerged from the being's mouth, at least six inches long by the time it had been extracted.

It didn't look like any mouth Matthews had seen; a circular hole with rings of small, curved teeth leading deeper.

The four tentacles snapped to life, extending and wrapping around the necks of the two doctors making notes. The remaining two grabbed the wrists of the woman who'd cut the mask away and lifted them all into the air with loud screeches and wails, drowning out their screams.

Matthews didn't hesitate in dashing to the door as Kayo commed for the two agents outside. The general entered at the same time as the guards burst into the room and the alien struggled to get to its feet.

Before anyone could open fire, the alien moved the two doctors, held by tentacles around their necks, between it and the two agents aiming their Enforcexes. The human shields stopped the pair from firing. Matthews grabbed the laser scalpel and pointed it at the alien, who dropped to its knees after finally leaving the table.

A gurgling noise broke through each wail and screech as the being's skin darkened. Its head swung from left to right as it looked for a way out, pushing back with its feet. It couldn't breathe.

All three doctors were slowly inching towards the floor, and Matthews hoped they could last a few more seconds until their enemy passed out. As if it could sense his thoughts, the tentacles tightened their grip in unison, snapping two necks and two wrists. The woman screamed louder as all three dropped to the ground, cradling her arms against her chest while the other pair remained in crumpled, unnatural positions.

With a final, fading screech, the alien slumped to the floor. Doctor Kayo rushed from the observation booth into the room and crouched next to her crying colleague.

"Was it worth it?" she snapped at the general as he checked the two bodies for a pulse.

"We'll make it worth it," he muttered, before issuing orders. "Get that thing back on the table and get another team in. I want reports every thirty minutes from the team here and the one in the hangar. No matter how small a detail, I want to know about it straight away."

CHAPTER TWENTY-THREE

His usual morning alarm started low, increasing in volume every fifteen seconds until it couldn't be ignored. The lights activated at a similar speed. The sequence was designed to be as gentle as possible but prevent the occupant from going back to sleep. There were a number of different noises to choose from and Ryan had chosen a simple tune. The tone changes helped him wake up quicker.

This noise blared from all sides, the volume and urgency dispelling any fog from his mind. It wasn't the normal alarm. Only senior officers and squad captains could activate it, and not for drills. This was real.

That didn't stop him from falling out of bed. His foot caught in the sheets as he tried to roll out and his head hit the floor. The cursing that followed was lengthy and loud. Straight away his skull thumped like a drum, the dizziness making him wobble as he pulled on his navy mech pilot uniform.

The alarm wouldn't turn off. After a few tries he was able to lower the volume but that activated red warning lights, blinking in line with the noise. He couldn't decide if it was better or worse. His head didn't care and continued to throb.

Another series of beeps drew his attention to the desk. The terminal blinked to life with a message to be viewed. It overrode all other functions until the high-priority window was opened and acknowledged.

Still groggy, Ryan saw the time on the display and groaned. He'd been asleep for three hours. His work with Mac kept him up past midnight when they both had the chance, like last night, and an alert coming through shortly after him falling asleep felt like torture. The noise was hurting his head as much as the impact.

"Flare Squadron!" Captain Ryder's face appeared. She looked as tired as he felt. "We have a mission. Meet in C-13-4's hangar for further instructions. This is not a drill. I repeat, not a drill. Move!"

It took him five minutes. The corridors were full of running agents. Everyone was reporting for duty.

The hangar was busier than Ryan had ever seen it but this time everyone made way for him as he jogged to the centre, where a shuttle was waiting with a group of pilots and techs near the steps. The mechs on each side of the hangar were being moved as he joined the group. Close to the entrance was a strange ship that looked like a wire frame with engines. The mechs were locked into place vertically for transport, with three already in position and a fourth being loaded as Ryan watched.

"Rough night?" Oaf asked with a grin. Ryan's blank stare made the bigger man succumb to hysterics.

"He's talking about your head," Teach clarified, also smiling. "Who knew the rook liked it rough?"

"Rough with the floor," he grunted, rubbing his head and feeling the bump.

That made everyone laugh, even those not in the squad. There was a tension in the hangar Ryan had never felt on the station before and laughter relieved it.

"It is a big bump," Jackson announced, poking it and making him wince. "Maybe it has its own brain?"

"That'd explain a lot," Rig added. "Maybe he'll act like a normal pilot if we cut it off?"

"Who's got a knife?" Wrecker called. More laughs.

Despite the pain Ryan smiled too. It was good to feel like part of the squad, even if it had taken time. Wisp grabbed his shoulder and gave him a gentle shake.

"Listen up!" Captain Ryder called from the shuttle's hatch. "The mechs are being loaded. Crew shuttles are moving out. This ship is bound for the *North Wind* so if that's not your destination, find another. If you're unsure, speak to Lieutenant Toomes. He'll direct you. We've lost more sensors, but the last scans showed multiple ships approaching Mars. From the *North Wind*, we'll pilot our mechs to the Warp Tunnel and travel through. We're to defend the portal and take out the advancing forces. Individual squad assignments will come before launch."

"Captain?" Sketcher called. "Why don't we just pilot the mechs to the *North Wind*?"

"No need to recharge them if they go by transport. There's enough to do already." Bishop said.

"Exactly," Ryder said. "I know you haven't had much sleep so use the journey to get some more. It's only an hour but take what you can. Any other questions?"

"How big is the enemy force?" Jackson asked.

"We don't know exactly but the sensor scans showed over sixty ships. We still can't pick up their mechs but expect a large number, with more probably docked.

They're in a wide formation. As we get further information, it'll be relayed." Ryder looked at the crowd again and when no other questions came, she continued, "There's no time to turn back so anything you leave behind will stay here. Make your final checks and get on board. I want to leave in ten. Flare Squadron on first. Rooks, with me," she added, and turned back to the shuttle.

Ryan and Jackson followed the captain on board and through the cabin to the cockpit.

"Fall, take the co-pilot's chair. Jackson, you're on comms," Ryder ordered.

A man vacated the co-pilot's seat and returned to the cabin. Ryan took his place and continued the pre-flight checklist as Jackson began coordinating with flight control at Orbital Station Delta. The captain watched them before taking her place in the pilot's chair.

"Relax, both of you. You've done this before in the sims. It's no different here. Tense up and you'll make mistakes."

As pep talks went, it wasn't inspirational, but the lack of warning in her voice helped the rooks settle. Any questions about why they were chosen for this instead of more experienced squad members vanished.

"Pre-flight done. Ready for launch," Ryan announced, and Jackson relayed this to flight control. The comm position wasn't vital as both pilots could open channels but Ryder wanted all three of them in the cockpit.

"Understood, Control. Standing by," Jackson said, turning to the others. "We're third in line."

"Fall, keep the engines warm. You'll be taking us out when Jackson gives the word."

"Sir."

The three sat in silence as the minutes ticked by until Jackson confirmed they were next. Ryan's hands flew across the controls and the shuttle lifted from the deck with only a small jerk. A quick glance at the captain revealed no reaction. She was flicking between the viewport and sensors to make sure their path was clear.

Ryan directed the shuttle forward. It felt like a crawl through the hangar but when they emerged from the station, he increased speed and turned for the carrier *North Wind*, which was orbiting the moon.

Jackson was already in contact with the ship's flight control team, updating them on their course and speed. Ryan locked in the coordinates and leaned back in his chair, letting out a deep breath.

"Well done, both of you," Ryder said. "I had no doubt you could handle this."

"Was that the real reason you chose us?" Jackson asked before Ryan could.

"No. I wanted to talk to you away from the others. I haven't had the chance to do so recently." The captain took a breath before turning her chair so she could see them. "You look pretty composed, but nerves will kick in soon. That's natural but we can't afford it. I wanted you to see your training has paid off. You knew what to do and have done well. Use this as a reference for what's to come. I'm not great at motivational speeches. All I'll say is if you perform as well as you have been in the sims, this mission will be a success. You may be rooks but you're our rooks. We've got your backs and I know you have ours."

"Thanks..." Jackson answered.

"Most importantly, remember why you were brought here. I've been hard on you both in the past for your creativity and lack of discipline. Maybe I shouldn't have been. We still don't know exactly what we'll find. Keep your eyes open and prove why you're two of the best pilots we've got."

"Is that an order?" Ryan asked slyly.

"You're damned right. I expect nothing but the best from my pilots, and that includes the two of you," she said with a small smile. "Jackson, I want you to go back and tell Lieutenant Toomes that the moment we've landed, we'll have about four hours before launch. I want everyone to get at least two hours' sleep before then. Three would be ideal. The twelve of us will be sharing a room so take your headset back and work with him and control on *North Wind* to get us one, close to the sim room if possible. I don't want to waste any time. Clear?"

"Yes, sir." Jackson headed to the cabin, throwing one last glance at the two of them before the door closed. Ryan let the silence return, waiting for Ryder to reveal the real reason he was in the co-pilot's chair.

"We haven't spoken much since you arrived. Not privately, at least," she said.

"Outside of performance meetings, no, we haven't," Ryan said.

"I'm sorry about that. Since day one, I've tried to keep my distance from you and that's not fair, especially as you're a rook. Even more so since you're such a gifted pilot. Mechs, fighters, shuttles – hell, I reckon you could pilot a battle cruiser and any other ship we have with a little time."

"I'm assuming there was a reason for the distance?" Ryan asked, aware Ryder was watching him, but he kept his eyes on the stars ahead.

"You remind me of my sister." That was enough to draw his gaze. "She was a hell of a pilot too, and she had this leadership coo down. I'm often compared to her; what she did and what she could have done. There have always been expectations on me, and I hate it. Trying to live up to that and be my own person isn't easy."

"What happened to her?"

"She died the first time we encountered these bastards. The footage you saw when you arrived on OSD… that was her squad."

"Oh," was all Ryan could think to say. "I'm sorry."

"I got a promotion, inherited her squad – the name, at least – and built it again myself. When Matthews reassigned most of my pilots I was upset. Then I got civilians. I know now what he was trying to do but it didn't feel like my squad anymore. Then you arrived. In your file there was a reference to Rebecca and it made me so angry! It said you had a ridiculous amount of talent and even more potential, but you were cocky and reckless. They said the same about her…and me, once. From watching you, I know you're a better pilot than both of us, but you have much more to learn. I should have been a better captain and helped you."

"You're talking about moderation. Knowing when to act, listen and obey," Ryan said, unsure of how to respond to the sister revelation.

"The general spoke to you?"

"Yeah. It makes sense."

"Good. I don't expect you to change overnight but this isn't training. It's not just us anymore and your actions could affect us and other squads. Keep coming up with ideas and tactics. I'll consider them all."

"I will." Ryan nodded. "Can I ask you something, sir?"

"Go on."

"All the information we have, and the training exercises we've been doing – I find it strange that our weapons are so effective compared to theirs. Do you know why?"

"We could only guess until recently. The last mission allowed us to bring home intact enemy mechs. We haven't figured it all out yet, but their mechs have smaller power supplies than ours – but they are more efficient in how it's distributed and used throughout the unit. It also means their energy attacks are weaker, and we do have stronger armour, as well. Their physical attacks will still do some damage, though."

"But—"

"Weapon research never stops, either. It may be done in secret, but weapons keep us safe as well as killing. We have more power and better armour, but they've probably been using mechs much longer than us – and there's a hell of a lot of them. It could be they think numbers will win every time. If we had the time and resources, I'd have liked more mechs and pilots, but it was easier to improve what we had. Even with weaker weapons, enough hits will take us down pretty quickly. Beyond that, I can't answer why."

"Yes, sir." Ryan hesitated before adding, "I won't let you down...or your sister."

"See you don't, Rook." She leaned back and closed her eyes. "Or I'll haunt you forever. Wake me when we're about to dock."

"Aye, Captain."

CHAPTER TWENTY-FOUR

THE FRAME SHIP TRANSPORTING Flare Squadron's mechs flew close to the *North Wind*. It was an engine on a frame with twelve docking points for the squad's mech units. As Ryan took his shuttle past the frame on the way to the *North Wind*, he saw dozens of techs in space suits completing the last bits of work on their units, finalising settings, loading armaments and checking for errors.

Ryan managed two hours' sleep once they reached the carrier. Such fragmented sleep wasn't great but it was better than nothing at all. From the look of her, Ryder hadn't slept much more than the short spell on the shuttle. Toomes and Jackson found them bunks easily enough and, while it was strange sharing a room with eleven others, it didn't stop him nodding off.

What followed felt like a race to reach their sims and get ready for launch. Physically, there was no difference between the pods on OSD and the *North Wind*, but they felt different. They smelled cleaner and looked more polished. Less used. He tried not to think about it, focusing instead on what was to come.

"Flare Squadron," Captain Ryder said over the comm. "Report status."

"Flare Two, ready."

"Flare Three, ready."

"Flare Four, systems online."

Each pilot called in. It seemed pointless since Ryder could use her sensors to see who was ready and who wasn't, but this was a tradition from years gone by, one senior officers wanted to uphold.

"Flare Eleven, ready," Jackson reported.

"Flare Twelve, ready," Ryan finished.

"Follow my lead, flight by flight, leaders in the middle," Ryder said over the comm. "We're going at half speed until we reach the Warp Tunnel. Keep comm chatter to a minimum."

All twelve mechs pushed off from the ship at once to prevent the frame from moving as much as it would if they launched one-by-one. Those unplanned movements could affect a squadmate's launch. It was a procedure they had only practised a couple of times but there were no problems.

They regrouped and joined the flow of mechs and fighters ahead of the ships on their way to the Warp Tunnel. There was no chatter on any of the channels Ryan had open. He wasn't the only one who was nervous.

The journey to the Warp Tunnel took twenty minutes and, in that time, Ryan ran another series of system checks. He didn't expect Mac to have missed anything, but nerves were kicking in. Before every race, Zack would do a final check to set his mind at ease. He could then focus on what was ahead without distraction.

When they arrived, Ryan saw a sea of ships. Hundreds of mechs were lined up in rows, fighters ahead and to the sides, with the larger ships drifting into place behind them.

In front was the Warp Tunnel – a metal ring large enough for even the biggest ship to pass through. Mac had tried to explain how it worked during one of the training sessions but all Ryan had managed to understand was that it folded the fabric of space and allowed anything that passed through to appear from another ring almost instantly. He tried not to think about the process. Their destination was the Mars ring. All the others had been destroyed.

It sounded like fiction, but they had been in use for over thirty years with no accidents. It was their only safe form of long-distance transportation but needed a very large power source. All around the area, large solar panels constantly collected power. After five activations, the cells would be drained and it would take two months to fully charge them again, so it was used sporadically. Sending a force to stop an alien invasion was a worthy cause.

"Listen up." Ryder's voice filled the sim again as she began relaying instructions. "The Warp Tunnel will activate soon. A recon team will go first and when they give the all-clear, the rest will follow. Our orders are to defend the Warp Tunnel on the other side. No enemy units should make it through. Once the area is secure, we'll move on to our next objective."

Weeks ago, Ryan would have asked what the next objective was. It had taken time, but he was learning not to question his captain over the small details he wanted to know but didn't need to. She had the responsibility of deciding what the squad needed to know and when. He had to respect that. No one else asked either.

"Rooks, when we pass through the Warp Tunnel, your system will cut out. The journey takes about three seconds, but it will be closer to ten before the sims reconnect with the mechs. Don't panic, and don't do anything stupid either."

Translation: don't shoot friendlies.

It wasn't the most exciting mission but it was real. Weeks of training were about to come to fruition, although waiting for everything to begin was as hard as waiting for the lights to go out on the racetrack.

With a blinding flash, the Warp Tunnel burst to life. The inside of the ring lit up white. The space beyond the ring was black. It was distorted, hazy. On closer inspection, the stars were tiny, blurred points of light.

The noises he could hear were fabricated – he and Mac had used the little time they had to get basic sounds loaded. There was no noise in space, but it helped him understand what was going on to hear as well as see. Depending on the distance, as well as the direction faced or where it was supposed to have come from, the sounds would be loud or quiet.

"Ryan." The voice was quiet and almost lost to static. Ryan checked the comm to find out what channel the noise had come from, but he couldn't make out who had spoken. "Don't ignore me."

There was a lot of static. Ryan cleared up the signal and repeated the message. The voice was familiar. His heart leapt into his throat as he put the pieces together. "Coo…"

"Coo? That's what I get? After all this time?"

"Where the coo have you been?"

"On OSD, you know that," Zack said, a little more life in his voice. It was still weak, feeble. Not like him. "It's been rough."

"We'll swap stories when this is over," Ryan said, relief flooding through his voice.

"Fine. I'm with Mac. He's briefed me. He's giving me the rundown on the mech. We're both keeping an eye on you."

"Good to have you back."

"You've been lost without me," Zack quipped. He left no time for Ryan to answer before adding, "The recon team is going through the tunnel now."

Ryan turned his attention to the screen and watched one ship, two squads of mechs and three fighter squadrons fly through the ring. The waiting was maddening. Every second dragged.

After what felt like an eternity, a gruff male voice gave the order to proceed.

Ryan took a slow, deep breath and imagined every other pilot felt the same. That's when things started. Fighters began diving into the ring one squadron after another while the mechs lined up and went through with the ships their sims were on.

It took fifteen minutes for Flare Squadron's turn to arrive. Ryder gave the order to move at twenty percent speed. Bishop's flight joined her on the front row while Tombstone's flight moved with Wisp's. Eventually the ring disappeared completely, and blurry, black space filled his view. On the other side were indistinguishable shapes moving around and a light flashed before the sim went black as the mechs went through.

A slow count to ten and the screen came back to life as the signal from the *North Wind* reconnected. Ryan's eyes widened as he processed the scene.

Chaos. The comm burst to life with frantic orders, questions and screams. Kicking his thrusters into action, Ryan moved away from the Warp Tunnel, taking a position on the left with the rest of his flight, and deactivated comm channels, leaving the flight, squad and tech channels open.

"Activate weapon systems," Ryder ordered. "Don't shoot unless you have a clear shot – you might hit a friendly. Stay with the tunnel; protecting it is our mission. We need to get the rest of our fleet through."

The sensor sphere was swimming with a sea of blue dots – allies – and swarms of red dots – enemies. Four clusters of yellow identified new signals before they changed to blue, red or vanished. More friendlies from the Warp Tunnel. The red dots would flash if they locked on to him.

It made no sense. Ryan couldn't see any enemy mechs on his screen, even when the sensors briefly showed they were there. That's when he remembered the video Matthews showed them on OSD – the enemy mechs were black. Dark silhouettes on a black canvas with white dots, only visible when those points of light vanished. It made them near impossible to find.

"Wisp, did you bring flares?" Ryan asked.

"Not this time. Why?"

"We can't hit them if we can't see them. If it's some sort of stealth, we're out of luck, but enough flares around the area might give us a way to find them thanks to the coloured light."

"Captain, did you—" Wisp started to ask.

"I'll put a call out now," Ryder said, cutting him off.

"I'll make a grid," Ryan said. "Zack?"

"On it."

A grid surrounding the Warp Tunnel arrived at his console and he sent it to Ryder. Flares launched around the area, offering a fierce, fire-red glow.

Ryan could see dark shapes moving. The sensors still couldn't pick them up but the display did pick out the shapes he could see.

"When a flare goes out, it needs to be replaced," Ryan said as his view was blocked by another battle cruiser passing through the tunnel.

"Obviously," the captain replied.

"Permission to engage?" Toomes asked.

"Only targets within our area. Do not hit a friendly!"

"All flights, cut loose," the lieutenant ordered.

The maelstrom intensified as Flare Squadron added their blue lances of light to the field. The targeting systems on each mech were meticulous and reduced the risk of hitting a friendly significantly but couldn't keep up with increasing numbers of units.

Ryan, Jackson and Wisp kept together to keep enemy mechs away from the tunnel. In place of arms, the enemy mechs used extendable tentacles or whip-like appendages. That didn't stop them holding weapons and their lasers flashed as buzzing red needles.

There were a lot of them, more than Ryan expected. Their weapons didn't seem particularly powerful; the first couple of hits barely registered on his unit's diagnostics sphere. Whether that was down to their weak weapons or his strong armour, Ryan couldn't tell. His weapon was much more effective but for every mech he destroyed another took its place.

"This isn't getting us anywhere," Bishop announced. He was right. Instead of spreading out from the tunnel, they were being boxed in, but so far, the losses weren't significant. "What are they trying to do?"

"Looks like they're testing us," Jackson said. "Seeing what we can do."

"You're not wrong," Ryan muttered.

"Speak up, Rook," Ryder snapped.

"Nothing," he said quickly before thinking it over. "No, they're boxing us in. It doesn't matter why, but if we don't spread out, whatever they're planning will come. We need to push on."

"That's not our mission."

"Then tell whichever squad has that mission to get on with it. The longer they wait the bigger out losses."

Ryan was sure he was going to face Ryder's wrath but the channel stayed silent. She must have switched channels.

Some of the blue dots on his sensors raced away from the tunnel into open space. The screen showed them turning and opening fire on a number of enemy units before resuming their journey.

That provided a boost to everyone. More shots found their mark and flares were replaced with increasing speed. Other ships and mechs were able to push the area of engagement into a wider space and the number of enemies around the Warp Tunnel dropped.

"Ryan, something's wrong," Zack said over the comm. "Are you seeing this?"

"A little busy; spell it out."

"The mechs furthest from the tunnel are shutting down."

"Coo! Why?"

"We're looking into it, but ships and fighters are not being affected."

"Captain, recall the mechs!" Ryan yelled after switching channels.

"I've sent the order but they're not responding," Ryder said, her voice tense. "What's going on?"

Ryan switched back to the general comm channel and was overwhelmed. The complaints and questions told him no one knew what was going on. All the while, mechs were shutting down and fighters were being picked off.

"Captain, we can't do anything if we shut down." Wisp's voice was barely audible over the rest of the noise. Ryan switched the general channel off again. "Recommend we withdraw through the tunnel and guard against any enemies coming through."

"Agreed. Flare Squadron, back to the other side."

The retreat left a bitter taste in his mouth, but it made sense. Ryder would be getting orders and information direct from whichever ship was in command, as well. The seconds it took to reconnect after passing through felt longer than the first time, although they relied on the *North Star* keeping up. When the signal reconnected, they were on the other side and Ryder was ordering them into a wide position with their weapons trained on the space inside the ring. Other squads operating from the same ship were with them, organising themselves into similar formations.

Ryan armed missiles. He wanted options since the battle wasn't going well. His left trigger would launch them – the right was still controlling the rifle although he tried not to look at it; holding empty space threw him off.

It became a waiting game again. He couldn't resist turning the general comm channel back on. It wasn't easy to make out what was going on and the sensors weren't accurate enough to show the situation on the other side of the ring.

Within minutes, they called a full retreat. Mechs, ships and fighters began streaming through in no order.

When an enemy unit came through the tunnel, Ryan and his squad were quick to pick them off. Debris gathered but no one deemed it important. Other mechs joined them in a defensive formation while fighters and ships retreated towards OSD, but more enemy units were appearing and it was getting harder to keep up.

"Shut down the Warp Tunnel." The order came from one of the ships.

"We still have units on the other side," a captain pointed out.

"We can build more. Shut it down."

"What about the people still on the other side?" a fighter captain yelled. "We can't leave them there!"

"More enemy units are coming through and our forces are already weakened. We need to stop them now while we can, buy ourselves more time." Ryan found it hard to keep up with the different voices, most he didn't recognise.

"Colonel! The Warp Tunnel won't shut down!"

"What?" the Colonel exclaimed.

"The enemy are accessing the system."

The channel descended into static as everyone fought to be heard. There was no order in terms of who spoke and when, but Ryan didn't hear Ryder speak once.

One thing became clear quickly: the tunnel needed to be shut down. More enemy units were coming through. Soon they would overrun the small defence they had established. More friendly mechs and fighters were succumbing to increasing weapons fire. Ryan knew what to do. He freed his left arm from the gauntlet, started keying in commands to his console and opened a private line to the captain.

"We need to destroy it," he said.

"What?"

"The ring. We need to destroy the Warp Tunnel. Now!"

"That's not our call – only General Matthews can authorise that plan."

"Then get authorisation. The longer we wait the more we lose."

"People will die."

"They're dying already. Can't you see that?"

He switched back to the squad channel but no one was talking. The targeting system identified six areas of the ring and he sent the information to Wisp and Jackson. They responded with a click on the flight channel but no questions. They knew what was at stake.

"Destroy the Warp Tunnel," General Matthews said over the comm. "Now."

Without waiting for Ryder, Ryan sent a signal to his flight and launched his missiles. Wisp and Jackson fired theirs seconds later. They each carried eight warheads, which meant four missiles to every location targeted.

The seconds ticked by. He watched, holding his breath, as they raced to the metal structure and created large orange clouds on impact. The distorted space disappeared as the ring broke apart. Several large fragments and many smaller pieces mingled with the rest of the debris.

It didn't take long to destroy the last of the enemy units. Ryan's head was swimming. They'd stopped the invaders, but the aliens had a way of shutting down their mechs. As their main defence, that was a big problem.

Ryder ordered the squad back to the *North Wind* as the fleet returned to OSD. Compared to how large a force they'd started with, only two thirds remained.

That was because of him. He'd fired the missiles. Agents, officers and pilots left behind were likely being killed right now.

Zack was talking but Ryan could barely focus. Without thinking, he switched off his comm and guided the mech to the ship and to his spot in the hangar. After the shutdown procedure, Ryan climbed out of the sim and landed with a thud on the floor, dropping to his knees. Ryder, Wisp and Jackson ran over to him while the rest of the squad crowded behind. Every face was white. Like ghosts.

His eyes watered and he threw up. The retching lasted over a minute, even after his stomach was empty. He slammed his fist against the deck every few seconds. Only his sobs punctuated the violent affair.

One thought kept repeating over and over: he had killed them.

CHAPTER TWENTY-FIVE

IT WAS THE RIGHT call.

Five words that had been said more times than he could count over the three days since the battle – the Mars Massacre, it was being called. Ryan didn't believe those words. Couldn't believe them. Doctors, officers, mechanics, pilots and squadmates all said it. They looked like they barely believed it when they said the words. Would it feel different if someone else had thought of the plan or fired the missiles? Would they feel so empty... so lost?

Maybe. It was something Enforcer training might have prepared them for. Never before had he felt so unsure.

After being discharged from the medical centre, Ryder gave him an extra day to recover. He spent it looking out at the stars, thinking about humans and aliens, the purpose of wars and morality.

Zack was with him the entire time. They hadn't talked about where he'd been for the last few weeks. It was a conversation both wanted to have but neither felt up to. If Ryan felt awful, Zack looked it. His skin was pale and his hair matted and tangled. The bags under his eyes seemed to cover his cheeks. Regardless, it was good to have him back. There was no one he trusted more, but even his reassurances didn't help.

Returning to the sims was a challenge. Ryan arrived late on purpose to avoid pointless discussions. Getting through the door was difficult enough but when he eventually managed it, the hush that fell across the room was worse than anything they could have said.

Rather than waste time on small talk, he reached his sim and grabbed a rung but couldn't bring himself to climb. He stood there, staring at his distorted reflection.

It was his face but...unfamiliar.

A hand on his shoulder made him jump almost to the top of the sim. Captain Ryder stood behind him with a look of sympathy that seemed foreign on her. She nodded to the door and walked out with Ryan a respectable distance behind her. Just before the door closed, he could hear Toomes telling the squad he'd be leading training.

They walked in silence. Ryan had given up trying to navigate the corridors on his own. OSD's station interface got him where he needed to be. It seemed foolish not to use it.

Eventually they arrived at a door and Ryder motioned for him to follow her inside. The room was not dissimilar to his own but bigger and with more belongings. Pictures, ornaments and more. Any other time, he'd have been keen to explore and find out more about the captain, but there wasn't much he wanted to do right now except sleep.

"Sit," she said, taking a seat at the desk.

He did, sitting opposite the captain. Her frosty eyes bore into him until he looked away; at a wall, the desk, the door. Anything.

"What's ripping you?" It was clear Ryder knew but she wanted him to say it.

"I killed those people."

"Is that it?"

"What do you mean 'is that it'? Isn't that enough?"

"Like it or not, you're a soldier. How many mechs did you destroy out there? Whatever that number, at least that many of the enemy died."

"But they're not human." He paused. "How do you know they're not remotely piloted, like ours?"

"From the salvage we've recovered. And no, not human, but still a life. I'm not saying it's right but that's not our call to make. We follow orders and senior officers deal with the consequences."

"Matthews said we're all responsible for our actions," Ryan shot back before calming himself. "Does that help you sleep better?"

"I haven't slept well in months. Not without meds, anyway," Ryder said, folding her arms and looking into the distance. "Look, I can't say I've been where you are, but I have been lost."

"Is this where you give a motivational speech? I don't think it'll help."

"Why not?"

"You've not exactly shown yourself to be relatable. It's been clear from day one you're the captain and we're the pilots. We do as you say."

"Then shut up and listen." Ryder's face softened as she slumped in her chair. "For as long as I can remember, there have been expectations of me. Do this. Do that. Meet this goal. This target. And just when I thought I was done, something else came up. I shut people out while trying to make those same coos happy. Even making captain didn't help.

"As a pilot, I've seen people close to me die. After a while you learn not to let people get too close because you know they're going to die – or you will, and they'll suffer. Loss affects us all differently. You haven't lost friends, but you feel responsible for comrades dying. You didn't kill them; the enemy did. Yes, you destroyed the Warp Tunnel, but you saved everyone who made it through.

"You knew the order would be given. You were ready for it. You prepared your flight for it. It was the right call and you saved us valuable time. Should you have waited for my order? No, the general gave it. We brought you in for that reason. We brought everyone in this squad together for the same reason; you think differently and aren't afraid to act. You won't get everything right, but this is one call you did. Completely."

Silence settled again. Ryan didn't know how to respond although Ryder was waiting for him to say something. In the end, he managed one question in a very small voice. "Then why am I feeling so lost?"

"Are you? Or are you coming to terms with what's going on here? You're a racer – a good one from what I've seen – but you don't understand the gravity of a situation. When you're involved in a crash, you get up and walk away. The only consequence is your race is over, and everyone else involved stops racing, too. In the past, before sim technology was invented, you could have died. Spectators might have died. Marshals clearing the circuit were in danger. The fear is gone; it's just a game now. For you, for everyone. That's not the case here. Every decision you make in the sim has an impact out there. You've seen that first-hand. All pilots and agents learn that lesson in time, which is something you don't have. It tends to happen on a much smaller scale. Regardless, we all learn it. Every survivor will understand the gravity of what you've done. That will make them better pilots in the future. It will make you a better pilot."

"That's the last thing I care about right now."

"It shouldn't be. We slowed them down but they're still coming. We've analysed their tech and are upgrading ours. We've even discovered the reason for our mechs shutting down out there. It's a jamming signal, probably from one of the approaching ships. We're working on a solution."

"It doesn't matter. I'm done with this. I can't go out there again."

"We need you. I've seen how hard you worked to get here. You have talent. You're a better pilot than people with years of experience. You're one of us."

"I can't even face a sim. Think how I'll react against the enemy."

"We'll help you."

"That's just it. I don't want help." Ryan stood and walked to the door before looking back. "I appreciate what you've said but I'm not like you. I can't turn this off. I'm a racer, not an agent. That's what I'm good at... all I'm good at." Before Ryder could say anything else, Ryan left the room to return to his own.

By the time he reached his quarters, there was no doubt in his mind. He didn't belong on OSD or in the Mech Force.

He sent a message to General Matthews with his resignation and checked the schedule for the next shuttle to the surface. Supplies were transported to and from the planet regularly, so it wasn't hard to find one.

It didn't take long to pack his few belongings and Ryan was soon in the maze of corridors of Orbital

Station Delta again. The lights guided him through the labyrinth towards the hangar where the next shuttle was due to depart. It was on the other side of the station. A transporter ride later, he emerged onto the deck of a bustling hangar with Vulture and Vanga-class fighters scattered around and a shuttle in the middle. Mechanics, techs and pilots were running around to get the next patrol ready to launch, so no one paid him any attention as he weaved through.

At the base of the steps to the shuttle, Ryan found the captain and an officer discussing the itinerary for the journey. Once they were done, he stepped forward. "Got room for one more?"

"We're heading to Delta Space Port. If that's okay, grab a seat."

It was the same type of shuttle that had brought him to the station in the first place. As the only passenger, he had no shortage of seats and chose one closest to the window on the front row opposite the door. According to the schedule, it would be another twenty minutes before they left.

Ryan activated his MOB-I and sent a message to Zack. They hadn't talked about what happened on the mission, his friend choosing to be there in supportive silence or trying to distract him with light topics, but given how weak he'd sounded over the comm, and how frail he'd looked when Ryan returned to the station, he wouldn't be leaving for a while. This was the best place for him to be until he recovered.

The second message went to Jackson. His fellow rook didn't seem to be having the same crisis, but the mission had changed her too. He had given her the targets and she fired once given the signal. She wasn't one to open up either. That seemed to be a common trait of Flare Squadron, as well as being outsiders.

Wisp received the last message. It was a short one to say thank you. His blossoming relationship with Jackson – even if it wasn't public yet – would see them compare messages, he was sure.

"Giving up?"

Ryan looked up to see General Matthews board the shuttle and sit one seat over from him. They sat in silence before the general spoke again. "Captain Ryder tells me you're having trouble dealing with death."

"Not death; being the cause of it," Ryan said, ignoring the feeling of the general staring at him.

"Oh, is that all?" Matthews asked, most likely trying to get a reaction from Ryan. It didn't work.

"You're even worse at this than the queen." Ryan kept his voice deadpan.

"Have you called her that to her face?"

"I value my life, so no."

"Good instincts. That's one of the reasons I brought you here."

"And the others?"

"You think outside the box and you're not afraid to do what needs to be done," Matthews said, taking a breath and stroking his beard. "Listen, what happened out there is tragic. There's no doubt about it. You had a rude awakening to what we're actually dealing with here. For our entire lives, society shields us from danger. Fear is powerful – it keeps us from doing stupid things that might hurt or kill us. If I could make every fighter pilot use a sim, I would, but it's not feasible. Besides, suicide runs would be more common. Equipment can be replaced, lives can't. Ryder can attest to that."

"Is it always about her sister?" Ryan asked after a moment.

"They're big shoes to fill. It might have been easier with a squad of trained agents but given how good Rebecca was, I suspected Eleanor would do well too."

"And?"

"She's exceeded my expectations. As have you, and your whole squadron – it's a shame that this is the situation that brought you all together but that's where we find ourselves. If Rebecca had been your captain rather than Eleanor, I wonder how things would have turned out."

"What do you want from me, sir?"

"Stay," Matthews said, the pair finally locking eyes. "Get over this hurdle like you have every other. You can be one of the best pilots out there. You can make a difference."

"So can someone else. I'm sorry but I'm not that special. I won't be the reason anyone else dies."

Matthews sighed, closing his eyes while he thought of his next argument.

"Are you going to stop me from leaving?" Ryan said.

"I could. You knew leaving wasn't an option when you agreed to join. I think you've seen enough here to know spreading the word on the surface will cause nothing but panic. If you think it's best, and you give me your word you won't say anything about what we're facing up here, I'll let you leave. Just remember, Ryan. I made the decision, so, ultimately, any blame lies with me. The fact you care says more about your character than anything else. It was the right call and we still need you here. But you have to come to terms with it."

"You said on the way here that following orders is no excuse for doing the wrong thing. I don't know yet if we did the right thing or not. You saying we did doesn't help. You can't have it both ways, sir."

"I was like you once, thirty years ago – maybe more…" Matthews said, his words trailing off. "You have more to give, and I never took you to be someone who ran from their problems."

"Maybe you don't know me as well as you think," Ryan muttered, refusing to take the bait the general dangled.

"Or I know you better than you know yourself. It's your choice, but the threat doesn't end just because you leave, Ryan."

The general left when Ryan offered no reply. His words had sounded hollow, just like Captain Ryder's. Ryan settled in for the journey to Earth and home. He should make it back with just enough time to catch up before the end of year exams.

CHAPTER TWENTY-SIX

SARA'S MESSAGE ARRIVED SOON after the shuttle landed. Zack must have told her – he never liked wasting time. It was exactly the kind of thing he would do. Since he couldn't help directly Ryan hadn't expected a response, but he should have known his friend would do something.

Of all the people he could have turned to, why her? He knew the answer even if he didn't want to admit it. Both racers, they'd always been close. Rivals and friends at the same time. It did get complicated but it didn't stop them from being there for each other when needed. Sara was just as important to him as Zack, in different ways.

The message read: *Come to the Loop on Friday. Noon. Don't be late.*

Just what Zack said to her, he'd have to wait to find out as she didn't respond to his reply. It wasn't often Ryan found himself repeatedly checking the MOB-I for messages but what he didn't want was another pep talk, and if that was all she had to give it would be a waste of time.

One of Miss Kinni's lectures would be a better alternative.

An Enforcer agent was waiting for him at the bottom of the steps after they landed. The disapproval was clear and his tone sharp. "We've arranged for transportation. You'll take the same route used to get here. Say nothing about what you've seen, heard or done while on OSD. We'll be monitoring your communications. Don't make us get involved with your civilian life."

Ryan nodded and they walked to the gates, where he was signed out by a pair of bored-looking agents. From there he was left alone to make his way back to the Institute in Zone-714.

A week after he had arrived on OSD, Matthews informed Ryan he wasn't to be expelled and could return to finish his studies once his time on the station ended; once the threat was over. He was going back sooner than planned but he had nowhere else to go.

Compared to the first journey with Zack, there was no enjoyment or excitement. It was already dark by the time he boarded the first train, and the carriage was close to empty, so he easily found a quiet corner. Whenever someone walked past, Ryan turned away. During the slower parts of the trip, he closed his eyes and tried to sleep.

Any one of these people could have been an agent he let die. Any one of them could be a relative or friend of a casualty. Any one of them could die in the coming days if the rest of the Mech Force didn't stop the invasion, yet they knew nothing. They laughed and cried like nothing mattered. Ignorance really was bliss.

Each station they stopped at was close to deserted. Late-night travel wasn't very popular. Reduced services and increased prices caused that, but Enforcers had certain privileges to make sure they could complete their duties. A train waited for him in Zone-676, whereas after midnight only interzone trains operated. It was scary, the influence and control they could exert, but it was working in his favour.

There was only one carriage and two other people on board. Both ignored him and Ryan found a seat as far from them as he could. It was too dark to see anything outside, but his gaze was glued to the window all the same.

He hoped the guilt and remorse would be sucked into the abyss beyond the glass, but it didn't happen. Shadows sometimes loomed, making him jump. Ryan was sure they were enemy mechs at first, but they vanished in an instant, allowing him to hide his reaction from the other passengers. It didn't stop his heart thumping against his ribs. Nerves were added to the storm of emotions swirling in his stomach.

There were no stops on this part of the journey. Ryan and the two men disembarked together at Zone-714's transport terminal and he watched them walk into the night. There was no one else on the platform, not that he expected to see anyone. Only Sara knew he was back. That didn't stop it being disappointing.

On the few occasions he glanced into the darkness beyond the streetlights as he walked to the Institute, any movement got his pulse racing. Murky figures rushed past with heads lowered, vehicles passed overhead and the wind blew the branches and leaves of the trees around him. None of this would bother him usually but this wasn't a normal situation. Halfway to the Institute, he began mimicking the other people: hood up, head down and power-walking.

The curved building was bathed in light as he approached. An impressive sight but not one he had appreciated until now. The windows were mostly dark except for the entrance and some student rooms – there were always night owls – and the only noise was the water circling the structure.

One security guard stood at the reception desk and he spared nothing but a cursory glance as Ryan checked in. From the corner of his eye, he saw two figures standing a good distance away from the Institute as he turned down the corridor.

Then it clicked. They'd sent agents to watch him. Given all he had seen and what he was doing now, they wouldn't take any chances he would do something to compromise them. It might not always be the same pair but there would be people watching him for at least the next couple of weeks. The general thought of everything.

His room hadn't changed in his absence. It had been cleaned but everything was exactly where he'd left it. He dropped his bag to the floor and flopped onto the bed, falling asleep.

Like every other night since the mission, the nightmares pounced quickly. The same things happened but in a different order, making them more terrifying.

They always started the same, with him drifting in space, slowly tumbling away from OSD and Earth. There was no way for him to slow down or change direction. This time, the shadows appeared first. Their movements were quick, and it was impossible to track them for more than a second. He had no way to tell how many of them circled or what they were doing other than scaring the coo out of him.

Eventually, a flare appeared in his hand, and Ryan threw it at one of the moving shapes. It became a red ghost and the others nearby gained strong, orange silhouettes with the stars visible behind them. They didn't slow down, move closer or attack.

As he flipped over again, facing away from Earth, the ring of the Warp Tunnel came into view. It looked small enough to hold but it doubled in size the next time he saw it, after another flip. Then doubled again. And again. It took more than half a dozen flips before it was as big as he remembered.

It activated, filling his view with distorted black. More shadows emerged and vanished from his view. He tried to grab one of the closest before he passed through the tunnel. It was then Ryan realised he wasn't floating in space and he wasn't in a mech – he was a mech. His arms were metal. His legs, too.

Ryan tried to scream as he approached the tunnel but nothing came out. He kept trying, but mechs didn't have mouths and, even if they did, there was no noise in space.

He woke with a start and bolted to his feet, breathing heavily. The screams must have been going on a while because his throat felt raw and dry. After calming down and focusing on his breathing, he heard footsteps and whispers on the other side of the door. He'd caused a scene already and no one knew he was back yet.

"What's going on?" a voice shrilled, and Ryan's heart dropped. He did not need this.

"Someone's been screaming. It came from in here." Ryan recognised that voice. She was a student a few rooms down the corridor, but her name eluded him.

"I thought Ryan was gone?"

"We didn't know whether to go in or not."

"We'd know if Ryan was back."

"How?"

"We'd all know!"

"Enough!" Miss Kinni yelled, cutting off the students. "There's no one in there. He's not back and he might not be coming back at all."

"But we heard it!" the first girl said, her voice higher-pitched than anyone else's.

"Alright, alright." She sighed. "Calm down. I'll take a look inside." Ryan barely had enough time to step out of view before the door slid open. "See? No one here. Back to your rooms. Now. And if I catch the person behind this, exams will be the least of their worries. Move. Go!"

The mutters and whispers dispersed and the door slid shut. When he was convinced no one was listening, Ryan stepped away from the wall and found himself face to face with Miss Kinni.

Neither spoke. She looked at him in the way he had learned meant she wasn't sure whether to be angry, disappointed or to slap him. The last one had never happened…yet. She sighed, stepped back and leaned against his desk.

"When did you get back?" she asked quietly.

"Last night," Ryan said, his voice neutral.

"Any particular reason?"

"Yes."

"Are you going to tell me?"

"No."

"Were you the one screaming?" Miss Kinni asked, changing tack when it became clear he wasn't going to give her a substantial answer. Ryan walked to the balcony instead of answering. That seemed to be all Miss Kinni needed to know. "Was it that bad, wherever you were?"

"Not at first."

"I never expected you to give up."

"I'm getting really tired of people telling me that," Ryan snapped, turning away from the balcony. "Maybe you don't know me as well as you think you do. I'm not even sure I do anymore."

"Do you need anything?"

"Time and space. I'll be fine, eventually."

"If you change your mind, come find me," his teacher said, and she turned for the door. "I'll keep everyone out of your way as much as I can, but if you keep screaming in the mornings, people will figure out you're back."

"Yeah, got that." Ryan paused, debating whether to ask the question burning in his mind. "If I told you something bad happened, and I was involved, that meant a lot of people died...is it my fault or the one who gave the order's?"

Miss Kinni whistled. "Without details I can't really say. We're responsible for our own actions and the consequences they bring. That being said, what one person determines to be bad doesn't mean others will feel the same. It's subjective."

"Why don't other people understand that?"

She left without answering and Ryan was alone again. It was what he wanted to hear but it didn't help as much as he thought.

With two days left until he met Sara, there was plenty of time to dwell. There were no messages from Zack, but Jackson had sent him one saying she understood his decision, although his replacement was greener than grass. That brought a momentary smile.

Reliving the mission did no good either. No matter how many times he ran through it in his head, there was no other outcome – not knowing what they did at the time or the mission. He was searching for something, regardless of how small or slight, that would have made a difference.

If it was his mistake, that would make it bearable. It could be addressed and prevented in the future. But if it was the only option, that meant people had to die and Ryan refused to believe there was nothing else he could've done.

Frustrated with his conclusions, he turned to studying. He had missed a lot in the months spent on Orbital Station Delta, but Miss Kinni had been kind enough to send a study schedule. It was nowhere near as exciting as piloting mechs or racing but it didn't involve death and there were absolutes. It was dull and certain, which proved enough to numb his mind.

His terminal had a message from Principal Grove, dated shortly after he left for OSD. It informed him he wasn't to be expelled for his actions. It didn't say anything else, which probably meant Matthews was involved. Maybe his parents. Perhaps both. Ryan deleted all other messages since then to avoid any unpleasant news.

Despite the pit in his stomach, Ryan didn't eat all day. Exhaustion drove him to bed well after midnight when he couldn't focus any longer. The terrors returned just after he closed his eyes but, mercifully, he didn't wake up screaming the next morning.

That didn't stop him creeping to the door and listening for whispers, but he heard nothing. Until his stomach rumbled. In a cupboard, he found a stash of nutri-bars. They weren't a substitute for a real meal but after wolfing down two of them and feeling ill, all thoughts of eating more evaporated and he sat down to study again.

Only one thing kept him going. Sara was a friend, away from his troubles, and he needed that distance. They hadn't been to the Loop for four years. It used to be their regular haunt before they started racing professionally. She had a reason for choosing that location; not that he could figure it out.

The next morning, he set off before dawn. It wasn't far but Ryan wanted to get out of the Institute before anyone saw him. Thankfully, this was the one time where the early worms didn't cross his path. With the morning mist lingering, he made his way to a train to the Loop.

The footsteps might as well have been drumbeats in the quiet morning. The wind had stopped and the track was silent. Ryan hadn't seen anyone in the hour he'd been here.

"You're late," he said, as she stopped just behind him.

"Traffic was coo," Sara answered.

"You slept in again, didn't you?"

"Ooft. That hurts," Sara said, feigning disappointment and making her voice dramatic. "I would never choose sleep over you."

"Liar. Why'd you choose this place?"

"You'll see. Come on," Sara said. Without waiting, she walked towards the garages on the inside of the track. Ryan followed.

When Cyber Cycle gained popularity, a lot of circuits were built in or around major cities across the world. Every other week saw tens of thousands of people attend for the races, but over the years street races became more popular and purpose-built circuits were used for practice, nostalgia and by hobbyists.

Every so often, races would return to one of the old circuits, like the Loop, but it was rare. Street circuits could be redesigned at will, while these tracks had only one layout. The racers lost interest in such one-dimensional tracks during competitive seasons but for recreational use they were perfect.

Sara stopped at one of the garages in the pit lane, unlocked the door with a code on her MOB-I and waited for the doors to part. Inside were six motorcycles, recently polished and in perfect condition.

Despite his mood, Ryan walked to the closest and ran his hand over it while his friend stood in the doorway. "All of these are yours?"

"That's right. These models have no sim synchro – they have to be enjoyed in person. It means they can only be used on circuits like this. Every year, I come to the old school meets and I use one." She pointed to the one on the far left. "That was my dad's. He's the one who got me started on this."

"Okay, I'm jealous. Is this why you brought me here?"

"Partly, but I also thought we could give them a shot. You've never tried a real one before, right?"

"Not without a synchro, no."

"Then pick one. I think it's time we had a race of our own, with no interruptions or distractions."

Ryan looked at the six before him. A black-and-purple model in the middle had caught his eye the moment the doors opened. When he touched it, there was no question in his mind. Sara watched him and picked up on his choice before he could say.

"Here," she said, throwing a bag to him. "Zack told me where to grab your gear. You can get changed in the back."

CHAPTER TWENTY-SEVEN

THE ROAR OF THE engine cleared Ryan's mind.

These machines were built for speed, stripped to the bare minimum and beautifully simple. That was what Zack would have said if he had seen them. It was louder than in the sims. Cyber cycles were built to be seen; the bodywork was bright and flashy, not to mention durable to protect the bike from damage in accidents. It took Ryan a few seconds to get his balance while Sara watched him with her helmet on.

Without warning, she tore out of the garage, leaving Ryan to fumble with his helmet and chase after her.

He caught up quickly as she cruised around the corners, waiting for him to level. The gap Ryan left open on his visor let the wind whip his face. Cool and crisp. In the sims it was warm and soft. There were no settings he could change here; just man, machine and nature.

The track wasn't long. Three straights, sharp turns, two chicanes and long, sweeping corners took just over ninety seconds to complete as he relearned the track. His visor's display showed the current lap time, best time, wind speed and direction, but after the third lap, Ryan tapped a finger on the edge and turned it off.

He had no need for it. Tracks like this were designed to move away from all the technology so he could focus on racing.

Pure, simple adrenaline.

Sara increased her pace with each lap and Ryan did the same to keep up. More than once he found himself going wide around a corner and cursing into his helmet when Sara slowed for him.

It was coming back to him, the rush from racing and what he expected from the track, but she had clearly been here since their last visit, judging by how comfortable she was with the circuit.

The stands were mostly empty but for a few people who paid them little attention. Once, Ryan caught a flash of flesh as he rounded a corner but there was no chance to check again – seconds later he was gone. The next time he reached that corner, there was nothing.

"So," Sara called over the comm in their helmets. The engines made it hard to hear but after years of experience it was second nature to pick out each word. "Are you ready to tell me what's going on with you?"

Ryan's answer was to overtake his friend and streak down the straight, braking later than on previous laps, accelerating out of the sharp turn and straight into a longer corner. Sara spoke again but he wasn't listening.

Each corner was a challenge to get right and every straight a chance to brake later. It was tough on his body after a while, but the sims had prepared him well. The simulators had compensators to limit the strain put on the body from extreme g-forces and it was beginning to show that Ryan felt the effects more than his rival. He made a mental note to ride more outside the sim and train his body to handle it.

By the time he was confident enough to push, to take the tightest lines and hit the highest speeds on each lap, his time was down to just over ninety-one seconds.

"Don't ignore me, Ryan," Sara warned, but she still didn't get an answer. A few corners later: "Don't make me run you off the track."

It took another lap before he finally answered. "Let's race. Beat me and I'll tell you."

"Deal."

They cruised around the rest of the Loop and came to a stop at the starting line. Rather than using the grid slots painted on the surface, they lined up side by side against the chequered white-and-black band. Sara killed the engine and Ryan copied her.

"Ten laps," she said, lifting her visor. "First one across the line wins. Fair?"

"Fine by me."

"Good. No crying when I wipe the floor with you."

"Whatever," Ryan said, pulling his visor down and adding, "Let's get on with it."

The engines roared to life again. In front and above them were two rows of five lights. The top line lit up red and one by one the lights shut off. Ryan's breathing slowed as the lights blinked out until all were dark.

The green lights on the second row lit up. Ryan and Sara tore off into the distance.

They had raced plenty of times with others but never on their own. Sara had always been the more sensible racer but that didn't stop her taking chances when she saw a gap, usually successfully.

Ryan lost the lead after the third corner but took it back halfway around the lap. Knowing this was real made a difference. He had been thrown around in the sim plenty of times, but the safety systems and SafeNet stopped him from getting hurt. Those rules didn't apply here. Nevertheless, Ryan didn't want to lose.

Sara had beaten him more times than not, but a lot of those losses were his own fault. He was determined not to repeat the same mistakes here.

Neither were able to gain a substantial lead. From the stands, it must have looked like they were in total sync; an undercut on one corner, a tow down the straight, a daring run on the outside of another corner. He'd seen similar things happen on vids and in other races. They performed the same moves over the ten-lap race, staying within a bike's length of each other at all times. Occasionally they'd pull alongside each other and try to out-brake the other.

They knew each other too well and this wasn't a sim. Any mistake here could cause an injury to themselves or each other. Ryan's restraint surprised him but the pit in his stomach made sure he didn't do anything reckless. He was backing out of moves that normally he wouldn't have thought twice about. Being out of the sim, and on a machine with no synchro unit to stop serious crashes and collisions, made a difference.

The race was too close to call, even leading up to the home straight on the last lap.

"Spill," Sara ordered after the bikes were back in the garage and they had changed into normal clothes. "Tell me what's going on."

Guilt crashed down on Ryan's shoulders again. It must have shown on his face because Sara frowned as the silence stretched on. "Let's take a walk," she said.

He marched from the garage, his friend hot on his heels.

They walked in silence. Ryan led them back onto the main straight, stopping at the starting line and crouching down to run his hand along a black mark from his tyres. Life was so much simpler when his only worries were racing and studying. Tedious at times but he knew what to expect. Since piloting a mech, there was something missing. The race didn't provide the same adrenaline it used to.

"I don't know what Zack told you so I'll tell you everything I can. In brief," he added, before pausing and collecting his thoughts. "The morning of my last race, Enforcer agents turned up at the Institute. They wanted me to take some tests, but I turned them down."

"So I heard. And then you jumped from the balcony?"

"Basically." Ryan stood and started walking along the track as he spoke. "The race came and went. It didn't go too well."

"No kidding. Very reckless."

"Shut it. After I left the sim…" Ryan looked at the grandstands and spotted two men, one of whom turned to look at them. "Actually, I can't tell you all the details."

Instead of following the track around another corner, Ryan continued across the gravel and over the barriers. They climbed a hill on the other side, Sara listening intently.

"General Matthews told me what he was offering would be a challenge, something a track couldn't match. He was right. It was hard. But also extremely satisfying. Coo, I learned to fly! It's one of the best experiences I've had. If there's something better than racing, that's it. Sure, it was only a sim, but it felt so...free. Cyber Cycle feels real but isn't. It tricks you into thinking you're there, at a track. This was on another level completely."

"Sounds perfect for you. Something must have happened to bring you back. What was it?"

"Why didn't you take the tests?" Ryan said.

"How do you know about that?"

"The general told me, but he never said what stopped you."

"I didn't want to leave. I have a future here, my family and friends too."

"Not for much longer, maybe."

"What do you mean?"

Reaching the top of the hill, Ryan turned to look over the track. The sky was still orange – it had been since he landed at Delta Space Port – and it transformed the circuit, making it look exotic. At least from this vantage. It was a good view, so he sat on the grass. Sara took a spot next to him.

"I've seen things I never could have imagined before," he eventually answered, ignoring her question and returning to the story. "It's what made this so real. I think it felt like a game before, where there were no real consequences. Just like Cyber Cycle."

"What happened?"

Ryan told her everything he could. The Enforcer agents were likely listening to their conversation, so he avoided details and painted a scenario. He saw the confusion on her face, but she began to understand the sheer size of what he was involved in, the gravity of it all.

He told her of his plan and what it cost. Her eyes widened at the deaths.

"What happened to them?"

"What do you think? It's not like they were invited for tea and crumpets," Ryan snapped. He took a breath before continuing. "We've had no word, but they're most likely dead. There's no reason to believe otherwise."

"And you feel responsible?"

"That's a coo question! It was my plan. I fired first. Those lives are on me."

"You didn't give the order. You offered a solution and carried it out when told to do so. You're not to blame."

"That's what everyone's been saying. It doesn't help."

"But—"

"Look." Ryan raised his arm and activated his MOB-I. At the bottom was a file filled with pictures. He opened the first one then started swiping through the photographs. "These are the people left behind. Not the ones who died while the tunnel was open but the ones who couldn't make it back. This isn't survivor's guilt, Sara. It's the consequence of my plan."

"Someone else would have come up with it if you hadn't. More lives would have been lost without your quick thinking."

"Quick thinking? It was reckless. I didn't consider anything else, anyone else. I took in the situation and made a judgement call. I nearly fired straight away without calling it in. We could have held on longer and got more people through," Ryan said, switching off the MOB-I and standing. "I think I finally get what everyone's been telling me. I treat everything like a game. The consequences don't matter because no one gets hurt. I took sim racing to be the same as life. Up there was the first time my actions really mattered. I felt real fear.

"That's why I kept backing out of moves today. That's why I didn't take chances even when you offered them – I know you did it on purpose. I can't believe how coo I've been all this time. Now I'm playing catch-up, reviewing everything I've done to this point and imagining life without a sim, without the SafeNet. I'd be dead at least a dozen times over.

"Even though I was in a sim, I feared for my life. I worried about the pilots in the cockpit, but the bigger picture was already forming. They beat us. They'll do it again. I can't believe they won't keep coming. They could get close enough to meet our last line of defence any day now."

"And then what happens?"

"Unless they can stop them...we die."

"So why did you run away?"

"One person won't make a difference."

"You stupid coo!" It wasn't often Sara raised her voice, especially to him. That was more shocking than the words. "One person can make all the difference. One person saved lives in space – you. One person can rally an army with the right words, can win a race with the right pass, can save a life by asking a single question.

"Don't underestimate the power one person can have. Even if you don't believe in yourself anymore, other people do. Zack does," she continued before Ryan could interrupt. "He's been by your side for years. Have you ever wondered why? It's not because of your charming personality. He sees something in you. It's why the Institute's put up with your coo for so long. It's why you were chosen to join the Enforcers. And...it's why I've always been on your side."

The silence stretched as he searched for an answer. Ryan kept his gaze on the quiet track down the hill but could feel Sara's eyes on him.

"You don't have to be the hero or the centre of attention but if you make a difference to someone, then giving up is betraying them. Did you tell them you were leaving? I bet you didn't, other than Zack. If the fate of the world is hanging in the balance then you have no right to wallow in self-pity while people are depending on you, even if they don't know it. Billions of people need you. They matter more than your conscience. Once this is over, by all means go and lock yourself away until you find a way to deal with whatever issues you have, but don't you dare give up just because something is harder than you thought. Look at me."

Ryan was shocked to see tears streaming down her face when he finally dragged his gaze to her.

"I'm scared beyond belief at what's coming but I can't do anything about it. You can. I've been trying to keep up with you since day one; you never let anything stop you, no matter how hard or coo. Find that again...and if you can't – fake it. Let everyone around you think you can handle anything because maybe, just maybe, you'll actually be able to do it. In the end, it happens. We all screw up. Get over it and realise people are relying on you. When this all comes out, they'll be glad to have people like you protecting them. I know I am."

Faces flashed before his eyes. Not shadows and night-mares – the casualties. He had thought they were blaming him. It may have been true, but what if they were trying to stop him from running away? What if they didn't blame him at all?

There was no way to know. Maybe all that mattered was what he did now, instead of what happened before. That was a choice, not a consequence. Even thinking that way helped him shed some of the weight.

His MOB-I vibrated. A message from Jackson: *They're coming. Nineteen hours out. We're mobilising everything and everyone. We could use you.*

"What is it?" Sara asked.

Ryan didn't answer straight away. The last sentence tore him in two. He wanted to help, to be with his squad. Then again, the doubts hadn't vanished. It was another choice to make and his decision would affect thousands of lives in the short term – billions in the future. The sheer number of people involved, and Sara's words, helped his resolve.

"They need me," he muttered. "I have to go."

"About time. Even if, and I stress the if, you screw up, then do what you do best. Shrug it off. Scream it out of your system if you need to. Coo!" Sara yelled, turning to face the track. She wiped her eyes on her sleeve before continuing. "There's no magic cure to this. We all find our own way through life – the good times and the bad. You will too. Now get going. Don't waste any more time here. Go and do what you do best. When you come back, we'll talk more."

Ryan hugged her as soon as she finished. "Cha." It must have taken her by surprise, but she wrapped her arms around him. They stood there for what felt like a lifetime until he pulled away and ran down the hill.

He was making the same journey again but this time he'd be paying for it himself. Anyone tracking him must have thought he was crazy, although the Enforcer agents would probably send word of his movements. He didn't have time to pack anything; Ryan went straight for the trains. He sent a short message to Jackson and Zack on his MOB-I while running. It read, *I'm on my way.*

CHAPTER TWENTY-EIGHT

THE JOURNEY BACK TO Orbital Station Delta dragged. It was the third time he had travelled the same route in the last few months and the second time alone. Apprehension was Ryan's companion on this trip and to distract himself he thought about the reception he'd receive upon his return. Would they be angry or happy? Relieved? He'd get a lot of stick either way.

Around him, people were talking about holidays, weekend plans, health problems, finances and where to eat. It all sounded petty. No one knew the threat heading towards the Globe. No one on any of the trains he travelled on was the cause of so much death. It almost broke his resolve until he banished the thought from his mind.

Sara had done something no one else could: she'd made him realise what he had to do. *Get over it and realise people are counting on you...even if they don't know it yet.*

Not once in his life had Ryan thought people relied on him. He had gone out of his way to stop that from happening, but even with selfish intentions of meeting the ultimate sim and piloting challenge, he had become part of a cause and that mattered more than anything. That feeling of belonging helped make the decision to return easier.

When Jackson's message came through on the MOB-I that the enemy invasion fleet was closing in, Sara had done enough to convince him to go back. He hadn't dealt with the guilt, but if he did nothing, there might not be any time to deal with it at all.

The biggest regret he faced now was not making it in time.

Books, music, vids, none of it could hold his attention for long. Even sleep wasn't helpful.

Upon arriving at Delta Space Port, the officers on duty gave him strange looks as they signed him back in after only a couple of days. They asked no questions and pointed him to the hangar. The shuttle's captain, on the other hand, wasn't so reserved. Comments about not being a chauffeur and agents taking liberties floated between them, but he didn't stop Ryan from boarding.

Convincing the ship to leave immediately was harder and took a call to OSD.

Three Vangas fell into formation around the shuttle once it launched to escort it to the station. What purpose that served, Ryan didn't know. If they were attacked, one enemy mech would be enough to take out all three escorts and the shuttle. According to Jackson's latest message, they were getting ready to launch as soon as the invaders were in range. OSD's weapons would be essential in the upcoming battle, but by that point surface sensors would pick up on the situation.

Space was more dangerous but a lot calmer than the Globe would be when people found out about the invasion. Panic would set in. That would lead to chaos and who knew what would happen. In space, the enemy was obvious.

Ryan was at the door as soon as they landed on the station's hangar. He didn't wait for the steps to reach the hatch; he dropped to the deck with a roll. Zack and Mac were waiting with his uniform. It was good to see them both and he grabbed their shoulders before turning for the corridor. Mac made sure no one got in their way while Zack filled him in. He still used crutches to walk but moved much quicker than at their last meeting.

Ryan's mech was ready, and it was using the same loadout as on the last mission. Without attending the briefing, he had no idea what his squad's mission would be, but he'd adapt. Ryan hadn't told Jackson he'd arrived. Zack and Mac informed him a tech crew had come up with a way for the sensors to track the enemy mechs through their camouflage. They were working on a system to overlay the information on their screens but there was currently a two-second delay, so it wasn't active by default.

"Where are they?" Ryan said.

"The briefing will be finishing now so they'll be heading to the sims," Zack answered. "Head straight there; we'll finish preparing your mech."

"Cha, I appreciate it."

As Ryan stepped through the door into the corridor, Zack grabbed his arm. "Are you okay?"

"No, but I have my head screwed on for now. I'll deal with everything when we save the Globe." Ryan paused and smirked. "Who'd have thought we'd be doing that?"

"We'll send Miss Kinni a holocard once it's done."

"Yeah. See you soon."

One thing Ryan hadn't missed were the endless, identical corridors. The interface guided him to the nearest transporter, which took him close to the sim room. The door to the room closed as he rounded the corner and almost didn't open before he reached it. Twisting sideways, he staggered into the room to the gazes of twelve pairs of eyes.

Twelve.

"Well, this is awkward," Ryan said, breaking the silence and bringing smiles and cheers from his squad-mates. He didn't recognise the rook who'd been brought in to replace him.

"Welcome back!" Oaf roared.

"We knew you'd be back." Ricochet beamed.

"Well, at least someone here can make the hard choices," Wrecker commented. Rig nodded in agreement.

"Are you back to normal, Fall?" Toomes asked, his eyes narrowed. "We don't want wildcards on this mission."

"Actually, a wildcard might be just what we need right now," Captain Ryder said, pushing her way to the front of the group. The ice was there but her stare wasn't as harsh as he expected. She understood more than the others. "Over it?"

"Not quite. I'm not sure I'll ever be, not completely, but there's more at stake here than my feelings. I won't let you down again."

"Good enough." Turning to his replacement, she said, "Agent, I appreciate you volunteering but our squad is full. Return to your station."

"Yes, sir." The man fled through the door.

"Have you informed your tech?" Ryder asked.

"They're finishing the prep now," Ryan said with a nod. "My mech should be ready in a couple of minutes."

"Good. I think it's time we gave you a call sign. Any suggestions?"

Ryan was at a loss. He hadn't thought about a name since his first day on board OSD.

"'Wildcard' sounds good to me," Jackson said from the back. Wisp was just behind her, and both were smiling. His replacement must have been really bad. "He's a bit unpredictable, after all."

"Seconded," Bishop said.

"Done," Ryder declared. "You're now Wildcard. No more rooks in this squadron. Right, let's get to work!"

The captain gave him a small smile and took Ricochet and Sketcher to their sims after they congratulated him. Toomes shook his hand and welcomed him back. There wasn't quite a smile on his face, but it was better than anything Ryan had expected. Rig and Wrecker were much more enthusiastic.

Bishop also opted for a handshake and Oaf went for a bear hug. Ryan ducked under his arms and dived into Teach, who stopped him in his tracks. Oaf picked them both up.

Wisp and Jackson were waiting at the back and the three walked to their sims together. Wisp grabbed his shoulder, shook it gently and left the two of them alone. They stopped at Jackson's sim and she hugged him quickly.

"Welcome back, Wildcard," she said.

"That'll take some getting used to."

"Could be worse."

"Oh? What did you get?"

"'Sunshine.'"

Ryan tried, really tried, but hysteric laughter escaped. Jackson couldn't keep the grin from her face either. It was sheepish but he suspected she liked it. "Who came up with that?" he said.

"Our fearless flight leader, of course. Apparently, it's because of my bright personality, but I think it's because it's always sunny back home."

"Yeah, no one would say your personality is sunny."

"I know!" Jackson declared in feigned offence. "We'd better get ready. We'll talk more after."

"You bet."

Ryan stood before the sim pod, remembering the struggles he'd faced the last time he'd tried to get in, but there was no repeat of them this time. He scaled the rungs quickly and dropped inside the pod, changing into his uniform. It felt like putting on an old pair of shoes, if those shoes were metal braces for his feet, ankles and lower legs. The chair unfolded and the gauntlets swung around. Once all four limbs were in, he finished the power-up without missing a beat.

"Sound off," Ryder ordered.

"Flare Two, here."

"Flare Three, ready."

The process had annoyed him on the last mission, but it was nice to hear everyone together again, ready for another mission. Ryan found himself searching for the perfect response.

"Flare Ten, ready."

"Flare Eleven, standing by."

"Flare Twelve, back at last," Ryan said when his turn came, and everyone laughed. There were belly laughs from Oaf and Rig and chuckles from Wisp, Bishop and even Tombstone. A few cheers and whoops from some others. The tension dropped.

The screen activated and their hangar dominated

his vision. "Three by three," Ryder ordered. "We're bringing up the rear, so long-range weapons ready. Take the shot when you have a target. Don't wait for orders. We won't get another chance at this. Good hunting."

They marched out of the hangar in flights and by pushing off from the edge. The captain led the way, followed by Tombstone, Bishop and then Wisp. Once in open space, they activated thrusters and aimed towards a number of angular ships and miniscule dots. The enemy was still very far away.

"Flare Squadron, hold here."

Ryan's sensor showed seven hundred and twenty mechs forming a grid and over eight hundred Vanga and Vulture-class fighters – not the full force – joining them. Whether these mechs and fighters were spares or brand-new units, he didn't know, but pilots were more valuable than hardware, and trainees had been drafted in after the last mission. That was understandable, given their losses. The sea of red dots slowly approaching was enough to send butterflies fluttering around his stomach – and they got faster each second.

"I hate waiting," he complained to Wisp and Jackson. "Can't they hurry up?"

"Can we take the fight to them? They'll make it here eventually," Jackson added.

"We're close to the limit of OSD's weapons," Wisp said. "We'll need them to cut their numbers."

"Zack, a timer would be useful," Ryan said to his friend over their private comm channel.

A digital clock appeared in the corner. It showed twenty-five minutes. Waiting, again. Why was there so much waiting?

"Anyone for a game to pass the time?" Ryan asked on the squad channel.

"Quiet, Wildcard," Ryder ordered.

"Understood, Queen," Ryan said, relishing being back with the squad despite the situation they faced.

"Remind me to kick your ass when this is over."

"Noted." Ryan smirked, not that anyone could see it.

With nothing else to do and silence presiding over the comm, Ryan checked his armaments. The laser rifle, which had a scope to improve long-range accuracy, a scatter gun for close-range projectile shots, eight missiles, a beam blade and the rail gun attached to his shoulder. Unlike the last mission, there were easily identifiable targets for this weapon – the ships.

The rail gun used power from the mech's plasma core, while the beam blade used a much smaller version of the same system. If used for too long, the blade would become useless. The rifle had four power packs that recharged from the power system when not in use. Only the scatter gun and missiles had a limited ammo supply. There were no reloads for the missiles, but the gun could be reloaded with six shots ten times by storing it again. Not ideal, but there was no changing it.

Every minute brought the invaders closer but they still looked tiny. Only the sensor sphere showed how much closer they were.

"Is now a good time to ask what happened to you, Zack? Why you were kept in isolation for so long?" Ryan said.

"No."

"Are you going to tell me anyway?"

"No."

"I've been worried about you. Come on, spill. Stop me from going crazy here."

"They gave me an implant to help with managing the mech," Zack said, and Ryan could imagine the exasperation on his face as he spoke. "All techs have it."

"We didn't take weeks to recover from the MOB-I."

"My body rejected it and started shutting down. On top of that, I caught an infection while my immune system was compromised. In the most sterile facility on the station. Don't say it," he added before Ryan could make his traditional smart-arse comment. "They tried a different implant and that seems to work. It takes some getting used to."

"Sure, but it'll be useful – even beyond working on the mechs."

"Did you miss me?"

"They wouldn't tell me what was going on."

"There's a good reason for that."

"What?"

"If you knew I was in a bad condition, what would you have done?" Zack didn't wait for the answers Ryan was already thinking up. "Don't lie. You'd have spent your time trying to help me. Getting in the way of people who know better. Your own training would have suffered. Not telling you was the lesser evil. Matthews knew that. He needed you to stay focused."

Ryan had no comeback. They hadn't told Zack the lengths he'd gone to to find out. He replied with, "I'm glad you're on your feet again."

"Barely. Mac's been a big help. Hold on, we've got some work to do before the enemy arrives."

The comm fell quiet and Ryan stood in near darkness. Still waiting. He made a promise that if he was ever in charge of anything, waiting would be abolished. It was unbearable. No one should endure this. How everyone passed the time and kept quiet was beyond him.

"Look sharp," Ryder snapped. "Start your recon. The more intel we gather, the better."

Raising the rifle, he used the scope to zoom in on the enemy fleet. Visually, there was little Ryan could make out, but the sensors logged everything and transmitted it to OSD. Zack and Mac would forward it to the analysts, who would provide any useful information. Ryan wasn't holding his breath.

A beam of light appeared above the line of mechs, aimed at the enemy fleet. It illuminated the area and, looking through his scope again, Ryan could make out more detail. Combined with the improved sensors, this would make the enemy mechs easier to see and attack. No one else showed any sign of surprise so it must have been included in Ryder's briefing.

The swarm, for lack of a better term, stretched from end-to-end of his screen but they were still out of firing range. A line of static crossed the display and Ryan's heart skipped a beat. It vanished and he sighed.

Then it happened again. The third time, his screen cut out completely and his controls died. He was left in darkness. The comm wasn't working either.

Using his MOB-I, he sent a message to Zack. Five seconds later, the reply flashed over his arm. *They jammed us again. Nothing we can do. On my way.*

Ryan was glad no one could see him as he struggled to free himself in the dark. Eventually he managed to get loose and climb the rungs to the top of the sim with only the light from his MOB-I to light the way. When the hatch popped, it was blindingly bright, and he emerged to madness.

CHAPTER TWENTY-NINE

"What happened?" Ryan asked as his head escaped the sim.

"Damn it! How are we supposed to fight like this?" Sketcher yelled.

"What do we do now?" Oaf.

"Where's the captain?" Rig.

"She's on her way to the CC with the lieutenant," Bishop said. "She'll relay instructions when she has them."

"So, we're just supposed to wait?" Jackson.

"This is coo!" Rig again.

Zack hopped into the room as fast as the crutches let him. He wore leg braces to help give him more strength, too. "The fix didn't hold. They altered the jamming signal."

"Coo. What's the plan?"

Zack shrugged. The squad were heading to a screen at the end of the room. As they followed there was a shudder through the station. The lights went out for a few seconds and another tremor knocked Zack into the nearest wall, where he bounced off it and to the ground. Ryan picked his friend up from the floor and helped steady him on his crutches.

For an impact to reach them like that, it had to be something big. "I need you to find out what's happened to the mechs. Whatever it takes, just get me an update," Ryan whispered.

Without waiting for a reply, Ryan joined the rest of his squad at the screen. It was split into two sections: one with text updates of the situation and the other a sensor scan of the station and surrounding space. Advanced enemy forces had already reached them and were targeting their defences. They could move quickly when the occasion called for it. Vangas were engaging enemy mechs to try to slow them down.

There was no mention of what the mech pilots should do.

For the second time, Ryan feared for his life. The shudders were a real indication OSD wasn't a safe haven and that opened his eyes to a whole new reality.

The invaders were closing in by the second and there was nothing he could do about it. He was a pilot. He couldn't even jump in a fighter because there were better pilots available.

The silence in the room was broken by another shudder through OSD and Ryan looked at his squad. Ryder and Tombstone were nowhere to be seen. Bishop was in charge when both were gone but even he was at a loss. Everyone wore the same fear he felt on their faces.

He placed a hand on Ricochet's shoulder and gave a small smile. Before he could say anything, Zack appeared and tapped him on the shoulder. The two walked away to speak.

"What did you find?" Ryan asked quietly.

"Out of the twelve mechs, six have been completely destroyed. Another three are damaged but could still work. Maybe. The last three suffered minor damage but the fighters were more of a threat by then. They stopped targeting the mechs when they realised the jamming signal worked. It seems to be the same across the board but it's not been confirmed yet."

"Which three suffered the least damage?"

"Ten, eleven, twelve."

"Wisp, Jackson and me..." Ryan muttered. "We have longer range weapons than the rest. Are the weapons still—"

"Ready. If we could break the signal again, we could use them."

"Any ideas on how to do that?"

"None. Anything would take too long to implement." Zack shrugged. "We need another option."

Ryan looked at his squad, then the black sim pods. "The controls we use in the sims...they're replicas of the control units in the mechs." Zack nodded and his eyes narrowed as he tried to figure out what Ryan was thinking. "The settings we've put in are applied to the mechs themselves...so if we could get to them, we'd be able to pilot them exactly the same, right?"

"In theory, yes..."

"So rather than try to break through their jamming signal, what if we tried to get to the mechs and pilot them manually?"

"Do you realise how coo that is?" Zack asked, his eyes wide. "You could die!"

"We'll all die here, on this station, if we do nothing. I'd rather die fighting than waiting for death to come." Ryan saw another stream of blue dots leave the station from the map on the screen. "Head to the closest hangar and stop them from launching any more fighters. We need at least six, but more would be better."

"What if they don't listen?"

"Say it's on Ryder's authority. That should stop them from launching until the orders come down. Take Jackson and Wisp and explain on the way. I'm sure they'll agree, so have them geared up and ready to go by the time I get there."

"What are you going to do?"

"Get authorisation."

Without waiting, Ryan left the sim room and was instantly pushed against the wall by a line of passing agents. Normally he would have strong words for them, but they had orders to follow and he had a plan to put into action.

The nearest terminal was a mess of blinking lights, impossible to use. Even voice commands weren't working. The second was being used by another officer, directing people to their assigned stations. With the third, he was able to track Ryder to the Command Centre. Ryan didn't have the authorisation to reach that level on his own and it took a few moments for anyone to answer his call.

"What is it?" an officer answered.

"I need to speak to Captain Ryder."

"She's with General Matthews and the other—"

"I don't care if she's with the president. I need to speak to her. Now."

The screen turned black and just as he was about to try again, Ryder's face appeared.

"What is it, Fall? We're busy," Ryder said, turning from the display to whoever else she was with and back again every few seconds.

"I noticed. I have an idea."

"One the strategists haven't had?"

"Let me explain and—" Ryan started to say, before the captain cut him off.

"I appreciate the effort but it's in hand. Go back and wait with the rest of the squad."

"There's no time to—"

"Agreed, so let us get back to it. Our top minds are on it."

"This is why I was brought in, isn't it?" Ryan yelled before she could close the channel. "I don't think like you. If you're not interested, I'll go back to the sim room and wait for their mechs to punch holes in the hull; or you can get off your high horse and let me come up there."

"Fine," Ryder sighed. "I'll authorise your code to reach the CC but don't waste our time."

All the transporters were busy as people tried to get to their destinations. After waiting a few minutes, he pulled rank on some agents. Ryan half-expected them to laugh him away but they let him through. He selected the CC, and his access code took him to the heart of the station.

The doors opened to overwhelming activity. People ran around the room, moving from level to level, screen to screen, connecting wires for makeshift repairs and yelling over each other. In the middle, a hologram of the station and enemy units showed much more accurate information than the screen in the sim room.

Ryder met him at the door and led him to the inner ring, where Matthews stood with other captains and colonels. "What's your idea, Fall?" she asked, and they all turned to him.

"I spoke to Zack and he reported three of our mechs are still operational and fully armed. When their jamming signal worked, they weren't considered a threat, we think, and the Vangas drew their attention. We can use them to fight back."

"Have you got a fix for the sims?" Matthews asked.

"No, sir, and even if we had, it would take too long to set up. The mech control units are intact and we can pilot them just like we do in the sims...if we can get there," Ryan said, his voice trailing off towards the end.

"You're saying we can get some pilots to them and attack the enemy from behind?" Ryder said quietly. "We can pincer them between the mechs, the station's defences and our fighters. It's coo but they won't be expecting it."

"Good, get the three best mech pilots ready to—" Matthews said.

"That won't work," Ryan cut in, and winced at the glare Ryder shot him. "The mechs are calibrated for each pilot. It would take too long for anyone else to get to grips with them and we don't have that time. It has to be my flight that goes. We have the best chance of making an impact quickly." He turned to Ryder and said, "I've already sent Zack down to a hangar to keep some fighters for us. They should be ready to go by the time I get there. We need an escort to our mechs. We'll evac the fighters and reactivate the mechs before they can react. The weapons are primed and can take some of the heat off the station."

"Agreed," Matthews said, before turning to an aide. "Get word to every mech captain and have them find out the status of their mechs. If there are other usable units out there, I want to know, and I want pilots ready to go. If they have trouble, have them contact Wendall."

"General, we need the Vangas to defend the station, not fly out on a suicide mission!" Ryan didn't know her name, but she was in charge of the fighters and their pilots on board the station. She didn't like the plan but this was bigger than one person. He was finally starting to understand what Ryder, Matthews and Sara had told him since the last mission and his captain realised it.

"Colonel Granya, make sure all our pilots on OSD are briefed and ready to go at a moment's notice. They may be on escort duty. The pilots out there already will focus on the defence of the station."

"Yes, sir." The woman moved to the nearest terminal and began giving orders to her pilots.

"Captain Ryder, find Wendall and ships that can be used to escort these three to their mechs."

"Yes, sir." There was no salute; she just turned and ran to the transporter.

"Sir, there's something else," Ryan said, and when Matthews didn't shut him down, he continued. "I don't think we should just focus on defence. We can help take some of the pressure off you from that distance, but I think our goal should be to stop their advance."

"We're the last line of defence between them and Earth. If we don't stop them, who knows what they'll do. The defence of this station is your priority."

As if to emphasise his point, another shudder ran through the station. It knocked people to the floor, Ryan included, and the lights flickered again. Matthews offered his hand, and he didn't think twice about taking it.

"I understand," Ryan said, "but even if we clear the attacking forces now there's no guarantee we can stop them forever. They'll just send reinforcements. We need to find another way. If some of the fighters come and give us some cover, we can get close enough to do some serious damage. It may buy us more time. Sir," he added quickly.

"That's probably a one-way trip for everyone who goes," Matthews concluded, "and you're not an agent – can you handle this?"

"I don't see that we have a choice. I can't say the same for Wisp or Jackson but if they're not up for it, they can defend the station instead. I think it's worth the risk."

"Very well. We'll try and find some support if there are enough mechs to form a defence. This is volunteer only." He sighed when no one else objected. "Good luck."

Without waiting, Ryan ran for the transporter, activating his MOB-I and opening a line to Zack. "Which hangar are you in?"

"B-9-3."

"On my way." He entered the destination and enjoyed a few seconds of calm before the doors opened.

The hangar was worse than the CC. Pilots in grey flight suits were in constant motion, moving from ship to ship as they performed the necessary checks, occasionally running into mechanics and techs in their grease-stained orange overalls. The latter group seemed to be moving about at random between shuttles, fighters and a few damaged mechs, taking parts from some and attaching them to others. Fuel lines crossed over each other in a maze of pipes, against regulations, but no one cared.

At the far end of the hangar, the doors had been closed to prevent anyone, or anything, boarding the station. In the middle of the room stood eight fighters everyone avoided. The V-shaped Vangas must be for his group, and Ryan tried to make his way through the crowd.

It proved difficult. Everyone had their jobs and didn't care about anyone else. He pushed through a sea of black and orange, trying to reach the cluster of ships.

More than once he was knocked about like a ping-pong ball, but after a slow and arduous journey, Ryan reached the eye of the storm. Jackson and Wisp were talking to Zack, already wearing flight suits and holding helmets. At their feet were three cases. They waved him over with grim faces.

A small distance away, four other pilots gathered around a fifth. They had helmets on and were being briefed over comm, and Ryan had nothing helpful to offer. There was a chance none of them would make it back from this.

"Ready?" Ryan asked his flight. They nodded. "Good, I'll get changed and be back in a sec. Zack?"

There was no chance to talk as they made their way through the crowd to the locker room. More than a couple of elbows connected as people pushed their way to the next ship they were trying to reach.

When they arrived, Zack pointed to a bag on a bench and Ryan pulled out his flight suit. He started getting changed and asked, "Jackson and Wisp know what's going on?"

"They know you're going for the mechs. Not even I know what you plan to do after that."

"And the pilots?"

"The same. When their captain turned up, they huddled. I've not spoken to them since. The fighters are ready, too." Zack paused before asking, "Are you sure about this? It's reckless. Even for you."

"Have you got another idea?"

Zack shook his head.

"Neither does anyone else. We have to do this now, while we can."

The grey flight suit was as uncomfortable as he remembered. It was the right size but it felt strange, probably because he still wasn't used to wearing one. It would become airtight when the helmet attached and contained a thirty-minute air supply in case of emergency evacuation in space. In theory, that was long enough for a rescue shuttle to arrive, but there were no guarantees. In the sims, mech pilots had their own uniforms, but he had never checked if they protected pilots against a vacuum.

Ryan led the way back. In flight gear he was given more space than he would have in his mech uniform. No one wanted to get in the way of a pilot.

"Sunshine, Wisp," Ryan called as he returned to the group of Vangas. "Zack's told you we're going for the mechs. Our three units are ready to go. When activated, we'll use the first few moments to take out some of the enemy units attacking OSD before they can react. After that there are two missions. The first is to defend this station. The second is to strike at their heart and stop the advance. If we can't stop them completely, we can buy some time for the others to recover and repair their mechs and organise a better defence. I can't make this decision for you – even Matthews said the second option sounds like a one-way trip – so it's a volunteer mission. We can't bail out of either option when we start but I need to know now."

"You're going to attack them, right?" Jackson asked.

Ryan nodded.

"Then we're coming with you."

Wisp nodded his agreement.

"Okay, go get ready. We'll operate on our flight's comm channel."

"Hold up," Zack said, before they could put on their helmets. "In these cases, there are power cells for the control units – use them to run a cold start. That will bring the controls online in seconds. Replace the cells and disable the remote link first. That way you won't have to power up to do it and lose your element of surprise."

Both Wisp and Jackson picked up a case and climbed the ladders to their fighters to begin their pre-flight checks while Ryan walked to the pilots. "Have you been briefed?"

"Yes. The general has given us orders to protect you at all costs," the captain responded, her voice muffled.

"Good, we launch soon. We'll be on our flight's channel. We'll relay the code for you to use Flare Squadron's channel before launch. Thanks for your help."

As the pilots climbed their ladders, Zack grabbed Ryan's arm and spun him around. "I don't want to have to explain to Sara why you didn't come back."

Ryan laughed. "Don't worry; I wouldn't put anyone through that."

They looked at each other for a second before hugging. "Don't die," Zack said as they separated.

After climbing into the cockpit, he dropped the case at his feet and put his helmet on. A control on the inside of his left wrist attached the collar of his flight suit to the helmet and his breath caught until the oxygen supply kicked in. To his left, a small tube was inserted into the bottom of his helmet. He strapped and plugged in.

There wasn't much room to move around but the tube extended as far as he could pull it.

A pointless exercise. It had been tested countless times, but it made him feel better.

Another button on his wrist opened the comm system in his flight suit and matched it to the ship. There was already someone waiting for him.

"Fall, are you there?" Matthews.

"Wildcard here. Go ahead."

"We've found another nine mechs so far that have drifted closer to the station. Their pilots are gearing up now. Has your team decided on a mission?"

"We're going after them."

"I'll relay that to the other teams and have them return to the station. Don't waste the element of surprise by defending us. If you time your attack right, you'll do a lot more damage and have a better chance of success."

"Understood."

"We'll launch both groups at the same time. You'll have a couple of minutes to prepare yourself. What channel are you on?"

"The pilots will be on Flare Squad's channel and I'll monitor that. The three of us are on Flight Four's channel. I'll send the code now." Ryan punched the details into the system.

"Received. We'll keep locating mechs and sending pilots. If possible, you'll get reinforcements. Good luck."

"Thank you, sir." Ryan switched to both channels the pilots were using. "Listen up. Another team is launching at the same time with nine mech pilots. Ignore them. They'll be focused on defending the station so when we reach the mechs do not power up. Surprise is our best option here. As soon as we get the signal, we launch. Be ready."

He received clicks in response. The engines were warm and ready to go when the time came. Jackson was on his left and Wisp his right. There was a fighter on each side, two ahead and one behind.

Ryan's mind wandered. He had been lucky enough to return home before this battle. No one else on OSD had been given that chance and being able to see Sara again had helped him find his resolve.

He might never see her again.

There were a lot of things Ryan wanted to change once this was over. The whole experience had opened his eyes; he wasn't the same reckless Cyber Cycle racer from a couple of months ago. Despite that, he was about to go through something else that could change everything.

"If I make it out of this, there'll be no more running," he promised himself. "Thanks, Sara."

Ryan tapped another control on his wrist and his visor darkened. The visor lit up with information about his fighter's condition, the flight suit's data and more. A waypoint had already been set for them and it appeared as a blue cross to the right of his vision. Directly ahead were the crosshairs. These were only visible while the overlay was active and wouldn't move unless he changed the focus of his weapons manually. It was a good system, and the helmet's visor acted as a backup if it became damaged. Ryder had told him it had happened before.

The hangar doors opened slowly. The guiding lights changed to green and he fired up the rest of his fighter's systems at the same time as everyone else.

He opened the comm to both channels. "Let's go."

CHAPTER THIRTY

THE FIVE VANGA PILOTS proved to be quicker than their mech counterparts and waited for them outside the hangar. Once all eight regrouped they set off together, Ryan's flight in the middle.

His sensors showed the other team launching and heading away from them and the station, putting plenty of distance between the groups.

The fighter captain led them on a course for their target. It displayed on Ryan's canopy overlay as a series of blue dashes to a waypoint. A few seconds of being in open space and they accelerated to full speed. Ryan was pressed back into his seat and dialled up the compensator to reduce the strain. He was used to sims and mechs with a different centre of gravity. It was a strange feeling, but still familiar from his training exercises with Ash.

Enemy mechs were engaging the fighters defending the station but most were launching long-range ballistic weapons as they approached. Every so often a warning would flash, alerting him of a collision, but the station's defensive weapons picked them off before they got close. Judging by the shudders on the station and the black marks and holes in the hull, some made it through.

The fighters' weapons took longer to break through the mechs' armour, often requiring concentrated fire.

The few that made contact often were struggling to keep up.

The route the captain picked took them around the station and away from the battle. It would take longer but they would reach the mechs without incident. The main force of invaders would reach them about five minutes later.

It wasn't long, but it was all they had.

Circling OSD, Ryan got a clear look at the extent of the damage. Some sections were clear and others in ruins, with some outer sections exposed to space. A number of hangars had been hit. Bodies, ships and debris floated around the station. Wreckage from the hull was a medley of panels, girders and twisted scrap – some pieces the size of his hand while others were closer to a shuttle. If the enemy forces got too close and created more flotsam, it would be harder to manoeuvre. Rescue shuttles and salvage ships were working hard to clear the surrounding space, but more debris appeared faster than they could remove it.

The first half of the journey proved uneventful. They took a wide, looping path around the battlefield and avoided the enemy forces. Ryan suggested they dim the lights and keep their engines pointed away from the battle where possible. It probably wasn't necessary, but he felt better doing so.

An alarm wailed, and the red collision light flashed. The same was happening in the other fighters too. They had been spotted.

"Target lock!" one of the escort pilots yelled out.

"Incoming enemy mechs," another called.

"Escort Three, Four and Five," the captain called. Ryan still couldn't place their name. "Break and intercept. Don't let them get close. The rest of you, stay on our tail."

"Acknowledged," Wisp answered.

Three of their escorts swerved to engage the incoming attackers. The sensors showed five enemy mechs had split from the attack force, heading in their direction. Their ballistic attacks were slow to fire but laser blasts would start in a matter of seconds. All the missiles were destroyed by blue lances from the fighters.

Not long after, the three fighters were exchanging fire with the mechs. Their pursuit slowed as they targeted the immediate threats, but the fighters were too quick. The mechs weren't able to keep up with their speed.

One pilot cried out as a mech grabbed one wing and a partner hooked the other side. They pulled it apart. The ship erupted in a ball of flame but the other two fighters kept firing. One shot broke through the armour and hit an arm joint.

Ryan soon lost track of what was going on. They were getting close.

"Approaching the mechs," he called out over both channels. "Reducing speed and preparing to evac."

All three mechs were floating and Ryan slowed to drift alongside his unit, spinning the fighter and orienting himself so the mech was above him. He pulled the oxygen tube from his helmet and waited until his visor's display showed a seal lock. Releasing his harness, Ryan unlocked the hatch and pushed up. Grabbing the case Zack had given him, he kicked against the seat and dived towards his mech.

He hit the body and clung to it desperately until he calmed down enough to crawl up to the head and open the hatch at the back of the neck.

Ryan pulled it closed behind him and guided himself down the tube using the rungs. With no gravity, it was harder than he expected. The control unit was dark, with only a few blinking lights indicating the machine was active. They were the remote-control interfaces. The rest of the controls were dead.

He found the battery at the base of the main console and replaced it with the new one easily. Ryan's hands glided across the controls and switches as he disabled the link and performed a cold start. Flipping the two above him brought the lights on and air was pumped into the unit. He took off his helmet and stowed it under a floor panel along with the old battery and case before turning to look at the control system.

It was exactly the same as the sim, just as he remembered from his stints inside the mech at the beginning of his training and the sound configuration with Mac.

Ryan sat and locked his legs into the frames. Once secured, the chair pushed him into a standing position and the arm gauntlets swung around. He got his right arm in place but the left he kept free to finish the power up when the time came.

One key difference was that the mech accepted voice commands while the sim couldn't. It was a feature he had known about since training but never had the opportunity to use. It could be useful.

"Wisp, Sunshine, are you in?" he called over the comm, bringing up the holographic display of his mech's status on the right and the sensor sphere on his left. The grey dots were other mechs, all deactivated, and their abandoned fighters. The green dots were the remaining escort fighters, but three of the enemy mechs were still heading towards them – red dots.

"I'm in," Jackson replied. "All systems ready. Waiting for orders."

"Same," Wisp added.

"Okay. Continue playing dead and keep an eye on your sensors. We'll only get one shot at this."

His squadmates clicked their comms instead of speaking further. Ryan heard how nervous they were through that conversation, and he couldn't blame them. So was he.

Ryan switched channels to speak to the captain. "Escort Leader. Three mechs incoming. Can you stop them? If we power up, we lose our element of surprise."

A single click came over the radio and the two fighters peeled off to engage the enemy units. It occurred to Ryan that there was a good chance they wouldn't come back, and the thought made him feel queasy. He never wanted to be responsible for any lives.

He couldn't see the action clearly with his sensor sphere – and even if his screen was active, he was pointing the wrong way.

One red dot disappeared from the sensor and a second followed. A green dot got too close to the remaining mech and blinked out. The last green dot was coming from behind the enemy mech and its red dot vanished too.

"Target lock!" Ryan called out to the pilot as his collision alarm sounded and red lights flashed. "What is it?"

"The last mech launched a missile before I could take it down," she responded sharply. "I can't get a clear shot without risking hitting you. I'm trying to intercept."

"Wildcard, we can power up and take it out," Wisp suggested.

"No! Don't power up. If it hits, the explosion may knock you around a bit, but don't make a move until they're right on top of us. We need this to work."

The red arrow representing the missile closed in quickly, followed by the green dot. It was gaining but he wasn't sure there'd be enough time for it to turn and shoot.

The timer showed ten seconds. He reached for the comm system again. "Escort Leader, pull back."

Eight seconds.

"Negative. I can stop it."

Six seconds.

"Don't be coo, you're too close to escape the blast."

Three seconds.

"Fall, shut u—"

The explosion rocked his mech and sent him spinning. It was then he recognised the voice. The realisation made him numb and he was about to call out but stopped himself. Jackson and Wisp were listening. They didn't need the distraction.

"Escort Leader," he called. The sensor showed the green dots of his mech and his companions as their three fighters, grey dots, drifted away. "Escort Leader, do you copy? Captain Ryder?"

Nothing. Ryan closed his eyes and focused on breathing. He needed to be calm for what was to come. There were lives depending on them.

"I'm here. Evac'd the fighter...before impact," Ryder said slowly, her breathing laboured. "Drifting away from...you, but my air supply is...intact."

"You're coo!"

"I'm taking...lessons from you."

"Are you okay? Any injuries?" Ryan asked.

"Hard to say. Everything hurts. I'm pretty sure my head is...spinning but...so is the rest of me..."

"Hang on, I'm coming to get you."

"Stay put! You need to...surprise them. You're not the...only one on a mission."

"I can't just leave you out there."

"You can and you...will," Ryder said, still speaking slowly. "It's why I...didn't tell you it was me...because I knew you'd do something coo. How long until...power up?"

"Three minutes."

"Okay. Give them hell from me, Fall. Give them... hell." She closed the line.

Ryan slammed his fist against the wall behind him in frustration. He was responsible for four deaths so far and there were three more, as well as his own, that were going to be added to the list before this was over. He was missing four names and might never find out who they were.

It wasn't long before his sensor showed a sea of red dots approaching. Most of them were mechs but there were hundreds of ships of various sizes holding more mechs waiting to launch. Towards the back was the target. It still showed as a dot in the sphere, but it was huge; bigger than OSD and the main driving force of the fleet. Whether it held soldiers, supplies or something else, he theorised it was the pin holding their fleet together. *Stop it and save the Globe.*

The other two mechs were waiting for his signal. There was no guarantee the enemy wouldn't destroy them as they passed but their best chance was to risk it and get behind them before opening fire.

That would sentence the captain to death. They had a few minutes before the advancing fleet would be in range and he found his hand hovering over the remaining power switches. If he was quick, Ryan could get her to one of the remaining fighters. She could get to safety, or at least have a chance.

Doing so would reduce their chances of success and increase the likelihood that they would die. Over the last week, Ryan had been the cause of so many deaths. Those, apparently, weren't on his head, but these were.

Both options were risky and either could be the wrong call. It didn't help him decide. He was used to simple decisions, choosing right or left. That didn't apply here.

CHAPTER THIRTY-ONE

THE INVADERS DREW CLOSER. Ryan had to make a decision soon or it would be made for him, and that would be worse than making the wrong choice. Having control meant something to him; it was why he raced – at least his choices, successes and failures were his own.

If he didn't make the choice and the situation turned out worse than if he had chosen an option, he couldn't own it. That drove him to act.

Ryan's hands flew across the console as he finished the power up. It never occurred to him to tell Jackson and Wisp. They'd be watching the sensors, notice the activation and either follow suit or wait, playing dead until the enemy passed by. There was only one thing on his mind. He wasn't going to let someone else die if he could prevent it, even if it brought his own life to an end.

Ryan tested both gauntlets, checking their movement and flexibility before flipping the final switch and bringing the mech to life.

"Easy, easy," Ryan murmured as the screen came to life. His left hand darted to the console again and found the captain. She was drifting away but still in range. "Okay, let's go."

He pushed with his feet; the thrusters fired and he began to move. A quick burst from the left elbow thruster helped him spin into position before the other stopped him. He reached the floating body, swung his legs around and fired again until he stopped and scooped her into his hands.

"Escort Leader, do you copy?" No answer. He turned for one of the abandoned fighters. "Escort Leader, wake up!"

"I'm here…what are you doing?"

"Getting you to safety. Hold on, I'm going to take you to one of our fighters. Get in and set a course for OSD. Keep comm traffic down until you're close and they'll help you in."

"You're sacrificing the mission…"

"That's an order, damn it. This is our mission, and you will follow my orders. Clear?"

"Yes."

"Good. Brace yourself."

Ryan fired the thrusters again, keeping his speed as low as possible with his mech's hands wrapped around her. It felt like an age before they reached the fighter and his eyes kept darting to the sensor sphere on his left. The swarm kept coming. They were still out of weapons range, but it wouldn't be long.

Reaching the Vanga, he slowed until he matched its speed and alignment before opening his hands.

"I'm going to push you to the fighter. Don't hesitate," Ryan said to her as he ran calculations through the mech's computer. He nudged the pilot away. She hit the open canopy hard. Ryan winced, but she clung to it like her life depended on it and clawed her way inside. When the canopy closed, he turned to face the invaders.

There was still eighty seconds before his weapons would be in range. Both Wisp and Jackson had powered up and took positions on either side of him, but not close enough for an explosion from one unit to damage the others.

"Escort Leader's engines have fired. She's heading back to OSD," Wisp said.

"Okay, let's focus. We've made this harder on ourselves. Weapons status?" Ryan asked. He ran through a check of his mech's arsenal; the rifle packs and beam blade were fully charged, the scatter gun and missiles loaded, the rail gun at full power. "All ready here," he reported.

"All green," Jackson responded.

"Weapons ready," Wisp confirmed.

"Arm rail guns and lock on to this target. Wait for my signal."

The rail guns were some of the most powerful weapons they had available. No armour could withstand a sustained burst, but they used a large amount of power and the heat they gave off made them useless in the atmosphere after the first shot. Some mechs fitted stronger ballistic weapons, but with a limited supply of projectiles the launchers became dead weight once empty – and they could be intercepted.

Flare Squadron were equipped with mostly laser weapons. They lacked some of the destructive power ballistic options offered but they were lighter and faster. Considering the squad was mostly civilians – racers and sim experts – it made sense to remove as many restrictions as possible.

The shoulder missiles and scatter gun were the only projectile weapons he had, and it was the same for his team. They were medium- and short-range weapons but were helpful in taking on multiple enemies.

"Enemy mechs entering range," Jackson reported. "The sensor upgrades are detecting each unit now. Most are launching from the large ship at the rear but some of the smaller ones are launching them too."

"Coo," Wisp murmured. "Look at them all. Even if we had all our mechs with us, that's still, what? A lot to one?"

"That's not including the ones attacking OSD, any they have in reserve or if they have any fighters," Jackson added with a slight tremble to her voice.

"Our mechs can take a beating compared to theirs – that counts for something. Their armour is weaker, and if we had the defensive mechs we'd be able to take even more heat," Ryan answered, trying to boost their spirits. "It doesn't matter now; we'll do what we can. Our target is the big ship at the back and our rail guns will cut a path so we can get close. Move as soon as the blast ends. Don't wait."

Two clicks answered.

Ryan turned his attention to the sensor sphere to make sense of what he was seeing. A sea of red dots spread out ahead of the ships. They were forming a net to stop any escape attempt.

With thirty seconds until their rail guns could reach the ship at the rear, he activated the weapon from his console. The rail gun released from its position on the mech's back and rose up to settle on his right shoulder. The crosshairs on the screen turned yellow to indicate the parameters were loaded and the barrel had finished extending. It was ready to fire.

"Okay, Wildcard. Ready?" Ryan asked himself. Being in the machine made it feel more like an extension of himself rather than a piece of hardware. Even though his flight was with him, he felt alone. Surrounded by metal with an enemy fleet bearing down, it would be easy to get disheartened, to give up.

There was no way for him to know if this was normal or not, given it was his first time on the front line, and it wasn't the time to ask.

"If we make it through this, I'm going to look at installing some kind of AI for you. It'd be a good way to pass the time," he mused. Over the comm, he said, "Five seconds. Four. Three. Two. One. Fire!"

Ryan squeezed both trigger fingers and felt a shudder as the rail gun fired. The engines kicked in automatically to stop the mech moving backwards. The beam could last for up to seven seconds if he wanted it to, and he did.

His screen lit up from the top right with a bright green lance tearing through the enemy mechs until it reached the target and broke through the outer hull. Jackson and Wisp both fired at the same time; the three blasts converged on the same point.

When the beams ended, Ryan could see a cascade of explosions from where the laser had hit targets in the way. Debris, metal limbs and dead mechs floated along with parts of smaller ships they had made contact with, but the enemy were already regrouping.

Ryan's engines kicked in as he pushed down with his toes and raced for the hole. He deactivated the weapon and it locked into position on his back. It would take time before it recharged enough to use again, even for a short blast. He swapped the laser rifle into his left hand and drew the beam blade with his right.

"Don't stop for anything," he commed. "Remember, their armour's weakest at the joints so just slow them down for now. The big one is our target."

Ryan didn't hear any clicks of acknowledgement; he focused on his first target. Using his left hand lowered his accuracy with the rifle but enough shots hit to do some damage. When he got close enough, he slung the rifle into its slot on his back and drew the scatter gun.

He fired a shot, which split into six smaller projectiles. Half hit the body of his target, two hit an arm – but it was enough to spin it around. The last one missed.

Another approached and he swung his right arm across, squeezing his right trigger finger to activate the pulsing white blade. He wasn't close enough to slice straight through the mech but it cut into the outer armour and slowed it down.

Most mechs he attacked with the beam blade, saving his shots for tough spots – there was little time to reload. He could bury the blade into their mechs with enough time and force, but instead he followed his own advice and went for joints and limbs.

Ryan wasn't concerned about cutting them off, just damaging them to remove the immediate threat. That didn't stop projectile and laser strikes being aimed at him, as well as a few tentacles and blades, which slowed him down.

Enemy attacks were weaker than his but already the damage was mounting. With this progress, they should make it through before anything serious registered, unless a stronger projectile made contact or a blade got close enough to cut through before that.

The sheer number of them made that very likely. If enough swarmed him, or the metal tentacles got a firm grip, there wouldn't be much he could do other than try to cut them off – and in that time more would close in. A quick glance at his mech's status showed he was fine for the moment.

The silence was getting to him as he pushed through. There was no comm chatter this time, no curses or warnings. All he could hear were the arm and leg controls as they responded to his movements and they were surprisingly quiet. Every so often he'd hear a noise from elsewhere in the mech but didn't let it distract him. The programme he and Mac had worked on had been installed in the sims but not the mech itself. He was condemned to silence on this mission.

There was no end to the mechs in his way. They filled the gaps quickly to stop him ploughing through. Progress was slow and more than once a group of mechs surrounded him or flew into his path and he was forced to stop and dispatch them.

That was where the scatter gun proved its worth. One shot hit multiple targets and gave Ryan time to focus on the dangerous units. There were punches thrown and kicks landed, occasionally aided by the joint thrusters for extra power. His beam blade was working overtime and each time it made contact it drained a little energy. It was down to half power already and he'd need to let it recharge soon. After dispatching another group, he had only two shots left in the scatter gun.

Ryan saw on his status sphere that his armour was weakening. What'd started as a green three-dimensional model of his mech was turning yellow, with a few orange patches on his front armour and right arm. It wasn't enough to concern him yet, but he couldn't go on like that.

"Wisp, Sunshine," he said between swings of his beam blade. "What's your status?"

"I think they've caught on to what we're doing—"

"Or at least where we're going," Jackson cut in.

"They're just throwing themselves in front of us to slow us down and let loose a barrage. Have you noticed they keep hitting their own units too?"

Ryan hadn't, but as he looked it was obvious. "Why? They have us outnumbered."

"The rail guns have sent them into a bit of a panic," Wisp answered.

"Keep going. I'm recharging my weapons and putting more power into the engines. Take a longer route if you have to but we can't waste any more time. They're getting closer to the station each second."

He heard the clicks just before an impact threw him against his harness. There was debris floating around but no alarms ringing, and his sensor showed only one area had changed to red – directly on his back.

Ryan deactivated the beam blade and slid the hilt into the slot in his right leg. The scatter gun flipped into a vertical state and filled a slot in his left leg, where it would also reload. He flipped a few switches and kicked hard.

While moving, he increased the compensator and the pressure on his body dropped drastically. The sims should have provided a real experience but the pressure on his body was huge and it was possible the environment hadn't been precisely replicated, or he had never pushed this hard during training.

"Plot a course behind their fleet. Show me direct and indirect routes," Ryan ordered his mech. A square appeared on the display to his left, just above the sensor sphere. It offered four routes to get to his destination.

A collision alarm wailed. Ryan dived and spun his mech around the side of a small ship. The alarm cut off as the projectile hit it.

There was no time to think as six enemy mechs were already coming to intercept. Two launched projectiles. He continued his course around the ship to come back to his original trajectory. The gap continued to close. None of the routes displayed were inspiring and Ryan kept his feet on the thrusters, turning sharply to avoid enemy units or swinging around ships and debris.

He focused on nothing else but his destination and Ryan felt like he was racing again. It wasn't turning left or right but any direction he could think of, any space he could find. There was no track to restrict him, just a goal.

In a way, it was easier...if he ignored the projectiles, weapons, tentacles and other dangers in his way.

All sense of time disappeared as he made his way through the fleet, dragging along an increasing number of mechs trying to take him down. He spared a glance at the sensor sphere when he could and saw Wisp sticking relatively close to him, using his rifle to pick off any enemies that got too close. Jackson was further away, making her way through the outskirts of the fleet in a wider looping path.

When a mech got too close, Ryan punched it. It did very little damage, even with a boost from the elbow thruster, but it was enough to knock it back while he continued on.

There were no standout battles or mechs that caught his attention. It all became a blur and on the few occasions he got lucky and destroyed a mech, Ryan found he didn't care. There were no feelings of remorse for the lives lost, no anger at having his home threatened. He had found a calm place in the centre of the storm and focused on getting to the target.

After breaking through the final line of smaller ships, Ryan absorbed the immense size of their target. It was bigger than OSD. His sensors showed it was at least five times larger – a diamond-shaped vessel with more engines than he could count.

The front of the diamond had a large hole just beneath the point, with a swarm of mechs around it: some trying to plug the breach and others guarding against an attack.

He swung underneath the ship and it opened fire with defensive lasers. They were too slow to hit him more than once or twice after Ryan figured out their speed and patterns, but they were more powerful than the enemy mechs. Wisp caught up to him after he made it through the bulk of the fleet. Enemy mechs still chased them but kept their distance while the bigger ship fired. Jackson had made it to their destination first and was battling a group of mechs behind the ship. More were coming.

It would be a minute or two before Ryan and Wisp arrived to help her and the next part of their mission began; if they survived the maze of laser blasts.

CHAPTER THIRTY-TWO

RYAN GRABBED THE RIFLE resting at the small of his back, drew the scatter gun and opened fire with both as he closed in on Jackson and the attacking enemies. The closest three took hits from blue lances of light and spun away. Jackson led her attackers in a random chase, allowing Wisp to close in on them, using his beam blade to attack joints and stab through their armour with instinctual precision while Ryan flanked them.

"Any damage?" Wisp asked.

"Nothing serious," Jackson answered, breathing heavily.

Ryan was thrown against his harness as Jackson grabbed his mech and spun him around. She opened fire at the units chasing them and they dispersed to surround the flight. Ryan stored the scatter gun and held the rifle in both hands.

"Back-to-back," Wisp ordered. The trio moved into a small triangle with their backs to each other. They had their weapons ready and were tracking targets as they surrounded and closed in. "Fire at will."

There was no hesitation. Blue light filled the space around them. A wide spray from each rifle stopped the enemy from settling in one place and launching a clear attack.

It wasn't long before the collision alarm started again as the enemy mechs launched missiles, but their wide firing arcs cut them down before they got close. The explosions did help them move out of sight for a few moments but it wasn't enough to stop the trio hitting their targets.

Ryan's mech was taking more and more damage but they were cutting down the enemy units quickly. When the rifle's power pack ran out, he replaced it with a new one and continued firing. By the time they'd cleared the area, one pack was gone. Only three left. He'd have to be careful not to lose any more.

Most of the mechs were heading towards OSD. They were running out of time. Fast.

"Wildcard, my rail gun still hasn't recharged yet. It'll be a couple of minutes. What's our next move?" Wisp asked in their moment of calm.

"Do you have any missiles left?" Ryan said.

"I've got half left," Jackson answered.

"A full load here," Wisp said.

"Okay, we hit the engines. Wisp, find us targets. Don't stay still or these coos will hit us."

"There are so many engines on that thing. Will this even work?" Jackson said.

Ryan had to admit she had a point, but they had come this far and until the rail guns were ready this was their best option.

"Let's hope it buys us more time, until the rail guns are ready. Fire on my mark," Wisp answered for him.

Every second dragged until Wisp sent the coordinates. They raced to the rear of the ship but stayed beneath the engine wash.

"Set for double launch," Ryan said as he set both launchers to fire at the same time. The shoulder launcher would normally fire one shot after the other, but this mode allowed a quick-fire burst. The panels drew back in strips from the shoulder down and missiles were loaded into place from storage deeper in the mech.

If one of the exposed areas was hit before launch, it would be the end of the mech – and him. Another reason the sims were a safer option. The mechs were weapons themselves, even without the arsenals they carried. More weapons had been loaded onto each mech since there was no risk to the pilot while they were using the sims to control the unit. Piloting manually meant more risk to the pilot, especially with the explosives they carried. It didn't matter now. Without these weapons, they'd have no way of succeeding, and their armour hadn't let them down so far.

"Fire," Ryan ordered.

Ryan's screen flashed with light on both sides as four missiles streaked towards the ship's engines. Three of his projectiles were taken out before they could hit their target but one made it through, while about half of his companion's weapons connected, causing small explosions to spread along the rear.

His sensors showed that its speed slowed, but it didn't stop. As other engines powered up to replace the destroyed and damaged ones, it returned to the speed it had been moving at before. Ryan's stomach sank.

"That...didn't work," Wisp stated. "Next?"

Ryan didn't know. The fleet advanced towards the station and Earth and they could only guess what would happen when they got there. With a force this size, it didn't bode well.

"Wildcard." The voice over the comm system startled Ryan from his thoughts. "Wildcard, come in."

"Go ahead, General."

"What's your status?"

"We've made it to the far side of the fleet in one piece," Ryan said, looking at his sensor data before continuing. "We've taken some damage but nothing too serious, and we've taken out some of the engines on the lower half of the largest ship, but they activated more. Our rail guns are charging while we consider our next move."

"We saw the change in speed from here. Their forward ships have entered firing range and we've recovered one hundred and thirty-one mechs to defend the station. Their smallest ships aren't big enough to hold more than fifty units, it seems. If we can destroy or disable the big one, we'll be able to turn the tide."

"Any ideas on how we do that?"

"Given the size of that ship and the number of mechs it launched, our sensors have gathered data from the hole you made and the analysts theorise their mechs must be stored deeper in the ship – and they've only launched from the ventral sections," Matthews said, pausing before continuing. The hesitation in his voice made Ryan uneasy. "With that in mind, you may be able to board the ship and do some damage from the inside without leaving your mechs. We have no idea what conditions will be like or if there will even be room to manoeuvre, but it's our best guess."

"Understood," Ryan said, doing his best to hide his reservations about boarding the alien ship.

"We're running out of time. We're sending a support team to you. They have your comm channel and we've assigned you the call sign 'Reckless'. Their fleet will soon be close enough to Earth to land units and that could be disastrous. Whatever you do, make it fast."

"Yes, sir. Reckless One out." Ryan switched to his squad's channel and briefed the others. "I've just spoken to General Matthews. Our call sign for this mission is 'Reckless'. You can argue amongst yourselves about who gets what number la—"

"Two," Wisp said instantly.

"Damn it! Stop doing that!" Jackson said.

"Cut it out," Ryan snapped, surprised at how much influence Ryder had had on him. "We're going to board the ship, either through a hangar or a hole we're going to make. The analysts on OSD think at least part of the ship will have access for our mechs to move around. We go as far as we can, causing mayhem on the way, and look for a way to do some serious damage. If we stop it, we can win this. Reinforcements are on the way, but I don't know how long it'll take or how many."

There was silence as Jackson and Wisp mulled over the situation. The levity had passed.

"So, what you're saying is," Jackson said, choosing her words carefully, "we have to make a hole big enough to get through, hope there's enough room to move around, find something important to blow up, then get the hell out of there before the explosion kills us?"

"And get away from everything trying to kill us," Wisp added.

"Oh, yeah. That too."

"Pretty much, yeah," Ryan confirmed.

"Okay." Jackson paused. "What are we waiting for?"

"Power up rail guns and lock on to this point." Ryan smiled as he selected a point for them to fire on. There was too much activity around the first hole. Jackson and Wisp were the perfect team – crazy enough to be daring and skilled enough to succeed. It was one right call. "Three-second burst. We may need to use them again later."

The crosshairs were joined by another pair representing the other mechs', and once they lined up, he spoke again. "Three. Two. One. Fire."

Three green beams raced from the mechs and converged on one spot of the ship. It took two seconds before they breached the hull but the third second cut deeper, causing a series of explosions within. Atmosphere leaked into space along with debris.

And bodies.

The three mechs moved closer to the breach. Jackson and Wisp grabbed the broken metal and pulled it apart so they could make it through. Ryan fired at the mechs inside until he realised they weren't moving. Some were covered in scorch marks on the sides closest to the explosions and others had parts missing.

Bodies floated into space and Ryan saw the invaders for the first time. He found one close by and focused his sensors, bringing a larger image onto the screen. All the data was recorded and sent to OSD, but Ryan was mesmerised by what he saw.

It was larger than a human, with blood-red skin darkening with each passing second. The suits they wore made it difficult to see much more, but there were no hands, only tentacles – four of them – where a human's arms were, and two legs. It explained why the enemy mechs had tentacles.

As it rotated, he saw the eyes. Large, bulbous and black. Three of them on each side of the head and one in the middle of the forehead. The rest of the helmet blocked the other features.

Ryan's view was interrupted by a large piece of metal floating past. He turned to see the opening in the hull was wide enough to fit through and led the way inside.

The inside of the ship was big enough for two mechs to walk side by side. Ryan and Jackson had spent more time flying than walking during their training. It meant plenty of stamping and stumbling along the corridor as they found their footing. Wisp adapted first.

It might have been funny if the situation wasn't so dire.

"Scan for any power sources, surges or areas we can do some damage to. Keep your eyes open though, they could come at us from anywhere," Ryan ordered.

"How are we supposed to know what to look for? This wasn't covered in the training!"

"Just...just do what you can, Sunshine," Ryan shot back. "Every second brings us closer to OSD and Earth."

It wasn't long before they reached a door. After a quick exchange of words, they used their rifles to turn the door into a metal waffle and punched their way through. Bodies and debris raced by like Ryan was a race spectator but there was no time to stop and think.

The next section proved more chaotic. The aliens held onto anything they could to avoid the vacuum of space behind them while some active mechs were doing their best to shelter exposed comrades. Ryan and the others didn't wait; they opened fire while the disturbance worked in their favour.

It was cold but Ryder had drilled into them that this was war. They would take every chance before the enemy took theirs. It was different in the sims, as pilots weren't in danger, but now, piloting mechs manually, one second of hesitation could get them all killed.

The enemy mechs went down quickly under sustained fire and the explosions knocked the aliens towards the breach. More mechs appeared from around a corner and swarmed the trio. They were too close for rifles and there wasn't enough time to activate the beam blades, so they went in with fists flying. Using their main thrusters, the three of them were able to knock their opponents into the units behind.

"Sunshine, rail gun. Now!" Ryan yelled.

"Clear!" Jackson said. Ryan and Wisp pulled back and pressed against the walls as the green energy beam cut through all of the units ahead of her and into the ship. The explosions sent shudders through the deck for a long time, knocking both mechs from their feet and making it difficult for Ryan to stand again. Wisp made it to his feet quicker.

The artificial gravity gave up shortly after, creating a maze of floating mechs and metal that slowed them down.

"Wisp, why have you stopped?" Ryan asked, when he realised they were only a pair. He led the way back so they were together again.

"There looks to be some kind of junction for the power lines. The explosions must have done some damage and I bet that's what caused the gravity to fail."

"So, we hit more sections like this and hope for something big to break?" Jackson guessed.

"No. If I can get an accurate scan of this junction and combine it with what we've seen of the ship so far, inside and out, then maybe we can determine some critical systems to hit." Before anyone could answer, he added, "Just buy me some time."

In the sims, Ryan was sure there'd have been some back and forth about who was in charge before Ryder cracked down on them to stay focused. There was no command structure here. Wisp had the rank, but this was Ryan's mission.

The disconnect had never been clearer to Ryan than it was now, and it went as far back as when he started racing. He knew nothing would happen to him and consequences were nothing to worry about. A mistake was a way to learn without getting hurt.

Sim technology made you forget the risks and kept you safe, but Ryan knew there was a delay between what he did, what he saw and how he reacted in the pods. It was so miniscule he thought it was all in his head, but OSD, where there was a bigger delay, proved it existed and influenced how he acted.

In a perfect world, there should be no difference between the sim and the real thing, which was one of the goals of this initiative. Equipment could be replaced easier than pilots, but complacency was a problem – one Ryan was starting to understand. Their squad was a perfect example at various stages. Breaking habits was difficult, but Ryder was there to instil discipline, and judging from their current attitudes, she had succeeded.

The only reason Ryan had the time to think about this was the lack of enemy mechs. They may have been focused on sealing off the adjoining areas, but this gave them time to find a way to do even more damage.

"I've got something," Wisp announced.

CHAPTER THIRTY-THREE

"WHAT'VE YOU FOUND?" JACKSON asked.

"One junction isn't important but there are a number of them all over the ship. If we take out enough of them, we'll be able to slow this thing down," Wisp explained, sharing the wire schematic he had created. "The deeper we go, the more resistance we'll encounter. If they catch on, they'll try to stop us by reinforcing these points."

"There are over three hundred just in this quadrant," Ryan counted. "And four to work through. That's going to take too long. There's got to be something else."

"I'm working with limited information and we don't know how far inside the ship we can go in the mechs. I say we start with these, and if we find something else along the way, we go for it."

"Okay, then let's split up and take out as many as possible. Call for help if needed."

Ryan left the others at the next junction, while Jackson and Wisp would split up at the next one. Wisp's wire map rotated at the bottom of his screen as he navigated the corridors. There was no resistance at first but after breaking through the next door, his sensors flashed and alarms wailed. Each bulkhead concealed enemy units.

There wasn't a lot of room in the corridors. They were big enough for two mechs to pass by, but combat was another issue. It did stop Ryan from being overrun and he was able to use his rifle to thin their numbers before activating the beam blade and cutting down the enemy mechs, limb by limb.

At the back of one group, Ryan noticed something. A new mech model, larger, with heavier armour and weapons, but slower, lumbering into position. When they raised huge rifle barrels, he had just enough time to withdraw before a flurry of red bolts shot towards him. When one barrage ended, another began, stopping him from moving forward or taking aim.

"Not good, not good," Ryan muttered.

His status sphere recorded more damage from these lasers blasts than the weapons used by the other enemy mechs. His armour wouldn't last long against that fire-power. Shaking his head at his recklessness, Ryan armed a missile. He took a step back, then another.

When the barrage ended, he dived across the corridor to the other wall, firing the missile. A shockwave from the explosion hit and he slammed into the wall.

There was no time to rest. He used his thrusters to fly through the wreckage, bouncing off the walls, and collided with one of the bigger mechs.

Activating the beam blade, he brought it down to slash straight through the middle of its armour. Sparks flew and the blade stuck in the unit's armour.

His sensor sphere flashed once more as another large mech approached, bringing its huge weapon to bear. He let go of the blade and pushed off with the thrusters just as it opened fire; the lasers pierced the armour of its comrade and followed Ryan's course.

Ryan drew the scatter gun and fired two shots. The first hit the mech in the chest and caused no damage but did slow it. The second hit the barrel of the weapon and when the pilot fired again it exploded, launching shrapnel all around. Ryan took his chance and dived into his foe, slamming it into the wall with his shoulder. He passed the downed mech and grabbed his beam blade, freeing it from the enemy unit by deactivating it as the enemy lunged.

Without thinking, he activated the weapon, brought the blade up and allowed the bigger mech to impale itself on the laser blade, its speed helping pierce the thick armour. Sparks flew but the enemy unit kept attacking. Being so close, it used its weapon as a club, forcing Ryan to try to grab it, but he couldn't keep up with all of the tentacles also slapping against him.

It took a moment to find an opening but when the flurry lessened he kicked off the deck, pushing the mech away, but it dived straight back at him. Ryan grabbed the beam blade and pushed it further into the chest. He had a couple of seconds to jump back, using his thrusters to escape before the unit exploded.

A second explosion followed as the downed mech also detonated and the shockwave caused Ryan to lose control and crash into the next bulkhead.

More mechs arrived, all the smaller variety. Ryan wasted no time in launching another missile to slow them down and unleashed a storm of laser blasts from his rifle, but their numbers pushed him back.

The explosion had created a hole through two decks above and below, but one of the heavy rifles floated right into Ryan's reach. He picked it up and fired.

The red beams cut through the enemy easily but the recoil was too powerful and the walls were marked with holes before he was done. There was no way to know how many shots it had or how much power, but it would help.

"Two, Three," he called. "I've come across another type of mech. It's heavier armoured and it took a lot more force to damage it with my beam blade. Their rifles are also much stronger."

"I've just found a pair," Jackson said, grunting every other word.

"Why haven't we faced them before?" Wisp asked.

"How am I supposed to know?" Ryan said. "Maybe they didn't think they needed them?"

"Any tips for taking them down, Wildcard?" Jackson asked. It sounded like she was having a hard time.

"Get in close. They're heavily armoured but slow. That rifle seems to be the most trub."

"Got it."

"I'm labelling these 'Goliaths' and the smaller units 'Grunts'. Comm if you find any others."

They clicked in response and the channel fell quiet. Ryan turned his attention back to the map and made for the next power junction. A one-second shot from the rail gun destroyed it completely and the lights dimmed throughout the section. He carried on, coming across more mechs. The Goliaths were tough, but he had a handle on them – although stopping them from exploding proved harder. The next pair he fought left no rifle for him to use and the one he picked up stopped firing shortly after, so he dropped it.

With the trigger embedded in the barrel, it felt like holding a large pipe. It was designed for a tentacle to be wrapped around it and secure before firing but that didn't stop him from picking up the next usable weapon he came across. They were more powerful than his own rifle.

The number of enemy units he faced grew with every junction destroyed but he had no idea if their efforts were having any effect. The increased resistance was slowing them down and they were running out of time.

A large shudder rocked the ship, informing him they were in range of OSD's weapons.

"...ckless On..." The call burst through Ryan's comm system with so much static it was almost lost. "Are y... ving? Reck...ne?"

"Anyone picking up that message?" Ryan asked his team. "There's too much static."

"Hang on," Wisp answered. "I'm relaying it through my comm. You must be in too deep."

Another burst of static before the message came through. It was one of the operators on OSD. "Reck-less One, do you copy?"

"Reckless One here. What's going on?"

"The entire enemy fleet is in weapons range. Orbital Station Delta is attacking with everything we have."

"We noticed."

"Our forces are trying to keep them at bay but we're being pushed back. We're running out of time!"

"We're taking out power junctions to slow it down but there are too many and we're encountering heavy resistance. Our sensors aren't strong enough to find a better target."

"Fall." Matthews came on the channel. "We think each quadrant has a power core. Destroy it and the explosion will cause serious damage to the entire ship. We're transmitting the location of the closest one now."

"I've got it," Wisp confirmed, and forwarded it to Ryan and Jackson. "We should be able to converge on it from our current locations in a few minutes."

"You won't have much time before it explodes so make sure to have a clear exit route if you want a chance of making it out alive. Your reinforcements are close. We'll split them between the other quadrants."

"Okay, you heard the general," Ryan said to the others. "Head for the power core...and try not to bring any friends."

Any replies were lost as another group of mechs approached his location and he turned to face them. The alarm became a constant noise and he had no time to turn it down or off before attacking.

He fired his stolen weapon into the group and retreated down the corridor he had come from until another opening appeared. After firing his penultimate missile into them, Ryan turned and fired his thrusters for a quick exit. It took a few moments for them to regroup but they wasted no time following him.

After navigating a series of turns, Ryan blasted a hole through the doors at the end to reveal a shaft up seven levels to the power core. As his team closed in, they appeared on the edge of his sensor sphere, but more red dots approached from all sides.

A group of six Goliath mechs were waiting for him once he found the right level. They opened fire as soon as he appeared and the only way to escape the barrage was to keep going up, but his mech had taken damage in that brief encounter. His front armour wasn't going to take much more abuse.

There were no enemies on the level above, but his pursuers didn't give up. Explosions rattled bulkheads as some flew into the barrage he'd passed through seconds before.

It bought Ryan time, but he didn't wait for them to catch up. His left arm must have been damaged as he passed through the ambush – he had limited movement at the elbow. A scan revealed the joint's thruster was also damaged. The scatter gun was on his left side, which could be problematic. The diagnostic showed some power disruptions throughout his mech, but they weren't hindering him. Given how much contact there had been, the mech was going to need major paint and scuff work if his armour held out for the rest of the mission.

He continued forward. The corridors were narrower here, with just enough room for one mech and less space to fight. If he was surrounded on this level, there would be nowhere to go.

The sensors showed no enemies ahead as he continued towards the power core but more than once he had to turn down another corridor to avoid shots from his pursuers. Wisp and Jackson were closing in too, with swarms of red dots on their tails. They wouldn't have much time.

"Two, Three," Ryan commed. "Check in."

"I'll be there before you both," Jackson answered. "My mech isn't in great shape, though. Rear armour is almost out and thrusters are damaged."

"I'm bringing a large group but I'm mostly intact," Wisp reported.

"Oh, yeah. I'm bringing some friends, too," Jackson added.

"Okay." Ryan took a breath as he tried to come up with a plan. It wasn't easy, as enemy shots were getting closer. "Sunshine, find us a way out. It needs to be fast – we won't have much time after destroying the power core. Wisp, arm your rail gun. We won't have time to coordinate our attack, so find a spot and do as much damage as you can. We might not make it out of here…"

"Oh, yes! Fantastic time to mention that!" Jackson's quip made Ryan smile as he dived around the last corner and raced down the corridor towards the target. "I'm here."

"You know what to do. We're right behind you!" Ryan yelled, firing his last missile at the door.

He flew into the room just as Wisp emerged from another. Jackson's mech dropped out of view as it descended. The chamber took Ryan's breath away.

Ryan had avoided large spaces during his journey through the ship to reduce the number of enemy units he faced. Junctions in the corridors were the widest spaces he had come across, but as the centre of this quadrant, the chamber stretched from the outer hull at the bottom right to the top. Bodies and debris shot past him again as the vacuum penetrated the room. While there was plenty of room for mechs to move below, with walkways scattered across and connecting other areas of the ship, above were thinner paths for smaller beings without mechs. Lots of them.

It proved the section of the ship they'd entered was designed with mechs in mind. There was nothing like it on OSD, so enemy mechs wouldn't be able to get close to their central shaft without making a hole. Ryan wasn't sure which design option was better: having areas for mechs to move around the ship or not.

In the centre of the room, running from top to bottom, was the power core. A large cylinder connected to various sections of the ship on every level and was encased in metal, with clear panels showing what was inside. Whether it was plasma, gas or another substance didn't matter, but it was obvious these panels would be the easiest to destroy.

"Target those panels with the rail gun," he instructed Wisp. "If we can cause a leak it'll cause chaos. If it explodes, even better."

Wisp clicked in response. Ryan locked his own weapon onto panels above him. With three panels targeted, he fired at each in two-second bursts. The blue-gold substance was quick to force its way out of the cylinder and expand. Explosions lit up inside, which was Ryan's cue to move. Wisp was already heading for Jackson.

His sensors showed the explosions cascading out, and as the gold substance continued to spread, it consumed metal and flesh alike as it reached the closest aliens. Shockwaves wreaked havoc with his flying. It was hard enough to navigate around the mechs, walkways and conduits connecting the power core to the walls.

An explosion ahead opened a hole in the hull, leading to space. Jackson dived through, followed quickly by Wisp, who had already caught up. Ryan's damaged thrusters were making it harder for him to escape the continuing explosions.

"Wildcard, what's your status?" There was an edge of panic to Wisp's voice Ryan wasn't used to.

"My thrusters aren't at one hundred percent. Get clear, this thing is going to blow."

"We're not leaving you." Jackson sounded even more worried. Whatever they saw behind him, Ryan didn't want to know.

"Get away! There's nothing you can do. Go!"

The gold cloud overtook his mech and the fire engulfed him. He was still too far from the hole. At this rate, he wasn't going to make it.

"Wildcard!" The general's transmission was faint. "Fall! The ship is splitting into four sections. We're seeing explosions in your quadrant spreading. The other sections – ships – are retreating. You did it!"

That explained it. This section of the ship – a ship itself, it seemed – was moving, probably in the same direction as him. He had been too slow to make his escape. Nevertheless, the news brought relief. If the explosions damaged or destroyed the remaining quadrants, that would help the other teams.

It might save everyone.

Another explosion rocked his mech and the alarms sounded again. The opening was close but he was spinning, making it hard to aim. Ryan gave a burst of power to his thrusters before killing them and let the shockwaves carry him forward. His left arm stopped responding completely and his left leg became harder to move as the flames caused more damage to his weakest areas.

The spinning made him dizzy and his view turned gold, orange, red and white. Ryan closed his eyes and hoped.

Ryan was thrown into his harness by a hard impact and sudden acceleration, followed by more shockwaves.

Someone was calling his name, but his head was spinning faster than his mech, making it difficult to focus. Ten seconds later, he recognised Wisp's voice.

"I'm…" Ryan tried to answer but he was too dizzy to talk. "I'm here…I'm…okay…I think."

"What's your status? We're still too close to the explosions."

"My left side is almost completely coo; those explosions destroyed the last of my armour on the arm and leg. Those thrusters are barely working."

"Then we'll carry you," Jackson announced, appearing on his left as Wisp grabbed his right. "Two, match my speed or this won't go well."

"Obviously."

They fired their thrusters and Ryan activated his working engines. The three of them flew away from the explosions and the ongoing battle with other Mech Force units. It was only now he was able to breathe again. Somehow, he had survived. Not only that, his team had too.

His part was over, and Ryan was glad. He slumped against the metal frames holding his limbs and closed his eyes as the deaths sunk in.

Then he remembered Captain Ryder. Before he could reach for the comm system and find out what had happened to her, another message came through and interrupted his thoughts.

"Are you seeing this?"

Whatever was happening had caught Wisp by surprise. That was rare.

CHAPTER THIRTY-FOUR

Ryan switched to the rear view. The invading ships were reversing course, heading away from the station and Earth, but Ryan couldn't take his eyes off the ship they had escaped.

It didn't look anything like it had when they'd approached. What had been a massive, long, diamond-shaped ship was separated into five pieces. The four quadrants Wisp had identified earlier had become individual triangular ships, leaving behind a thin frame, which had once held them in place. There was a cylinder in the middle, like the one they'd destroyed, only bigger.

The bottom ship was erupting from within, explosions bursting through the hull as the blue-gold substance from the power core continued to spread. The other three were moving away quickly, leaving the frame behind. It looked like the frame needed the engines of the smaller vessels to move at a respectable speed.

"Here it comes," Wisp called over the comm.

"When I said I wanted to get back into surfing, I meant waves. You know, like at a beach," Jackson quipped. "Not shockwaves!"

That must have been a conversation she'd had with Wisp because Ryan had no idea what she meant. There wasn't time for a response as the previous explosions triggered a larger one, consuming the ship. The frame was engulfed in the explosion, too, and the closest of the other three lost momentum as the fire's fingers wrapped around its hull. The shockwave pushed it off course and a stream of mechs and tiny ships appeared from multiple exits, making for the nearest ship that could take them to safety.

Seconds later, eruptions breached the hull of the second ship from within. It exploded soon after but there was no sign of their fellow Enforcer mechs and pilots escaping. More deaths to add to the list.

Unlike the second ship, the final pair made it far enough away and escaped the explosion, but the shockwave pushed them further from the battle. The third team sent by Matthews succeeded in destroying that quadrant and three mechs escaped from the hull just before it exploded. Once they regained their bearings after the shockwave, they made for Ryan and his team.

The latest shockwave reached Ryan's team's location and sent them tumbling until Jackson and Wisp were able to bring them back under control. Ryan stayed out of it. He could fly in a straight line, along with long, sweeping turns, but a sharp spin or quick direction change were out of his power now unless he wanted to fly in circles, due to the damage he'd taken.

"We need to get back to OSD," Ryan said, once they had returned to a stable position. "We're in no shape to keep fighting."

"I reckon I could keep going," Wisp responded calmly.

"That's because you let us do all the hard work," Jackson complained. "Freeloader."

"Save it for when we get back," Ryan ordered. He found it strange how easily he was giving orders now since it was something he had actively tried to avoid. "Their fleet is breaking up and retreating. Unfortunately, we're going to have to get through them."

"And if I were one of them, I'd be glad to take out some enemies, regardless of who won or lost," Jackson added.

"Exactly. Let's get moving."

With Jackson and Wisp's help, Ryan's damaged mech cleared the danger zone. The battle had become so chaotic, unlike anything the training exercises had showed him. It was mesmerising, and he gave it his full attention while the others focused on keeping them safe.

Orbital Station Delta, littered with holes and surrounded by debris like a minefield, loomed ahead. Fighters and mechs darted in and out of the spaces too quickly for him to track. Some enemy units made desperate runs towards the station, others to the Globe. It was hard to say at this distance, but it looked like they didn't last long before burning up in the atmosphere.

Ryan had very little to do on the journey back. They took a longer and wider route to avoid the bulk of the enemy fleet as it retreated. The three mechs that had escaped their exploding ship joined them halfway back to OSD but said little over the comm. Of the other two teams sent on the same mission, one team of three didn't make it out of the second ship before it exploded and the last trio hadn't been able to complete their mission, with that section leading the retreat.

A couple of times an enemy mech came their way but the three newcomers would break off and destroy it before it got too close, and re-join them.

When they had passed the majority of the fleet, they were able to take a more direct route to the station. There were still battles going on but most had ended. Fighters patrolled the area, looking for units lurking for a stealth attack, and the mechs were trying to create a path through the debris field to make it easier for incoming and outgoing ships.

Ryan's alarm went off again as the station opened fire. Jackson and Wisp moved him clear of the lasers aimed straight at the retreating ships.

The barrage continued for over a minute, each weapon targeting a different ship. Some exploded while others were disabled, and a few of those blew up later, but the fleet kept retreating and Enforcer forces weren't pursuing.

A concentrated burst drew his attention to some drifting wreckage. Three triangular ships had been destroyed but the wrecks were dangerous. By the time the lasers stopped, his screen showed a haze of dust and debris. As exhausted as he was, all Ryan could think was that he didn't want to be the one to clean it up.

That's when he saw it. One part remained.

It wasn't big in comparison to the whole quadrant but it was large enough to survive the drop to the planet's surface – exactly where it was heading. The barrage and explosions had pushed it close enough to be caught in Earth's gravity.

Ryan's sensors measured it at over sixty kilometres long. An object that size would cause serious damage no matter where it landed, but the shockwave and after-effects would also be devastating.

"Orbital Station Delta, Reckless One," he said over the comm.

"Go ahead."

"There's one piece of a ship still intact and caught in Earth's gravity. It'll be a disaster if it reaches the surface."

"We're already working on a solution. Your orders are to board in hangar—"

"Fall!" Matthews cut in, his voice ragged. "Ignore that last order!"

"Sir?" Ryan said.

"OSD is suffering power surges whenever we try to use core systems. Emergency power is keeping us going but firing that last salvo shorted out more systems. Even if we could fire again, our rotation cycle means our remaining weapons are not in range to target the debris. By the time they are, it'll be too late."

"So someone needs to stop it before it hits the ground?"

"That's right. Our simulations indicate it's going to land somewhere in the western Eurozone," Matthews continued. "We need to destroy it or deflect it until it's over water. That will minimise the damage."

"Can the fighters do it?" Ryan asked, a sinking feeling growing in his stomach.

"No, even all of their missiles together wouldn't be enough."

"So, it has to be the mechs…"

"Correct. The jamming signal is still active. It's stopping us from using the sims. By the time the source is out of range it will be too late. I've sent out a message to all mech pilots but no one has volunteered and we need the debris cleared. I know your team have been through a lot and I won't order you to do it, but…"

"Hang on a second," Ryan said, switching channels to speak to the five other pilots. "You've been listening?"

"Another suicide mission?" Jackson asked. "You know, people are going to think we like them."

"No point turning back now," Wisp added. "If no one else is signing up, someone's got to do it."

"I can't ask you to do this, not after all you've been through," Ryan started.

"But you're going to go anyway," Wisp finished. "Before this, I'd never have pegged you as the self-sacrificing type, but you've changed. A lot. Besides, without help you'll never get there in time."

"If I make it through this, I want a raise!" Jackson said.

"Deal." Ryan smiled. "Reckless Four, Five and Six, what do you say?"

"We're with you," a man's voice answered. They must have been speaking on their own channel. "We signed up for a one-way trip and we're still here. Let's try again."

Ryan tried not to think too much on that, hoping it was a poor joke. He switched back to the channel Matthews was waiting on. "We're on it, sir. Have your simulations come up with a way for us to destroy or deflect that thing?"

"You all have my thanks," Matthews said. "Our analysts have determined your rail guns have enough force to deflect it while breaking off smaller pieces that will burn up in the atmosphere. We're transmitting the data to you now. You'll need to override the firing controls to enable bursts longer than seven seconds, as well as reroute power from other systems to sustain them. How to do that is included in the data stream."

"Sounds simple enough," Ryan said slowly, although he wasn't sure.

"One last thing...your mechs should be able to with-stand entering the atmosphere at high speed but you've taken a lot of damage that could make it a rough ride. If your engines are damaged, you may not be able to reduce speed before impact, if they don't fail first."

"Understood," Ryan answered. The data stream flashed on his screen and the pilots changed course for the debris. "Wish us luck."

Without waiting for a response, he closed the channel and studied the information OSD had sent. There were a series of calculations and targets to fire at. He entered them into the targeting computer before bringing up the virtual interface for his mech's systems and diverting power to the rail gun.

He reached for his helmet and put it on before rerout-ing life support into the weapon as well. Once done, Ryan sent the new setup to the others so they could apply it and input the targets and course into their own systems.

"Ryan." Zack's voice was a welcome distraction. "You reckless idiot! This is coo...but I'm not surprised. Not really. Your engines are damaged; Mac and I have a patch. Listen carefully..."

Ryan followed the instructions as Zack relayed them – with Mac's occasional interruptions – and a few min-utes later he had partial power in the left side's engines. It wasn't perfect and his limbs didn't move well but it gave him speed. He still needed one pilot to help him but it freed the other to do other things.

"Thanks, Zack. See you soon," Ryan said.

"I hope so. Good luck."

It didn't take long to reach the atmosphere. There wasn't time to slow down if they wanted to catch their target and the mech's sensors recorded the increase in hull temperature as they dived.

They hadn't spent much time on atmospheric entry during training. Space missions took priority, with a little time devoted to surface movement and combat. This was new territory for both Ryan and Jackson. They would soon rotate and rely on other areas of armour and deflect some of the heat, but it would slow them down. Ryan was being helped by Wisp. His engines worked but he didn't have the control needed to fly alone and the heat would cause more damage if he didn't pay attention.

The debris grew larger each second. According to the information from OSD and General Matthews, they needed to be ahead of it to succeed. There were traces of the blue-gold substance from the power core but it was burning off in the atmosphere.

"Everyone know the plan?" Ryan asked.

"Keep going until we're ahead and then use the engines to match speeds," Wisp answered.

"Then we the blow this coo out of existence," Jackson added.

It was simple and effective and, according to the data, should work. "Any damage from entry?"

"I'm noticing some glitches but that could be from rerouting the power to the rail gun," Jackson responded. Wisp remained silent, being in the best shape of all of them.

Ryan didn't like being a passenger but there was nothing else to do. Twice, Ryan had to increase the compensator to account for velocity and gravity, but there was only so much it could do. He was straining against the harness.

"Hang on," Wisp called out to them. "We're almost in position. Brace for a sharp turn in three, two, one…"

Even with the compensators set high, the speed of travel was intense, but it had to be as they pulled ahead of the debris. The spin to get the mechs around and in front was dizzying. Ryan's body swung to the opposite side and he just about dislocated his shoulder. He had no time to think as they matched their speed with the debris, which now filled almost his entire view. It was a fiery arrowhead shooting straight at them.

"Don't wait for orders. Fire when ready," Ryan said, and armed his rail gun. Wisp let him go and the six mechs spread out in a line ahead of the wreckage, staying a safe distance in front.

Immediately, Ryan's alarms went off and he cursed them for the hundredth time since leaving the station. They were protesting at the hull's temperature, with the weaker and thinner sections reaching higher temperatures than others. He silenced them all with a voice command and fired at the first target.

Wisp fired a moment later and Jackson a few seconds after. The other three fired together. Using four-second bursts, they were able to ignite the remains of the gold substance and cut through sections of the hull, breaking them off into smaller fragments that would burn up on their own.

"I've got a problem here," Jackson announced. "I'm seeing overloads in a number of systems. My rail gun is failing and engines are losing power. I'm not going to be able to keep up."

"Pull out, Sunshine," Ryan said instantly. "Shift power to engines and get low enough that you can eject safely."

"If I fire one last burst, I can—"

"No!" Wisp yelled. Silence answered him – both Ryan and Jackson were too stunned to speak. It was the first time they had ever heard him raise his voice. "There's no need; we can finish this. Too many have died today. We're not losing you."

"If we don't stop this then it won't really matter who lived and who died," she responded, making no move to leave.

"Your mech can't stand this much longer. Get to the surface and help people evacuate. We'll do our best to stop this thing," Ryan said, surprised at how logically he was able to think.

"I..." she started, clearly unhappy. "Okay. Just don't screw up. And don't die either!"

Ryan didn't have time to answer. He was quickly updating his targeting computer to make up for Jackson's absence and sending the data to the rest of the pilots.

They attacked in unison, cutting through the object and reducing its size, but it was still too big. They were running out of time. It was a feeling Ryan was getting used to but not one he enjoyed. They were descending over Eurozone, one of the most densely populated areas on the planet.

His rail gun failed to fire at the next target. A quick scan showed the heat was disrupting the power. His engines were functioning, but it would soon evolve into the same problem as Jackson's. Wisp must have noticed as he fired at Ryan's target before continuing his own sequence. Ryan checked his projectiles. No missiles. The others might have enough to deflect it.

"Anyone have any missiles left?" he said.

"I've got two. Why?" Wisp asked.

"Five," one of the other pilots said, before the other two added their own tallies.

"One."

"None."

Ryan's simulation wasn't promising. The results gave him enough data to ensure they moved the impact point closer to the coast, but it would still cause major damage.

"We're running out of time," Ryan said, but in his head, he could hear Jackson adding, "again!" "Our missiles might help push it over the water. Keep firing everything you've got and try to ignite whatever remains of that power source. If you manage to destroy it, even better, but we have to limit the damage this thing will cause if it lands."

"Where will you be?" Wisp asked.

"I'm losing power, just like Sunshine. You know this already."

"I was hoping it was just a glitch. Pull out now. I'll finish it."

"No way. We need every bit of help to do this. Activate launchers and aim for these coordinates." Ryan transmitted the new target and powered up his launchers. "Fire."

Missiles streaked towards the fiery target. Before they could impact, Ryan fired his rail gun and hit one. The first explosion set off the others and while there was no notable difference he could see, his sensors showed the new impact zone was a couple of miles from the coast.

That was a start.

The blue dot heading to the surface, Jackson, vanished from his display and Ryan swallowed a curse. It took everything he had to keep his focus on the object ahead. He knew any of them could die but he had hoped his squad would make it through. He debated informing Wisp but chose not to. If he didn't already know, he didn't need a new distraction.

Wisp started firing again but more often than before. After a few shots, he stopped, and Ryan saw his friend's rail gun snap from its mount and soar towards the metal mass. It exploded on impact, taking out a massive chunk from the front and further deflecting its course.

"Wisp, get out of here," Ryan ordered.

"I'm fine, losing the rail gun is my only problem," Wisp said.

"It's a big problem and you know it. You need to lock that unit down before a power surge rips it apart."

"We need everyone to do this," Wisp countered. Ryan knew he was right.

The rail gun failure was a massive problem, especially for it to happen on Wisp's mech, which was in the best condition of all. Ryan continued firing in short bursts but had no luck in igniting any of the remaining gold substance.

Ryan fired a burst from his engines to increase his speed and close in on the debris before cutting power to his engines and transferring it to the rail gun. The others followed.

He fired again, a long and continuous shot this time, and dragged the green lance across the hull. Twelve seconds later he hit a pocket of gold trapped inside the wreck. The explosions penetrated deeper through the debris, pushing it further from the coast. The shockwave knocked him back and his rail gun mount snapped as well. The barrel hit the side of the object and detonated.

"My rail gun snapped off," Ryan said.

"My weapon's gone too." This was confirmed by

another explosion as each of the other three pilots reported in.

"Mine's failed."

"And mine."

"What now?" Wisp asked.

"I don't know!" Ryan yelled, frantically thinking through their options. "Push it!"

"You're kidding!" Wisp said.

"That's coo!" another pilot said.

Ryan wasn't kidding. He closed in on the debris and pushed against it from the side, away from land. Wisp and the others joined him but it felt like they were making no progress.

"It's not working," one of the pilots shouted.

"Reckless, this is Shadow and Gale squadrons. We're ten seconds out and have no weapons but can help you push. Stand by." Ryan recognised the voice over the comm as Captain Dixon of Shadow Squadron. Nine mechs joined the five and transferred all their power to the engines. The temperatures continued to rise and his mech's metal hands melted into the debris and broke, but he pushed on with the stumps. Streaks of white could be seen as they descended through the highest clouds. They were running out of time.

The effort was causing more problems. Two mechs exploded during the push but no one stopped. The compensator was maxed out and it still wasn't enough; his right arm broke under the pressure and through his scream he locked the gauntlet in place.

After what felt like an eternity, Ryan's engines cut out.

The mech tumbled and he frantically tried to restore power to his engines as his collision alarms went off.

He was approaching the ground too quickly and there wasn't enough time to slow down even if he could eject. Voices were calling to him but he couldn't focus.

He finally got power back to the engines and kicked them to life but he was pointing at the surface. He pushed hard on the controls as he tried to avoid the ground, aiming for the ocean. Ryan yelled but these soon turned to screams as the compensator failed and the pressure ripped through his body. He couldn't hear anything. His vision blurred. Still, he pushed down on his thruster controls to slow his descent.

Darkness crept across his vision, but he could see the fiery metal mass above him, with eleven mechs still pushing against it.

With a crash, his mech hit the ocean. Water flew up on all sides, as he plunged deeper. It took every ounce of his energy to ease off the thrusters. The last thing Ryan saw was a wall of grey, white and blue pressing in from all sides, and he lost consciousness as the mech hit the water with such force it crashed straight to the ocean floor.

CHAPTER THIRTY-FIVE

"What's his status?" Doctor Crine asked as the group approached.

There were six of them. Two wore long white coats over blue tunics, two were in black flight gear pushing a rectangular chamber along the corridor, and the last wore blue and was staring intently at the screen on the left of the hoverpod. Crine, also wearing a white coat, asked the question. He had grey-streaked brown hair and beard and flushed skin. Deep breaths with his every step interfered with his composure.

The woman in blue didn't break her gaze from the display, even when they approached a door or turned a corner.

"Vitals are weak but stable. We had to sedate him during the journey, he was in so much pain," the woman said.

"Did he say anything coherent before you sedated him?" Crine asked.

"Yeah," one of the pilots answered. "He kept screaming about his right side – especially the arm and leg."

"The scanners are ready for him," the woman in the white coat said. "We'll know more very soon but it's clear he needs surgery ASAP."

"We can't prep until we know what it is," another doctor said. He was the youngest of the group.

"You can get everything ready that we might need," Crine answered. "He'll be with you as soon as the scans are done. Once we know more, we'll have to act quickly. Go. Get a move on!"

The young man turned off down another corridor, leaving the five running with the pod and its occupant.

They moved in silence, navigating the corridors until they reached a room with a large machine and a dozen people around it.

One of them hurried to Crine and handed him a PCT. After studying it, he nodded and turned back to the hoverpod, which the two pilots had already unlocked, and watched them lift the lid.

On the mattress, Ryan slept peacefully.

He was covered in blood and his flight suit was torn to shreds. The people in the room swarmed the open chamber and cut away the remains of the grey flight suit with laser scalpels before sponging blood, dirt and dust from him. The right side of his body was odd, misshapen, lumpy in places. Most of his skin was bruised – black, purple and yellow. Only a few patches of uninjured skin remained. There were cuts on his arms and legs and they trickled blood.

Every screen and terminal was occupied but the newcomers replaced the other staff and continued working. Only the older man didn't stand at a console. He looked from the PCT to Ryan and back again, waiting for the two pilots to get into position.

A circular hatch slid open and the topless pod was pushed into the opening by the pilots. Metal claws reached out and grabbed the base, pulling it into the machine.

The hatch closed and the machine hummed to life, running scans of Ryan's body. Everyone made notes at their stations, picking up on every injury. There were a couple of gasps but no conversation. The orders for this case were specific and came from the highest level.

The woman in the white coat called out, "Make sure the surgical team is informed of this immediately. The moment the last scan is done, take him down and get started. We'll be sending the biggest problems direct to their screens."

"Have standby staff ready to relieve anyone who gets tired. This is going to be a long night," the older man added.

A few minutes later the humming stopped. The machine released Ryan as the claws pushed him out and he was taken from the room. The two women followed him while the man gathered the last of the data and sent it to the surgical team.

When the man left the room, General Matthews and Captain Ryder knocked him into the wall as they ran down the corridor towards the operating theatre. The man sighed and chased them, catching up just before they burst into the room.

"You can't go in!" he said between breaths, grabbing their arms. "This is a sterilised environment and surgery will begin imminently."

"I want to see him!" Ryder screamed. She looked beaten too. "Now!"

"That's enough, Captain," Matthews snapped, rubbing his brow. He took another look at the doctors around the bed Ryan lay on before the doors closed and turned back to the man. "I'm sorry, doctor...?"

"Crine. Please, come with me and I'll explain."

Matthews and Ryder followed Crine to a waiting room, where he sat on a white sofa and waved them to the suite opposite him. He asked the nurse near the desk for some water and after she left, he started speaking.

"I'm going to be honest; I'm surprised your pilot is still alive. The extent of the injuries throughout his body is severe. There's internal bleeding and damage to a number of organs. All of the bones on his right side are broken but the arm and leg are another story. Half his left ribs are broken too, and his left leg has five breaks: three lower and two upper. Those are easy enough to fix; it'll just take some time for him to regain his strength. His left arm is relatively undamaged – some bruising and dislocated joints to contend with, but they'll heal if he pulls through. If we can repair the damage to his organs – which I have to warn you is a big 'if' – then his right side will still take a lot of work."

"What's wrong with his arm and leg?" Ryder asked, about to stand, but Matthews' hand on her arm stopped her. The nurse returned before Crine could speak again and placed glasses of water on the table before taking a spot at her desk.

"The bones in his right limbs have been completely shattered. I've never seen this kind of damage before and there's no way it can be repaired. There isn't a piece of bone bigger than a couple of centimetres. We had to sedate him on the journey here because the pain was so intense. I'm surprised he was conscious at all."

"What are the options, Doctor?" Matthews asked, his hand squeezing Ryder's arm, but she didn't seem to notice. Her eyes reminded him of the times he had delivered news of a patient's death to their family: the eyes are always distant and red.

"At this stage, I'm not sure," said Crine. "The only option I think might work is nanite replacement, but it's never been done to such an extent on one patient. We'd have to run more tests and bring in specialists from around the Globe. It would be one of the biggest medical feats in the last fifty years, at least."

"Try not to sound so happy, you shite!" Ryder yelled. "He isn't an experiment!"

"I'm sorry, Captain," Crine replied, and he had the decency to look abashed. "I got ahead of myself. The first stage is to repair the damage to his organs and then we can consider further treatments going forward." He stood up, leaving his water untouched. "I must ask you to wait here until the surgery is done, and it might take a while. The nurse at the desk will see to your needs."

Crine walked to the door and stopped. He looked back, and even though Ryder and Matthews weren't looking at him, he added, "Like I said, there's no guarantee he'll make it through but given how he's still alive after this, I wouldn't give up hope just yet." Crine left the room.

"He'll survive, Eleanor," Matthews said. "He'll be okay."

"Surviving isn't the same as okay," she replied curtly. "Sir."

The first thing Ryan noticed when he woke was the beeping. His eyes felt glued shut but he could feel heat on a patch of his face, so he knew there was daylight. That meant he was on Earth. It took a few more seconds before he managed to open his eyes, but it was too bright and they snapped closed.

His chest felt like he had belly-flopped into a pool, there were pins and needles in his left arm, and his left leg was in a hard cast strapped to the edge of the bed. Thankfully, his right arm and leg weren't sore. In fact, he couldn't feel a thing from them.

Ryan opened his eyes, slower this time, and kept them narrow to adjust to the light. It was a hospital room, devoid of colour, crisp and clean. On his right was the machine beeping, monitoring his vital signs. He had no clue what it meant but it seemed steady.

Sara slept in a chair on his left. She was pale, her hair was a mess and someone had draped a blanket over her. It looked like she had been there for a while and he smiled as he remembered their last meeting.

Only a wheeze escaped when he tried to speak and he realised how thirsty he was. There was a drip connected to a tube inserted into his wrist but it didn't help his throat. He coughed and Sara bolted upright. She looked at Ryan and smiled, almost tumbling out of her chair to move closer.

"Hey, sleepy," she said, brushing some hair from his eyes. "How're you feeling?"

Another wheeze escaped him and she laughed, pouring some water into a tumbler and pointing a straw to his mouth. A couple of sips and he felt able to talk.

"Why are you here? How long have I been out?"

"Captain Ryder commed me," Sara said, taking a break between each sentence so Ryan could process it. "You've been out for eight days. You were quite a mess when they brought you in," she said, turning stern. "What the coo were you thinking?"

"Did it work?"

"Mostly…but that's not the point! You could have died. You nearly did!"

"And a lot of people would have if I hadn't done anything. When I was up there, I think I started to understand what you were trying to tell me," Ryan answered slowly, and her stern looked faded. "I think the responsibility finally caught up with me."

Being careful not to pull on any of the tubes or wires around him, Ryan placed his left hand on Sara's and they locked eyes. Neither spoke, and she smiled and placed her other hand on top of his.

Ryan leaned back against the pillows, feeling tired already. The silence in the room was different than in the mech. He was able to enjoy the moment and Sara's presence.

A knock at the door a few minutes later drew their attention and a doctor walked inside the room, standing at the end of the bed with a tired smile.

"Glad to see you're awake, Ryan. I'm Doctor Crine. I've been in charge of your treatment since you arrived."

"Eight days ago?" Ryan said.

"That's right." Crine nodded. "I saw Captain Ryder outside. Has she been in and spoken to you yet?"

"Not since I woke up," Ryan said, starting to shake his head but stopping with a wince.

"She looked pale. I don't think she's slept much since you got here. She's been very worried about you. How do you feel?"

"Which bit?" Ryan answered, prompting a chuckle from Sara. Crine was unmoved – he had probably seen this all before – but before he could speak, Ryan changed the subject. "What happened to the debris? Did it land in the water? How many died?"

"You pilots managed to make sure it landed offshore but the resulting tsunami wreaked havoc on the coast. Over two hundred thousand people confirmed dead at the last count; a fraction of the number had it hit land."

Ryan closed his eyes and took a breath. It was small consolation that only that many had died, but they were a result of his failure to complete the mission. Damaged mech or not, they should have done better.

"What about Wisp and Jackson? The other pilots? At least two mechs failed..." Ryan said.

"There were three casualties from the team tackling the debris. Andre Tanner is fine but Kendra Jackson, she...she didn't make it. Her body was found in a mech off the coast."

"She didn't evac?" Ryan asked. Sara squeezed his hand and he closed his eyes to stop tears from forming. He had suspected this already, given how Jackson's signal had vanished from his sensors during the descent, but hearing it poured ice water on his heart.

His thoughts turned to Wisp and how his flight leader must be feeling. It was no secret he and Jackson had been growing closer. Had he noticed what'd happened to her at the time, when Ryan did, or after?

"No, I'm sorry," Crine said. "The other two pilots are called Gr—"

"How's Wisp doing?" Ryan cut in, his eyes still closed.

"I'm afraid I don't know. You were the only pilot to be brought to this facility, so physically I'd imagine he's in better shape than you, but I can't speak to his emotional or mental states. I can ask Captain Ryder if you'd like?"

"N-no. I'll ask her when we talk. It's a squad matter," Ryan said, taking a couple of deep breaths to steady himself. He'd known there would be casualties. He'd accepted that, but hearing the numbers, and that his friend was included, hit him harder than a gut punch.

Unlike the Mars Massacre, where people had tried to convince him the responsibility lay with those at the top, this time it was on him. He had led the mission to stop the debris. He should have done better.

"Hey, Doc, why can't I feel anything on my right side?" Ryan asked, changing the subject again before those thoughts overwhelmed him.

"That's one of the things I want to talk to you about," Crine answered, and he pulled up a chair on Ryan's right. "We've stabilised your internal injuries. The broken bones have been set and your bruises are healing. Your right side is another story, but I do have some options for you. Before that, I noticed something strange in your test results when you arrived, but I didn't have time to really interpret the data. Since then, I've been over it half a dozen times to make sure, but I wanted to ask you a few questions, if you're feeling up to it?"

"Sure. Shoot."

"Okay, let's take a look at this to begin with," Crine said, handing over the PCT he was carrying. Ryan's eyes widened and when Sara leaned over for a look, she gasped.

"What does this mean?" she whispered.

"That's what we need to figure out," Crine answered. "I've never seen anything like this before and it does change what we can do about your right side. I need you to start from the beginning – don't leave out any details and tell me exactly what's happened over the last six months."

EPILOGUE

SIX OPERATORS SAT AROUND a small table in the middle of the room, their backs to the consoles they were meant to be monitoring, playing cards. When the door opened, they looked up to see another agent enter with a tray of drinks. She set them down and joined the game, picking up triangular cards and studying them intently.

"Just so you know," she said, "Matthews is reportedly wandering this level."

"Who told you that?" the dealer asked.

"Gonzo."

"Heh. Figures," he replied, dishing out another card to everyone. "Gonzo is a coo. Says the same thing every couple of days and it's never true."

"If he's on this level, shouldn't we be working?" the youngest asked.

"Chill, Rook. Even if he is, he's not likely to come here," the dealer said, pointing to a terminal showing a sensor scan. "There's nothing out there anymore."

"Besides, the general has enough going on," another continued, reaching for a drink. "The publicity from the invasion has seen a surge of applications from people wanting to become Enforcers, especially in the Mech Force."

"And with most of the pilots on leave, it means we need bodies, even to watch space dust," the dealer grunted.

The rook turned away from the game and checked the closest terminal. Nothing. A flash caught his eye as he turned back to the game. A white spark trailed orange as it descended towards the surface.

"Just a piece of debris," the dealer said, looking over his shoulder. "You should see a group of pieces burn up. It's mesmerising."

"It won't take long for you to see it," one of them sighed. "For all the pieces salvaged and collected, more still appear. Makes you wonder where it all comes from."

The rook stayed quiet. He'd been one of the transfers from the surface to OSD and the Mech Force after learning about the battle over the planet five months earlier. It had become all too clear how jaded a lot of the station personnel were with no threat looming over them. It made him wonder if the general's appearance would change any of their attitudes. Until he could complete his rotation as an operator and join the pilot training programme, he had to keep his head down and ignore the cavalier attitudes of the operators.

In the middle of the next hand being dealt, every monitor in the room flashed red and an alarm wailed. Panic set in as each operator scrambled to their station. Cards dropped to the floor and drinks were knocked over as they rushed to identify the cause.

"Multiple contacts!" the dealer yelled.

"Is it debris?" the rook asked.

"No, they're too far out – and moving towards us," the woman who had brought the drinks answered.

The alarms kept blaring as the number of contacts increased. Just as the dealer was about to comm for support, every single screen went blank and a single word appeared.

"What is this?"

"I don't believe it..."

"Where's it coming from?"

"Go and get the general. Now!"

"It doesn't matter. This is on every screen in the station. Maybe the other stations too. Possibly even on the surface," the dealer said, sitting back in disbelief.

"I guess we have an answer, then," the rook said.

The alarm continued but no one seemed to hear it. They were all captivated by what they saw. Just one word.

THE END

THANK YOU SO MUCH for reading *Reality Check* – I really hope you enjoyed it!

I'm proud of getting my debut novel out into the world, but it hasn't been easy. There's no publishing house or marketing team helping me as an indie author, so I'm learning and doing everything myself. I know there's a lot of competition out there, so I'm honoured you've taken a chance on me and my book.

It'd mean so much to me if you could let other readers know what you thought – it'll help them decide if *Reality Check* is right for them, and I read every review, no matter what it says. If you have a few minutes, please head to Goodreads or Amazon (using the QR code below) – or wherever you bought it from – and let everyone know. If you have the time, feel free to do it on both!

It's a big help, even if you have questions or think things can be improved.

If you'd like to keep up to date with the latest news and releases, join my monthly newsletter (https://dave-mccreery.co.uk/newsletter/) by visiting my website. You'll also get an ebook copy of *Introductions: Volume One* as a thank you, which includes some short stories set in the *Weight of the World* series.

Thank you again.

About the Author

DAVE MCCREERY IS A British writer born in Edinburgh. He loves to create vivid and engaging worlds for readers to fall into and become engrossed in the stories held within them. In between these stories, he seeks adventures and experiences from across the world to broaden his horizons, which are shared in his writing. Dave studied English and Creative Writing at Manchester Metropolitan University before beginning a career in digital marketing to support his ambition to publish books. He often shares his experiences, with writing processes and exercises, challenges and obstacles and insights from his journey. You can read more on his website and social media channels:

https://davemccreery.co.uk
https://www.facebook.com/DaveMcCreeryAuthor
https://twitter.com/DaveMcCreery